A Fire's Beauty

JASMINE RICHMOND

A Fire's Beauty

Copyrights © 2022 by Jasmine Richmond

All rights reserved.

For my sisters, Kanani, and Karla
To whom gave me my love, and fire for writing

Chapter One

When she pulled into the driveway, the address matched but not the picture. She called the real estate company and confirmed this was her house.

A cute little cottage style with a loft. Two bedrooms, two baths on a half-acre with creek frontage. It was a little run down, but with some new curtains, some plants, and a little bit of elbow grease, she convinced herself it was going to be an amazing fresh start.

Though she had a neighbor on either side, she could only see her left-side neighbor. A little bit bigger than hers, cabin style and a new black F-150 sat in the driveway. She rolled her eyes. Male.

She sighed and hoped he was married or at least left her alone. She was here for peace and quiet, to be left alone. She didn't want loud, obnoxious, or nosy neighbors.

She turned off the car, sighed, and got out. She opened the backdoor and pulled out her suitcase and a pillow. She didn't have much but figured the four small boxes and black trash bag of clothes could wait till tomorrow. As she spent the last week driving, she was tired.

She walked a few steps up the porch to her front door and unlocked it. When the door opened, the musty smell hit her, making her wrinkle her nose.

"No one said starting over was going to be easy." She whispered to herself as she walked in. The natural sunlight was good as it beamed in to illuminate the dust everywhere. Small but perfect for her. She loved it.

She shut the door behind her and walked over the creaky wood floors to the small kitchen with a small island and breakfast bar. She turned on the sink and it sputtered brown water before running clear. She turned it back off, then ran her fingers over the rough wood countertops.

"A sander... check." Making her own mental checklist of things to get.

She would run into town tomorrow and ask what the local shops would have for supplies. Though she didn't expect much, being a small town in the middle of nowhere, surrounded by mountains, she had to find out. She then opened the fridge and though cleaner than the rest of the house, it was still going to get a good scrub with bleach before she would trust it.

She walked into the small dining and living room area. Eventually, she would buy a small table for some guests maybe someday, but she would be good with the bar seating for herself for now and save the extra room for a nice couch in the corner against the wall. Maybe even splurge on a Chaise lounge, as she always wanted one, to sit in and read her books with a glass of wine.

She smiled and looked over at the cute small bay window with dirty windows that overlooked a small creek in back and dead bugs in the window seals.

"Traps and more bleach." She continued and opened the back door taking in the running creek down a small slope through some trees and bushes. The lawn would use a good trim, maybe weeding some bushes out so she could have a better view from her bay window.

It was the end of July and the creek flowed swiftly past her house; the sound was soothing. She closed her eyes and took a deep breath while listening to it. The sun beat down on her face. It was warm. She smiled again before opening her eyes and going back inside.

She scanned the rest of the house looking over the basic bedroom and bathroom that also had some dead bugs in the tub. She enjoyed seeing the open section of wall with washer and dryer hookups.

"Washer and dryer." She left the bathroom and climbed the small narrow stairs to the loft. She opened a door she thought might be a closet, only to find out it was a bathroom crammed into a closet space. She laughed at the tiny tub and sink with sloping ceilings with a toilet in the corner, then shut the door.

The next door wasn't any better. Small bedroom, small closet, and even smaller window also with low sloping ceilings. She took a step and the nearly brown carpet squished under her clogs. She looked down at the soaked carpet then looked up at the dripping ceiling.

"Contractor. Check." She grumbled.

She walked to the small dirty window and looked out over her back yard to the creek. "Well, tour is over Daphne." She took a deep breath. It wasn't much, but it was home. After a goodnight's rest, she will start in the morning on rebuilding her life.

"Coffee pot. Check."

She went back down the stairs and dug into her small suitcase for a matching silky purple tank top and shorts, a book, a small blanket, and her pillow. She used a dirty shirt to clean the dead bugs from the dirty bay window and changed into the Pjs and climbed into the small window with the blanket, pillow, and book.

Each pop and crack of the house kept her awake till nearly midnight. When the sunset got dark enough to let her drift to sleep as she was watching the stars coming out and twinkle through her window. In a ball in the window, she never felt more alone than she was now, and cried herself to sleep. Tomorrow held more promises.

When she woke, she dreaded it, at least the hotel rooms had coffee. She got dressed for the day in a sluggish, tired mood. She checked herself in the mirror and didn't think she looked homeless, so she deemed it good enough with what she had. She prepared herself for a big shopping day as she walked to her car and unloaded the four small boxes of keepsakes and trinkets and the black trash bag of clothes and set them on the counter.

The amount of work she had ahead of her made her grumble, shut the front door, and lock it with more attitude than usual. The sun was back out today shining through her long, chocolate brown hair as it bounced all over the place. Maybe she should dye it. New place, new look... mmm, maybe that would be more work and time she didn't want right now.

She unlocked her 2011 candy apple red Jeep Grand Cherokee Laredo with a click on her fob and got in and set her ordinary small white wallet and cell phone in the console. She did a double take, then picked up her cell, and hit speed dial number 2.

The other end rang as she took a deep breath. Click. Voicemail.

"Hey, its Dani! You've reached my voicemail. Leave me a message and I'll call you back." Beep!

"Hey Sis, it's me. I made it. The house is cute. Gonna do some shopping today. Wish you were here to help me. About to visit town and see what it's like. Wish me luck. I'll buy a new phone today and get one that actually works up here."

She closed her eyes as they started to water. "I'm so sorry. I love you guys so much. Give kids a hug from Auntie. I'll keep in touch ever so often. I'll be peachy. I love you. Goodbye."

With a click she hung up the phone. Looked at it then turned it off and put it in her center console. She broke. Letting the tears fall as she quietly sobbed to herself over the steering wheel. She was officially alone now, but she knew it was for the best.

As she wiped at her tears, the neighbor's black truck passed her house slowly and sped up after it passed. She didn't care. She cleaned her face off and ran her fingers through her hair, deemed it good again, and put her car in reverse.

She drove through the small neighborhood back to town and wandered the streets finding her way around and getting to know it. She found the middle school where she would be the new school nurse at the end of August and the single-story fire station in the middle of town. It had a small mini mall with some cute boutiques. The small grocery store that she assumed was the only one, along with the only gas station. A few run-down restaurants, and a better looking one that was more crowded than the rest called "Mike's Diner." A small clinic that looked older than the mountains themselves, and the police station just off a couple corners from her neighborhood.

As she drove around people were getting curious and watching her. It was a small town. Outsiders were not welcomed or at least accepted very easily. She had a purpose and reason to be here, so that made her the new gossip. Fine, she could deal as long as no one dug.

She took a deep breath and pulled into the "Mike's Diner" parking lot. Coffee at least and maybe some breakfast before shopping and maybe she could talk to someone about where to get some stuff for her house. Mikes was the only sensible diner within 50 miles. Beside a cheap Chinese place that was notorious for having bad company and a bar. Mikes had everything a small hole-in-the-wall diner needed. In this small town, Mike's was the local hangout for kids after school. The seniors for Sunday brunch, even late-night dates, at least until 11pm, Monday through Friday, and open until midnight on Saturday and Sunday. Though a small town, they were mostly night owls. The quietest you'd ever see the town is 7am on the weekends. Birch Valley was a family, and she was its newest member.

She ran her fingers through her hair and checked herself again. If she was going to be the new gossip, then she wouldn't give anyone more ammo than what she could handle.

As she walked in and spotted an empty booth closer to the back of the restaurant, she was already getting curious looks, gawks and even heard the whispers.

"Who is she?", "Phh City girl, she'll never last here." "That I think is the new nurse, what's her name?"

She passed a table of firefighters and police officers half dressed in gear, who watched her with curiosity over the rims of their coffee cups. One with more genuine curiosity than the rest, a firefighter. When she reached her booth and sat down, a waitress took her drink order and returned with an empty coffee mug and coffee pot to fill it up.

"Hi, I'm Kayla." The young girl stretched out her empty right hand in front of her, still holding the coffee pot with her left.

"Hi Kayla, I'm Daphne."

After the waitress took her breakfast order, she left and she felt the looks again, but chose not to look up, and instead, drank her coffee letting it seep into her bones.

Staring into her coffee, the sounds of glass shattering and metal crunching in her head made her stiffen her spine. Then the pleading screams to stop, rang through her ears. Jerking herself back to reality making sure it wasn't real, she immediately looked up and caught the gaze of the curious fireman as he watched her intently while drinking his coffee ignoring the group he was sitting with.

Dark blonde, clean shaved, and rough hands that held the cup. A plain black T-shirt with bulging sleeves from his biceps. A turnout pant leg and boot showing from under the table. When she looked back up to his golden eyes, the edges of his lips were curved up as he still watched her.

When their eyes connected, she felt something. She didn't know what, but it scared her. The thought of running crossed her mind for a split second until a plate of food hit the table in front of her, making her look at Kayla.

Then alarms rang out echoing through the restaurant, making her jump as the table of first responders all stood up and grabbed their turn-out coats then checked the pager message. The curious one, though standing now, still drank his coffee, holding his coat over his shoulder. He gave Daphne one last look, set the cup back on the table, and broke the connection jogging after the rest of the crew heading towards the door. Everyone gave them arm pats or a "Be safe!' as they passed by their tables.

Now watching Kayla refill her coffee mug she asked, "Where would someone go to get some furniture and decorations for their house?"

Kayla smiled, "Not here. We're too small for those stores. You need to go to Freeman for those. We have just a simple grocery store. Though Gale and Earl I think carry soil and some plants and maybe a rug or two on occasion when their sellers have good prices but mostly, they are your normal grocery store with seasonal fruits, veggies, bread, and milk."

Daphne nodded, "Okay. Thank you."

After she ate and cleared her check, she made a better mental list of what to get today. "Bed, couch, cleaning supplies, curtains, groceries, and especially coffee."

Guess she would have to make the hour and half drive back to the town she drove through yesterday.

When she returned home, her car was full to the roof with everything for her house from groceries to small furniture, linens to rugs, she was exhausted. She still needed to bring all this in. With a mumble, she started taking in the first few bags of groceries.

One trip at a time, she packed her house with lamps, dinnerware sets, blankets, bed sheets, curtains, small rugs, and small end tables she had found at a cute antique shop along with the black leather set of barstools. Everything she bought never had a theme or design - simple, functional, and cozy. She loved cozy. She loved her bay window, 90% of the time she would choose to sit there, rather than some big sectional or hard couch. She was the girl that would rather sit in the corner than the center of a room, in a crowd, or alone or would prefer to lay on a big soft rug rather than stiffen her spine to sit in a chair. This time around she would make it her life and not conform to anyone, society, and trends. Besides, who out here would care. Most everything ran along the darker color scheme with the occasional pops of color, usually in violet and maroon to keep it light and cheery but loved the relaxed and calming feelings she got from her decor.

When she bought the bed, couch, and dresser, she didn't think about delivery, leaving her to curl back up into her window and watch the stars again for another night which she was okay with knowing there were worse places to sleep than in a cozy window in her own house.

When she went for another load, she felt the gaze, but saw no one when she walked around her car to grab groceries. Her pulse raced, feeling the tension crawl down her spine. Trying to shake it, she kept moving, as she grabbed the bag and bucket of cleaning supplies. Her mind ran through possible people until it came across the hot fireman at the diner. She smiled, relaxed, and took the bags and bucket into her house forgetting about the gaze.

Taking the last item out of her car was a pretty hanging pot she bought that was filled with various flowers in purple, red, blue, pink and yellow. She smiled at it and set it on the porch railing with the hopes to hang it up soon. She went in, got a cup of water, watered it then smiled, and walked back inside ready to clean.

Music bumped through her new phone for the next few hours while she danced around and cleaned, working her way from room to room until the sky lit up pink through her now clean windows. She walked to her bay window and kneeled in it watching the treetops above the creek light up in a rosy, orange color. Hope. It gave her hope. Today was a good day, but tomorrow will be better. She looked at her cell phone, 10:35pm. Oh! She would have to get used to this if she were to stay here for a while.

She put away a few more bags of stuff and looked at the bag of bed linens and couch pillows. Telling herself it was coming tomorrow; she smiled and went to change into a pair of soft PJ pants and a tank top before curling back into her window after shutting the house down. She looked at her new coffee pot on the counter before going to bed and told herself it was going to be a great day tomorrow and drifted to sleep.

In the morning she sat on her new barstools drinking her cup of coffee from an Outer Banks cup with a smile. By afternoon, the house was as clean and organized as she thought it was going to get. She beamed with pride walking around the rooms to look at everything she had cleaned and bought. She sprayed ocean scented air freshener around the rooms to get the last of the musty smell out.

Daphne smiled at the new plush rug she bought for her living room and enjoyed walking barefoot around her house feeling the mixed textures of carpet and wood flooring under her feet. She walked through the kitchen running her hand along the newly sanded wood counters. Smooth. Remembering the work of scrubbing and sanding and polishing the counters, she took a deep breath and told herself that she did that.

She smiled, opened the fridge for her bottle of wine, opened it, and grabbed a tall plain stemmed wine glass from the cabinet. She deserved it. As she drank it, she walked to the front window wondering when her furniture would arrive and saw the neighbors truck pass by in a blur.

She watched it pass then turned around to look at her house completely. She bided her time walking from room to room making mental plans for upgrades and changes to each room. New paint in the bedroom, all new counters in the kitchen, maybe new tiles, and fixtures in the bathroom to brighten it up. The upstairs would need all new carpet and flooring after the contractors fixed the roof on Friday. She sighed, still being a week away, it was the only time she could get. Days blended together as she hadn't had a set schedule to run off in almost a year. She looked forward to finally being able to put down roots and settle into a place of her own.

She tipped up her wine glass and chugged the last of the wine, letting it release the tension in her muscles from cleaning and unpacking. She then decided to grab a light sweater off the hook by the door and slip on a pair of old flip flops and walk out. She folded her arms across her chest. She was dirty with dust and cobwebs she cleaned and shivered from the thought of what she cleaned today. Daphne then saw the old wooden bench down the small slope to the left of her house, hidden in the overgrown bushes that overlooked the creek.

She looked back at the house and decided against a shower. She wandered down to the bench pushing the bushes down making her path to it. She ran a hand over the weathered wood and pushed on it to make sure it was sturdy enough for her, then took a seat. She took in a deep breath and sat back to watch the creek running by in front of her.

A metal door clanked shut making her jump. Looking around for where it came from, she noticed around a few big trees, a little brunette girl coming towards her from the neighbor's house with two Styrofoam cups stacked on top of each other. Daphne watched her as she made her way across the shared yard and down the small slope.

"Hi" She spoke with a soft voice. Daphne smiled and returned the greeting.

The girl walked to the other side of the bench from Daphne and smiled.

Oh, she's adorable. Daphne thought.

"I'm Kada. Your neighbor. I brought you some hot cocoa." She spoke as she took the seat on the far end from Daphne. Thinking about the wine already on her stomach then mixing Hot cocoa didn't make her smile but took the cup anyway as the warmth would help sitting beneath the shade of the trees. She stretched over the seat and took the cup of hot cocoa from her.

"Hi Kada, I'm Daphne. Thank you!"

Over the next hour only making small talk, never giving any real information out, Daphne noticed, someone taught her well. Daphne, working as a middle school nurse, pegged Kada to be around 12-14 years old and was right when Kada mentioned she was 12. Daphne was careful not to ask too much to spook her but from the looks, it would take a lot to change the 12-year old's demeanor.

When the black truck pulled back into Kada's driveway and disappeared behind the porch, Daphne pointed towards the driveway.

"I think your parents are home."

Without looking, she spoke softly "It's only my dad. Mom...."

She paused and looked down, ".... isn't here."

Daphne saw the sadness not only in her tone and eyes, but her posture as she leaned forward.

"Oh, I'm so sorry." Daphne frowned

"Dad is a fireman, so he is on calls or down at the station a lot, so I cook and clean for us."

This was the most information Daphne got out of her but judged her term of "A lot" as it was probably very different then her own but smiled and nodded.

"It sounds like he is a really cool dad."

"Yeah. At the station they are all pretty close, so it's like having a lot of uncles and aunts." She giggled.

When Kada's back door clanged again, a tall man stepped out wearing black pants and a dark colored sweater. From the distance Daphne couldn't see his face yet but with the squared shoulders and straight posture, knew he was walking with a purpose. Relaxed but stern, he spoke about halfway across the yard.

"Kada, I told you to leave the new neighbor alone."

Daphne stood up as he walked towards them, and his face became clearer. The curious fireman from the diner. Her eyes widened as he made eye contact with her. She froze as he walked down the slope with his hands in his pockets.

"But Dad, you said it was my new school nurse, so I'm gonna meet her soon anyways."

His eyes got fierce as he looked from her to Kada and back to her.

So, he did know her but yet she knew so very little about him. She took a step back and labored her breathing.

He noticed but did nothing.

"I did but she's not at school yet. Give her time to get settled in." he spoke to Kada then turned back to look at Daphne.

His eyes connected with hers again. Though cloudy today his golden eyes glowed in the daylight. Her breath quickened. The musky cologne, the warmth, comfort, and soothing voice in place of her fear. The flashes ran through her head, making her jerk back and then quickly drop her head, hoping he didn't notice.

He stood next to Kada now still with his hands in his pockets. When Daphne got up the courage to look up, His eyes were a little wider and held more intensity and curiosity.

"Sorry Kada can be nosey sometimes."

She straightened and tried to relax but couldn't, so she folded her arms across her chest, still holding the cup of hot cocoa. "No, it's okay. I don't mind the company. I was just taking a break from cleaning."

He smiled to purposely ease the tension that you could cut with a knife.

"It's Daphne, right?"

That didn't last long. Her chin went sideways as her eyebrows lowered.

"The diner this morning. I heard you talking to Kayla." He reached a hand over the full length of the bench.

She nodded and reached across, having to lean forward to shake his hand.

"Luke, Miss Nosey's dad." He nodded to Kada standing next to him.

"Hi Luke."

Kada watched the sparks and energy with a wide smile not understanding what was happening just that Dad was acting differently.

Who was the guy shaking Daphne's hand? Because it wasn't her dad anymore. Dad said a lot more words to a stranger, he would rescue or to the random women that he always turned down who hit on him. Until now. He stayed quiet and tense as she saw it.

Daphne and Luke held each other's hands over the bench as they watched each other for a few more seconds until they were snapped back to reality by the sound of a diesel truck coming down a dirt road then the beeping of a commercial vehicle backing up in front of her house.

She let go of his hand as they both looked towards the front of the house.

"Oh! My furniture is here." She spoke.

Luke looked from her towards the house and back.

"Do you need a hand?" He asked.

Kada crossed her arms and put all her weight on her left foot watching her dad.

Daphne took a couple steps up the slope, looking back at them both. Kada smiled.

"Umm. Sure."

Luke turned to Kada and told her to go pull out the chicken for dinner and he would be there soon to help make dinner. Kada smiled and did what she was told without objections and headed for their back door. Daphne then walked up the slope and around the side of the house as he followed.

When they rounded the corner, the company men were prepping to unload the small box truck of furniture all new in plastic wrap.

"Ms. Daphne Kimble?" One of the men asked.

She walked up to the truck now getting excited. "Yes! That's me!"

"We have a loveseat couch, king bed set, a dresser and washer and dryer set for you?"

"Yes!"

The older man made a few marks on a clipboard and stretched it out to her.

"Sign at the bottom please."

Daphne gave a couple of skips over to the back of the truck and took it from him as he pressed a button to unfold the loading dock. Luke smiled big as he watched her from behind, seeing her hair bounce all over the place. Daphne took the clipboard and signed it, handing it back to him as they lowered the dock to the top of the porch over her steps leaving a half inch of space before touching the porch. Luke then walked around her and hopped up on the dock and porch and helped the men twist and turn the small loveseat through the door as Daphne directed them.

"Over in the corner by the far wall please!"

Daphne gave a hand helping slide the mattress across the wood floors to her bedroom as the men followed with a high-rise frame box into her bedroom. Next came the small dark wood dresser and her gray washer and dryer that went into the bathroom in the corner by the hookups.

Luke jumped over after getting them close enough to reach the connections and plug-ins. Then got them all connected and plugged them in as the units beeped and came to life.

"Yay! I can do laundry!"

Luke smiled at how excited she was about her new furniture and appliances.

When he jumped back over trying not to damage the new washer and dryer, his boot caught the edge of the washer sending him forward.

Daphne's eyes went big as she leaned forward and put her arms out to catch him. Not even thinking about the difference in size, her left arm caught his chest and her right arm wrapped around his left arm that wrapped around her waist. His right foot landed first, making his right-hand land on the floor to brace them both.

"Oh shit!" She gave a small scream waiting for the floor. Nothing.

Still wincing she opened her eyes and saw Luke within a few mere inches from her face, smiling and looking down at her. He was crouched over her holding her waist up with his left arm bracing them both with his right flat against the floor, her legs stretched out straight. A position she had only seen in professional salsa dancers.

"Nice reflexes." She whispered

His lips twitched, "Comes with the career."

Realizing how they looked, she quickly released her tight grip on his shirt and arm and got her feet under her to stand up with his help. They paused, searching each other's faces for any reaction.

"Alright Ms. Kimble. Everything is unloaded and you should be good." The company man spoke walking through the open bathroom door looking at his clipboard.

She frowned and turned to face him, taking a deep breath trying to shake off the secure and safe feeling she felt again.

"Thank you."

Then walked out with the guy to show him out the front door and shut it behind him as he left. When she turned around Luke sat at her bar on the stool, watching her. She folded her receipt and slid it on the kitchen island as she took the other bar stool then turned to face him.

"We should probably put your bed together."

She straightened before answering.

"Oh. No. I can do that myself tomorrow. Don't worry about it, as long as I have at least the mattress to sleep on I'll be fine. Besides, it will be a nice change of pace from sleeping with the bugs in my window."

His face became confused. She pointed to her little bay window, and he turned around to look. How did he miss the bay window with a dark purple pillow and blanket that he could nearly fill just by sitting in it, and she had curled up and slept in it.... for the last two nights? He had so many questions, but only nodded and smiled at her. His eyes searched hers for answers she knew he couldn't find and with hope, never would.

When his pager activated and lit up with an alarm, it made him jump forgetting it was on his side. He pulled it off his belt and checked the message then looked up at her.

"Sorry I got to run."

Daphne stood up to walk him out the door. "No. It's fine. Thank you for your help." He tried to move faster but his feet only walked to the front door.

"Yeah. Let me know if you need any more help. I'm usually around on evenings and weekends."

"Okay. Thanks Luke."

When he stepped out the door, she closed it and he took a deep breath and started his jog across the yard to his house. He went into his house and came back out a minute later with his radio and small duffle bag. He talked into the handheld mic as he looked over at Daphne's on his way to the truck.

Daphne watched from her kitchen windows as his truck lit up with red and blue lights that were hidden in his windshield, front grill, headlights, and along the side running boards. After he passed her house, she took a needed breath and went for another glass of wine.

Luke's thoughts were scattered as he did CPR on a patient. He tried to shake them off and focus but she clouded his head and made it nearly impossible to do his job. He sat back telling another fireman to take over as he prepared the patient for transport. His Captain watched him carefully.

After returning to the station, he worked on some paperwork in his office. A knock sounded on the door.

"It's open." he shouted over his desk.

The door opened and a tall darker skin man walked in, shut the door behind him, and took a seat in front of Luke's desk.

"Hey Cap, just finishing reports from yesterday. What's up?"

Captain sat back in his seat, "You looked a little distracted on the call, Lieutenant."

Luke's half smile fell flat as he looked up from his paperwork.

"Don't give me that look, Luke..."

He took note of the informality now.

"...I know you. We grew up together, man. What's going on?"

Luke inhaled sharply to talk but the captain cut him off.

"And no bullshit. I know you better than Kada."

Luke rolled his eyes and chuckled at the statement.

"Heard of the new girl yet?

The captain nodded.

"Yeah, Kayla told me she already ate at the diner. I heard she was the new middle school nurse and replacing Mrs. Adams."

Luke now adjusted in his seat and sat back resting his arms on the armrests and worked his jaw.

"Then you've heard of my new neighbor."

"No shit." His eyes got big as he sat forward bracing his arms on Luke's desk then gave a confused look.

"Wait. There hasn't been anyone in that house for a couple years and our middle school nurse moves into it, and you can't focus at work?"

Mentally following the clues, Captain raised his eyebrows and gave a nod.

"There is something about her, Mike. I can't put a finger on it. She has a history and she's terrified of it."

Captain tilted his head sideways and now sat back in his chair again.

"Figure it out man. But don't bring it to calls." He spoke with a relaxed but stern tone.

Luke gave a nod. "Yes Cap."

Mike stood up, took a breath, and placed a bracing hand on Luke's desk.

"And Luke, you're the last person I need to tell but be careful."

Luke smiled and nodded. "Kada first." he replied.

Mike turned and walked out

Why did she stir him up? How could she get under his skin especially on a call. He always held a heavy hand separating work and personal and was able to flip the switch when duty called for it. He picked up his pen again and looked down at the paperwork in front of him. It was now foreign to him. Frustrated, he put his pen down and grabbed his coat and walked out, locking up his office.

CHAPTER TWO

At dusk, Daphne unwrapped her mattress that leaned against the wall of the bedroom and flopped it down with a thud against the floor. She opened her new bedding, put on the dark purple and gray bed sheets and soft comforter with her stack of six new pillows. All with alternating purple and gray colors. She splurged on the pillow top mattress telling herself she deserved it as she paid for it. When she laid down on the bed, stretching to cover as much of the bed as her little body could, she went limp and sank into the softness. Oh, no. Her eyes got heavy as her mind wandered to Luke. His smile. His voice. His hands...so rough but yet so caring. Soon she drifted to sleep still in her dirty jeans and tank top.

After morning coffee and a small breakfast, she finished decorating and adjusted a few things to her liking with what was left in the last few bags and unpacked the small box of trinkets and keepsakes she traveled with.

She unwrapped a glass sign that had painted irises on it and held a quote between two, " Life is not measured by the number of breaths we take but the moments that take our breath away." She smiled and pushed a tack into the wall between her bay window and the door and hung it up. Then stepped back to admire it, then did a turn and admired her home. She did it. This was hers and only hers. Though a little bare, she would fill it as time went and was excited to see it in a year from now.

She then stepped out on the front porch and saw her hanging flower basket still on the railing. Oh. She needed to hang that up. She went back inside to grab her foot stool and small power tool set she bought and set the stool next to the wall on the left side of her front door. On the tallest step, she stood on tiptoes and tried to drill in the screw to the house siding through the bracket. The drill wobbled and the screw fell to the porch and rolled through the cracks of the porch. She sighed.

"Need help?" The shout came from across the yard. She looked over and saw Luke on his porch watching her.

She rolled her eyes and replied "No, thanks!"

She then got down and walked off the porch to crawl underneath. It was dark and colder. She crawled through the cobwebs, overgrown grass, and weeds feeling for the screw on her hands and knees ducking under the low rafters of the porch that hung only a couple inches from her head.

"Daphne?" Luke spoke from behind her.

She looked back at the opening and saw the silhouette of him against the background of the yard and his house.

"What do you want Luke?" she spoke with a soft gruff tone as she still felt the ground for the screw.

"Thought you could use a magnet." He spoke

She heard him crawling in behind her as his hands, knees, and feet scraped at the gravel, dirt, and weeds under the porch.

"Where you at?" His voice got closer in the near pitch-black darkness. Soon a hand touched her calf through her jeans she wore today, making her wish she had the thickness of turnout gear to keep his hand off her. The hand let go and she heard him crawling up next to her left side.

"Here. Where's your hand?"

She sat back on her heels keeping low to refrain from hitting her head and faced the direction his voice came from.

"Right here." She held out her hand in front of her. When his arm bumped her hand, she felt him use his other hand for guidance to place the palm size heavy magnet in her hand.

His hands were rough but warm and gentle. After he placed the magnet in her hands he didn't let go of her hand.

"What are you doing, Luke?"

He let go of her hand and replied, "Helping you find a screw... under your porch."

She knew he tweaked the truth to his liking. She took a breath and went back to searching for the screw rubbing the magnet through the tall grass and weeds till the magnet clicked. She used her other hand to feel it and it felt like a screw to her.

"I think I found it." She nearly shouted with hopes to get out from under the porch. "Good." He replied.

When she started to turn around something crawled up her arm, made her scream, and hit her head on the rafters above. Crawling fast to get out, she made it to the shorter softer grass in the daylight, in a panic and brushing her arm repeatedly. Luke appeared in the daylight after her.

"Hey it's okay. It's gone now whatever it was."

When she looked at him his golden eyes brightened in the daylight as he smiled.

"How's your head?"

Oh. Yeah. She remembered now that she hit it. Her chocolate brown hair hung loosely over her shoulders and chest. It had pieces of dead grass and twigs in it as Daphne now pulled out what she could see. She touched the top of her head and winced.

"It's fine." She showed him her hand. "See, no blood."

He smiled, "Can I look?"

Her brows shot downward.

He held up his hands. "I'm a medic too. I just want to make sure it's clean of any debris and no slivers of anything."

He tried her patience, but she took a deep breath and lowered her head. He got up on one knee and parted her hair. His hand ran down the full length as he brushed through her hair to move it out of his way. He tapped his fingers around the bump but didn't see an open wound.

"Just a bump. No open wounds. You're good, but you should ice it for the swelling."

She scowled at him.

"Let me hang up your basket while you go ice that."

Again, she scowled which he ignored. So, she handed him the magnet with the screw still attached to the bottom. Then got up and dusted off as she walked inside while he stood on the stool, effortlessly screwed in the bracket, and hung her basket up. The front door was left open, so he knocked.

"Come in!" He heard her but didn't see her.

"Daphne, your flowers are hung up. Where you at?"

"Bedroom"

His eyebrows drew together, as he set the stool by the door and walked past the kitchen. Her bedroom door was open, and he saw her trying to lift the king size mattress on the high-rise bed frame, bent in half with it on her back. In a rush now, he just made it through the doorway when the mattress slid off her back and onto the frame crooked.

He stopped immediately when she stood up straight. "I could have helped with that."

Daphne's eyes got big and fierce as she snapped. At nearly a shout she turned and stepped up to him. "See that's the thing Luke, I don't need any help! I don't want any help and I definitely don't need a man!"

He propped a shoulder against the doorframe of her bedroom and crossed his arms across his chest but didn't smile.

"You see me as broken, right?"

She didn't give him time to answer before continuing

"I'm the furthest from broken and if I ever need help it wouldn't be because I lack the muscle or height!"

He should have been mad, or sorry but for some reason everything he had felt for her just amplified. Trying not to smile, he kept a straight face. He unfolded his arms and put his hands in his pants pockets to keep from touching her and then stood straight.

"Is that it?" He asked

He watched her unclench her muscles and relax a little.

"I'll leave you alone if that's what you want. I don't have a problem with that..." But he did because he couldn't. He turned to head for the front door walking out through the living room past the kitchen then turned around taking a few steps backwards still working his way to the door,

"...But for the record, I never thought of you as incapable, just though you shouldn't have to be capable as your demeanor and house shows your strength of having to manage alone... for at least a couple years." He clearly looked around her house noting the decor and space.

Her face went from anger to shock. He gave her a rueful smile and turned around, walking out of the house closing her door behind him. Her confidence in him not knowing her dropped a couple of notches, along with her heart and stayed watching the door for a couple of minutes.

Over the next month, they kept their distance, only seeing each other through their windows or in passing. Though Kada visited often, it was for small things like helping Daphne plant some flowers, visiting Daphne on her bench, or raking the leaves that started to fall in Mid-August. Luke kept keen on her comings and goings, watching her load in groceries and things for her house. The last week of summer vacation before school was to start, Daphne was finishing students' files and paperwork for her new job as school nurse. She talked with other school employees and got to know them and got to know more about her job and the school. She was gathering a few small decorations for her new office when there was a knock on the door. Expecting Kada, she jogged to the front door, and opened it, finding Luke looking a little worried.

"Hey Luke."

"Hey Daphne, umm Kada's locked herself in the bathroom crying. I think she started her...."

Before Luke could finish, Daphne turned around and jogged to her bathroom. She came out with a small makeup purse, kept jogging to the kitchen to open a cabinet, grabbed a chocolate bar, and stuffing it in the purse before zipping it closed.

Luke thought she looked cute zipping around her house in leggings and a long gray cardigan over a white tank top with reading glasses on top of her head while biting her lips in concentration. Leaving her keys and cell phone behind she jogged back to Luke as she watched him.

"Let's go!" she spoke.

He stepped back as she stepped out and closed the door. Daphne walked fast; Luke had to jog to nearly keep up with her as they headed for his house.

"We had a fight about her coming on my training trip to Freeman this weekend and she got upset, I noticed the blood, and tried to make sure she was okay, not realizing. Then, she bolted in hysterics and locked herself in the bathroom and now I can't get her to come out. She keeps asking for you."

Daphne rolled her eyes and looked at him, "Do you expect anything different? Luke, she's confused, embarrassed, and upset. She's not a little girl anymore."

Oh, that hit him harder than he would have liked. They jogged up the porch steps and he opened the front door for her. When she walked in, it smelled like a clean man getting out of the shower. Fresh, woodsy, and masculine. His home decor spoke simple, efficient, and neat with a couple girly touches.

Luke closed the door behind them as he spoke, "Up the stairs to the left." He pointed to the staircase on their left.

Daphne toed off her shoes and jogged up the stairs to the carpeted balcony that overlooked Luke's big living room with big windows. Then turned left and saw the two doors as Luke came up behind her.

"She's gonna need a clean set of clothes."

Luke frowned and pointed towards the far-left door that had a pink sign on it, 'Kada's Room, Keep Out!' Daphne rolled her eyes and swatted Luke's chest, then headed for the bedroom door and opened it.

Two windows covered in purple, and pink shadowed the room in the girly colors. Stuffed animals and sparkles with a small desk and a soft pink chair in the corner opposite of the bed covered in soft blue. There was also a wide dresser against the wall next to another door to which Daphne assumed went to the bathroom. Luke leaned on the door frame as Daphne found her way around and to the dresser crouching down to the bottom drawer and opening it find Kada's Pjs and pulled out a soft light purple pair of PJ pants, then to the top to her underwear and the middle drawer for a tee shirt. Daphne, holding the clothes and the purse, walked to the bathroom door in the room, and knocked on it.

"Kada, it's Daphne. Open the door sweetie."

Daphne didn't hear anything and looked at Luke still leaning on the doorframe watching her, giving her no help, and keeping a straight face.

She knocked again, "Kada, open the door please. I have some things for you."

The shout through the door came as a shock, "Tell him to go away!"

Daphne looked at Luke, who just threw up his hands in surrender and turned to walk out.

"He's gone Kada, now open up."

The door opened a crack and Kada peeked out then opened the door for Daphne, then closed it again and locked it. A pair of bloody jeans lay on the floor and Kada with her damp hair, wrapped in a bath towel. She then walked back to the tub and sat on the floor next to it and started to cry.

Sobbing, Kada spoke to Daphne. "Dad doesn't understand."

Daphne took a deep breath and mentally prepped for the talk. She had to remember though Kada was one of her students, this was a more personal home visit to a friend.

"He's not supposed to."

Kada grimaced and looked up at her.

"He sees you as five years old and his little girl." Daphne bent down in front of her and handed the clothes and purse to Kada, who took it from her and then wiped at her tears. Daphne reached over and picked up the bloody pants, stood up and walked to the sink.

"Cold water. Soak blood in cold water and then wash in cold water. That way your dad can save for another car in a few years and not pants every month."

Kada giggled.

Luke sat outside on the balcony stairs as he smiled and leaned against the railing.

Daphne turned around, letting Kada change in privacy as she filled the sink with cold water and added the pants until they were submerged, then turned off the water.

When Daphne turned around, Kada was finishing pulling her shirt down over the waistband of the clean pajama pants and pulled her hair free from the collar of the shirt. Daphne walked over to her and picked up the purse off the side of the tub and pulled out the candy bar and handed it to her.

"Chocolate is always the cure. If your dad throws a fit, my back door is always open for you, and the left cabinet to the kitchen sink always holds something chocolate in it."

Kada smiled again.

"You put a pad on?"

Kada nodded.

Daphne pulled out the Midol from the purse and took out two and handed them to her.

"Two of these will help you....and those around you survive the day, especially in gym class. Have Dad pick you up a heating pad or hot water bottle to help with the cramps. And Kada, never and I mean never let anyone make you feel less for being a woman cause every single one of us bleeds once a month. You are no different than anyone else. This is natural and scary but I'm here and .... so is your dad even if he doesn't want to admit it. Keep your chin up, and Kada, enjoy sending your dad out for pads and chocolate every month."

On the stairs still, Luke chuckled quietly and rolled his eyes with a smile.

Daphne cleaned up Kada's bathroom and sat on the edge of the tub next to Kada and took a deep breath.

"Now the hard part, talking to your dad."

Kada shot up in shock.

"No! He won't listen to me. He won't let me stay home alone. I can stay here nearly all day by myself, but not while he goes training?'

"I can see his side Kada...."

"Oh, so you are taking his side now?" she shouted

Daphne held up her hands trying for patience with the ever so emotional preteen.

"Instead, why don't you see if he'll go for a sleepover at my house and we'll veg out, pig out and watch chick flicks all weekend, till your dad gets home? I could use a relaxing weekend with some girl company anyway."

Kada's eyes lit up as she smiled.

"But Kada, be nice to your dad, he's just as lost as you, except you have more help than he does."

Kada nodded, opened the door, and sprinted down the steps to Luke who was now in the kitchen. Daphne drained the sink, wrung out the pants, put them in the dirty clothes basket by the bathtub, turned off the lights, and shut the door.

Luke sat at his kitchen bar on the stool facing Kada while they talked, so Daphne sat on the bottom of the stairs by the front door out of view.

"Kada, It's okay. I know I miss mom too. We will figure this out as we always have before."

"But Dad, Daphne said I could go to her house for the weekend while you're gone and have a girl's weekend. Please Dad, please!" She begged.

Luke took a breath, "Let me talk with Daphne, alone and you go pack a bag for the weekend, no matter where you are staying."

Daphne sat on one step, leaned against the wall, feet against the railing, while holding the makeup purse in her lap. When Kada rounded the corner and hopped the step over Daphne's legs, Daphne spoke up, "Pack a blanket and pillow for the couch. My guest room isn't finished yet!" as Kada kept jogging up the stairs to her bedroom.

When Luke walked over and leaned on the rail in front of Daphne, she looked a little more tired now.

"You sure you're okay with this?' He asked

"Yeah! We'll be fine at home. We'll bake brownies and watch girly movies all weekend."

Luke smiled, "Do I need to run to the store and pick up pads and chocolate before I leave?" Letting her in on what he was listening to.

Daphne smiled now, "No. I'll run her and at least show her what to look for."

He shrugged, "Okay, well at least let me...." He pulled his wallet from his back pocket making Daphne straighten.

"No! Luke, I think I can afford a box of pads."

He watched Daphne as he pulled out his business card, handed it to her, then finished, ".... my number just in case."

She relaxed, took it from him, and read it as he put his wallet back in his pocket.

"Birch Valley Fire Department, Lieutenant Lucas Richmond." As she spoke a flood of memories hit her.

"Richmond! Get the gear put back in the truck. We are out of here!"

She opened her eyes and instantly connected with him. Hers still held a hint of shock as his chin tilted sideways a little, while he attentively watched her.

"Something wrong?"

She shook her head as much from the memory as it was an answer.

"No." She lied. "Just never pegged you for a Lieutenant."

He read the lie just as he read the shock of a memory. He just chose not to push it. Kada came out of her room with a small duffle bag holding a soft pink and purple blanket and pillow then walked down the few steps to Daphne and Luke.

"Can I go Dad?"

Luke broke eye contact from Daphne to reply.

"Yes. Just be good."

Daphne stood up and took a couple of steps down to the floor as Kada passed by and opened the front door, looking back at them.

"My door is open." She told Kada who nearly sprinted to Daphne's without saying goodbye to her dad.

"Thanks Daphne. For today and Kada this weekend."

"You're welcome." She walked down the porch stairs as Luke leaned on the railing.

"We might even see you for lunch in Freeman, if Kada is up for it. I still have a few things to get for the house."

"Sounds good. Keep me posted."

Daphne gave a nod and turned to walk back to her house. Luke watched her until she got inside, then sighed.

By the evening, after a quick run to the store for supplies, they had a tray of caramel turtle brownies Kada had made from a box and a bag of random sweets and salty treats. After their long talk about puberty and hormones from a school nurse, Daphne texted Luke the updates, then settled on the couch for a season of Gilmore Girls.

At nearly 8 O'clock, Daphne's phone lit up and chimed on the end table next to the couch.

"Richmond" popped on the screen.

Daphne grabbed it as Kada watched her from the end of the couch. Daphne opened the message, read it and then looked at Kada.

"Your Dad wants to know how you are doing?"

Kada rolled her eyes, "Of course he does. I'm good, Dad!"

Daphne texted him that exact reply and hit send.

Luke replied right away. A smiley face and "Okay. Good night, ladies."

Daphne smiled. At least he was trying to accept that Kada wasn't a little girl anymore. "Good night, Luke - Dad!" She answered back.

Daphne put her phone back on the side table, picked up a popcorn bowl, and ate some watching Kada and her sour mood.

"Hey Kada, he's trying. Give him some credit."

She stopped watching tv and turned to face Daphne on the small couch, so that their bare feet touched under the blanket they shared.

"That's the thing, Daphne. He's not! He hasn't been on a date ever. He never does anything fun. He goes to work and comes home to me. Him and Uncle Mike go out sometimes when I stay with Aunt Jen and Sarah, but usually, it's to hang out at the station. I want him to be happy and he is not getting any younger worrying about me all the time."

Daphne laughed at that.

"Yes....He does worry but that's what parents do and even more so when they are the only parent. He is a firefighter, so he feels like he has to help everyone first, so that is true though."

"Yeah, I know!" Kada replied with an attitude.

Daphne smirked then ate another pinch of popcorn.

"Just be patient with him. Okay?'

"I'll try, but I have at least 6 more years before I get freedom." Then rolled her eyes and went back to watching TV.

Luke set his phone back on the nightstand in his hotel room, looked over in the bed next to him, and watched the naked sleeping brunette woman. He got out from under the covers and slipped on his boxers, then looked around the room at the two sets of turnout gear strewn all over the room. He took a deep breath and decided on a shower. His muscles clenched thinking of Daphne and the puzzle.

While water poured over him, sending steam into the air, his mind wandered.

She knew his name. How? Why? He had never met her. Maybe someone in town told her about him, but the body reaction to her memories told him those were brutal memories. The tag... on his coat says Richmond. A call! But she didn't look like she was hurt, maybe someone close to her on a call. No, because if she wasn't on the initial call, she wouldn't know his name. His mind flipped through as many victims' faces as he could remember.... nothing. There is no one even close to looking like her. He was at a loss and now even more frustrated than before.

He finished washing up and got out. Tomorrow was going to be another long day of training and he needed sleep. He slipped on a pair of clean boxers and heard movement in the room. When the door opened, he looked at the brunette woman standing in the doorway.

"Hey, Luke, I'm gonna take off. I need a shower and sleep before tomorrow."

"Okay, yeah I'm headed to bed too."

She gave him a frown and turned to walk out.

"Oh, and Reid?"

She turned to look at him.

"Yes, Lieutenant?"

"Don't wear yourself out in the first portion tomorrow. There will be four parts including the smoke house and forceable entry."

She smiled and nodded then turned to walk out. A couple of minutes later he heard the room door open and close.

Luke brushed his teeth, shaved, and then climbed back into bed falling asleep thinking of Daphne, the only woman that could occupy his mind besides his daughter.

When Daphne woke and walked out of the bedroom, Kada was curled into a ball on the couch under the blanket. She smiled and walked to the coffee pot to make coffee.

After Kada woke up they got ready for a girl's shopping day in Freeman. Ready to lock up the house, Daphne slipped on a pair of thigh high, black suede, high heel boots over her fitted jeans and wore a loose cowl neck gray sweater that showed off her collarbone.

After putting on some mascara and lip gloss, she fluffed her hair. The first time she felt pretty like a girl in a long time. Kada took notes and with Daphne's help picked out a cute outfit in similar style to Daphne's. Loose jeans, long black sleeve shirt, and Daphne's small dark gray crop top sweater over top with Kada's short black ankle boots with a one-inch heel. Daphne then dug out her gray tote purse from the hall closet and packed it with the small makeup purse of Kada's, her wallet, cell phone, lip gloss, and other random girly necessities.

"I think we need to buy you a purse today, but a small one. Your dad is gonna hate me already."

Kada frowned at the statement, "No he won't. He likes you too much to hate you, Daphne!"

Daphne batted her now heavier lashes at Kada with a smile, then reapplied her lip gloss, and handed it to Kada, while she rubbed her lips together. Kada smiled and ran to the bathroom. She came out a minute later like she was walking down a runway.

"How do I look?" and did a turn.

Daphne's eyes got big, but replied, "Gorgeous!"

Gathering up her purse and coat.

"K. Out to the car!"

"Can I sit in the front? Dad, lets me!"

"If your dad lets you, I guess it's fine with me."

Kada ran out to the car and jumped in the passenger seat.

Daphne locked up the house and looked over to a dark and empty Luke's and whispered.

"Your dad is gonna kill me anyways, might as well live for the both of us." Then turned and walked to the car.

After Daphne and Kada hit a few stores in a big mall. Luke texted.

"Almost done with morning training. Got an hour lunch break soon. We still meeting up?"

"Yeah. When and where?"

"Doie's? 12:30? It's off 20th and C Street."

"Sounds good! We'll be there!"

Daphne looked at Kada. "Ready to bat those pretty eyes at your dad? We have to meet him for lunch in 30 minutes."

Kada smiled big and gave her a demonstration.

"Yeah, like that. I'm counting on it!"

Kada laughed, Daphne didn't but smiled.

Luke waited by the restaurant entrance a couple minutes to 12:30 and watched the cars pass by on the busy road in front of him.

Daphne's Jeep pulled up behind Luke's truck next to the sidewalk and saw the girls' faces laughing as Daphne parked. Daphne swiped at her face in the mirror and said something to Kada that had her smiling big. Luke smiled as their doors opened and Daphne got out first and jogged around the car onto the sidewalk to help Kada.

The glimpse Luke got of Daphne dressed up nearly floored him as he adjusted his stance to better support his own weight.

When Kada got out and closed the door Luke's face went into full shock as Daphne and her new mini me strolled down the sidewalk towards him. Daphne had noticed him first and rolled her lips inward to bite on them with a half-smile. She held hands with Kada as Kada skipped alongside her. When Kada looked up and saw her dad and his facial expression, it nearly stopped her dead in her tracks, and she walked the rest of the way.

"Hi Daddy."

"Hi. Who are you?" Then he looked at Daphne, "Where is Kada? My little girl... that you took home with you last night....Where is she?" Being more serious with Daphne but light enough for Kada.

Kada just laughed, but Daphne didn't. He gave Daphne a look from over Kada's head as he hugged his daughter. Daphne just smiled. When he crouched down to Kada's level he spoke softly.

"Hi, Baby. You look very beautiful. How are you feeling?"

"Good! Me and Daphne have been shopping all morning. Oh, and she let me pick out the bed for the guestroom......"

Luke's eyebrows dropped a notch.

"And Daphne bought me some new clothes for school...."

He looked at Daphne.

".... Oh, and she bought me a purse to hold....my things. See!"

She showed him her new plain small black purse. He tried to smile as he looked up at Daphne then turned back to Kada.

"That's awesome, Baby. I'm hungry, let's get something to eat." Trying to end the conversation before he found out anymore.

Daphne led the way in, letting Kada hang out with her dad. The Hostess asked how many and Daphne replied, "Three."

She grabbed three menus and headed back outside to the side patio to seat them at a small round table in the sunlight. Kada sat across from Daphne and Luke in between them on Daphne's right. They ordered drinks and quickly chose food. While waiting for the food, Luke looked at Daphne and asked before drinking his sweet tea.

"So, when does your bed come in?"

When Daphne gave him a look, Luke held up his hands.

"That's two flights of stairs, Daphne. I'm just saying."

Daphne drank her sweet tea and put it down.

"That is not two flights of stairs. That is four steps up the porch and...."

She thought about the narrow steeper set of stairs to the loft with a switchback turn.

Luke grinned from ear to ear and took another sip of his tea. Daphne bit her lip and swatted at Luke.

"Fine! But you are only helping me."

He gave a smug smile and shrugged a shoulder. When Luke turned to Kada, Daphne felt Luke's foot hook hers and pull it towards him. Luke continued to talk to Kada about her night and day as she excitedly told him all about it.

Within a few minutes her knee was over his. Sitting perfectly still at the table, Daphne drank her tea and gave the occasional nod or agreement when Kada or Luke looked at her, Luke usually with more of a smile.

When the food came, Luke scooted his chair closer to the table, reached under, and pulled her leg further up his thigh as Daphne watched Kada smile at the waiter who served her food to her. They thanked the waiters as they served the plates of food, Luke then pulled out his wallet and placed his card on the waiter's tray.

"Just clear the tab now please. We'll be leaving soon. Thanks"

The waiter nodded at him.

Luke looked at Kada happily eating her food and then mouthed a silent "Thank you" to Daphne as he gave a nod towards Kada. Daphne gave a nod and smiled back. Luke gave her leg a small bounce under the table while watching her take a bite of her food.

After eating, Luke signed the receipt, and they left walking back to the vehicles.

When they reached Daphne's Jeep, Kada gave her dad a hug, thanked him for lunch, and said her goodbye, then jumped in the car.

Luke turned to Daphne. "I should be home around 2ish tomorrow. We got training and a couple of quick tests in the morning, but I should be done by noon, maybe one." He played with his keys in his hands nervously.

"Good. That should be the time the bed comes." She smiled.

Luke smiled and his eyes intensified.

"So, when will I get my little girl back?

Daphne looked to be in thought, then bunched her lips together giving him a grin.

"Hmm, never. I don't think *that* Kada will be back, but if you give the new edition a try, She's fun and happier, at least 3 weeks out of the month."

Luke smiled and laughed.

"Alright, I gotta get back to training."

He watched her for a second.

"Thank you, Daphne."

With keys in his left hand, he wrapped his free right hand around her waist, pulled her in close, and gave her a kiss on the cheek. When he released her, she placed a hand on his shoulder, gave him a smile, and let it fall as she turned to walk to her driver's side and get in.

Kada rolled down her window to shout at her dad.

"Love you, Dad!" as she waved to him through the open window.

"Love you too! Be good! I'll see you tomorrow!" He spoke.

Daphne smiled at him, gave him a quick wave, and pulled out into the street and drove off.

CHAPTER THREE

When Luke returned to the training center in gear, firemen and women were lined up in their individual station uniforms. Luke joined the three Chiefs in the front. One spoke to him.

"What's next, Lieutenant?"

Luke smiled, "I don't know. Lunch was pretty heavy. I think we need to do a warmup."

The Chiefs all gave him a nod.

Luke spoke loudly so all the sixty firemen and women could hear him.

"The training center is one mile around! You have forty-five minutes to come, get a forty-five-pound weighted vest, and do two laps, Starting...... Now."

Several moans and complaints broke out as they ran to the large tote behind Luke, got a vest, and started jogging the perimeter of the training center.

Chief Greyson bumped Luke to show him a picture on his cell phone. Luke leaned over to look at it. It was a picture taken from behind him and Daphne today at lunch of Daphne's long black boots over Luke's leg, hidden under the table, as Luke held a hand on her leg. Both Luke and Kada watched Daphne with smiles.

Luke looked at the Chief in shock, who just nodded towards a small group starting to jog. A younger fireman looked over his shoulder smiling at Luke.

"Jackson! You now have 3 laps!"

The Chiefs watched Luke.

"Who is she?"

Luke tried not to smile. "No one."

His phone chimed in his turnout pants pocket. He undid the Velcro and reached for it watching the various groups running, then looked at the message.

Mike Davis: *You're supposed to be training up there not playing hooky with the neighbor.*

Luke didn't bother to reply before stuffing his phone back in his pocket, grabbing a vest and throwing it on. He started off in a full sprint to Jackson's group, until they heard him coming and Jackson saw Luke homed in on him.

"Oh shit!" Then took off smiling and laughing in a full run leaving the group behind.

"Jackson, you're dead!"

The group cheered and yelled with laughter as Luke chased Jackson around the edge of the training center the full two laps.

When the girls got back to Daphne's and unloaded their shopping bags, they were exhausted. Daphne and Kada immediately changed into pjs to lounge on the couch. They then made pancakes and hashbrowns for dinner, watching more Gilmore Girls, and laughing about Luke with his shock and dismay.

As morning came, they got dressed and decorated the guest room while jamming to music. Daphne and Kada both danced to happy upbeat tunes as they hung some blue curtains over the small window. Daphne began singing soprano with her amazing voice, as Kada danced with Daphne. They sang in harmony, swung their hips and hands to the beat and lyrics as Daphne twirled Kada around the small room.

Daphne had her back to the door, so she didn't notice Luke watching her with wide eyes and a smile. He was taken back on how well she could sing matching the pitch and tone. When Kada noticed, Luke put a finger to his lips and smiled at Kada just to watch Daphne sing and dance with his daughter in the small confinement of her guest bedroom, as her hair fell and bounced around her shoulders.

When she reached for Kada's hand and spun them both in a circle, she saw Luke standing in the doorway smiling as they made eye contact. She froze for about two seconds before she reached for Luke's hand and pulled on it, spinning herself under his arm as her hips and shoulders moved to the beat. Kada laughed and smiled at Daphne dancing with her dad. Kada joined in, Luke then spun and dipped Kada while he rocked his hips back and forth slower than the girls did. With the music on full blast through the little Bluetooth speaker on the window seal, they danced, laughed, and smiled until the song ended.

"Wow! You can really sing, Daphne." Luke spoke as his hands went safely back in his pockets.

"Oh that? That's just singing to the radio and, maybe some high school choir lessons." She smiled

"You're back early." She was watching him over Kada who ran to hug her dad.

"Yeah. I about killed the crews last night on training, so we just did tests and left." He smiled and thought about him and Jackson running the full two miles.

Daphne smiled. "Ugh, I need some water. I haven't danced like that in a while."

She pushed her hair back and smiled at Luke, then walked around him and Kada hugging and walked down the stairs to the kitchen.

As she filled up the glass with cold water, her hips were still moving to the music in her head on repeat. Kada and Luke came down and took seats at the bar as she swayed her hip while drinking the water. When Daphne turned around, they just watched her with big smiles.

"What?"

Luke laughed. "We just haven't seen you this happy."

Unenthused, she frowned.

"Yeah? Well, it's been a few years."

He didn't like that reply.

Kada spoke up, "Hey Daphne, you know it's Dad's birthday next weekend?"

Daphne tilted her head and looked at the uncomfortable Luke with a forced smile.

"No.... No I did not! Well, it looks like we might have to go shopping again, won't we?! Do you have any ideas or know what he likes?"

Kada smiled big and looked at her dad, got off the stool, and ran to Daphne. Then stuck up her hand as Daphne leaned down to put her ear close to Kada as she whispered in her ear.

"Dad likes the fire department and you."

Daphne smiled big and turned to whisper back to Kada.

"I know."

Luke watched Daphne go blush in her cheeks and smiled at the two of them whispering back and forth.

"Hey, Dad doesn't need anything." he gave a soft shout across the kitchen island.

Daphne smiled again.

"Hey pipe down over there and let the girls talk."

Luke laughed.

"We'll figure something out."

"Okay!" Kada then faced Luke to say, "I'm gonna take my stuff home and get ready for school tomorrow."

"Okay, Baby. I'll be home as soon as I'm done helping Daphne."

"Okay." She looked at Daphne and gave her a hug. "Thank you, Daphne. I had a blast and thank you for the clothes and all the stuff too!"

"Of course. Just remember what I told you and if you need anything, my back door is open for you and your dad anytime."

Both Kada and Luke smiled at the same time.

"That goes for you and our house too, Daphne." Luke spoke.

Daphne just smiled at Luke from across the kitchen.

Kada jogged around the house piling up a load to run over, then took a small arm load home.

"I really don't need anything, but if you want, the crew is having a barbeque at the station this Saturday, you're welcome to come, if you want."

She didn't know if she was ready to meet his crew yet, but smiled and nodded, "I'll think about it. Thank you."

He placed his elbow on the counter and braced his chin in his hand, then gave a quick glance to the pile of bags next to the door, then back to Daphne.

"So how much shopping did you actually do?"

She smiled at how uncomfortably confused he looked, then replied, "It's what girls do best. Plus, I needed it. I don't exactly have a best friend these days to run to, so shopping is a stress release. Even if I can't talk to Kada about my more mature problems, I can at least relax and smile with her."

Luke smiled, "I'm glad she can make you smile. But you know I'm an adult and a friend.... you can talk to me. Come on, try me. What's the worst, that I wouldn't understand what it's like to set my house on fire to talk to the hot firemen."

Daphne drinking water while he talked nearly choked on some when he finished that sentence.

"It amazes me that, *that* was the only scenario you came up with to describe a woman. Not everyone needs to be rescued, Luke." For her own guilt, she left out the 'needing a man' part on purpose.

Kada walked in and picked up another arm load to haul over and walked back out the front door leaving behind the last four bags, then closed the door again.

"You're wrong. Everyone needs help. Even the heroes. Here, I'll show you. I need help with some problems I'm having. Maybe you can help me figure them out."

She raised an eyebrow. "What a bromance at work not working for you anymore?" She laughed and smiled.

Luke actually laughed at that. "No. My new neighbor."

Now Daphne stood still as her eyes got more intense. "Umm, Okay. What about her? You like her or something?"

"I don't know yet. But I know she stirs up something inside me. I know she knew me prior to moving here, but I don't know how." He searched her face as he still leaned on his hand on the counter.

She swallowed, leaned back on the counter behind her, and braced her hands on either side of her hips on the countertop.

"She has a past she is running from either out of fear or guilt or both. I don't know. The what and why I haven't figured out either. But I know it's not criminal and whatever it is keeps her building walls just as fast as I keep trying to tear them down. She doesn't trust easily, even me, except a 12-year-old which is the only thing I have found that makes her smile. "

Nearly on the edge of breaking, she looked at him, "Luke, I'd *never* put Kada in danger."

He still watched her and took a breath preparing for whatever came next. "I know that and honestly I'd be willing to bet your protective instincts are probably just as sharp as any parent's is, if not sharper given your... situation, but Daphne, I'm also a firefighter. It's a need to care, protect, and save, But you...."

He got up while keeping eye contact and moved around the kitchen island to lean against it, leaving only a couple feet of space between them, but put his hands in his pockets, relaxing more than Daphne.

"......are stirring up something in me that is far beyond any need and has been pushing on my instinctual boundaries. I felt it in the diner, and nearly every day since and I don't know why."

The fabric of his cotton t-shirt stretched over his chest rising and falling with each breath he took. He looked at a nearly frozen Daphne that searched his eyes. He saw the raw emotions she dug through to reach for a calm reserve.

"Daphne, talk to me please."

He noticed her hands on the counters, not holding any real weight, started to shake and a single tear fell from her face.

"I'm sorry Luke." She stood straight and crossed her arms over her chest.

He let out a breath and pulled his hands free of his pockets then took a step forward and she took a single step to her right, making him freeze where he stood.

"Daphne." he spoke softly.

Her stiffer posture told him that the conversation was over.

"I'm gonna help Kada take the rest of the bags over. The bed should be here soon."

She walked away, picked up the last of the bags, and walked out the door leaving him right where he stood. He took a deep breath and let it out, then walked to where Daphne stood to pick up her empty glass, fill it with water from the sink, and drank it. He watched her through the kitchen window, as she walked across the yard to his house and greeted Kada on the porch. Daphne passed her the bags and gave her a hug before Kada said something, making Daphne smile and nod.

Luke heard the diesel truck rounding the corner as the front door was left open.

He watched Kada put the bags inside the door and start the jog across the yard with Daphne. He walked out the open front door as the truck backed in next to Daphne's Jeep. When the crew got out of the truck, they waved at Daphne. "Hello again."

Daphne waved and walked to them and took the clipboard again to sign as they dropped the loading dock again. Luke helped them unload into her entryway the full-size bed, box spring and low metal frame with a small dresser and matching nightstand.

The three of them stood on the porch to watch them leaving as Kada spoke first.

"It's here!!"

Daphne smiled at Kada then looked at her with the same smile. Luke smiled back and mouthed "I'm sorry" over Kada, to Daphne, who gave him a half smile.

"Let's get a move on. We all have a busy day tomorrow."

The three of them moved the furniture upstairs to the guest room as an efficient team. Daphne said her goodbye and thanked Kada for the fun weekend together, then Luke gave her a hug and kiss on the cheek before closing the front door between them.

Over the week, Daphne kept busy with her new job, meeting the parents, students, and staff of Birch Valley Middle School. She only saw Luke in passing a few times and on the second day of school with the second wave of parents bringing their students in to meet the teachers and new staff that couldn't make it the 1st day. Him and Kada stood with another group of parents and kids.

"Hi, Luke Richmond. Kada's Dad."

"Daphne Kimble, Birch Valley's Middle School neighbor.... I mean nurse."

Kada giggled while Luke smiled.

She smiled and tried to play it off as the other parents looked on and shook his hand. When she let go, he didn't. He gave it a couple seconds, then let her hand slide out of his. Kada just smiled holding her backpack ready to walk on to the next classroom.

"Thanks, Ms. Kimble!" Kada spoke as she pulled her dad away.

Luke smiled at her and turned to walk away with Kada. Daphne could overhear Kada whisper while she greeted other parents.

"Dad, you are gonna get both of us in trouble. You might as well date my principal or heck even the mayor. Thought I was the cool kid in the third grade when the teacher told everyone that My Dad and Uncle were bringing fire trucks to school for fire safety day but now, I'll really never be homecoming queen."

Luke just laughed and put an arm around her as they walked down the hall and leaned over to kiss her head.

"Dad! Stop! Oh my God....just go to work. Please. I love you." She leaned away pulling out of his grip to walk on the other side of the hall from him. Then, they turned into another classroom and out of view.

When Daphne's group left, she smiled and laughed. Poor Luke. As she thought about her first year of puberty and the handful she was, with half the attitude of Kada.

By the weekend, she was exhausted and used it as the excuse, she told herself, to skip out on Luke's station barbecue. But took Kada after school from the house to Freeman to go shopping for Luke. Kada found a nice, fancy, black metal fireman's watch at this little shop dedicated to all the Emergency services departments. Luke was looking a little worse for wear and thought it was perfect from Kada but found her own gifts to give him.

Saturday, Daphne worked on some files and flipped through her textbooks at her kitchen island with a glass of wine.

When Luke's truck passed her house, she sighed and looked at the small rectangle package wrapped in a silver iridescent paper with a blue and silver ribbon that sat beside her. She grabbed it and walked out her front door, across the yard to place the present by Luke's front door and stuck a folded piece of paper under the ribbon. She smiled, then kissed her hand and touched it to the wrapping.

By nine o'clock, the sun was setting, and she turned off her lights and curled into her bay window with a book and blanket dressed in PJs. When Luke's house lit up with headlight beams, she got up to walk to her kitchen window. Her house was completely dark besides her small book light. So, she had her doubts that they could see her in the window watching. Kada got out of the truck with a bag and plate of food and walked up the steps. Kada in the porch light, said something while looking at Luke getting out of the truck with his keys and radio in hand. Kada set down the bag and plate to pick up the present and walked it to her dad just coming up the steps.

Holding his radio and keys he pulled the note out and read it, while walking up the steps. When he reached the door, he looked over towards Daphne's house. Kada jumped up and down next to him with questions and pleas. Luke smiled and unlocked the door to go inside.

Daphne took a deep breath and walked back to her window to settle in again with her book, setting her phone on the small bookshelf next to it.

"What's the note say, Dad? Is it From Daphne? Dad, open it!" Kada begged next to Luke who put his keys and radio next to the door and walked over to the kitchen counter. He picked up the note again and read it out of Kada's view,

I'm sorry. This is all I have right now.
Happy Birthday Luke.

He folded it, stuck it in his back pocket, then untied the ribbon, and tore the paper off. Inside was a silver 4x6 picture frame that held a picture of Daphne and Kada at the mall. Both dressed up and smiling big while raising arm loads of shopping bags into the air. Luke smiled at it, propped it up on the counter next to him, and looked down at the thick book that was under it.

"Father-Daughter relationships: A Dad's Survival Guide to Raising a daughter."

Sticky notes stuck out the top, so he flipped to them as Kada watched him.

Chapter 24: Puberty

Chapter 26: The Beginning of the Teenage years.

He gave a soft laugh and closed the book as Kada grabbed it from him with her own complaints and comments about the book, none of which Luke heard as he pulled out his cell phone from his back pocket and pulled up Daphne's texts.

"Thank you, Daphne. I love it."

In a near instant, his phone chimed with Daphne's reply.

"You're welcome. Happy Birthday, Luke. Hope it was great."

He started to type a message, then erased it. As he started typing again, he looked up at Daphne's blacked out house.

"Kada goes to bed in an hour, can we talk?"

A longer wait for a reply.

"Sure."

He smiled and tucked his phone back in his pocket.

After Kada took a shower and got tucked into bed, Luke turned out the bedroom lights and closed the door. He walked down the steps and straight out the back door. With steps slow, but big, he made it across the yard in about half the time to her back door.

Her bay window now empty and no backdoor light, he took a deep breath and opened it. Daphne nearly jumped off the bar stool by the kitchen island in sheer panic dropping her glass of wine as the glass shattered on the wood floor spilling the red wine everywhere.

Luke immediately stopped in his tracks just inside the door, realizing what he had done. But he didn't care. They were going to talk, and he was going to get some answers. He continued walking towards the frozen Daphne, stepping over the glass and puddle of wine, to grab her and kiss her. He held her neck and used his thumb to push her chin up. He could taste the tartness of the wine on her lips. Her eyes closed; her lips parted for the air he kept stealing. His free left hand reached behind her touching the small of her back pulling her closer. For a second she did nothing as her hands stayed in the air not touching him, yet not pushing him away. Well, that answered one of his questions.

She didn't know what to do. She imagined what kissing him would be like, but this was far from what she could dream. A very satisfying loss of blood and air. All she could feel was his three contacts of warmth, both his hands and his lips. Here was the safe and secure feeling again that she had known. Nothing could hurt her, except him. Only her lips made any movement. Her brain began to fog when he turned his head sideways to fit better. Time now, stood still.

When he released her, in a delayed second later, she gasped for air and nearly shouted.

"Luke! What the hell?"

"How do I know you, Daphne? Tell me how we met.... the first time!" He nearly shouted back out of frustration.

Her eyes got big as she took a step back. Her hands clenched and released the tension. She then turned and walked around the kitchen island to get a rag and the trash can, breathing deeply.

Luke took a deep breath. He knew better than to scare her, then kiss her, but it was a pure reaction he had little control over. He bent down to help her pick up the broken shards of glass as she wiped at the wine. She noticed that he was wearing the new watch her and Kada bought and gave a slight smile. They stayed silent as they cleaned up the mess together. He then walked over to her, keeping his distance but close enough to reach her.

He spoke very softly now, "Daphne, was it a call?"

She stiffened her spine and hung the rag over the faucet and looked out the window to his house unwilling to look at him.

"Yes." She gave a whispered reply.

"Did you lose someone close? Did I lose someone in my care? Where was it? When?"

"No."

She paused, then continued.

"I only came here to thank you. I never expected to move in next door to you, or to fall in love with your daughter, or to find you so single and....."

She turned to him now and waved a hand from his head to feet and back up,

"That hidden under all that gear after knowing what you are capable of in gear."

Luke smiled and let out a breath. She continued, almost at the verge of breaking.

"Nightingale syndrome, white knight, rescuers romance...whatever you want to call it, there are a hundred names for it. I did the research, Luke. It's not that, despite what you think. But I need answers as to why the only thing I see in my darkest fears, happiest moments and before I close my eyes every night, are a set of golden eyes and still the only thing I see when I look at you."

His eyes darkened as he watched her.

"Well thank you, but Daph, I'm also capable of trust. Why won't you trust me?"

She gave him a sad look and wrapped her arms around herself.

"I do. I did then and I still do. I just don't trust myself."

Luke grew confused and lowered his eyebrows. Instead of stepping to her, he held out his hand. Her eyes grew sad as a few seconds ticked by, she grabbed it, and he wrapped her into an embrace. Her arms tucked in between them, and her head laid on his chest as he just held her. He wrapped his right arm around her waist and left arm around her back placing his hand on her head, resting his cheek on the top of her head.

"I'm sorry, Daphne."

"Don't tell anyone please."

He kissed the top of her head and held her tighter in response.

Over the next couple months to Thanksgiving. He didn't push anymore. The three of them shared home cooked meals on occasion, split between their houses as friends and the occasional friendly message to check in and kept their friendship light.

At least a couple nights on weekends, Kada spent the night in Daphne's guest room and on the occasional longer call of Luke's, Kada found company sharing dinner or movie with Daphne before returning home for the night for school in the morning.

Daphne found friendship in a couple of co-workers especially in Jeannie, the school secretary and often spent lunch together laughing and smiling over a cheeseburger from the Diner or their lunch from home. Though Daphne talked about Luke and Kada, she never let Jeannie know of anything more serious than a simple friendship with the neighbor kept outside of work.

Though Daphne saw Luke three to four times each week, she still missed him. She was enjoying their time together though and noticed even the memories started to fade. She built a comfortable life within the short few months she was here but never let herself forget her past as thoughts and questions kept her awake most nights.

She got invited to the station for a family Thanksgiving at the firehouse and was asked to bring a dish. It was starting to freeze solid at night with snow during the day then melting the next sunny day. Daylight got shorter putting her on a more natural sleep schedule at least on the days she was able to sleep.

The night before, she had dinner at Luke's and then stayed up half the night texting Luke, talking until she fell asleep. It was beginning to feel natural and almost needed, at least the small talk.

On the evening of Thanksgiving on the way to the station with Luke and Kada, she held her bowl of potato salad in her lap with the force of a bodybuilder nearly crushing the plastic bowl, as Luke watched from his driver's seat next to her.

"Daphne."

She looked at him, taking her focus off the road.

"Relax. Most of them you already know as the parents of your kids. Breathe."

Kada popped her head between their seats and spoke up,

"Besides Uncle Mike."

"Kada!" Luke shouted.

Daphne forgot about Luke's best friend, brother, and Captain, Mike Davis. She had already met Sarah, his daughter and Jen, his wife, but the famous Mike that Luke and Kada both talked about often, not yet. How much did Luke tell him about her? Would Mike remember her even if she couldn't remember him? Thoughts raced and she clenched the bowl again.

Luke held his hand out over the center console as he weaved through the neighborhood headed for the center of town. Hidden from Kada by her seat, Daphne lowered her eyebrows and looked at Luke. She then placed her hand on the center console as he wrapped his hand around hers, hoping to calm her nerves a little. Knowing how much a simple hug or touch from him could calm her after a bad memory or bad day at work, it was getting to be the same for him. After a bad call or day, he could only think about Daphne.

Luke didn't care what Kada saw but doubted she would say anything to anyone else. He glanced in his rearview mirror at her and saw his 12-year-old with a big grin and a secret, as she stared at their hands on the console. Even if he knew it wasn't what she thought it was, he let her keep it. At her age he figured boys had cooties still anyways so the concept of adult friendships of the opposite sex would be foreign to her anyways, plus save him the trouble of any future corrections or changes, hopefully.

At the station, Luke gave her a tour, greeting people and making introductions as they passed people. Kada and Luke, both introduced her as " Friend and neighbor, Daphne Kimble" or "Friend and school nurse, Ms. Kimble" which she loved.

Though not as bad as she thought, she could still feel the gazes and questions in various forms as to why the Lieutenant brought his daughter's nurse to their Thanksgiving. She definitely felt out of place and tried not to ask herself the same question. She was not family, girlfriend, wife, or knew anyone else here longer than four months.......at least that they knew.

Luke went to get them something to drink from a big cooler near the buffet table of food as Daphne stood next to a hallway watching the crowd mingle. Kada pigged out with Sarah at the dessert table as Jen watched over them nearby. Luke was dressed in black Tactical pants and a nice station sweater and black boots. Clean shaved today, he wasn't the same Luke she had met a few months ago, without the gear. He was different. Same professional demeanor that saved her more times than he knew. Though, now she saw the two men merge into one while she watched him pull two water bottles out of the cooler, turn to look at her, and make eye contact. He froze and his soul smiled watching her glowing from across the room, though her arms were still wrapped around herself, she kept eyes on him. When he took a step towards her, he heard his name.

"Lieutenant."

He turned his head to the direction of the shout and saw Mike walking towards him through a small crowd of people. He looked at Daphne who still watched him and gave her a small smile before turning to face Mike.

"Hey Captain."

"Hey. Happy Thanksgiving!"

"Yeah, Happy Thanksgiving! Hey, I want you to meet someone." He looked up at Daphne, who now wasn't smiling and saw her glow begin to fade. He walked towards her, and Mike gave short greetings to people he passed. Daphne straightened her spine. Luke walked over and stood next to her.

"Mike, this is Daphne. My neighbor and the girl's nurse."

Mike looked at her standing next to Luke holding herself and rigid, giving her a smile. He held out a hand, " Hi Daphne. So good to finally meet you."

She loosened a little and took his hand, "Hi Mike. Same."

"So, you are the new school nurse that took Mrs. Adam's place, huh?"

"Yes, sir. I hear she is an icon and will be missed at the school."

Daphne talked, though her posture still stayed stiff. So, Luke tried to ease her tension and wrapped his empty hand and arm around her waist, pulling her close as he spoke to Mike. Trying to make it as natural as possible and almost immediately felt her muscles loosen.

"Daphne is an amazing nurse and has helped me with Kada. So, I have no doubts Daphne will fit in Mrs. Adams shoes perfectly at the school within time."

Mike smiled at Luke. "Oh, no need to tell me. Sarah and Kada love her, so she has my blessing already."

"Oh, Sarah. How is she? She came into my office a couple weeks ago for a bump on the head from a ball in gym class. I think it was your wife, Jennifer, I talked to her over the phone and came in later that day."

"Jen, yup. Sarah is great. They are pretty resilient at that age. Usually, an ice pack and Tylenol works best. You definitely have your hands full. "

"Meh, 200 preteens finding their hormones is an adventure, but I wouldn't compare it to the older kids...." She looked up at Luke who just chuckled at her. ".... you train to help complete strangers on the worst days of their lives."

Mike laughed and looked at Luke and gave him a nod. " I like her! Keep this one."

Luke smiled and tilted his head. "She's not mine."

Daphne put her hand on Luke's back and stood straighter.

"Well, she should be. If she can take care of that many kids with hormones and still hold a sense of humor, then you should be a piece of cake."

He looked at Daphne who just laughed. "If you need more Kleenex and band aids for the man-child here, just let me know. I'll gladly turn over my med kit with gold stickers and lollipops."

Luke chuckled and worked his Jaw. "Alright, let's get Jen over here and compare notes, shall we?"

"Oh, no, no, no."

The guys laughed at each other in good humor as they poked at each other. Daphne smiled at the friendship base they had and had no doubt that it was at least part of the reason Birch Valley slept easy at night knowing they ran the fire department together as family, friends and co-workers. She now knew how she survived that day.

When Mike had to turn and greet others, Luke turned her around to head down the hall.

"Where are we going?"

They passed others in the hallway.

"My office is right down here. Last door on the left."

Daphne followed.

Luke pulled keys out of his pocket and when he reached the door, he handed Daphne the water bottles he still held onto, to unlock the door and hold it open for her to walk in. Luke walked in behind her and shut the door, without turning on the lights, making her jump and drop the water bottles.

When she turned around to find him, he grabbed her waist and the side of her neck kissing her again. He turned them and backed her into the closed door. In the dark office room only a small computer power button shined on his desk.

Her pulse raced with his. She gasped for air. "Luke."

He didn't release her mouth but braced both his hands on the door above her head. His hungry kisses made her near breathless. Her hands found his waist covered by his sweater and gripped it. His mouth moved over her jaw and down her neck letting out a soft moan. "Luke."

She pulled at his sweater making him give a soft throaty moan. He took his hands off the door to grab her wrists, folding his hands with hers, and then pinned them to the door. His mouth slipped down her cardigan and off her shoulder and he sucked at the dip between her collarbone and shoulder. She grew weaker by the second trying to resist him.

"Luke, stop."

But he didn't. His hands pawed hers against the door as he gave her soft love bites. He was holding most of her weight now with his and her hands. He growled as he gave one last bite to her shoulder and snapped away, stepping back and releasing her.

She could hear him breathing hard in the darkness.

"Luke. We can't." She tried to regain her strength.

"I know, I'm sorry. When I saw you standing next to the hallway smiling at me, something snapped in me."

"Buttons, maybe?"

They both laughed.

"See, stop that. Or half the town is gonna know tonight that we are not just friends."

She searched for him in the dark but didn't get a good enough mental picture of the room beforehand to know the layout well, making her not leave the door, but a few steps. Her hands hit his chest and worked up to his face.

"Someday, I hope I can give you everything you need, but right now, I'm sorry."

She felt his hand touch her face and lips cover hers. She gave into one last deep kiss before his hands gripped her jawline then jerked back, then the lights came on making her squint and letting her eyes adjust. She heard the door open behind her and turned to see Luke propping it open with the door stop. She watched him like a flip of a switch, turning back to a professional with no indication besides the bulge in his pants, that anything happened. He smiled and walked around her taking a seat behind his desk and slid his chair up to it keeping his legs covered by the desk as he readjusted his pants.

"This is my office. I'm mostly on call but if I'm not home, I'm here almost every day."

She looked around at the simple office that reminded her of his house with only a few more helmets, firefighter awards, and certifications that hung on the wall and shelves. The office was brightly lit with overhead lights and one big window behind a big "L" shaped dark wood desk which held a computer monitor, various files, paper stacks, and office supplies.

To the left, held a simple modern dark gray futon that could fold down to a bed if needed and a filing cabinet in the corner. In front of the big desk, sat two chairs. She noticed the backs of the picture frames on his desk and walked around to his side to see them. A pink picture frame with "We Love You Daddy" written in sparkles, of a dirty blonde woman smiling with a small two-year-old, Kada in a pile of leaves. A smiling Kada had her arms outstretched in the air as leaves fell around, as the sun shone through the falling leaves. She frowned at it.

"This must be Kada and her mom?"

"Yeah, that's Jasmine. My late wife." he replied with a soft tone.

"I'm sorry, Luke."

"That was a long time ago."

He sighed and leaned back in the chair now revealing the other picture next to it, hers. The one she gave him for his birthday of her and Kada. She smiled and ran a finger over it as he put a hand to her back.

"The only two women that have ever loved Kada."

She didn't think that was true but understood what he meant.

"Aren't you worried about your crew asking questions about that picture?"

The corner of his mouth twitched up and he shook his head.

"No, no one comes behind the desk to see it and if they do, no one is stupid enough to ask questions about my life and personal business at work, except Mike. He knows enough to keep from asking too many questions, but without any real information. Even though we are a family here, unspoken knowledge is, you'll get personal information when we are ready to tell you. Don't ask. Don't tell. So, whatever happens with us will not go public till we let it. Until then it's just rumors and jokes between firefighters that have nothing else to do between calls."

She smiled at that.

When Kada came through the door a minute later, Luke kept his hand on Daphne's back.

"Hey Dad?"

"What's up sweetheart?"

"Can I go to Sarah's tonight and tomorrow?"

When Sarah came in behind her with Jen following, Luke dropped his hand and placed it back on the chair arm rest.

"Hey Jen. Did she wrangle you into this?"

She smiled at Luke who relaxed in his office chair as Daphne stood next to him.

"Well, this time it was mine, but I'm fine with it. I'm just starting on Christmas decorations tomorrow and could use the extra help. Plus, I know Mike is coming in tomorrow, so you can come to work or.... take the day off for projects you've been working on *around* the house. " She grinned at Luke.

"Okay, yup. Bye, Sweetheart. Be good. Jen, stop talking to your husband, you two gossip more than Ms. Bellwood."

Daphne just smiled at Jen.

"What else is there? No theater or bowling." She shrugged her shoulders as she shoved the girls out the door.

"Plus, it's both your job security, kids, and other accidents happen because of boredom."

Luke worked his jaw, glaring at her as Daphne stood in shock, then gave a laugh.

"Love you, Bro!" She smiled and walked out laughing down the hall.

"Love you too!" he replied, "Somedays at least."

He looked up at Daphne and smiled, then the entire station sounded like one big alarm. Luke pulled his pager off his hip and read the message before standing up.

"Gotta go!"

He dug into his pocket and pulled his keys free and handed them to her.

"Take my truck home, I'll catch a ride back from Mike."

"What? No! I'll catch a ride home with Jen."

"Not a good idea! Just take the truck. I'll see you there in a bit."

She took the keys from him and smiled.

He placed a hand on her arm and kissed her forehead before running out back to the bays. Before she knew what had happened, she was left standing alone in his office and then running after him.

When she got out to the bay and out the man door to the parking lot, Luke smiled at her through the window of the Command vehicle with Mike riding passenger as Luke spoke on the radio pulling out of the parking lot. He watched her until he turned off the station property and onto the main street through town.

Through the darkness, she watched him, and a line of fire trucks disappear down the road as the sirens got distant. The pit of worry and emptiness kept her frozen to the same spot even after they were long gone.

CHAPTER FOUR

S he stood in the snowy parking lot in the cold darkness when Jen, Kada, and Sarah came out the man door.

"Daphne!" Kada came up behind her giving her a hug acting like nothing happened.

"Hey Daphne. Do you need a ride home?" Jen asked, coming up from behind her.

"No, he told me to take his truck." She showed Jen the keys Luke gave her as she still watched the main road.

Her shoulders squared off as she smiled. "Ok. Well, have a good night." as her and Sarah walked to the parking lot.

"Dad gave you the truck keys?" Kada asked, still wrapped around Daphne.

She finally snapped out of it and looked down at Kada to see her smiling and nodded. "I guess."

"Dad loves his truck and won't even let Aunt Jen drive it." Kada whispered.

Daphne frowned at that then looked at Jen now halfway across the parking lot.

"But Jen has wrecked a few vehicles so he's probably just careful."

Daphne smiled. "Yeah probably. Be good. I'll see you soon." she kissed the top of Kada's head and watched her run across the parking lot.

When Jen left the parking lot, she sighed and clicked the unlock button on Luke's key fob, lighting up half the parking lot with his LED headlights.

"It's just a bigger ass, Daphne. You can drive a truck... a couple of miles... in the dark and on snowy roads." She said to herself with dread.

She walked over to the Lieutenant parking spot and got in the driver seat. She adjusted the seat and mirrors and then started it before buckling up and taking a deep breath to put his truck in reverse.

When Mike pulled up to Daphne's nearly five hours after Luke left Daphne, he saw his truck parked back at home a few feet from his usual spot, but close enough. He smiled and got out.

"Need me to stick around till you get in?" Mike asked

"Na. I'm just gonna get my keys and head home. Thanks Mike."

"Yup. Have a good night."

Luke got out and shut Mike's Dodge door and he drove down to Luke's and turned around in the cul-de-sac and drove back towards town. Luke walked up to Daphne's and tried the door. Locked. He knocked. No answer.

He peered in the window, and it was dark.

He looked over at his house and it was black.

"Where is she?"

He turned around and her car was here too. So, she was home.

He knocked again. No sound or answer.

The chill of the ten-degree night started to reach him through the sweater. He jogged around the back and opened the back door.

"Daphne? You home?"

He walked in and closed the door. Through the darkness, he knew his way around by his memory of the layout of her house. His eyes adjusted to the darker house, then the moonlight outside, and didn't see a figure on the couch or bay window. He walked to the bedroom and her bed was still made. He then jogged up the stairs to the guest room and only saw a few of Kada's leftover clothes on the bed.

"Where is she?"

He jogged back downstairs and out the back, cutting across the yard to his house. He jogged up his steps and checked his door. Locked. Shit, his house key was on his truck keys. Kada and Mike had the only spares.

"Shit!" He glanced around.

"Where is she?"

He jogged down to his truck and grabbed the driver door handle to open it and saw Daphne curled up in his front seat asleep through the window. He inhaled the crisp air and let it out, then slowly opened the door. The truck dinged, so he reached over and pulled out the key from the ignition, put them in his pocket, and then clicked the cab lights off on his dashboard. She was curled in a tight ball with his station coat over her in the driver seat, with her head on the console. Her bare feet, by the door, curled when the cold hit them. Her shoes laid on the floorboard.

"Daphne." He whispered leaning over brushing her hair out of her face.

"Daphne, Wake up." He gave her arm a rub.

She took a deep breath and sat up.

"Luke?"

"Hey, what are you doing out here?"

"I didn't want to go home, and it was just awkward going into your house without you or Kada and your truck smelled so good and it's so big in here." She shrugged a shoulder at him and smiled.

"Well, it's freezing out here. Let's go in. You can sleep on my bed tonight. I'll take the couch."

She wanted to argue but was too tired and comfortable.

"What time is it?" She whispered.

"Almost 1am. Here wrap your arms around my neck."

Without argument, she did until she figured out, he was going to carry her. Now she argued

"No. I can walk." She mumbled.

"You have no shoes on and you are dead. Come on."

She wrapped her arms around his neck, and he slid an arm under her knees after pulling the keys from his pocket to have on hand. He lifted her up and let her head rest by his neck. He pushed the truck door with his hip, walked up the stairs, and unlocked the front door without rattling her too much. He got into the house and closed the door with his foot.

"Mm, I remember this smell. Richmond. So warm and comforting. My head hurts." She mumbled against his neck.

He paused by the door trying to look down at her. Asleep. So, it was a memory.

"It's okay Daphne, I've got you."

"I know. Just put away the harness before they yell at you."

Her arms dropped as her body went fully limp. He had to adjust his grip with fast reflexes to account for adjusted weight that was around his neck a second ago. His hand went from her head to her hip in a flash to hold her up and raised his arm to move his arm further up her back to catch her shoulders. He took a deep breath and kept walking through the dark house. They turned the corner by the kitchen to open his bedroom door. He set her down on his side of the bed and let her hair fall on his pillow.

"Richmond, stay with me. Please." Her voice cracked between deep breaths.

"Daphne, You're safe. It's okay."

He tried to soothe her, but she was in too deep of a sleep. Whatever memories or fantasies she had couldn't be stopped now, he knew the feeling very well. His own nightmares and memories kept him awake many nights, only he never had anyone besides a very young Kada who had her own troubles sleeping.

He sighed and folded the comforter over her. His heart gave way to the feelings of her calling for him and knowing he never stayed for whatever reason.

Harness? Rigging? He only used that in steep rescue calls. His head flashed through hundreds of rescues and still nothing of Daphne. He scrubbed his face with his hands. Puzzle pieces. That is what he had.

"Darryl? Where is Darryl?" she mumbled out. Her shoulders moved and knees came up. He brushed a hand through her hair. As he watched her. Who was Darryl?

He then turned to lock up the house and the truck. On his way down from Kada's empty room, he heard her scream. His heart clenched as he began in a full sprint skipping steps down and around the corner to the bedroom. She sat upright looking around the room as he came through the bedroom door and sat next to her pulling her in.

"Shh, Daphne. It's okay. It's Luke. It's just a nightmare."

She sobbed as she breathed hard.

He gave half a thought to assuring her of his presence now more than ever.

"I'm here now."

She pressed her face into his chest against his sweater.

When she finally quieted down. He didn't ask questions, just took off his sweater and tossed it at the foot of the bed. He undid his boots, put them by the foot of the bed on the floor, and laid down with her, holding her close to his chest, in his arms, still fully dressed. He ran his hand down her hair.

"Go back to sleep. I'm not going anywhere."

She gave a few more sobs and slowly drifted to sleep.

He laid awake for a little bit longer trying to figure out the Daphne puzzle but gave in to his own comfort of actually holding her in his bed and drifted asleep himself.

When she finally woke, daylight poured in through Luke's small bedroom windows that stretched the whole wall across the top by the ceiling. She felt no weight next to her. No Luke.

She then got up and smelled eggs and bacon cooking. She shivered and looked down at her tank up and dress pants she still wore. Where was her sweater and purse?

She saw the Station sweater down at the foot of the bed and put it on. Almost reaching her knees she was tiny in it. But it was warm and comforting. She walked barefoot to the bedroom door and opened it. Luke immediately looked at her.

"Good morning." He spoke cheerfully, as he smiled at her in his station sweater.

"Ugh, you're a morning person."

He laughed.

"Coffee?"

She bundled in his sweater, walked to his kitchen stools similar to hers and took a seat. "Yes please! I feel like I have a hangover."

Luke laughed as he poured her a cup of coffee in a Fire department mug then asked, "Creamer? Sugar?"

"A dash of cream, one spoon of sugar."

"No, you didn't drink, but what do you remember?"

He watched her as he added the cream and sugar and stirred it for her.

"Driving your damn truck home after you left me at the station."

Oh, she was feisty in the morning. "What, you don't like my truck?"

"No! I don't know how to drive a truck! Then you might have to talk to your sister. She saw me with your keys...."

Luke's face went into shock. "Oh shit!"

"... and I don't think she liked it. Kada mentioned you never let her, or anyone drive your truck."

He put the coffee cup down in front of her and rubbed his face with the freed hand, still holding his own cup with his right.

"Yeah. No one drives my truck."

"So, why let me?" She shouted. "None the less from your station!"

"I thought she was gone already. But she has wrecked a few vehicles so mine is off limits to her especially and Mike....well thank god he owns a diner to pay his insurance."

"Wait, he owns the diner?" The name finally clicked. " I guess it is Mike's Diner."

Luke just laughed and drank more coffee.

She finally took her first sip and let it sink down to her toes.

"Oh, this is so good."

Luke smiled as he walked over to the stove and turned it off.

"Made breakfast."

He watched her drink coffee so he made her a plate, pushed it across the counter to her, and went after his own plate.

"So, what else do you remember?"

She thought a little harder,

"Falling asleep in your truck."

"Yeah, I had to wake you up and carry you in."

Her face went red as she drank her coffee and put it down.

He walked over to the counter with his own plate and propped up a hip on the edge to eat.

"Anything else?"

"No, why? What happ...." When she spoke, the flashes of the accident came back and woke up in a full panic to Luke next to her. She turned her lips inward and bit them.

"You remember, don't you?"

"The accident."

"Took you a while to settle down, I had to lay with you.... fully dressed, so you could go back to sleep."

She drank more coffee and ate a slice of bacon off her plate to keep her hand busy.

"What did I say?"

He took another bite of his food and shook his head.

"Not much other than screaming for some Richmond guy."

He chuckled and smiled.

She frowned and drank more coffee.

"Sorry Daphne. I know I wasn't there when you needed me most. I don't have the full story, but the terror in your voice, is rare, as shock has different effects on people. But I'm here now. Whenever you need me, even if it's just as a friend."

She smiled. "Thanks."

After breakfast, she thanked him, and he got her shoes, purse, and cardigan from his truck. She gave him a hug and soft kiss on the lips before she walked out and went home.

At the beginning of December, there was four feet of snow on the ground. The temperature stayed in the teens during the day and dropped to -10's at night. The sunlight now lasted only about five hours a day from about 11am to 4pm, none of which was direct because Birch Valley sat in the shadow of a 6,500-foot-tall mountain. Daphne was surprised at how well she dealt with the dry cold climate, but the lack of sun made her make a weekly trip to Freeman for at least a couple hours of direct sunlight. She used it as an excuse to go Christmas shopping.

Luke took her to get a set of studded tires on rims and switched them over for her at the station as Kada gave her all the girly tips.

"Lotion, lots of lotion. A good conditioner, lip balm 24 hours a day even at night, a good humidifier and lots and lots of blankets." She remembered Kada telling her on a girl's night.

The first Sunday of December, the power went out. Luke woke her up in the middle of the night under a pile of blankets on her bed. After Luke insulated her pipes to keep them from freezing overnight, he kidnapped her. Letting her take the couch, as his house had a full generator that ran most of everything in his house including a few lights and heat. His stove was gas making it still usable without power.

Luke and Kada woke up in the morning like it was another day except with flashlights and battery-operated stationary lights for common areas. Luke had his and Kada's needs, and necessities covered from morning coffee and food to a small board game cabinet with hours of entertainment and fun, to a closet of emergency supplies including jump and bug out bags.

Whatever he couldn't supply, the rest of the town could. It was the first time she had seen the town come together as a community to help those in need, which weren't many. Mostly the newer residents. Luke left to help an elderly woman with insulating her pipes just as he did with Daphne's. Daphne and Kada stayed at Luke's playing *Monopoly* and *The Game of Life* until Luke returned in a few hours. He made chicken tortilla soup for dinner and spent the rest of the evening watching a movie on the TV with a library of DVDs available, until the power came back on at nearly 9 at night. She hated for the power to come on as she got comfortable at his house.

The second weekend of December, Luke played hooky from work not even telling Mike where he was going. After Luke dropped Kada at Sarah's for the weekend, he headed for Daphne's with a smile. Mike texted and called several times that morning and Luke ignored everyone. When he pulled into Daphne's driveway, she smiled as she closed the front door and locked it, bundled in a thick coat and boots with her small purse. She walked down to his truck and jumped in the front seat with a smile.

"I feel like a teenager skipping school to go to a party with my boyfriend, which my parents don't approve of. What are you doing to me?"

Luke just smiled, put his truck in reverse, and headed for town.

"Shh, get down. You are supposed to be at home sick, remember."

She crouched down below the window and leaned over the cup holders in front of the console. Her hair fell over Luke's lap and console. He safely placed his arm on the console and leaned on it as he drove through town.

As he passed the fire station, Firefighter Hastings was out shoveling snow and waved to Luke. He pretended not to see him.

"Stay down. We're passing the station and through the center of town."

Daphne giggled. "Oh God. What am I doing?'

"Well, I don't think you are younger than 18, you aren't skipping out of your parents' house and unless I'm missing something, I'm not your boyfriend, but yes we are being sneaky in a small town."

Daphne giggled again and turned her head to see Luke driving. Luke, without moving his head, looked down at her and smiled, his hand twitched on the console, so she reached around the stick shift to place her hand on his knee over her hair. He smiled even bigger now and with his right hand, moved her hair, and placed his hand over hers. She laced their fingers together. With curiosity he squinted his eyes and looked at her as he came to a stop sign. She smiled and softened her eyes.

"Oh shit! Red alert! Red alert!'

She almost jumped up as if Luke didn't hold her hand making it impossible.

"What?! What's going on?"

"Mike just passed us. I don't think he saw you, but my phone is gonna blow up now."

Just as he finished the sentence his phone rang on the center console. Daphne reached up and grabbed it.

"Daphne? What are you doing?" Don't do it! Don't answer it!"

She smiled devilishly and swiped to decline, making the ringing stop.

"Now he's really gonna know I'm ignoring him."

"Well...."

She paused as she opened Luke's phone. The picture of her and Kada was his background. She turned her head up to look at him in curiosity, but he only smiled at her as he watched the road and rubbed a thumb over her fingers still on his knee.

She clicked on the camera and with her right free hand, held it back as far as possible, turning it sideways for a wider picture of her laying over his console and holding hands with him as he drove. When Luke noticed what she was doing, he gave a small smile as she snapped the picture.

".... Now when our secret breaks out, you have proof."

Luke just smiled as she felt the truck slowing down to a stop as he turned on his blinker.

"Where are we?"

He didn't answer, but when he put the truck into park, he leaned over and planted a hard kiss on her lips making her give a soft moan, then released.

"You can get up now. We are far enough out of town now."

She sat up and looked around. The side of the highway on a road. She smiled at him and leaned over to kiss him again. He smiled again and put the truck back into drive still with his right hand holding hers, but now over the center console. They talked as he drove, working out the agreement. Daphne spoke first.

"It stays out of public view...."

"And away from Kada." Luke added

Daphne nodded and thought for a second,

"Keep it light.... for now." She added warily as she looked at Luke.

He was focused on the road, but smiled, gave her a simple look, and kissed her hand he held.

"Hey, as long as I'm the only one you're kissing, that's all I want."

She smiled as he held her hand close to his mouth as he leaned over the console and drove.

"No promises. If either of us wants out, everything falls back into a friendship.... of neighbors."

"And my daughter's nurse." He gave a sly smile.

She watched him as he drove the highway.

"Keep it out of texts and calls as Kada answers my phone a lot when she is with me, and you call or text."

Luke chuckled and nodded. Yeah, he understood that because she did the same with him when Daphne called.

"Can we do this, Luke? Can we really keep this a secret?"

"I don't think we have any other choice. I mean, I would be the happiest man alive, walking through the center of town, holding and kissing you right now and not giving a damn what the town thinks...."

He looked over at the shock and fear on her face,

"....but that is why we have to and honestly it's gonna be fun, stealing kisses at the opportune moments."

He smiled.

"Just promise me something."

"Anything." She answered a little too quickly before she knew what it was.

He looked over as he slowed down coming into Freeman's icier roads.

"If you get scared or have another nightmare or flashback, come to me or at least call or text. That's not how you should be screaming my name. I'm sorry I wasn't there, Daphne."

He gave her hand a small squeeze as he turned off the highway and onto a main street through Freeman.

"Luke...." She paused and took a breath."...I'm only here because of you."

Pulling up to a stop light, he gave her a scared and shocked look.

"Daphne, tell me what happened please. I don't know you or anything about this call before July. Why are you running? Are you hiding from something or someone? You don't have to. I can help you."

The light turned green, and he gave the truck a little more gas than he normally would.

"Luke, just don't please. Let it go."

"Never. But for now, for today, I will."

He pulled into a big parking lot and parked in a spot, then put the truck in park. He quickly turned to face her. His phone rang. He looked down at it on the console.

Mike Davis.

"Uhh, he is relentless." He growled out in frustration.

He picked up the phone and answered it.

"What do you want?" he growled out with irritation.

Daphne could only hear Luke and stayed quiet with a smile in his passenger seat as she watched him.

"No! Daphne is at home, hopefully in bed where I told her to stay.... I don't know, probably Mono!"

Daphne dealt with a lot of mono as a middle school nurse, it's nicknamed the kissing disease for a good reason. She laughed quietly in the front seat.

"No! Mike....okay a week off sounds great, but you wouldn't last the first MVA or Structure."

He smiled and looked at Daphne, then rolled his eyes.

"I'm Christmas shopping...... In Freeman."

"Hey, the fact that you can't play hooky is not my fault. You jumped at the position when the Chief retired and moved to Florida."

"Hey, Mike, I gotta run. There is a sexy woman standing next to a truck lot with a Dalmatian. I'll pick up Kada tomorrow. Thanks."

He hung up on Mike as Daphne heard the protests coming through the phone.

"You're so mean!"

"No, I'm not. Trust me, he'll dig a hole to China to find the answers he wants to hear. He knows something isn't right and has probably figured out that you're with me. Unfortunately, he knows me too well and when I start pulling stunts like this, he's usually pretty quick to catch on. But as long as I don't confirm or deny anything he can stew for at least another month or two."

He reached over the console to pull her nearly into his lap as he planted a hot kiss on her lips. When he released her and looked up at her. Her eyes were still closed, and lips parted.

"I'm kissing Richmond, in his truck. Don't wake me, please."

Luke smiled and kissed her again, more softly and lingered.

"Trust me, from where I stand, we'll never wake up. But for now, let's enjoy ourselves and do some Christmas shopping."

"Okay, that's just as fun."

Luke gave a short laugh and got out of the truck after Daphne did. He clicked lock on the fob and walked around to meet her in the front of the truck. He gave a couple quick glances around the crowded parking lot. Finding them being mostly covered with another vehicle, he pushed her into his truck grill and gave her a longer kiss with soft love bites on her lips, while he held her in place with both his hands now.

When he stepped back, he raised both his hands up.

"Sorry, I just had to get some water before I started walking through a dessert."

She laughed and started walking towards the mall while biting her own lips now.

Later that night, he drove back through town with her, but this time she was leaning over the console on his shoulder because most everyone should have been in bed, so they didn't worry too much about who would see them.

As he pulled into her driveway, she sat up, got her purse, and put her coat back on in the well-heated truck that she took off after leaving Freeman. She then reached in the back seat and pulled out the few shopping bags she had got.

When he looked over at her, he leaned over for a kiss, and she dodged it leaning to her right.

"Goodnight, friend."

He scowled and leaned back. "Goodnight, Daphne."

She got out and watched her walk to her door and go inside before he put it in reverse and drove to his house. He looked through the windshield at Daphne's.

"This is gonna get interesting." He whispered to himself, then got out grabbing the few bags he had in the back seat.

Over the next few weeks up to the day before Christmas, she kept her distance and limited herself to only a couple dinners and time with Luke and even Kada as she played it safe. Luke got grilled by Mike about the responsibility of being a parent. Luke laughed as Mike was only throwing darts in the dark now. So far no one knew anything different.

As Luke pulled out a roast from the oven, his phone rang.

"Dad, It's Daphne." Kada picked it up on the counter and answered it.

"Hey Daphne. Umm, no, he's busy pulling a roast out of the oven. You, okay? Oh yeah, he knows how to fix that."

She pulled the mic away from her face.

"Dad, Daphne's pipe is leaking under her bathroom sink and she can't get it tightened. Says she needs your help, but umm, she's laughing."

Luke looked at Kada in confusion, took the oven mitts off, reached for the phone, and took it from Kada.

"Hey Daph, what did you do?'

Kada stored another mental note that Dad now shortened Daphne's name and she watched them talking on the phone while Luke cut the roast with a wider smile then he had a minute ago.

"Umm yeah. When did you get back from Freeman? Okay. I'll be there in a few minutes."

He hung up the phone, slid it on the counter, and finished cutting the roast.

"What happened?"

Luke looked at Kada and tried not to smile.

"She has a puddle in her bathroom from the sink leaking. I have threading tape, I'm gonna take over and see if I can fix it quickly. Should only take a couple of minutes. I'll be quick. Serve up and I'll be back before you're finished."

He kissed the top of her head and walked to the back door slipping on his boots and coat and walking out.

Kada got a plate out of the cabinet and watched her dad jog across the yard but forgot the tape and tools to fix her sink. Kada smiled. Either Dad was keeping him and Daphne a secret or dealing with her Christmas presents, either way she liked the odds of a good outcome and smiled as she took a bite of the tender juicy roast.

Luke reached the backdoor and opened it, "Daphne? Where you at?"

"Upstairs!"

He jogged up the stairs, opened the bathroom door to a big puddle, and Daphne under her sink in the cabinet as water sprayed everywhere. He crouched down, looked under the sink, and turned the red handle, shutting off the water.

"What! No! How did you do that?"

She ducked getting out of the cabinet from laying on her back. She was soaked.

"You're so cute when you're wet." He grinned while looking her over from head to toe.

She took the soaked towel next to her and threw it at him. He just laughed as his shirt was now soaked.

"I'll come over this weekend and fix this. For now, Kada has my phone and dinner."

Daphne tried not to smile and shrugged.

"What's the chance that she one opens your phone and digs through your gallery to find that one photo of us in the truck?"

"Kada? My daughter... 90 precent"

Daphne laughed.

"She's a smart girl, she's already done the math, Luke."

"Yeah well, I would actually like to tell her and Mike about the total at least before the wrong math is done."

"Soon." she smiled "Go eat dinner. I'll see you and Kada tomorrow."

He smiled and leaned over to kiss her forehead and got up to walk out. Hopefully if he hurried fast enough, the soaked long sleeve shirt wouldn't freeze completely before he reached his house.

Christmas morning, though she woke up alone, she was happy. Her small fresh Christmas tree sat in the corner next to her bay window, the windows were frosted, and it was completely white out with all the snow they had got. The smell of a fresh Christmas tree was always something she looked forward to at Christmas time and this year she had friends to celebrate it with. Her plans to share Christmas evening with Luke and Kada was her Christmas excitement. Luke and Kada spent a couple hours in the morning by themselves and then shared the afternoon with Mike, Jen, and Sarah.

She remembered how full Luke's 12-foot-tall tree was with presents around it. She smiled and drank her coffee before shoveling the snow off her porch as Luke and Kada drove by saying "Merry Christmas Daphne!" out the windows as they passed by.

She smiled and waved.

Daphne loved the snow and had already been shown Pike Hill with Luke and Kada on a snowy afternoon, the week prior. It was the town's local sledding hill. Kada, Luke, and her had a blast for an afternoon even though it was short-lived because of a wipe out by Kada and what Daphne considered an overprotective father. Daphne had to smile at Luke being a father. She didn't see it as often as she would have hoped.

By the afternoon, she wore a red, hi-lo, flowy Chiffon dress with long sleeves that hung off the shoulders. In the right light, it sparkled with silver glitter that looked like snow dust. She wore red, strappy high heels with silver painted toenails and fingernails.

Her makeup looked like it had been professionally done, but with a simple elegance that she learned from her sister years ago. Big thick lashes shadowed her blue eyes and silver eyeshadow brightening them up, making the blue pop with a dark tint red lipstick a shade darker than her dress.

She couldn't wait to make Luke speechless. She was excited when she had found the dress in a little thrift store in the mall she and Luke went to. She had bought it and hid it before Luke returned with afternoon coffee from the corner shop. But she had to return to find shoes the next weekend.

Her hair was curled into big sections with a wide curler, it framed her face and shortened her hair a few inches to show her bare shoulders and collarbone.

She was drinking a glass of wine at her kitchen island when she heard Luke's truck coming down the road and pulled into her driveway. She got up and flicked her hair to let the curls bounce and watch out the window for Kada getting out and Luke shortly after her. Kada in a pretty black and white dress with red ribbon and short heels, bounced up the steps. Luke wore black dress pants with a dark red dress shirt that nearly matched Kada's dress. Before Kada knocked, Daphne opened the door and stepped out holding a small purse and paper bag with presents.

"Daphne! Oh my god you look beautiful!" Kada yelled.

Luke closed the truck door, looked up, and like Daphne hoped for, went speechless with big eyes and a sexy smile.

Kada hugged Daphne, "Merry Christmas, Daphne!"

She looked down at Kada and smiled. "Merry Christmas, Kada."

Luke now walked forward, never taking his eyes off Daphne, and tripped up the steps to her porch. He froze about three feet from Daphne, as the girls giggled.

"Merry Christmas, Daph."

"Merry Christmas, Luke."

"Do you have anything else... to grab?" he fumbled his words, making Daphne laugh and smile.

"Just one more bag of presents by my tree."

"Kada, will you grab it for Daphne, please."

Daphne's eyebrows lowered in curiosity.

"Yeah!" She ran inside and Luke's eyes got fierce.

"Luke...."

She was cut off with a hot possessive kiss that plastered her to the house exterior wall, the mix of cold on her back and warmth of his lips, made her head spin. His hands grabbed at her waist.

They heard Kada shout from inside. "Daphne, do you want me to turn your Christmas lights off?"

Daphne laughed and tried to get Luke off her, she freed her mouth to turn her head, "Yes please! Thank You!"

Luke kissed down her neck to her bare shoulder.

"Luke, stop. We're gonna get caught."

"Then stop playing with fire." He laughed and kissed her lips softly and she giggled against his lips.

Kada came running out to catch them in a lip lock just as Daphne freed her hands.

"Dad!"

He stepped back trying his hardest not to smile while stuffing his hands in his pockets as he still watched Daphne.

"Sorry, I thought it was New Year's Eve. Just stealing a kiss."

Kada didn't believe it for a second and Daphne knew it.

"I told you." Kada said to Daphne with an evil grin as she crossed her arms while still holding the other bag of presents."

Luke looked from Kada to Daphne.

"Told you what?"

"Nothing." She said to Luke with a wide blushing smile.

"There is one more bag on the counter of wine and sparkling cider with a container of Christmas cookies, will *you* grab it please."

Then turning to Kada, she flicked her purse at Kada, "Truck. Now. Before we get in trouble."

Luke took Daphne's keys from her, "I'll lock up."

"Thank you."

"Careful of those steps, they are icy." He warned before he rushed in to snag the bag and back out in a hurry and locking up before Daphne started down the steps holding on the railing. He pocketed the keys and swooped Daphne off her feet carrying her down the steps and nodding at Kada to open the front passenger door.

"Oh, my God! Luke! I can walk!" She had to think fast and wrap her arms around his neck to steady herself.

Luke set her in the front seat and smiled, "But you shouldn't have to."

He kissed her forehead then shut the door after he put the wine bag by her feet.

Kada jumped in and smiled at them as Luke jumped in and shut his door.

"You two are so cute!"

"Don't get any ideas, Kada. It's Christmas, nothing more!" He smiled at Daphne and went back to Kada.

He backed out of her driveway and down the road to his driveway.

"That was a quick trip!" Kada laughed.

Daphne opened her door and Luke watched her closely. "No, down boy!"

Kada rolled with laughter in the back seat as she opened her own door.

"Take the bags, if you want to help!" She pointed at Luke.

He smiled and got out as she passed the wine over the console to him, then she got out and disappeared below the truck with a scream and thud.

"Daphne!" Both Kada and Luke screamed as Luke ran around the truck and Kada shut her door.

Daphne laid on her back in the snow laughing hysterically with her dress and hair spread out over the driveway around her. She raised her hands in the air. "I'm Good!" Still laughing. Kada laughed with her as Luke reached them and saw them both laughing.

He rolled his eyes and crouched down beside her. "The couch is inside the house."

Still laughing and trying to catch her breath, she looked at Luke.

"I'm just checking your tires, they looked flat. Nope, just me!"

Now all three of them laughed together. After they caught their breath, he reached out a hand to her.

"Let's get you up."

He helped her back up to her feet, brushed off her snowy dress then took a couple steps into the deep snow to get her purse out of the yard a couple feet away, and handed it to her.

"Let's get you in the house first, then I'll come back for the rest." He laughed and smiled at her holding her hand as they walked across the icy driveway to the sanded porch steps and up to the door with Kada following closely. When she got inside the door, Luke looked at her.

"I'm good Luke. I swear I didn't just learn to walk unless you just waxed your floors."

"No, you're safe till spring at least." He smiled at her again as Kada walked around them and took a bag of presents to the huge Christmas tree.

He kissed her forehead and walked back out to get the rest of the bags and came in as Daphne took her heels off leaning against the stair railing. She set them down and went tiptoe barefoot to the couch and sat down. He keenly watched her while he took off his dress shoes and took the bags to the kitchen counter.

"Wine?"

She smiled, "Yes, please. I assume you have wine glasses."

He frowned, "Umm, let me check, but I don't think so." he lied.

"I can get mine from home."

Bingo! He smiled, "Nope, I will get them. We don't need you checking the trees and creek to make sure they have air." He chuckled.

"Kada, show her your makeup kit. Maybe Daphne can teach you how to use it."

Kada jumped up excitedly. "Oh, yeah, Daphne, Dad got me a big makeup kit. Can you show me?"

Daphne stood up. "Of course!"

When Kada headed for the stairs, she looked back at Luke pulling out the wine and cider.

"My backdoor is unlocked. The wine glasses are above the fridge."

"Okay. I'll be back in a few minutes. Daphne, don't teach her too much please."

Luke scowled at Daphne, and she just smiled devilishly back as she walked around the corner and up the stairs. He made sure she was out of sight, then ran to his room and pulled out a paper bag of presents out of his closet. He saw a locked wood box on his nightstand and soft plush Fireman's blanket on his bed. He stopped dead in his tracks and walked over to them.

He smiled at the blanket and ran a hand over the soft plush material with a flame design and fire department Maltese Cross in the middle. Then walked to the box and used his thumb to turn it towards him. It had his Birch Valley Fire Department patch design hand painted on the top and sealed into the wood. The front had a gold metal plate with 'Lieutenant Lucas Richmond' etched into it. He could break the small lock on it but left it and turned to head out with even a bigger smile than when he came in.

Kada ran fast into her bedroom to the pile of stuff on her bed and picked up the big makeup box on her bed, unopened and showed Daphne.

"Wow! That is a big kit!"

Kada handed it to Daphne and smiled. Daphne's heart smiled watching Kada hand her the box, knowing she looked to her for mom tips, she couldn't really get elsewhere. Daphne took the box from her and took a deep breath.

"Okay, but we need to do this in the bathroom."

Daphne got up, walked to Kada's bathroom, and opened the box on the small counter next to the sink. She spent the next 30 minutes teaching Kada everything in the box from eyeliner to blush. Though cheaply made, Daphne did her best to work with it and applied just enough makeup to make a difference, but not overdo it for the young 12-year-old. She lined her eyes with a shade darker than skin tone, some of the cheap clumpy mascara and brushed it thinly, with some blush-colored shadow for her eyes to brighten up her darker dress, then brushed her cheeks with the plaster textured blush and use the decent pink gloss on her small but perky lips that were the same shape as her dads.

When Kada looked in the mirror, she glowed with excitement. "Wow. thank you, Daphne." as a tear fell from her face.

Daphne bent down and took Kada's hands.

"Hey, what's wrong?" She asked, even if she knew the answer already.

Over Kada's shoulder, she saw Luke walk to the door frame before Daphne held a finger up to him behind Kada.

"I miss my mom!" She spoke as more tears started to fall.

"Hey, it's okay. I'm here and so is your dad. You also have your Aunt Jen who is an amazing mom and aunt."

"It's not the same. Dad is so lonely, and I feel like half of me is missing all the time. Mom would know how to do this stuff too, she was so pretty, Daphne."

Luke dropped his head and tried for a composure that was just out of reach.

"I know sweetheart. She was gorgeous! I saw a picture of her and you in your dad's office at the station. He loves you both very much and I know he misses her just as much as you do. Maybe you should ask your dad to tell you more about her. Sometimes it's good for people to talk about their loved ones."

Kada started to sob and threw her arms around Daphne's neck holding her tight.

Luke leaned against the frame with his hands in his pockets and watched Daphne with a frown as his head hung a little lower.

Daphne spoke for reassurance as she watched Luke. "I'm here for you, Kada. Whenever or whatever you need." She held Kada tight.

After a silent moment holding each other, Daphne spoke, "Hey, wanna see what I got you for Christmas?"

Kada backed up and tried for a smile through the tears as she looked at Daphne and nodded her head.

"Okay. Then why don't you give your dad a hug before he breaks down also and let's go open presents before dinner."

Kada jerked around to see her dad in the doorway with a soft smile and ran to him. He opened his arms and pulled her into a hug and lifted her up.

"I love you, Daddy!" she cried to him.

"I love you so much and so did Mom. Daphne, Aunt Jen, and Uncle Mike do as well. You have a lot of people who love you. We will be okay, I promise."

Kada kissed Luke's cheek and he kissed hers before he put her down and she ran out and down the stairs. Daphne folded her arms over her chest and frowned at Luke.

He walked into the bathroom and pulled Daphne into a hug and tilted her head up for a soft kiss before he pulled back.

"You're not Jasmine, but you're doing an amazing job with your cute feet filling her shoes."

Daphne backed up in shock.

"That's not what I was trying to do, I can't replace her mom, I won't."

"Hey, Daphne, it's okay. You couldn't replace her if you tried, but Kada has found her in you and believe me, she does know the difference."

Daphne closed her eyes, remembering her own mother brushing her hair after a bath before bed while humming a soothing tune. She remembered the soothing comfort feeling, something she didn't know if Kada had before her mother passed. Her heart sank, remembering the loss of losing her own mother.

She walked up to Luke and gave him a hug. He held her and kissed her head.

"Let's go open presents before we get caught again."

Daphne laughed and walked down the stairs with Luke following.

As she sat on the couch in the middle of the living room, the Christmas tree was decorated with colored lights and colored ornaments. Some were handmade by a small child and also held other older fragile ones, along with new shatterproof colorful ones. It stood between the two biggest windows in the middle of the living room a couple feet from the couch. Luke walked over to her with a glass flute of the sparkling white wine she brought and had one himself. Kada searched the presents under the tree until she grabbed a small hand size box wrapped in sparkling purple and pink paper with a silver ribbon and handed it to Daphne.

"Here this is from me and Dad!"

She set her glass down on the side table and took it looking at a smiling Luke.

"Kada picked it out." He spoke.

Kada danced around on the floor on her knees in her dress with excitement.

"I hope you like it!"

As Daphne untied it, Daphne spoke.

"Okay, Kada grab the big square one over there with red wrapping. That's for you and your dad, you both can open."

Kada reached over, grabbed it, handed it to her dad who grabbed it, but held it on his lap as he watched Daphne open the small present.

She ripped open the wrapping to reveal a small flat jewelry box and gave Luke a wide-eyed look,

He grinned with a slight scowl, "It's not a ring, Daphne. Just open it."

She swallowed and opened it to reveal a teardrop Amethyst with a small diamond accent in a rose gold setting necklace and matching drop earrings.

"Oh wow! You guys didn't have to. This is too much."

"No. It's a small comparison to what you've given us." Luke spoke as he reached over, took the necklace out, wrapped it around her neck, and clipped it together.

"Oh, my gosh. Thank you. I love it. It's so pretty. I love amethyst! It's my favorite." She leaned over and pulled Kada into a hug, then turned to Luke and gave him a hug as he kissed her cheek.

As she undid the earrings from the box and put them on, she nodded at the box he held, "Open yours."

Kada sat across from Luke and tore at the paper on one end as he tore the other side and opened the big cardboard box and slid out a shiny red tinted steel cut fire department Maltese Cross with "The Richmond's" across the middle.

"Oh Dad, it's for our door! Me and Daphne saw one at the mall for the police with a badge."

"Wow. This is nice and its weatherproof. Thank You Daphne."

"Oh, and Kada...." She got up and got her purse by the door and came back pulling out a small red envelope with Kada's name on it and handed it to her. "...here this is for you."

Kada smiled, took it, and opened it. Luke watched on with curiosity. Kada pulled out two - $50 Gift certificates to a women's spa and salon in Freeman and looked at Daphne.

"You said you wanted your ears pierced, and nails done. There are two there, so you can use them all, or share with Sarah, or maybe even turn it into a girl's day out with your Aunt Jen and Sarah."

"And you!" Kada spoke up.

"I can do that."

Kada smiled now and looked at her dad, dropping her smile almost immediately.

Daphne saw Kada's smile go flat, looked to a concerned Luke then gave him a swat and mimicked his tone, "It's just her ears, Luke."

He smiled now. "Fine, but one in each."

Kada jumped up and hugged her dad! "Oh, thank you, Dad!" and then jumped into Daphne's arms, "Thank you, Daphne."

"You are very welcome, Kada!'

Daphne put her phone on the coffee table aiming the camera at her and Luke.

"Kada, jump up here!"

Kada jumped in between her and Luke as they snuggled in close to get in the frame. Daphne hit the timer button and leaned back next to Kada, and the photo snapped.

After a few more presents and a prime rib dinner, Daphne sat at the counter drinking more sparkling wine as she watched Luke put away dinner and wrap her up a to-go container of some leftovers. Kada was in her room playing with her presents.

She turned the stool to look at Luke's Christmas tree lit up in the dark windows that lit up in the moonlight.

Luke came over to stand next to her. She looked at Luke.

"Turn off the kitchen lights."

He reached across the hallway and flipped the switch.

The colorful tree lights glowed in the living room and moonlight shined through the windows and over the white fluffy snow outside making it even brighter.

"It's so beautiful! I love the snow and how pretty and quiet it gets outside. I didn't get it the last couple places I lived."

Luke looked at her and frowned. He would never get used to the pieces she gave him and yet he wouldn't ask for more. He enjoyed how much the simple things in life made her smile, and lost part of his heart to her because of it. He pulled her in close and whispered, "Your other presents are in your bedroom, at your house."

She whipped around to look at him.

"What? When?" Then it clicked, "When I was with Kada, upstairs." She nodded then replied, "Well so are yours. But in your room, not mine."

He grinned. "Damn."

She laughed softly.

"I know, I saw them earlier. I love the blanket."

"For colder nights." She smiled.

"And the locked box?"

She smiled again, "The key is hidden. You have to find it to get the treasure."

He dropped his eyes.

"Any clues?"

"Me."

He reached over and gave her a quick pat down search as she laughed.

"No. I'm the clue. It's somewhere in your house. Better find it, or you'll never know what's inside the box." She got off the stool grabbing her Tupperware of leftovers and headed for the door.

"That's it? That's all I get?"

She gave him a wide grin, "Yup! Kada, I'm headed home! Merry Christmas!"

Kada came running down the stairs and gave her a hug.

"Merry Christmas, Daphne!"

"Goodnight!"

Kada ran back upstairs as Daphne grabbed her bags and purse. Luke put on his station boots and coat.

"I better at least walk you to your door."

She smiled, "I was hoping you would."

She walked out and he followed. They walked the plowed road back to Daphne's driveway in silence. Luke kept his hands in his pockets but kept an arm's length away in case she fell again. When she reached her door, she unlocked it, and turned around.

"Goodnight, Luke."

"Goodnight, Daphne." He glanced over at his house, decided against kissing her and getting caught again, so he just smiled. She leaned up, kissed his cheek, and walked inside, closing the door.

She got ready for bed and turned on her Christmas tree lights and then opened her bedroom door. An iridescent crystal rose in a glass dome was lit up that sent rainbow sparkles across the room. A sticky note on it, *To brighten your day.* His station sweater lay on her bed also with a sticky note, *For comfort, when I can't be.*" and the picture in a frame of them in the truck with her over the console with also a sticky note. *For better memories.*

She sent him a text. "Thank you, Luke. They are amazing. I love them. Merry Christmas!"

He instantly replied.

"Merry Christmas Daphne!"

When Luke got ready for bed, he saw the locked box still on the side table. He was too tired to think about finding the key she hid but wondered what was inside. He took his shirt off leaving just his pajama pants on and ran a hand over his new blanket before he took it off to fold his comforter up and replaced it with his new one. It smelled like her ocean and floral scented house. He folded down the bedsheet and found the small key where she laid the night he held her. He picked up the small key, sat on the bedside, grabbed the box, and unlocked it. When the lid flipped up, he immediately saw the picture of them in the truck she took and a note taped to it, *For all your secrets*

He gave a soft laugh thinking how they gave each other the same picture hidden in each other's rooms. When he picked up the picture, he saw the silver key on a silver dog tag keychain under it and read the engraving, *The only fire you can't put out, is the one you started in my heart. Be safe and always come home to us. Love, Daphne*

It had a Maltese Cross cut out at the bottom. He looked at the key attached to the ring, rubbed his thumb over it, and smiled. Her house key. He immediately got up and walked out to the dark living room and to the front door, digging in his station coat, pulling out his keys, and attached the new keychain and key to it. He smiled, put it back in his coat pocket, and headed for bed.

Kada watched over the balcony standing still in the dark, out of sight as she watched her dad attach another key to his. When he left, she snuck down and pulled out the set of keys out of his coat, read the dog tag keychain and did a little dance in the entryway as quietly as she could with the biggest smile and whispered to herself, "Best Christmas ever."

CHAPTER FIVE

For New Years, they had a small bonfire on the dry bank of a wide section of creek bed behind Luke's house. Luke and Mike set off fireworks, in the night, for the town who watched from their houses every year, just before midnight. Sarah and Kada made smores and Jen and Daphne talked about the men over plastic champagne flutes as they rang in the new year. At the stroke of midnight, Mike and Luke lit off the biggest ones and with loud bangs and pops, as the sky lit up with all the colors. Mike walked over to Jen and planted a midnight kiss on her lips in the cold colorful night.

Daphne smiled and yelled, "Happy New year!" into the sky above. Everyone except Luke followed and did the same. With hoots and screams, Luke watched Daphne over the fire, walked around it to Daphne, and grabbed her for a hot midnight kiss, not caring what the others saw. He kept it safe by wrapping his arms around her upper back as heat and intensity fueled them both. Daphne grabbed a fist full of Luke's coat to keep balanced. When he pulled back, Daphne smiled with raised eyebrows and played it off with the others watching.

"What was that for?"

He shrugged with a straight face, watching her closely, "No one should ring in the new year alone, that includes us."

She bit her lips, "Got plans for next New Year's?"

He laughed and walked away to light more fireworks as everyone watched them. Mike followed Luke with a scowl. Jen walked over next to Daphne, who gulped down more champagne from her glass.

"Forget the bonfire and fireworks, I have all the heat and sparks I need watching you two! Damn, Daphne!"

Daphne casually laughed.

"How long has that been going on?"

Daphne lowered her eyebrows, "What? We are just friends, Jen."

Jen lowered her eyebrows to squint at Daphne. "Uh, huh."

Kada and Sarah walked over and Kada smiled at Daphne.

"Dad has had a thing for her for a while."

"I thought I saw something at Thanksgiving." Jen gave Daphne a sly smile. "Come on, there must be something going on?"

Daphne smiled and tried not to blush. "No. Nothing."

Now she understood why Luke said riding home with Jen after Thanksgiving was a bad idea.

"Uh, huh. Go ahead keep your secrets, but if there is one fire, he can't stop it's the wildfire that is gonna start when whatever...." She paused as she waved a finger back and forth between Daphne and Luke. ".... that was, gets out. Fuck it, I'll be first to light it and give Ms. Bellwood the heads up."

Daphne didn't know Jen well enough to tell if she was just tipsy or if this was just Jen normally outside of the station and school, but Daphne had to drink a lot of champagne to keep herself together. As she refilled her champagne flute next to Jen, who was still talking, she caught Luke watching her over the bonfire and saw more heat than what she felt from the fire. He smiled and looked from Jen and back to Daphne then gave her the slightest shake of his head. Daphne smiled and turned her lips inward then chugged a glass of champagne and filled it again. Luke's eyebrows raised as he smiled then mouthed, "I'm sorry". She shrugged and smiled then turned to listen to Jen. Kada and Sarah sat on wood logs roasting another marshmallow by the fire.

Once the fireworks were over, Mike and Luke drank hot cups of coffee next to Daphne and Jen by the fire, as the girls played in Daphne and Luke's shared yard, making a snowman under the bright moonlight.

Luke asked Jen to distract her from Daphne, "Did Sarah bring her bag?"

"Oh yeah. She already put it in Kada's room. So....." She clammed up as she pointed to Daphne and scowled at Luke, "....That was some New year's kiss for just friends, Bro?"

With a dead straight face, he looked her in the eyes and spoke, "We're just friends Jen."

Oh, he was good and knew how to handle his fierce sister in-law. Jen raised her hands, "Okay, whatever you say."

Daphne smiled and took another sip of her champagne. Luke bent and grabbed a water bottle out of the snow next to the creek and handed it to Daphne taking the champagne bottle from her.

"That is a slope to the house and there are no tires down here." He smiled.

She nearly choked on her gulp of champagne from laughing and had to lean forward and grab Luke's arm for support, to get air.

Without even looking behind him at Mike and Jen watching them, he spoke as he watched Daphne gasp for air, "She fell out of my truck on Christmas, sober, and told me she was checking for a flat tire."

Mike winced at the thought and Jen laughed. Daphne took the bottle of water, opened it and drank some while Mike and Jen began their own conversation.

Daphne looked up at Luke who was just smiling at her.

"You ready to go inside and warm up?"

Daphne smiled and giggled, "I feel fine."

Luke shook his head. "You are cold, don't make me carry you. They will have too many questions."

"You carry me and something close to two bottles of Champagne is gonna come back up."

Luke looked at her and bent down to grab a hand full of snow and smiled.

"Luke, don't you dare!"

He gave it a soft lob at her coat, as it broke apart and fell to the ground.

"Luke!" She smiled. She picked up a handful of snow, packed it into a ball and threw it hard towards him. He moved to the left, making it fly past him, and hit Mike in the jaw as the snow crumbled down and in his station coat.

"Oh My God! I'm so sorry, Mike!' She smiled and laughed at him now in shock and tense from the cold.

"Now you just pissed off the captain." Luke laughed at Mike.

Mike picked up a handful of snow, packed it into a ball, and watched Luke.

"We're doing this, huh?"

Luke stepped back, "Cap, Daphne did it not me!"

Mike took aim and threw it hard, hitting Luke in the chest.

"Okay, that's it. I'm taking aim at everything you love!" Luke looked at Mike and walked over to him and tripped Jen into a snow pile next to her with his foot and a soft push.

"Lucas Richmond!" She screamed from her spot two feet deep in a snow pile to her neck and feet up. Luke gave a full laugh.

"Bro!"

Mike stepped around Luke to look towards Daphne, Luke ducked, and drove his shoulder into Mike's waist grabbing him and efficiently taking him down next to his wife. Mike sprang back up in a quick instant and went after Luke as they laughed and wrestled in the snow. Jen got up and walked to Daphne as they watched the antics of the best friends in a battle of strength versus agility. She drank the water and they laughed at their men.

Luke showed more speed as he dodged Mike's grab, tripped Mike with his leg and a push of his forearm against his chest, but Mike had the smarts to counteract it grabbing Luke's arm and taking him down, then used the motion of the fall to twist his bigger thick frame and pin Luke in the snow. While pressing his palm into Luke's collarbone, Luke wrapped one arm around Mike's neck, and trapped Mike's free arm with his arm wrapped behind Mike's back, making Mike drop his shoulder.

They both laughed, "Draw."

Mike smiled and nodded and released Luke as Luke let go of Mike. Then Mike gave Luke a hand up. Both shook and brushed off their coats to free the snow trapped in it. Jen turned to Daphne, "This is common and so far, it's been pretty even with neither of them winning, yet!"

Mike spoke first, "Yet."

Luke laughed. "Maybe if you get out of the truck and actually join the action on calls, you might pick up some speed and reflexes, Captain!"

Mike made a jump for Luke who showed his speed and ducked his reach.

"You're lucky."

"No. Just faster." Luke smiled and gave Mike a pat on the shoulder, then walked over to Daphne.

Mike walked over to Jen and gave his wife a kiss.

"Michael, don't you put those cold hands on me, I swear....."

Before she could finish, Mike wrapped his hands around her bare neck and kissed her again to stop the silent scream coming from her. Daphne laughed, watching them.

Luke looked at her and smiled. "You ready to go up now?"

She smiled and nodded. "Yeah, it's getting late."

"Alright, let me put this fire out and I'll help you up the hill."

Daphne smiled, grabbed the last bottle of champagne, and started up the shoveled path, watching Luke with a smile.

After Mike and Luke put the fire out and cleaned up the creek bed, they met the girls inside Luke's house.

"Friends or more, I'm happy for my brother. He is happier now than I've seen him in years." Jen spoke to Daphne, now bundled in Luke's soft couch blanket as they sat at the counter. When the guys came in the back, the girls were already in Kada's room and settled in, thanks to Jen. Mike looked at Jen, "Ready for home. We got the house to ourselves."

Jen smiled. "Yup. Let's go!" She slid off the stool and gave Luke and Daphne a hug and said their goodbyes.

After Mike's headlights left the driveway, Daphne looked at Luke, "Wow. She is a handful."

Luke laughed. "Yeah, that's why she is married to Mike." He continued, "But don't worry about her, she is a lot of talk, but mostly she is just being the protective sister, knowing Me and Kada and our past."

"I can understand that. I have an older sister too." She spoke as Luke walked into his bedroom and came out shirtless as he put on a dry shirt.

"Sister? You've never mentioned a sister. Where is she?"

Daphne frowned, "Not here."

Luke tightened his lower lip and nodded. "Right. When was the last time you talked to her?"

"July, my first day here, or at least her voicemail, but before that I saw her in April for a week."

"Are you two not close?"

"Oh, we are as close as sisters can be, but I can't put her in the middle of my life right now."

Luke frowned and got concerned.

"Daphne..."

"Luke, don't. Please, just leave it alone. If you want me here, this is the way it has to be."

He walked over, tilted her head up, gave her another hot kiss, and even dipped his tongue in and tasted her before pulling back just enough to feel each other's breath. Letting the blanket fall over the stool she sat on, she dipped her hands under his shirt and felt his ribs down to his waist and hips where his pants hugged. He pulled her off the stool, sat her on the counter, and pushed her legs open to wrap around him as he now was the one looking up at her.

"I don't want you anywhere else." He spoke. She leaned down to kiss him again before he pulled back to place a small kiss on her collarbone.

"Luke, the girls are here."

He took a deep breath. "I know." Then slid her off the counter to let her feet touch the floor but didn't let go of her. He gave her one last soft kiss, let go, and put his hands in his pockets. "Happy New Year, Daphne."

Now a little disappointed she replied with a slight frown, "Happy New Year Luke."

In March, Daphne looked up at the stars, bundled up head to toe, grocery bags in hand, standing on the front porch with a wide smile. The crisp, cold air floated ice crystals down from the glowing blue and green ribbons in the sky, with a near full moon and sparkling stars in the night sky above her. The lights danced and stretched across the sky, as her slow faint heartbeat was the only sound in the silence. Even being alone, the beautiful winter scene could make her smile with her heart. She closed her eyes as the snow fell on her rosy cheeks. For a moment everything was right in the world. She took a deep breath, opened her eyes, then turned around and opened her door.

Now simply decorated, her small house was only lit with a couple small nightlights in the hallway and the kitchen. She slipped off her clogs, hung her keys up while holding the bags of groceries. She walked to the kitchen, flipped on the light above the sink, and put her groceries on the small kitchen island that was also used as a small breakfast bar. She pulled her phone out of her coat and sent a text, "I'm home." A few moments later her phone chimed.

'Richmond' popped up on her screen before opening the message, " I saw. It's hard to miss that smile, even in the dark."

She smiled and replied, "How's my girl?"

While putting groceries away, the phone chimed again, "I got her fever down and she is sleeping. So, I guess better."

"Sounds like it. Well good, I got more soup and crackers if she wants."

"You're the best. I'll let her know when she wakes up, but you might want to get some rest soon, you need it too."

"I will. Goodnight, Luke."

"Sweet dreams, Daphne."

With that she finished putting away everything, got into her pjs, and curled into bed, while turning off the lights.

Daphne woke in the middle of the night to Kada crawling into her bed and snuggling in close. Daphne smiled, pulled her in closer, threw the blanket over her, and fell peacefully back to sleep.

At daybreak, her eyes opened to a handsome Luke in a new fire station sweater and hands in his pockets leaning against the door frame of her bedroom. With a big grin he spoke softly, "Now I know why we haven't seen any bears around the neighborhood in a few months." He said with a hearty soft laugh.

She smiled and rolled her eyes as she slipped out of bed, dressed in her matching deep purple satin tank top and shorts. She tip-toed passed him as he watched her with keen eyes.

He followed her out to the kitchen after closing the bedroom door.

"So?" she asked as she went to her coffee pot that had brewed a fresh steaming pot of coffee. She snagged two cups off to her shelf of souvenir mugs from her travels.

"So.....?" he replied, too distracted to understand the question she was asking.

"So, what does the jury say about my sleeping style these days?"

"Hot! If my daughter wasn't sleeping next to you, I probably would have had more of a pulse."

Grinning over her shoulder as she poured the cups of coffee and doctored it to their liking. She turned around to press a hot cup into his chest as she walked past him, taking her own cup across the small kitchen and living room to the small bay window seat. It was cozied with soft fuzzy blankets and a small bookshelf next to the window with small books and knick-knacks and random girly items.

She curled up in it, yawning and pulling the blanket over her lap, as she pulled her knees to her chest, and looked out the window. So familiar with this look, he's seen it a thousand times before, but from the other side of the window and through his windows across the yard. So peaceful looking, but if he knew anything from the past six months since she moved in next door to him, her head was anything but peaceful.

Though most subjects were kept light and playful, most of her life was still a mystery to him. Except for a few puzzle pieces about an accident that he supposedly saved her from which he couldn't remember, but he still felt as if he'd known her for years. Watching her still in a trance, he knew if he didn't speak now, she could be lost in thought for most of the morning.

"So, how was Kada?"

Snapping out of it as she looked at him in a confusion still holding her knees and coffee.

"Sorry. She was asleep till I got a call. I tried to sneak out of the house, but pager tones must have woken her up. I assumed she was over here when I came home and found her bed empty."

Both took sips of their coffee as Daphne smiled first.

"She is good. She crawled in with me late last night and has been there since."

"I think she is starting to feel better. I checked for fever last night before I got the call and she didn't have one, but she still hasn't eaten much."

Taking another sip of coffee in hopes to wake her body up now, she looked at him with better vision than before. A dark blue Birch Valley Fire Dept sweater and medical grade tactical pants with a couple of bulging pockets with trauma shears and pens sticking out. He looked sharp and ready to save anyone's life. She memorized his facial features. The soft lips, dark blonde hair, golden eyes that she knew got brighter in the sunlight, and a smile that could warm her skin. You would have to be blind or have the short attention span infant to miss him walking down the street. Luckily for the last three months, he only wanted her attention.

Shaking her head, as in much to a reply, as to shake those thoughts, "She felt fine all night with me. But if you want to go home and get a quick nap in, I'll feed her and send her home a little later."

How could she do that to him? How could this woman curl up in a frosted bay window in a blanket with her hair crazier than Medusa's herself, make his stomach tie into knots? Like she has done since the first day she moved here and worse, since they started sneaking around.

Although Kada was 12 years old, very capable of taking care of herself and being responsible while he was away on short calls, Kada had Daphne. He wasn't sure of any feelings with Daphne and how she fit in the picture. All he did know was, she did. But now he was unable to tell if his twinge of possessiveness was over her or Kada or both. He moved to the window and sat down across from her, and she immediately looked at the bedroom.

"Don't worry. You won't get cooties today." He smiled.

She smiled over her coffee cup and her eyes darkened. His right foot in a big black boot, set next to her bare left foot and he stretched out his left leg next to her.

A squeak of her bed frame made him pause as the bedroom door opened. Both turned to the sleepy-eyed girl in fuzzy, soft, blue snowflake pajama pants and white tee shirt, with her hair all a mess. She dragged her feet to the bathroom and closed the door behind her. A few moments later they heard the flush and sink turn on and off.

When she emerged from the hallway, wiping the sleep from her eyes, she wandered over to her dad, and gave him a peck on the cheek. Daphne patted the cushion in front of her between her and Luke. Kada sat facing her dad as Daphne grabbed the brush from her bookshelf next to her and began brushing Kada's beautiful long hair that was quite a few shades darker than her dad's.

As Daphne began to brush, her thoughts began to drift. In the silence of the house, she began to hear a familiar humming as the world faded away. Watching the brush bristles moving through Kada's soft hair, she began to copy the tune, unknown to herself. Kada and Luke made eye contact and a small smile as they listened to Daphne.

Curious as to what Daphne was humming, he was well aware that she was in her own reality, just as Kada would be put back to sleep soon if she didn't stop brushing her hair. Kada with a curious but soft look on her face, was getting more relaxed by the minute. Luke smiled at both of them as he took the last couple of sips of his coffee and glanced out the window to the small frozen creek still trickling with water. It was covered in snow and ice around the banks, which held more water during the summer months.

If Daphne kept humming, he might just curl up on her couch and take a nap. It was soothing to him as it was to everyone else in the room. Realizing the severity of his tiredness, he looked up at her and noticed she watched him with curious eyes.

"I think I'll head home for a couple of winks." He spoke to Daphne before looking at Kada, "You gonna be, okay? Daphne said she had more soup and crackers for you."

Daphne stopped humming.

Looking at her dad like she was just told how to walk, replied in the casual sarcastic tone, "Yes Dad, I'll be fine."

With a smirk and giggle, Daphne looked at Luke, who had a less than pleased look on his face now and gave him a wink and nod towards the door. He smiled because he knew whether she realized it yet or not, she inherited his daughter and she was gonna be just as deep if not deeper than he was, trying to raise her.

He leaned forward and kissed Kada on the forehead as he watched Daphne continue to brush the bedhead knots in her hair. Then he stood straight and headed for the back door after placing his empty coffee cup in the kitchen sink.

Leaning now to her side around Kada, with a grin from ear to ear, Daphne asked, "What should we do today?"

Gaining a grin back, she replied " Sledding? Hot cocoa, then Gilmore Girls?"

With pressed lips and a raised eyebrow, Daphne tapped the brush to Kada's shoulder and waved it at her, "You better dress warm, if you get sick again, your dad will kill me, then bring me back, just to yell at me." Both of them giggled like little schoolgirls.

"Why don't you go get something to eat quickly, while I run over and grab your snow gear, so I don't get yelled at for starving you, at least.

Kada drew both eyebrows together watching her but nodded her head as they both stood up. After watching Kada put the bowl of soup in the microwave above the stove and tap two minutes on the keypad and push start, she finished getting her coat, and scarf on and then slipped out the front door.

She walked down the path covered in snow. She watched her feet, throwing the snow as she walked and shivered in her coat. When she finally looked up, she was over halfway to Luke's and got nervous. Two paths were well made through snow going from Luke's to her house. One for the front yard and one for the back. Though his house was a quick stroll across their shared yard, the cold made the walk seem longer. Her heart started to race as much from the nerves as the cold.

"Warm thoughts. Warm thoughts." she whispered to herself.

A warm beach, waves lapping the shore in front of her. Arms from behind her holding her tight, two sets of bare feet in the sand. A soft peck on the back of her neck and a whispered "I love you," over the sounds of the crashing waves.

Her heart melted and warmed her to her toes.

The sound of a door opening snapped her back to reality of walking through the snow and crisp air and stopped her in her tracks. He stood on the porch, in soft flannel snowflake pants similar to his daughters this morning and dark gray tank as heat waves rose off his chiseled chest and broad shoulders. He had quite the smirk on his face when he finally asked, "Miss me already?"

Realizing she was frozen in her tracks; she regained her pace and reached the steps before answering him. "No. I just came to sneak out Kada's snow gear. She wants to go sledding at Pike Hill after she is done eating her soup." She wasn't planning on telling him she was eating soup, but she watched his demeanor change at the mention of sledding, so she needed backup and a defense.

"She'll be fine. I'll make sure she dresses warm and plus you can't tame her spirit, she got it from you."

Softening up his scowl now, he raised an eyebrow and held out a hand to his open door. She jogged up the couple of steps through the front door with her Richmond sign she gave them for Christmas, and into his bright house. As she passed him, she smelled his delicious body wash from his freshly showered body. Her stomach fluttered as he closed the door behind them.

The house was built to a similar style as hers, except bigger, a lot bigger, except he had a full-size bathroom and bedroom upstairs, instead of her tiny, little loft with a bedroom and bathroom. But even with similar builds, they both felt very different. His house spoke with efficiency and easy access to every area. It had family pictures and an old, blackened fire helmet on the wall next to the front entry. Tactical pants and station gear sat on a chair by the front door.

Daphne knew that even Kada's voice was never louder than Luke's need for efficiency and comfort. He still allowed his daughter to have a few girly luxuries such as pink and purple soft couch pillows on the dark gray couch, or the floral printed kitchen canisters on the counter next to the microwave. Though tough and by his own right, he was still a softy at heart when the only woman in his life was around.

Brushing her as he walked by nearly made her heart stop. Smiling as he walked towards the back door and through the mudroom interior door, he pulled Kada's gear off a hook. Then snagged the boots next to it, opened the small bench to pull out a soft, white hat and pair of white and silver winter gloves.

In anticipation, he turned quickly back and nearly ran into her, standing in the doorway. It suddenly felt like he was floating in space with nothing to hold onto and no air to breathe but still kept his composure as they made eye contact.

She watched him and searched his eyes for answers.

"Don't get us into trouble." he spoke softly.

Her smile widened as she remembered the sensation she got every time they kissed. "I'm trying not to."

If his hands weren't holding snow gear, he'd have reached for her. After that thought had passed, he finally took a breath and clenched the gear tighter in his hands. Without losing eye contact, he saw the shake in her hands. Their gaze deepened; her lips parted. He took a step up and came within an inch of her and softly connected their lips that she deepened by tilting her head sideways. Her hands ran over his chest through the soft fabric. He gave a slight sound as he closed his eyes and let out a deep breath. When he leaned back to look at her, she spoke, "Luke...."

He took a deep breath in, to prepare for anything.

Her hands dropped back to her side.

"Maybe when you get up, you could join us? I think Kada is missing you." Releasing his breath, he licked his lips in disappointment, and took a smaller breath to answer. "No."

Her eyes widened and her heart clenched, before he finished, "She misses her mother. That's why she is wrapped around you."

Daphne took in a deep breath to correct him, but he wouldn't let her. "It's okay. It's what she needs right now. If you're okay with it, so am I." He leaned back and held out the snow gear for her to take, then smiled. "Like you said, Kada is gonna do what Kada wants and neither of us are gonna be able to stop her."

Even on a step higher than himself, he still had to look down at her to catch her eyes wandering his body. His muscles clenched. If she didn't stop doing that, he might have to go jump in the freshly shoveled snowbank soon. He leaned down and kissed her forehead before he lost complete control, which he still hadn't gotten used to.

Taking another breath, he walked inside before he did something he might regret later. Which reminded him, he needed to talk to Kada soon. He had no plans with Daphne, but he never messed with his daughter's emotions, knowing him and Daphne would not be able to keep this up much longer.

Walking to the front door again, he didn't know where he was going. Daphne had every part of him in a knot and it was time to cool off. Slipping on his boots, he didn't bother to lace them or put on a coat before walking outside on the front porch. Bracing his hands on the snowy railing, he looked up at Daphne's house. He couldn't see Kada, but knew she was watching.

Kada was an observant one, even as a baby, she watched everyone else before testing the waters herself. Whatever she was seeing, he didn't know if she would talk to Daphne about it or not, but she surely would not talk to her dad about it. And though he understood why, it still stung that he could never have that connection with her, not like her mother used to, or the connection like Daphne had with her now. His heart broke.

Catching movement in Daphne's small kitchen window, he squinted hard to see Kada's face shape and her eyes staring straight back at him. Luke turned and grabbed the small snow shovel by his door to shovel off the snow on the steps as the dread of uncertainty set into his bones faster than the cold.

He heard the door open, as Daphne stepped out, more bundled in her coat than before. He paused for a moment leaning an arm on the shovel, to watch her. She held the snow gear in one arm and closed the front door with the other.

Acting as if nothing had happened. She paused in front of him, three small steps above him almost eye to eye now. Trying for a smile now, she spoke softly. "I hope you join us later. I'll give up the Gilmore Girls for a more family-friendly movie or show. We'll have hot cocoa and popcorn, and I could even make dinner. I'll even share my blanket on the couch with you."

His eyes deepened and his soft smile made her heart flutter again. Without letting him answer, she walked down the stairs past him and back onto the trail, leading to her house. She didn't look back, instead, quickened her steps and made it back to her door in half the time it took to get there. Opening the door and stepping inside, she finally gasped for air that she didn't know she needed.

Kada was leaning back against the kitchen counter in front of her window that faced Luke's, eating a bowl of soup, as she watched Daphne come in. Daphne smiled like she just had been busted for robbing a bank.

Kada spoke first, "How cold is it out there?"

After putting the gear on the little bench by her door, she shrugged as she took off her coat, "I don't know, I didn't check the temperature, but I'd say about 10 degrees. Why? It should be warmer by the time we go out."

Nodding her head with a smirk, Kada answered, "You're pretty pink for spending less than five minutes outside and ten minutes talking to Dad."

Drawing her own conclusion as to what Kada thought she saw, she smiled. She was getting to know Kada's keen awareness and thoughts. After putting her own boots and gear to the side, she walked over to the coffee pot, and refilled her cup again. Now leaning against the opposite counter, she smiled back. She took one glance at Luke through the window, over Kada's shoulder, before giving a slight frown.

"Kada, your dad is not ready for a relationship and right now, I'm not either."

"But he's always looking over here, whether you are here or not. He never looked over here until you moved in. But also, the last people in here were like 90 years old. He likes you, Daphne." She raised her eyes as she finished her soup and put her bowl in the dishwasher.

Daphne took a sip of coffee and felt the warmth reach her toes, while thinking of how to reply. "I know he does, but only because I care for his daughter. That is friendship, not a relationship. We help each other, Kada. I didn't have any help until I moved out here.... to the bush. I'm so happy I get to spend some girl time with you, whether your dad needs alone time or not, and I'm happy I know I can rely on him for help, when I need it. It's a lot for any parent to raise a child, but to do it alone after losing the one person they thought they would have forever...It's not only difficult, but it changes someone forever."

Seeing the sadness in Daphne's eyes growing, she stopped pushing, smiled, and turned around to watch at her dad still shoveling snow. Daphne walked over to wrap her arm around Kada and watch with her while sipping coffee. They both saw the same man, but not the same person. Both of them, smiling at Luke for very different reasons, yet still similar.

Thoughts, memories, dreams, and fantasies all molded into one.

Luke in his station wear, kissing her neck with her back to his office door, in the dark. His scent filled her head and his skin heated under her hands. Soft purrs escaped as her nails dug into his shoulders. Her mouth trembling at every small love bite he gave her as his hands grip her hips then braced hers against the door. She pushed at him with weakened muscles, gasping with one stray breath to regain strength, she pushed hard until his mouth released hers.

"I'm sorry, Daphne."

They haven't spoken of it since, but a lot has happened since then.

Luke held a small Kada in his arms on a bright sunny day as a couple tears fell against her pretty black dress, watching her mom's casket getting lowered into the ground. Later that night she would see him, elbows to his knees on a soft floral print couch sobbing into his hands as quietly as he could, through her cracked bedroom door after she was tucked into bed. The same night, she would wake to him folded around her, holding her in the small pastel pink twin bed.

Both Kada and Daphne took a deep breath and watched Luke go inside his house.

Daphne turned to Kada, "Go get ready for sledding. I want you dressed super warm, cause if you get sick again, your dad will kill me, Kada." That made them both smile again.

Luke finished shoveling the snow off the porch and stairs. She made him crazy with what he didn't know yet. He wandered inside and decided if he wanted a nap or another shower except this time it'd be ice cold. He turned on the water in the shower and stepped in. The icy water hit his skin and seeped into his veins. He got ready while thinking of her. An hour later, as he slipped on his boots ready to go sledding and his pager toned.

Grabbing it off the charging dock on the counter, he read the small text on the screen. Grabbing his coat quickly and running out the door to his truck. He hopped in and started it. He looked over at Daphne's to see the girls' hauling sleds to her Jeep Grand Cherokee. Watching them, he turned on his radio and held his mic. With a click, he told dispatch "BV 6-1 responding." He hung up the mic, threw his truck into reverse, and hit his emergency lights. He passed by as both his girls watched him.

"Dad must be going on a call." Kada said, loading her sled on Daphne's roof rack on the Jeep.

With a lower tone, she responded while watching Luke drive by, "Yeah, must be."

She threw the ratchet strap over the sleds, looped them through the sleds handles and tightened it. Turning to Kada, all dressed up in white and light blue snow gear, she asked, "Ready?" Kada nodded and jumped in the front seat. Already in her snow gear, Daphne turned out the lights in her house and shut the door.

Within 30 minutes, they pulled up to a snowy hill with kids and parents sledding down it. Chaos ensued as kids went tumbling down the hill. Parents racing to check on them while others narrowly miss them coming down from the top.

The most crowded part was the middle of the hill. The left side was for smaller kids and beginners. The far right was for the experts as it was taller and steeper, infamously called "Death Row" by the daredevils of the teenage sorts.

Kada turned to Daphne with eyes as big as a child's on Christmas morning. Daphne gave a grin before jumping out and shutting the door and unlatching sleds from her roof.

Almost an hour later, Luke pulled up next to Daphne's Jeep. Looking for them, he finally spotted them at the top, almost ready to go down on a sled together. Kada with a grin ear to ear, gave a nod to Daphne sitting behind her, as she tightened her grip on the handles. With one big push, it was too late for Daphne to see the little boy walking up the hill in their path.

About halfway down, they bailed off the sled to keep from taking the boy out. A big cloud of snow flew up and a flash of blue and purple mixed with sparkling ice crystals, came tumbling down the hill.

Luke grabbed the door handle ready to jump out and help, when the cloud cleared near the bottom and saw Kada sprawled out in Daphne's arms, both laughing hysterically. He let out a breath and shook his head. Daphne said something and Kada pointed to the bottom of the hill to their sled. As they stood up, he got out of the truck. In his thick work boots, thick jeans, and a thick winter station coat, he reached to unlock his toolbox in the back of the truck, pulled out a thick pair of gloves, and put them on.

Walking around his truck to Daphne's car, he pulled the extra sled off the top and headed for the hill. Making sure to stay behind them as they climbed the hill to the top. Kada and Daphne loaded up on the sled again. From behind them, he heard Daphne tell Kada, "Now, no more aiming for the small children." Both giggled as Daphne tucked her feet in under Kada's legs and gave a push off.

Before Luke gave it any thought, he took a running leap off the top of the hill with the sled, landing on his stomach and flying down the hill past Daphne and Kada.

In a blur, he heard a mumbled shout from Kada, "Dad!"

He smiled as the cold stung his face and his heart raced. Within a matter of a few seconds, he reached the bottom and slowed to a stop. He got off quickly to turn around and watch the girls just hitting the bottom and smiling. From the ride or him, he didn't know, but either way he liked it. Kada jumped out before the sled even stopped and ran to him and hugged him.

"Dad, it's been a blast. We almost hit this one kid and we dove off the sled and rolled down the hill. It was hilarious."

"Yea, I saw that. You, okay? How's the head cold doing? Are you cold yet? How are you?" as he turned to Daphne, picking up her sleds' rope and walked towards them.

With a grin and a scowl in place, she replied, "She's fine, I am fine, we are good."

Eyes connecting in a moment of heat that warmed her soul to her toes. He smiled as he released Kada from his grasp. "Good."

Kada watched Daphne and her dad for a second. "You two should go together." In a state of shock, Daphne and Luke looked at her in question.

"It'll be fun. I'll take my sled and follow. Both of them smiled and shrugged at each other.

At the top, Daphne climbed into the sled first. Luke sat behind her and wrapped his legs around hers. Leaning her back on his chest, he gave a hard push that had them flying down the hill, faster than she had gone all day. The snow hitting her face, made it sting, but felt joy she hadn't felt in a long time. His arms around her tight as she held onto his legs was a sense of security that she always felt in his arms. Seeing a small berm at the bottom, her heart sank, and her muscles tightened.

Going too fast to bail off, Luke tightened his hold around her and shouted, "Hold on!"

She closed her eyes in hopes to shield herself from the disaster about to happen. They hit the berm and went flying. For a split second, she couldn't tell you where the earth was. When she landed, it was softer than she thought it would be. When she opened her eyes, she saw a blue sky with clouds. Her muscles loosened to take count for any injuries but the tightness around her chest stayed.

"Ow! You, okay?" His soft voice spoke from underneath her.

He still held on and used his own body to break her fall. She took a deep breath in and rolled to her side off of him. He was laid out staring at her, taking in every inch to check for any signs of bleeding or injury.

Kada slid up to them with a smile. "Having fun yet?"

Luke sat up, "Oh, I'm getting old."

"Dad! You're not old!"

Smiling and laughing now, Daphne slowly got up and brushed the snow from her head, that was now missing a hat. Kada took a few steps, picked up Daphne's purple and silver hat, and handed it to her. "Ready for some more?"

Luke and Daphne glanced at each other, then at Kada, as Daphne got up and ran towards the hill. Luke began the chase after her with their sled in tow, Kada following with her sled.

Another hour later, parents were turning on their vehicle's headlights at the sounds of their pleading children for one more run. At the bottom, Luke waited for the last run for Kada and Daphne. On their sleds they raced to the bottom, Daphne winning of course. Once they reached the bottom and walked over to Luke with vehicles already running and warmed up, he told them, "Let's go get dinner."

Kada gave Luke a huge hug and thanked him for letting her out of the house with Daphne. With an arm around her shoulder, a kiss to her head, he walked her over to Daphne's car and opened the passenger door to help her up the step, and into her seat. With a scowl, he reminded her to buckle up and then he shut the door.

The ratchet strap thunked on his side, so he reached up and clipped it to the roof rack over the sleds. After helping Daphne strap, them down, he walked around to the driver side and pushed her against the car, trapping her with his big body and holding her there.

"What we want for dinner?" He asked, rubbing his hands down her sides. In rhythm with his hands, she inhaled the cold air as deeply as she could.

"Well, we always have Mike's." She looked up through her long thick lashes at him.

The thought of a nice big bread bowl with Mike's homemade daily soup sounded amazing, but not ready to put their relationship on display for the town gossip, he'd suggest taking it home.

Luke and the rest of the department were some of Mike's biggest customers, but in Birch Valley, if you needed a hand to fix your roof or leaking pipes, and if Mike helped you then you at least ate dinner at his diner.

Birch Valley Fire Department weren't just a group of Firefighters, they were the town's handymen and heroes of every variety, making the captain's restaurant, Mike's Diner, the local hangout. For everyone from teenagers after school, to local hobbyist groups, and even for Ms. Bellwood's late brunch with her weekly local gossip on Sunday mornings. Mikes had the food and usually half the town at any given hour of the day from opening till close.

"How about my place? We can have a glass of wine and watch..." He winced, "......G ilmore Girls. I'll call in an order for pickup and snag it on my way home. You and Kada go home, warm up, get comfortable, and meet me at the house, say in an hour?"

Daphne didn't even notice the cold anymore. She was getting warmer by the minute. "Okay, but under one condition."

Luke's hands fell to his sides, then to rest on his own hips. He raised one eyebrow. With a probing look, she spoke in an assertive tone, "You talk to Kada, soon."

He saved lives, he worked on cars, built houses, and could even cook. But talking to his daughter about a personal life he never thought he would have again after her mother, was not his best quality, at least not when it was on his own terms. He took a deep breath and pursed his lips.

Even if it was his more recent thought too, Luke had mixed feelings. Happiness that at least him and Daphne were on the same page of letting Kada know. But also putting his daughter on a page that he wasn't even sure, he was on. He needed time.

He spoke softly, "Okay. Fine. I will tomorrow, during breakfast, before I go to the station."

Daphne slid her hands under his coat and up his shirt to his abs. She dug her nails in just enough to feel his whole-body clench tight.

"Good! Thank you!" She responded as she let go, turned, and walked to her driver door.

"See you in an hour." He spoke with a stiffness as he played with his keys.

With an evil grin and wink, she jumped in as the heat hit her like a sauna. Still with a smile, she buckled her seat belt, and turned to see Kada in the front seat. She was fast asleep, curled up, and had stripped off her snow gear that was now piled on the floorboard just below her feet. She smiled even more, put her Jeep in drive, and left the parking lot.

Watching her leave, Luke pulled out his cell phone and hit speed dial #2 as he got in the front seat of his truck. When the other line rang and Mike answered, "How was sledding?"

"Good. Hey Mike, can I get a to-go order of two bread bowls with your daily soup and a mushroom burger and fries for Kada?"

"Sure, But hey Luke..."

"Yeah, Mike?"

".... This is three meals."

"Shut up and get on it. I'll be there in 20 minutes."

Mike's chuckle rolled through the phone. "Okay, okay. See you in a bit."

Luke now put his truck into drive and headed back onto the main road. He turned to look at the empty passenger seat during the drive. He should be upset that Kada was spending most of her time with Daphne, but he wasn't. Whether with Luke or not, he was happy all the way to his soul that Kada had someone to look up too. Daphne could never take the place of his late wife, but better to fill those shoes with Daphne's cute feet, than his own. It was hard being two parents, especially to a little girl who only knew how to be tough.

Somedays, it even broke his heart to come home to a clean house with a new screen door installed and a leaky pipe fixed, and now she was off at neighbors, getting her toes painted and watching "Gilmore Girls," and not much else could make him smile more than Kada smiling as she would show him her freshly painted pink toes and fingers with braids in her hair and smooth and shiny, glowing skin like women get after a facial.

Soon, he pulled into the back parking lot of Mike's Diner. He pulled his wallet out of the center console where he put it before sledding and got out of the truck and entered through the back door. The smell of greasy French fries, salty beef and fruity pies wafted through the air. He walked down the short hall and turned left into an office where Mike sat in a chair hunched over a big desk and paperwork.

"Man! How do you do it?" Luke spoke first.

Mike looked up with a big smile and replied, "Oh, what? Whoop your ass at training?"

Luke pulled out the chair on the other side of the desk and sat propping his elbows on the desk. "Ha! Please, I pulled Bob out of the smoke house three minutes faster than you!"

"Well, yeah, cause Bob, the dummy, is 50 pounds lighter and doesn't give any lip like Magar or Whitte does."

Both with a couple of chuckles each.

"True! But I was talking about being good at cooking, paperwork, and CPR, but I'll give you the benefit of the doubt, I guess."

"Well, these hands are good for a lot more than that, but we'll keep the conversation shorter, considering you have a date waiting for you." He spoke with a shallow tone while raising an eyebrow.

Luke jerked his chin to the side and held up his hands in a surrender.

"Kada has been with her since last night, we just got done sledding, I just want to feed the woman and my daughter."

With a raised eyebrow still, he didn't seem convinced, "Uh, huh! That's bullshit and you know it. But alright, just don't go rewriting the will yet. There's a lot we don't know about her."

He knew a lot more than Mike knew but wouldn't let him know that.

"Down Captain, she's just an interest."

With a half grin, Mike replied, "Yeah, and you're damn lucky if you get off the home base considering your batting average." He laughed as he got up and out from behind his desk and started down the hallway to the kitchen.

Again, he knew more than Mike about his dating history, but kept a lot to himself.

Mike reached for a brown bag with a paper stapled to it marked "Luke," off the top shelf of the server's racks and handed it to him. Then walked around to the servers' counter, opened the cooler, snagged a bottle of wine and half a gallon jug of "Mike's homemade sweet tea," and handed those to him. Luke started to reach in his back pocket and Mike stopped him by putting his hand up.

"Don't worry about it. This one is on me, in hopes it will help you get laid, soon! Kada isn't the only newly hormonal one in the Richmond house. But I'm happy to see you smiling again."

With a chuckle and a nod, he took the wine, tea, and bag of food and escaped the way he came in.

CHAPTER SIX

A s he passed Daphne's cute, little cottage, which was far more decorated than his own, he noticed her in the kitchen window, probably doing dishes.

He pulled into his driveway and put his truck in park, then picked up his phone and sent a text, "I'm home. Got food and Mike sent wine." Then he grabbed the food and drinks and got out. By the time he got his door unlocked and bags on the counter, his phone chimed. Immediately grabbing it almost made him feel foolish like a love-struck teenager.

"Okay, we'll be over as soon as Kada gets out of the shower."

He smiled and mumbled under his breath, "Okay, see you tomorrow." he spoke to himself as he laughed. He knew his daughter well enough to know she took a shower more to warm up, than to get cleaner, plus add an extra hour to every task cause the world ran on preteen time.

He walked down the hall and opened the bedroom door that had a sign on it saying, *Break, in case of emergency.* A birthday joke from Kada two years ago.

Opening the door, he walked into what a woman might call a "dungeon." Dark gray bedding with matching curtains and black, soft rug with a design and layout that screamed efficiency and simple but also dark and cooler than the rest of the house.

The right side, bedside table held a photo of Jasmine holding a newborn Kada on her chest. Jasmine dressed in white lace and Kada in a sheer purple wrap, in an intimate and emotional photo. As well as the lock box Daphne gave him for Christmas that held his and Daphne's photo.

He pulled his wallet out and dumped his change in a bowl on the dresser, put his pager on the charger, and plugged in his phone. He changed into a plain black t-shirt before walking out to start setting out food.

Just as he was plating the bread bowls and burger, the girls walked in the door. Kada shouted, "Hey Dad!" as if she hadn't seen him just under an hour ago. Kada slid off her shoes and tossed her coat next to the small bench, which made Luke clear his throat pretty loudly as he continued to plate food.

Kada let out a breath, grabbed the coat and hung it up on a coat hook, then stomped away and up the stairs to her bedroom.

As Luke poured Kada's fries onto the plate next to the burger, he asked the stunned Daphne still standing in his entryway holding her coat, "Please tell me she doesn't do that at your house?"

Now looking at him, she gave a single nod as she unzipped her boots and slid out of them. "She does, but I don't spend all day picking up after kids nonetheless the same kid for 12 years, so I don't mind as much."

She reached over and hung her coat on the last available hook next to the door. She quickly pulled up her sleeves ready to help Luke, then turned around and ran into a warm, soft wall.

Gasping quickly, his scent was intoxicating. Her hands started to tingle, her eyesight fuzzy, her heartbeat skipped, and her legs weak. She felt hands grip her waist as she regained her senses. She tried to look up at him, but his head was coming down. Then she felt warm wet lips along the corner of her jaw on her neck just below her ear.

She thought her knees might give when her shoulders hit a wall and his grip tightened. "Luke." She whispered the breathless name. Her skin sparked with energy and electricity. Her hands reached up to brace on his arms.

Another soft kiss to her neck. An even more breathless name escaped, "Luke." She gave a weak push, and he took a step back releasing his grip.

With racing heartbeats, she pried her eyes open to look at him. He stood there with his hands on his waist, looking at her with eyes that told her, "Desire and disappointment". The stretched t-shirt over his broad chest moving up and down with his deep breaths made her hands spark with renewed energy.

He spoke first, "I'm sorry, Daph. I'm trying not to push."

With heavy eyelids, she peered up at him still plastered to the wall in the entryway. "Luke, I told you. Friendship...."

He raised an eyebrow at her.

".... okay, Stronger friendship, but that's all, while we both process this."

Luke smiled, laughed, and licked his lips.

"I know and I'm sorry, but it's getting harder to process anything."

She smiled at him.

"Trust me, it's not only you, Luke."

He widened his stance to relax a little more and smiled. He leaned back on his right foot and put his hands in his pockets. Took a deep breath, then turned a bit and gestured to the plated food on his kitchen counter.

"Let's eat before it gets cold."

Daphne wrapped an arm around herself, and her other hand played with the silver anchor pendant on her necklace as she walked to the counter.

"Kada, dinner!" Luke shouted as he grabbed the wine to open and gave her a glance. They both smiled at each other.

Kada leaned against the balcony railing in the dark corner just above the entryway, smiling like a kid on Christmas morning. Everything she just saw and the conversation she overheard, gave her hope that she hadn't had before. Plus, any more heat in the house had potential to melt the snowbanks outside.

She took a deep breath in and let it out, pressed her lips together and got rid of the smile. She walked down the stairs, turned the corner, and immediately got a probing look from Daphne. Both girls grabbed their plates from the counter as Luke poured the wine. They gave each other a look, until Kada went blush and grinned like a busted criminal. Daphne's mouth dropped with a wide smile and shook her head as she rolled her eyes at her. Kada did a little happy dance in place.

Clueless, Luke turned around and handed Daphne her wine glass. Daphne winked at Kada as Kada grinned and grabbed for the sweet tea and poured herself a glass. Luke smiled at Daphne as she thanked him for the food and wine.

They sat at the small counter bar in between the living room and kitchen. They also talked about the day and plans as they ate. When Kada mentioned school tomorrow, Luke glanced at Daphne over his wine glass, looking for some kind of reaction. Daphne hid any reaction by looking at Kada and asked her how she was doing in school.

"Fine. Our new social studies teacher is..." She paused and second guessed her planned words, ".... a pain."

"You'll always have at least one, and for your information Mr. Everett is having family issues. Don't be too hard on him." She looked at Luke, "Aren't you due for a promotion soon?"

Finishing the bread bite in his mouth, he swallowed and nodded. "The second round of promotions are to come in after the new training, but we'll see if I get the captain's slot or not. Mike is also overdue too and a few other good men. So, we'll see."

Daphne spoke up in a quick reply, "You'll get it. You're a great firefighter and wonderful Dad, Luke."

Kada nodded her head in agreement.

Luke smiled at Daphne and took another sip of wine.

After dinner, Kada and Luke did the dishes together while Daphne ran home to grab her Seasons of *Gilmore Girls* on DVD. In that time frame, Luke thought it might be good to talk to Kada.

"Kada, what do you think about Daphne?"

Drying a plate and putting it away, she nodded her head at her dad with a soft smile. "She's great, Dad! But I wonder where her family is?"

"I don't know, but I feel like she'll let us in when she's ready. We just need to be there for her, like she's been there for us."

"Dad, I can only make her smile, but you can make her happy. She's more relaxed around you and she seems to like you and for more than just your lips."

Luke stopped scrubbing the silverware to scowl at Kada, but wasn't surprised his daughter noticed, then replied in a questioning tone. "Yeah? You think so?"

"Yeah, Dad. Like today she was smiling when we were sledding but she laughed more after you showed up. Then she got quiet on the way home, like she didn't want to come home. You make her happy and for some reason other than the kissing I've seen you two doing, I'm happy she has us. No one should be alone."

Luke grabbed the dish rag off the counter, walked over, and gave his daughter a hug and kissed her on the forehead. Just as he returned to the sink to rinse dishes, Daphne walked in.

Daphne started to take off her boots and looked up to see them both looking at her, "What? Is my hair messed up?"

Luke dried his hands off again, walked over to her, and plastered a hot kiss on her lips. When Daphne sank into it, he wrapped his arms around her waist and gently lifted her off the floor till her feet dangled.

Still holding the DVD's, she was caught off guard as she wrapped her arms around his neck.

Kada walked over to snag the DVD's out of Daphne's hands. "Told you dad liked you." She spoke with an attitude as Luke and Daphne giggled against each other's lips. Kada took the movies to the living room and put one in the DVD player.

Luke's hands wandered under her coat and finally got working at taking the coat off her. Her mind wandered on the why's, how's and what ifs, but soon gave up as his kiss got deeper and hotter. The second he pulled back; he saw her soul in her eyes. Open like a wound. He brushed a hand against her jawline and got a smile out of her.

For whatever reason, he felt like it needed to be said while both of them stood emotionally naked, "Daph..." shortening her name just sounded better at the moment and her look didn't show any disappointment, so he continued. "I'm here. I'm not going anywhere."

Her demeanor changed in an instant. He spooked her and in a second, he regretted saying it. Though she still had a small smile in place, her posture was frozen until she inched closer, and slowly placed her hands on his face and gave him a slow gentle kiss and whispered, "Thank you." Then she turned and walked the few steps to the living room to join Kada on the comfy couch.

Within a few seconds after she walked away, he already tied himself up in knots kicking himself mentally for saying anything. He took one last deep breath as he watched her sit on the couch and he turned to finish dishes.

After a few episodes, he noticed Daphne and Kada both were asleep against him. He reached over and pulled the DVD remote out of Kada's hand and clicked the power button. Knowing he wasn't getting up, he reached behind his head and grabbed the small plush black blanket off the back of the couch, threw it over them and then pulled them in closer and closed his eyes.

His phone rang. Leaning over new station blueprints, he pulled it out of his pocket and looked at the name. "Jasmine." The crew's laughter tuned out the ringing. He wanted to decline the call, but his gut told him not too. He swiped at the answer button. "Hi, Hun, I'm in the middle of a project with the crew. Can I call you back?"

The sound of Kada's blood curdling screams in the background caught his full attention along with Mike's. A shaky breathless woman's voice on the other side spoke with fear.

"Luke, baby, there's been an accident. You need to save Kada. I love you."

He looked up at Mike across the table, now frozen watching him keenly, before he saw Mike's pager light up on his side. The world went silent, and time froze for a single moment.

He gasped awake, nearly throwing himself off the couch if Daphne hadn't been laying on his chest. Kada was gone and now a full-size purple and blue blanket lay over him and Daphne.

Breathing deep now to slow his racing heart, he rubbed her side and felt her snuggle in closer. He could be happy again, he knows he can, here was this precious life of a loving woman in his arms sleeping so silently, it felt like a sign to him. Not wanting to read too much into it, he pulled her closer into his chest, kissed her head and snuggled into the couch, smiling. Life was going to be better for him and Kada, he would make sure of it, somehow.

The sound of cracking grease woke him. The sun shone bright through the window behind the couch he laid on.

Glass clinked and whispers came from the kitchen. The smell of bacon and coffee wafted through the house. He could barely make out two figures in the kitchen as he realized the lightweight of Daphne was no longer on top of him, disappointing him for a second, until he rubbed his eyes and got a clear picture of his kitchen.

His favorite black hoodie dancing around in the kitchen. The woman with bed tossed hair and no makeup, flipped bacon on the stove and pancakes on the griddle. She instructed Kada how to flip an over easy egg without breaking the yoke, as low music played from Daphne's cell phone on the counter.

His heart skipped a beat.

Thankfully, he had a blanket covering his lower half because he did not want to give Kada a male anatomy lesson right now.

When he sat up, hanging on pretty tight to the blanket, both the girls looked at him.

"Morning, Daddy." Kada spoke first.

"Morning, Baby! Making breakfast, I see."

Daphne spoke quickly. "She wanted to learn how to cook eggs, so I told her I could teach her." She paused a second and continued, "I hope you don't mind, I didn't bring any clean clothes with me, so I went through your closet. Kada helped me pick these out." as she moved from behind the counter and did a quick turn in his flannel snowflake pajama pants and big hoodie that made her look so tiny in it.

For the split second she blocked his view of Kada, he didn't have time to think before he moved quickly in one smooth motion from the couch, out of the blanket, to her. He reached for hips and squared hers with his, so they were face to face. She felt his erection under the tight stretch of his black tactical pants and the thin t-shirt displayed everything underneath.

He gave her a quick light peck on the lips and whispered, "Don't move. This is not a lesson I want to teach her about right now." As he twitched the corner of his mouth up.

Her eyes deepened as she turned into a devil's glare and gave an evil grin.

"And if I move to the right?" She bumped her hips a tap to the right and his grip on them tightened.

His stare now matched her evil glare as his thumbs dug into the waistband of his pjs she was wearing.

"You wouldn't dare!" She whispered in a drawn-out breath. The corners of his mouth curved up further. She held her stance and rose to her tiptoes and kissed him. "Go shower, breakfast will be ready soon."

She glanced down.

"No.... don't do that unless Nurse Kimble wants an entirely different talk with her favorite student."

Daphne swallowed, looked up to his darkened eyes, and tried not to grin.

His smile turning sinister, he dropped his head to whisper next to her cheek as he keenly watched Kada cooking in the kitchen, "All my clothes are pretty easy to remove and change for my job, but these are a little loose to hang onto your curves while you tease me in my favorite hoodie and pjs."

He gave her a kiss on the cheek when Kada looked over at them.

He now spoke loud enough for Kada to hear "I'll be quick so I can take Kada to school."

"Yeah, I have to go back to work today too."

His eyes spoke volumes of disappointment.

She tried not to smile. Then straighten her lips.

"You good?"

He forced a smile, "Yeah."

He gave her a soft lingering kiss then headed down the hall to the bathroom. She turned back to the kitchen to finish making breakfast with Kada, who now was smiling like a fool at Daphne, while she plated some toast with jelly.

"You and Dad are so cute."

Daphne brought her brows down and the curves of her lips curved up as her cheeks blushed. With a pause, she replied, "Don't burn the bacon, I like mine still soft." She got two coffee cups and took them to the counter.

Luke towel dried off, got dressed in another t-shirt and jeans. He had some house projects he could do today while the girls were gone. He sure as hell wasn't going to the station so Mike could poke at him. He shaved the edges of his jaw and down his neck, cleaning up his 5 o'clock shadow as he went. He threw on his baseball cap backwards, ready for breakfast, then reached for his cologne, sprayed it twice across his chest, and shrugged. Checked himself in the mirror, deemed it good enough.

After work as she pulled into her driveway, a boombox played hard rock music from across the yard on Luke's porch. Wood, sawhorses, and a few power tools scattered a small section of his side of their shared yard.

Daphne smiled, grabbed her books and purse, and walked up her porch to put her keys in the door lock, then looked back over to his yard. Luke stood there with a construction pencil in his teeth and a small piece of a 2x4 board in his hand watching her. Jeans, work boots, and the same hoodie she wore this morning.

There was snow on the ground so why did she feel like she was in an oven? She smiled at him, then turned the key, and walked into her cottage.

She took off her coat and hung it on the rack next to the door after shutting it. She put her purse and books on the kitchen island then walked to the fridge and pulled out a half empty bottle of Rosé wine to pour herself a glass.

Kada would be home so she couldn't go help him without getting herself into trouble. She's safer at home with her wine and a good book for the evening. After a shower, she would curl up in her bay window, and try and finish her book, and that's what she did.

He lost focus after seeing Daphne coming home. He made one last cut on a 2x4 and measured it. Three quarter inch off. "Damn it!" The board went flying across the saw table, to the ground, into a melting snowbank.

He packed everything into his shed and took another shower. When he got out, he heard Kada's bedroom door shut. Then her voice on the other side of the bathroom door. "Dad, can I go to Sarah's and work on English homework?"

He slipped on his dirty pants and opened the door.

She loved the smell of her dad's cedarwood and musk smelling body wash, as did her mom.

"When will you be back?" He grabbed the toothpaste on the back of the sink, put some on his toothbrush, and stuck it in his mouth.

Kada, now leaning against the bathroom door frame, crossed her arms. "It should only take a couple hours, but Aunt Jen said she could drive us to school in the morning. If it gets too late, I can crash there."

He watched her as he brushed his teeth. Judging her expressions, he deemed it the truth and gave her a nod.

She smiled and kissed her dad on the cheek. She grabbed her duffle bag from the couch, took the coat off the rack, and ran out the door.

"Now what?" He finished up, changed into a clean pair of pants, and walked out to the kitchen to find something to eat. He picked up Kada's sweater, and random clothes as he crossed the living room, and threw them at the bathroom door where the washer and dryer were.

A beer. That's what he needed. He opened the fridge, and pulled a beer, and popped the cap on the edge of the counter.

He looked at his pager on the docking station on the kitchen counter and told himself it was going to be a peaceful night. He took a gulp of his beer, then set it down on the counter. He walked back into the bathroom, pulled a clean tank top from the dryer, and put it on. He walked into the living room and looked out the window towards her house, no lights. He walked to the mudroom, opened the door, and stepped into the frosty room with windows all around. The sun was starting to set. He peered over to her bay window that faced the creek they both shared.

The creek was trickling during these winter months, but still a gorgeous sight and peaceful to watch and listen to.

Her reading light showed through very faintly. She was awake. His heart skipped again. He could imagine her reading her book with her cute reading glasses and glass of wine. He just wanted to hold her while she read. He didn't care if they talked or not, he just needed to be near her to keep his head straight. He shut off all the lights and grabbed his sweater...the one that still had hints of her scent on it and walked out the back door through the mudroom and followed the small foot trail through the snow to her back door. She saw him coming before he even knew he was coming.

He looked up at her little bay window and saw her curled up in a soft, blue blanket with a book and a small reading light on as she smiled at him. When he reached the back door, he looked for a sign that he would be welcomed. Still in the tiny bay window, she watched him and smiled as he opened the back door and walked in. He let out a sigh of relief as he took off his boots.

She pushed up her glasses and put her book and blanket to the side, showing the station sweater she wore. Then she stood up as she finally pulled the glasses off completely. "Hi." She spoke softly.

He smiled at her as his eyes drifted over his older station sweater, he gave her.

"Hi. Kada went to Sarah's, so I thought we both could use company tonight."

The curve of her lips went up just slightly. Still standing by the doorway, he closed the door and put his hands in his pockets waiting for anything to happen.

She walked quickly to him and laid her lips on his and in reaction he deepened the kiss and wrapped his arms around her waist and lifted her up off the floor. When they pulled back, they both smiled, and she dropped back to the floor. She reached for his hand and led him to the window to sit him down and curl into his lap and arms.

Both looking out the window, they both relaxed. His legs stretched across the small seat around hers. On her side, shoulder to his chest, his arm wrapped around her, she pulled the blanket over them. The last of the pink glow was now touching the treetops surrounding the creek bed. For a couple of seconds, the world was glowing pink with hints of orange and glistening in the last rays of sunlight.

"It's so pretty out." She spoke softly, holding onto his right arm wrapped around her.

He couldn't see most of her face but didn't need to hear the happiness in her tone. Her hair was freshly towel tumbled and he felt slight dampness in the thicker parts of her hair when he kissed the top of her head. Moroccan oil shampoo, small, blue bottle. He knew it well because it was the same one his sister in-law used. In a small town with only one store to choose from without driving further then needed, grocery selections were limited. When he could reach his phone in his back pocket, he'd put it on his shopping list and stash a bottle at his place for her when or if she ever needed to take a shower. He hoped she would, soon.

"There are better views in this house." He spoke as he felt her cheek tighten into a smile against his arm but got no reply.

As the sun finished setting, the sky lit up in a black and silver glittering glow so bright, it lit up the treetops in the distance. She moved deeper in his arms to get more comfortable and snuggle in closer. Now she was completely in his lap, her ear on his collarbone, nose pressed into his neck, knees up to her chest and arms tucked in. He leaned to his right side to raise his left leg up to keep them both from falling out of the small window seat. He glanced at his watch on his left wrist, almost 6:30pm.

He noticed the half empty bottle of wine and empty wine glass on top of the small bookshelf next to the window seat. Has she eaten anything for dinner yet? He hadn't yet, but his starvation was far beyond his stomach right now.

All her scents on her and in her house would make any man starve, but he had a lot to learn about her still. Luckily for him his reservations matched his speed. He liked that they were comfortable with each other without having to be intimate. It was nice to hold a woman in his arms and not have any expectations, even if his jeans got tight sometimes. Hey, he is a man, nobody would argue with that. But he always felt better just being with her and for whatever reason, whether she could admit it or not, she enjoyed his company too.

She looked up at him. His golden eyes deepened when they made eye contact. Everything told her to stay right here and never leave. She felt his chest rising and falling with each slow breath. She pushed up to reach his lips, then twisted until they were chest to chest and their lips connected. His hands gripped her hips and moved up to her waist for a better grip to deepen the kiss. If she didn't stop, she knew she would regret it, but she couldn't. He was like a wave, pulling her into the depths of an ocean that she could easily drown in.

He tilted his head and sucked on the edge of her lips and caught the tart taste of her wine, which only brought out the sweetness in her skin. Her hands clung to his sweater. His pants began to tighten, if he didn't pull away now, he'd be lost to her forever. He felt the silky, satin tank top under his sweater and matching bottoms she wore. *Thin*, he thought.

He felt the dampness of her tongue on the edge of his lips and opened his mouth a little wider. Her taste seemed to get sweeter with each passing second. He heard a near silent moan release from her and knew he was a goner. He tightened his grip and tried to readjust as her shirt came up off her hips. His hand brushed against her skin making her jump out of fear, releasing quickly from his grasp and falling off the bench. His heart stopped a second and his eyes widened with shock. Daphne, now standing next to the window and holding herself, stared at him like he was a ghost.

"What's wrong?" he asked quickly.

"I'm sorry, I almost forgot who we were."

"Daphne, it's okay. It's me, Luke..."

He reassessed his words and spoke again, "...Richmond."

She looked down at his now straining bulge in his jeans and spoke with a defined tone.

"Are you hungry? Want a beer or glass of wine?" She turned and started to make a move for the kitchen, but he snagged her hand and just held her there, leaning forward as he watched her from the bay window.

His eyes softened. She hoped he wouldn't ask any questions and he didn't. He very softly tugged on her hand to sit back down. He held up the soft, blue blanket to her and when she walked to it, he gently wrapped it around her and pulled her back into his lap. His hold was a little tighter than before, but oddly more comforting.

He whispered next to her ear, "I'm sorry."

"It's not you."

Flashes of bright lights, doctors, and alarms surged through her head. Her entire body clenched tight, and her knees came up to her chest again. He brushed his hand up and down her back for comfort. He felt the tears land on his arm, pulled her even closer and tighter, and just held her without saying a word.

They watched the snow begin to fall outside.

His body began to relax, and his breathing slowed. She kissed his arm that rested under her head. He rubbed her arm through the blanket over it.

A dark haired, tall man smiled at her and reached out his rough hand and put it on her cheek, "You'll live." He spoke with a soft temper.

She woke up with a startled jerk. Her eyes adjusted to the darkness. She was in her bedroom on her bed. Fully clothed still in the blue blanket. She sat up and softly spoke, "Luke?" The house was silent. Her heartbeat raced as her stomach turned and hairs raised on her neck.

She got up and walked out to the living room. She didn't know she was holding her breath until she saw him asleep on her couch and released it. He looked so peaceful on her couch, on his back, feet over the armrest and the slightest smile in place. She hoped he was dreaming of her. She walked over to him and bent down to wake him gently till his phone rang in his back pocket. He jerked upright and saw her instantly. Keeping his gaze locked on her, he pulled out his phone and answered it.

"Richmond. Yeah... Sorry, it's at home..."

A short pause, as he stood and pulled the microphone away from his face to give her the softest and gentlest kiss on her lips. Again, she didn't realize she was holding her breath until she finally let it go.

He searched her eyes, but she didn't know what for. Maybe answers to why panic and fear clearly showed in her expression.

"No, I'm not home. Don't worry about it." He said in a snappy tone that gave him the faintest twitch of a smile while he watched her. "Yeah, I'll be right there. Engine? Okay. Yeah."

He hung up the phone and stuffed it in his back pocket again and pulled her in close, holding onto her waist to make sure she didn't pull away.

"I have a call. It's medical, so it should be quick, and I'll come right back. I promise."

As much as she wanted to be disappointed, she tried not to show it, and straightened her spine with a half-smile and nod of her head.

Her eyes showed fear, but he knew it wasn't because of him. He hated leaving her, but another life was on the line, he had to go.

"Go back to bed and I'll come back as soon as I can." He gave her a kiss that deepened for a couple of seconds then he turned and headed for her back door, slid on his boots, walked out and jogged down the path back to his house.

Now she felt more alone than ever, and never had she felt so scared of her own shadow. She wandered back into her bedroom and laid down again. She remembered the comfort she felt in his arms, watching the snowfall outside her own window and slowly drifted back to sleep with a smile.

Mike and Luke loaded the patient into the back of the ambulance, shut the doors, and sent the rig leaving the scene with lights and sirens.

Mike, with crossed arms, looked at Luke with a curious look.

"Don't look at me like that." Luke spoke with a sharp tone.

"Well, you said you weren't home at ten o'clock at night. You have your truck and station sweater and now your pager which you did state was at home, and yet you still got to the station under the five-minute response time from *your* house."

They gathered their tools and gear used for the call and loaded them back into the sparkling clean gold and white fire trucks.

Without a response from Luke, Mike continued.

"Did you at least figure out the fear?" Mike's look softened as Luke showed sadness.

"No. Working on it."

Luke paused a second before putting the medic bag back into the truck compartment and shutting it.

"Sorry, Luke." He would drop the conversation. Mike patted him on the back. "Let's head back. You can fill out the report tomorrow."

Luke's jaw tightened with a grin while Mike gave a soft laugh as he walked back to his command vehicle.

The crew loaded up as they turned off the emergency lights and headed back to the station.

On the way home, he thought about how Daphne flinched and shut down at a simple touch of skin and he cringed thinking how it might have hurt her.

When he turned down his road, he had every intention of going home first, but his arms turned the steering wheel into her driveway. He put it into park next to the red Jeep. It was dark and cold out, but yet the warmth crept through his body as he watched the quaint, little cottage through the windshield. He shut off the truck, got out and pocketed his keys. He looked over at his house to see it blacked out, and everything in order. He jogged up the stairs to the front porch. When he reached the front door, he swallowed hard before reaching for the doorknob and turning it.

Locked. *Shit.*

Before he could reach in his pocket for her house key, the knob rattled, and the door opened.

If it wasn't the heat wave coming from the house and warming him up, it was definitely the sight of her, with her hair in a cute mess falling around her shoulders and sleepy eyes while still holding onto the same blue blanket he left her in. She was still wrapped up in it as she clung to the top of it, holding it together.

"God, I could come home to this every night." When she gave a sleepy smile, he realized his thought came out of his mouth. And dove to her mouth for a long, yet deep kiss.

Her blanket dropped to the floor, revealing his station sweater and her girly satin shorts in dark purple. Not knowing where to place his hands without scaring her again, he wrapped both arms around her and took a couple steps into the house so she could push the door closed behind him.

He slowly let her feet touch the ground but didn't loosen his hold on her. He pulled his head back to look at her face and her small smile she still had before he finally let her go.

"You hungry now?" She said as she picked up her blanket off the floor and wrapped up in it again.

He hadn't thought about food and through his stomach told him otherwise, he replied, "No, but thank you. I'm just exhausted."

He glanced at the clock on her wall which told him it was nearly midnight.

"I figured you'd still be in bed." He said as he removed his boots and tucked them under her small bench by the door, then continued to remove his coat and sweater.

"Confession, Mrs. Adams is our closest neighbor, and she is 500 feet that way...." She pointed East down their street. ".... Making the sound of your truck, the only other one coming this far down, soothing. Especially after heading home from a call." She watched him with a poker face waiting for a reply. He crossed his arms in an inquisitive look that turned into a grin.

She stepped to him, reached for his hand, and led him back to her bedroom. He took off his shirt and pants, leaving him bare chested and in boxer briefs, leaving his curves and bulging sections on display. She folded down the blankets and sheets and climbed in to scoot across. He climbed in behind her and pulled her close to him. She snuggled in close.

Her pillows smelled like her shampoo and body wash, woodsy, fresh with a hint of sweet florals. His body relaxed more than he's felt in a long time. Her skin was so soft and warm, her hair tumbled around her gray pillowcase. He felt her take a deep breath and her body go limp, and he smiled and closed his eyes.

Chapter Seven

T he sun shined directly at him and the soft, warm body he was snuggling all night was gone. He listened for any sound, but nothing. He opened his eyes and let them adjust to the brightness. His heart sank a little when he found the bed empty. Something told him she was gone.

He got up and got dressed and straightened the bed sheets and blanket and walked out into the living room. A note on the counter was the first thing he saw. He walked over to read it after grabbing his sweater off the hanger by the door. It read:

Luke,

Let's keep this simple for now. Friends first, please. I had to go to work. There is a breakfast burrito in the microwave I made for you. Thanks for staying last night. I'll see you soon.

Daphne

His heart sank a little deeper. He took the pen next to it and drew a heart on the bottom and signed his name.

He grabbed the burrito out of the microwave and wrapped it in a paper towel. Snagged his coat, keys, and pager, and walked out more disappointed than he's felt in a long time.

She sat at her desk doing paperwork, thinking of nothing else except last night. It was getting harder to do paperwork as the day went on till a shy voice from behind her spoke.

"Daphne?"

She turned to see Kada leaning against the doorframe, holding her foot off the floor.

Reality snapped back to her.

"Ms. Kimble, when we are at school, please Kada."

"Sorry. Ms. Kimble, I sprained my ankle playing kickball in the gym. It kinda hurts. Mr. Parks sent me to get it looked at."

Jumping up and walking over to her, she helped Kada limp to one of the beds in her office and propped her foot up on a pillow.

"Can you take off your shoe for me, please." She said as she walked to her fridge and pulled out an ice pack from the freezer.

Rolling up her pant leg to look at and tap around her foot and ankle. She saw the bruising already starting to color.

"Yeah, you sprained it, alright. Do you want me to call your dad, or do you want Tylenol and go back to class with the ice pack?"

Kada eyeballed her ankle and then searched Daphne's face.

"Yeah, I'll go back to class. We only have a couple more hours and I don't want to get behind on schoolwork."

"Okay, well, rest here for a bit until some of the swelling comes down and I'll get you the Tylenol."

She got up, went to her medicine cabinet, unlocked it, and pulled out the Tylenol, taking out two and handing them to Kada with a small cup of water from the sink.

"I still gotta call your dad and tell him what happened." She almost choked on her words, getting them out.

"Okay." Kada replied as she looked at Daphne watching her facial expressions.

A bleach blonde woman smiled and leaned in the doorway, looking at Daphne. "You have a message at the front office." She spoke with a wide grin in place.

Daphne pulled her eyebrows down in a questioning look, then turned back to Kada who was taking the Tylenol.

"I'll be back in a sec."

Kada nodded.

She walked out to the front office and rounded the corner and instantly saw the pretty pink vase with dark pink roses, purple irises, and big yellow sunflowers with a small card in an envelope in the middle.

The young secretary on the phone nodded her head towards the flowers as Daphne walked towards them and pulled out the card and read it.

You trusted me once, trust me again. Stop running.

With a grin now, she whispered to herself, "I don't know how, Luke."

She picked up the vase and walked back to her office.

Kada nearly startled her when she gave a whistle. "Who are those from? Your boyfriend?" Poking fun at her with a grin while knowing exactly who they were from.

"From a friendly neighbor, that's all." As her grin grew to a questionable smile. She put the bouquet on her desk next to her computer and turned it as she sat in her chair to admire them before turning her chair around to look at a smiling Kada.

"Guess I should call your dad now and let him know what happened to you."

"Uh, huh." Kada said with her smile still in place.

Daphne turned her chair back around and thought it was safer to use the office phone instead of her cell. She picked up the headset and dialed Luke's number by memory.

A deeper, "Richmond." answered on the other side, knowing she caught him off guard with an unknown school phone number.

"Mr. Richmond? Nurse Kimble from Birch Valley Middle School..."

She could hear the release of a deep breath under the rumble of his engine idling. "....I have Kada sitting in my office with a sprained ankle."

"What? What happened?" She heard a hint of worry in his tone.

"She's fine. Just some swelling and bruising that's all, but she wants permission to be released back to class for the rest of the day. I gave her an ice pack and two Tylenol, and I'll lend her a brace I have here in my office to help her get back to class, but I think it best if she gets a ride home instead of taking the bus."

He took a deep breath and agreed.

"You can pick her up after school or I can drive her home after I'm done with work, it's up to you."

"Yeah, she can stay with you. I have some work to do at the station today and I don't know how long I'll be there."

"Sounds good, Mr. Richmond. I'll have her home before dinner. And Luke...."

He now held his breath and all she could hear was the rumbling idle of his truck.

She turned away from Kada. ".... Thank you, for the flowers."

He let his breath out and in a soft tone, said, "You're welcome."

When the line went silent, she hung up the phone and turned back to Kada.

"Your dad wants you to ride home with me and I'll drop you off after work. So just come back down here after school and I'll take you home, okay?"

Kada smiled again and nodded. After bracing her ankle and getting a fresh ice pack, she headed back to class. Daphne decided paperwork could wait until tomorrow, she'd be too distracted to do anything else besides stare at her flowers now. For the rest of the day, she was the speculation of the entire staff of Birch Valley Middle School, and she didn't mind at all.

When she turned down her road and rounded the corner, her heart sank a little when she found both their driveways empty.

"He's probably at the station." Kada said, looking at Daphne's disappointed facial expression.

"Nah, it's okay. I have a ton of paperwork and some house chores to do." She said quickly to hide her shock and disappointment as she pulled into Luke's driveway.

Daphne turned off her Jeep and started to open her door when Kada spoke up. "It's okay, I can make it on my own, it's not broken."

Daphne raised an eyebrow and closed her driver door to point at Kada.

"Okay but rice it! Rest, Ice, Compression, and..."

"Elevation. I got it."

"And take the brace off tonight before bed. Ibuprofen every six hours. If you need anything, call me."

"Okay, okay, thank you." Kada got out and closed the door.

Daphne would normally wait until she got inside before leaving the driveway, but she could see her front door from her window at home, so she backed up and went home.

She didn't know what to expect walking in her own door, but she didn't expect to find it how she left it. After taking her coat off and putting her purse on the counter, she saw the heart and signature left by Luke. Through the open door, she saw her bed was made.

"Get over yourself, Daphne. It's better for both of us. He'd just get hurt." She told herself.

She crumpled up the note and threw it towards the trash can, missing the ledge and landing on the floor. Then she went for a glass of wine and her books where men were predictable and the lives, she read about weren't hers.

Over the next few days, she kept herself busy, never going outside unless it was to leave for work or coming home. She chose to sit on the couch instead of her little bay window. In a fit of anger over the weekend, she made the split-second decision to redo her bathroom and update the old tile and bathtub, so she took some aggression out with a sledgehammer. She pounded out an hour of smash therapy and instantly regretted her decision, wondering how she was going to take on this big of a project alone.

She dropped the hammer and took off her protective goggles and went for a glass of water, only to look out her kitchen window and see Luke pulling in his driveway as Kada stood waiting at the front door. She seemed to be getting around better as long as she still had a compression brace on.

A tired looking Luke walked up to his door and gave her a hug. Both of them looked to be sharing some words before Kada disappeared back inside. Luke looked over to her house and gave a small smile. Even knowing he couldn't see her; he knew she was watching. He walked into his house and closed the front door.

For dinner she made herself some Alfredo Fettuccine and wondered what it would be like to have a dog, someone to play with. The little golden retriever puppy came to mind, the one she had as a little girl. She recalled "Puddles" sleeping on the foot of her bed almost every night, but she also remembered the big messes he made too especially after running the beach outside her childhood home.

The big snowflakes falling outside her bay window caught her attention. She smiled walking over to it and kneeling on the seat to peer out at the snow falling onto the creek bed out back. She ran to the back door, slipped into her snow boots, put on her thick winter coat, then the knitted gloves, hat, and scarf. Peering out the back door down the little hill to her bench just above the creek bed, she smiled. She walked out and closed the door behind her, then turned and started down the hill to the bench as the fresh snow crunched under her boots.

The moonlight sparkled off the snow-covered ground and each snowflake fell from the dark partly cloudy sky above. The air was crisp, but fresh. Through her skin tingled from the cold, she loved it and everything about a cold, dark, starry night. She made it to the bench, dusted it off, and took a seat. Beyond the sound of trickling water under the icy creek, it was completely silent. Her thoughts wandered from her childhood to life choices, to her current position in life.

How'd she get here? She didn't even know, but she knew it's been a long road, and for now, she was content. Terrified but content. She didn't feel any guilt about telling Luke to back up, but she was lonely, even if she had gotten used to being alone.

She had remembered the decision to move here. The cabin in the picture of the magazine was not the same cabin that was at her address. Now thinking about it was... or is Mrs. Adams, her other neighbors, but she didn't mind. Though a split-second decision, so far, she hadn't regretted it and hoped to never have to.

The soft crunch of footsteps in the snow made her whip her head around and see Kada and Luke approaching with thermos and Styrofoam cups in hand.

Kada was following the small, buried path through the snow, as Luke, a step behind her, made sure she didn't fall.

When they got close enough, Daphne spoke first, "Kada, what are you doing out here? You're supposed to be resting that ankle."

Kada, stopped in her tracks to reply and cross her arms as she spoke with a gruff tone, "Dad has kept me on the couch or in bed and doing nothing, but mother-hening me. I needed out and so did he. So, when we saw you out here, we made some hot cocoa and figured you could use a cup."

Daphne slid to the far side of the bench as they started again and walked around the bench to sit next to her. "Aww, that's sweet. Thank you."

After Kada took a seat, Luke shoved her down next to Daphne, and she took measure of the gesture, from both Daphne and her dad.

Luke opened the thermos, poured three cups, and passed them down. Daphne looked at Kada after blowing on the cup of hot cocoa and asked, "How is the ankle doing?"

Kada nodded and stuck her right leg out to show her winter boot looking a little bit thicker in diameter than her left. "It's good. The swelling is gone, but it's still bruised."

"Yeah, it will be for a bit. If you're at home resting, take off the brace and let circulation back and the bruising will heal faster."

"Okay." She nodded.

Luke just watched the creek, occasionally sipping and blowing on his cocoa. Daphne didn't have to watch him to know what he was doing. His presence alone was like a fog in her head. Undeniably there but confusing all her senses.

In the uncomfortable silence, Daphne spoke while watching the twinkling stars above the creek, "So, I decided to redo my bathroom."

Kada and Luke turned to look at her, but both with very different facial expressions. Kada's held a kind of excitement to it and Luke's had a shock to it as their questions began. "Can I help design it? The theme, I mean. Are you changing the tub? Dad won't get me a big jet tub." Kada spit out in a fast pace of excitement.

While Luke was more worried, "Do you have time to do a project that big...alone? Do you know how? Mike renovated his bathroom a year ago, I can see if he has any scraps, we...I mean that you could reuse, if you'd like?"

Daphne looked at Kada and with a smile replied, "I'd love some help on design, but I'm not putting in a jet tub." With Kada's smile in agreement, she looked at Luke and continued. "I'm pretty sure I can do most of it on my own, but there might be a few things I could use a strong arm or two on. Most of the materials I'll have to order, but some of the designs I have in mind, I might be able to use reclaimed materials. Depending on what Kada and I come up with. It will be fun, I think, and it'll help me stay busy for the rest of the winter."

"Well, if you need help with anything, let me know."

"Okay."

They all took sips of their hot cocoa and watched the creek and bright stars. Within the hour, they made small talk and drank a few more cups of cocoa. Kada now leaned up against Luke. Daphne spoke, "You should get her inside. I'll probably head in a bit myself."

"Yeah. It's past her bedtime. You gonna be up later? I need to talk to you."

Daphne swallowed and didn't need to ask why, but instead nodded. Luke tried for a smile that fell flat but his eyes told her more then she knew he wanted to. He patted Kada's back and told her to head for the house and get ready for bed.

Without argument, she got up, gave Daphne a hug and told her, "I'll see you tomorrow." Then turned and headed for the house.

Luke got up and gathered the cups and thermos and tucked them under his arm and then hands in his pockets, looking at Daphne. He took a couple steps to her and leaned over and kissed her forehead and whispered, "You're not alone." Then turned and headed back for the house.

Daphne watched him until he made it to his back door before, she got up and turned to head back inside. After turning on the lights and stripping her gear off, she looked at the kitchen and at the bedroom. Then with a chill in her bones, decided on a quick hot bath.

She walked to her bathroom, opened the door, saw the destruction before she immediately shut the door again. She walked to her bedroom, gathered her soft, purple pajama pants and black tank top out of her dresser, and headed for the tiny upstairs bathroom. Though very tiny like it was meant more for a small child, she could make do for now.

She hardly used it, so she would have to pack what seemed like a truck load up to this bathroom, but after a sigh, she got to it. Making a few trips with arm loads of makeup, toiletries, hair tools, and clean towels.

After filling the small bathtub and adding in some bubbles, she climbed in. Although a lot to handle, she tried to think of the positives of redoing her much bigger downstairs bathroom. She could really make it hers.

This whole thing was a fresh start. New town, new house...if you could even call this a house, and now a new bathroom. Next, would be that old run-down kitchen of hers. Though everything worked, the old wood cabinets were going to be the first thing to go, along with those wood countertops. There was definitely a lot to do, but it was hers. She kept reminding herself, and only hers.

She sank under the water and heard her heartbeat. *I'm still here.* She thought to herself. She opened her eyes and saw the swirl of blood drifting through the water.

She panicked and rose so fast out of the water, gasping for air, that water spilled out of the tub on her floor. She grabbed for whatever she could reach for help, as a hand grabbed hers and helped raise her out of the water, holding tight to her hand and now another under her other arm.

Coughing up water and gasping for air, her eyes started to clear to see white bubbles and clear water. Though her heart sank, she was relieved. So, were the hands real? She looked behind her. Yup. There was Luke looking just as shocked as she was and just as wet.

"Breathe. It's okay."

Coughing up the last bit of water. She took a deep breath in and felt her heart steady.

He reached for the towel on the rack next to the bathtub and handed it to her without even drying his face or body.

She let go of his hand to grab it and wipe her own face, then covered her bare chest.

"Thanks." Pausing for a moment to gather her thoughts, she continued. "What are you doing here?"

Now taking a corner of her towel, he wiped his own face, and sat on the edge of the little tub.

"Well, I knocked on the back door, but didn't see any lights on so I walked in. When I saw the lights on in the stairs, I came up. Then when I saw the bathroom light on under the door, I started back down the stairs, until I heard the flood of water and gasp for air, now I am here."

His face was straight with no emotion as he stared at her.

She wrapped the towel around her a little tighter and unplugged the tub to drain and stood up. Though enough room for her, he had to duck a little when he stood up to help her out.

"Slow." He warned.

After stepping out onto the white and soaking wet floor mat, she tucked in her towel and grabbed more towels off the small bathroom shelf and laid them over the pools of water.

"You, okay?" He asked with a soft tone.

She looked up at him, and the swirl of blood flashed again. She jerked away, grabbing for another towel to wipe up the excess water and discard all the wet towels in the hamper by the door.

"I fell asleep." She lied.

Now he crossed his arms and leaned back against the sink as much in reaction to her lie as to relieve his tight neck from the low ceiling.

"I don't buy it. They are called flashbacks, Daphne. A symptom of something we first responders see frequently, called PTSD. Your accident is only a fraction of the story, isn't it?"

She sighed loudly. This is why she moved here. To get some peace, right? She grabbed her pjs off the counter, turned off the light and headed back down the stairs to her bedroom as Luke followed. Cooler down here, goosebumps started to rise as she put her pjs on her bed. He leaned in the doorway, hands in his wet pockets. She couldn't help but smile at him in his soaking wet black T-shirt and jeans. Except his expression hadn't changed.

Her smile fell flat as he watched her, so she took a deep breath, straightened her spine, and lifted her chin. Watching his expression closely she undid the towel and let it fall to the floor. His eyes widened then closed as he let out a drawn-out breath.

More than a dozen scars, no more than an inch long stretch across her body from her breasts to her belly, and one faded but visible wide cesarean scar on her lower belly.

Her voice started breaking as she spoke softly. "He wanted to surprise me. We took a couple of flights here and drove. I don't even remember how he lost control of the car, but the scars are from the glass and debris that shattered when our car slammed into a big cottonwood, 150 feet from the bottom of the cliff. A fireman they called 'Richmond', pulled me out. I can remember the sharper scent he wore as he pulled me from the car, the Richmond name and his golden eyes that told me I was going to be okay."

He gave a rueful smile as he crossed his arms over his chest and searched her face for all the emotions that were pouring in those few seconds she paused.

"When I woke up from surgery, I couldn't have told you why I was even at the hospital. But the first thing they told me was that I was almost three months pregnant, and it was a girl that I lost. Anything else from that day has been blocked or lost, but that's all I can remember."

Luke walked over to sit on the bed by her, but she got up and stepped back from him. Her voice broke as tears started to spill down her cheeks. He watched her closely as she tried to say more.

"Over the next few years, we tried 100 times. The more we tried and failed the more he drank. For a long time, I just put up with the arguments, screaming, the fact that my body was broken, even the taunts and torture after a bottle of whiskey, and pinning me down to the bed."

His eyes widened as his elbows touched his knees and his face landed in his hands. The anger inside was building as he tried to control his breathing.

"It wasn't until he broke three of my ribs and dislocated my wrist, that I packed up in the middle of the night and ran. It took exactly twelve months at my sisters for him to find me, then again at an apartment I had for a little less than a year in Minnesota. When the state troopers finally took him, I found this cute little cabin in the middle of the woods with an idyllic little community about as far from him as possible. I needed to disappear for a while, so I bought it and haven't looked back."

Now she truly felt naked. She crossed her arms over her body, covering her breast and some scars. He stood and she tightened. His hand reached out to her, she took it and kept her head down till he pulled her closer. He softly ran a thumb over a couple of the scars, then up over her jawline, then gently under her chin to look up at him.

"Listen to me. I'm so sorry you had to go through that. You are beautiful and amazing, and I know Kada would say the same."

Her soft tears became sobs.

"Hey, I don't remember the accident and it kills me to know that I walked away from you knowing I could have done more than just my job, but your ex will get what he deserves and no woman, especially you Daphne, should be treated like that. I can't imagine what you went through and now living in fear. I'm so sorry and these.... "

He touched a few scars beside her breast with the back of his fingers. "Just shows your strength and how far you've come to find me. You know I'm different. You saw it. Just like I don't see anything but a very beautiful and brave woman."

She struggled for a smile and nodded as she wiped the rivers from her eyes. He pulled her in closer to hold her as she let it all out. He held her tight and laid his head on hers as he tried to control his breathing for her benefit. When he released her, he gave her a slow sensual kiss. He picked up her pjs off the bed before he handed them to her and told her to get dressed before he left the room, closing the door behind him.

He took a deep breath as the pain and anger he felt for her, stirred inside him. He walked to the back door as he tried to loosen his jaw and worked it and then grabbed her coat off the rack. When she emerged from the bedroom, looking more delicate than when he left her, he tried for a smile watching her shattered appearance.

"Put on your coat. You'll spend the night with me tonight and tomorrow we'll start working on your bathroom."

She didn't argue and did as she was told. The Daphne he knew would have argued. When she went for her boots, something inside him snapped. Giving a huff to fight his own insecurities, he picked her up and headed for the door. Again, she didn't argue. He carried her across the yard to his house as she snuggled close.

Feeling broken and beaten down again, she found the warmth that she needed, the same warmth that held her on one of the worst days of her life.

He felt the dampness of her hair against his neck, so he hastened his steps to reach his back door and open it with his hand that held her legs and hip.

Getting inside his warmer mud room, he set her bare feet on the floor and shut the door behind them. He helped her out of her coat and hung it up. She walked to the inner door and opened it and walked inside. He followed until she froze on the door mat, so he picked her up again and carried her to his bedroom. He gently placed her on the bed and pulled the covers over her.

"Let me shut down the house and I'll be back."

Feeling humiliated, she curled into a ball and tucked her head deeper into his pillow. His scent on the pillows was just as comforting as him, if not more.

When he returned, the bedroom door opened, and the house was now as dark as his bedroom. She couldn't see anything but heard his footsteps and the beep beep sound of his pager turning off. His phone illuminated when he plugged it in and put it on the dresser next to the bedroom door. She heard the metal buttons of his pants hit the floor next to the bed and the familiar dip of the bed as he crawled in next to her and pulled her close.

"Get some sleep. I'm not going anywhere tonight. I'll be right here."

He felt a tear hit his arm under her head and kissed her forehead. Her burdens drifted almost as fast as she fell asleep. She was safe and loved for tonight.

When morning came, he was still there, wrapped around her. Unable to see his face, she tilted her head back to see his face. His eyes looked down to see her and he smiled.

"Morning. How'd you sleep?" He asked while rubbing her back gently.

She smiled sweetly.

"Amazing. The best in years actually."

"Good. What do you say to some coffee and breakfast while we toss some ideas around with Kada for your bathroom?"

Understanding he wasn't going to push the subject about last night. She nodded but didn't smile.

"What are we gonna tell Kada?"

He looked confused.

"That I'm helping you with your bathroom and we need to order supplies soon?"

Now she smiled.

"No, about last night."

Still rubbing her back, he replied. "Oh! Right. I'll leave that to you, but for today, might I suggest that you had a rough night and wanted to be with us?"

Pursed lips, she nodded before propping her head up on her hand.

"That will work."

He leaned over, kissed her forehead, and propped his own head up on his hand while moving his other hand from her back to her face.

"You're so beautiful, Daphne, scars and all and you do have support here, you have us."

Her heart and lips smiled.

"Thank you, Luke."

She appeared to be in thought, so he asked, "What is it?"

She looked at him with curiosity. "Can you do me a favor today?"

"Anything."

"Can you call my sister and give her a message?"

His eyebrows drew down, but understanding why she couldn't call her herself, he agreed. "Sure. Just let me know what to tell her and I'll call her after breakfast."

"Just tell her, I am peachy. Our tree is still standing, I'll see her on Valentine's Day, and I miss and love her."

His eyes widened in more confusion as she smiled.

"Peachy means it is me. A tree still standing means, I'm still in Birch Valley, and seeing her on Valentine's doesn't mean I'll actually see her, it means I'm happy..." She took a deep breath, "and I'm falling in love."

He smiled really big now, leaned down, and gave her a soft kiss on the lips.

"Coffee?" He asked.

She gave a soft moan. "Mm... please."

He rolled over to the edge of the bed and stood up, then slipped into his jeans he left on the floor. He buttoned and zipped them up, but left the belt undone while grabbing a clean tank top out of the dresser across the room from the foot of the bed.

He unplugged his phone to stick it in his back pocket, and grabbed his watch Kada and Daphne bought, then headed for the bedroom door as he slid the watch on his left wrist and latched it. He opened the bedroom door and before walking out, he turned and looked at her curled up in his bed and smiled at her before walking out, closing the door behind him.

When he turned around, Kada was at the counter on a stool eating a bowl of cereal while watching him.

After chewing and swallowing her bite, she smiled and said, "Morning, Daddy."

"Morning, Baby."

He walked into the kitchen, picked up a ripe apple out of the fruit basket and took a bite out of it before kissing Kada on the head and running a hand down her hair.

As he took a step to the left, he grabbed the coffee pot and filled it with water from the sink. When he got it, all set up to brew, he turned to Kada, who was still watching him.

"Daphne's here."

He waited for her reaction, but got nothing, so he continued.

"She had a rough night last night and wanted to stay with us."

Now she was shocked.

"Is she okay? What happened?"

Pushing the "Brew" button on the coffee pot, he turned to lean against the counter.

"She's okay, but give her some space Kada, and she'll tell you when she's ready. Okay?"

He glared at her with a stern look and finger now pointing at her.

"Don't push, Kada Jasmine!"

She threw up her hands, "Okay, okay, geez."

Kada put her hands back down when Luke's bedroom door opened and Daphne appeared still in soft, purple PJ pants and black tank, holding herself as she walked over to the counter. Kada and Luke, both watched her as she grabbed a banana out of the bowl and gave Kada a hug from behind.

"How's the ankle?"

"Great! I can finally walk on it without the brace... which I have for you in my room."

"Good! Can I see it?"

Kada obliged by throwing her foot up on the counter just to annoy her dad. Daphne smiled and rolled her eyes as Kada gave her dad a devilish smile.

Luke shook his head and grabbed two coffee cups, cream and sugar dishes, then poured coffee in both the cups. He poured a dash of cream in one then a half spoon of sugar and stirred it, then pushed it to Daphne as she tapped on Kada's ankle with her fingers and turned her foot to look at it in the light above the counter.

"Looks great. How does it feel?"

"Good."

Daphne grabbed her cup of coffee after Kada dropped her foot back to the floor and took a sip. The caffeine surged through her veins.

"Mm." She closed her eyes as she swallowed another gulp, then took a seat on the stool next to Kada and started to unpeel her banana.

Both Kada and Luke observantly watched her as she drank her coffee and ate her banana. Luke broke the silence and spoke to both the girls with a smile, "You girls want to drum up some ideas for the bathroom renovations while I jump in a quick shower. Then I have some paperwork to fill out quickly at the station. I figured you could tag along, and we can talk to Mike about what he has that we can reuse."

Daphne watched Luke over the rim of her coffee cup as Kada smiled in excitement.

"Yes! I have so many ideas for Daphne. Let me get my book." As she raced across the living room and up the stairs to her bedroom. Luke took another sip of his coffee as Daphne watched him.

Since she said 'book', Daphne knew her ideas were going to measure up to the same thickness as one of her medical textbooks. But didn't know if what she felt was dread for renovations or excitement for change and watching Luke on the other side of the counter watching her, stirred extremely different feelings, even some heat that wasn't coming from the coffee.

The energy sparked in the room, and he felt it. Her long hair and bed tossed, no makeup, plain black tank with no bra. Her cool, blue eyes doing nothing to cover the heat behind them as they reached his soul and gave him more energy and heat than the coffee did.

If he didn't speak now, he'd need more than just a cold shower in a minute.

"You gonna be okay today?"

He noticed the obvious redirection in her eyes from his body to his face.

Her smile turned to being forced now.

"Yea. I'll be fine."

Though he didn't believe her, he replied, "Okay." as not to push her, then added, "I'll be with you all day, if you need anything, just ask."

She nodded before she took another sip of coffee, still watching him and then replied, "Thank you, Luke. Oh, hey, give me your phone quickly."

He looked confused but obliged, pulling out his phone from his back pocket and handing it to her. She took it with a smile, "Dani's number."

Now he smiled and nodded. She looked back to his phone and saw Kada's picture on the lock screen then swiped up to unlock it and saw their picture on the back screen again. She would never get used to that as it gave her a short pause, he just drank his coffee and watched her. Raising his eyebrows to her.

She smiled at him as she pulled up his contacts, entered Dani's cell number in a new contact, and hit save before handing it back to him.

He looked at it, "Dani Morrison" and locked the screen before tucking back in his pocket.

"I'll call her in a minute."

She smiled, "Thank you Luke."

His body moved before his brain did. He pushed his coffee cup to the side and leaned over the counter. He saw a slight smile before locking lips with her. She leaned in and tilted her head to deepen the kiss that got a reaction from both of them.

He gave a soft moan, at the sweeter coffee taste when her tongue opened his lips.

The sound of Kada's bedroom door closing hard and footsteps down the stairs jolted them into reality as Daphne sat back in her stool and Luke straightened his spine, took another sip of coffee, and licked his lips.

Kada rushed into the kitchen with a binder filled with sketches and magazine clippings of pictures of lavish bathtubs and vanities, oblivious to the tension in the room that hung like a heavy fog and sparked like lightning.

Luke rolled his eyes and spoke before Kada could. "I'm gonna jump in a shower." Jerking a thumb behind him down the hall towards the bathroom.

Still with stars in her eyes, she watched Luke as she nodded and took the binder from Kada and opened it.

Adjusting his jeans before leaving the safety of the counter, he turned and headed down the hall past his bedroom.

The icy water helped tamper down the heat and his erection. After getting out, he dried off and slipped his jeans back on after discarding his boxers to the laundry hamper. After shaving and brushing his teeth, he cleaned up the bathroom, wondering what Daphne might think if she needed the bathroom.

Opening the door, he heard the laughter in the kitchen and the whisper soft talk about colors and style of floor tiles. He smiled and headed back down the hall.

The girls got silent at his sight, just before he reached his bedroom door.

"Dad! Daphne likes my nautical and ocean theme ideas!" Kada spoke with an enthusiasm in her tone while he just stared at Daphne, who now watched him with keen observance as he reached for his bedroom doorknob and paused.

Even from ten feet away, Daphne could see the water droplets running down his neck, over his pecks, and over his washboard abs to the seams of his jeans that hugged low on his hips. Her heart raced now as she chewed on her nails as she propped her head up on her palm and watched the water turn the color of his faded, blue jeans at the waist seams.

What was he like in bed? She bet he'd be amazing. What would he really think about her scars though? Did he have any? Maybe accidents at work? He was definitely a lot sexier than she'd ever feel. He never had issues showing his bare skin as she just got comfortable seeing her own skin. But he was the first person to see her, and he still called her beautiful. Now that she wasn't completely naked or upset, she could actually smile at that statement that steadied her pulse.

The shout actually made her jump.

"Daphne!" Kada spoke with a loud tone that snapped her back into reality.

Looking at a grinning Luke and to a confused Kada, she answered, "What? Sorry, guess I'm still waking up." She blinked a few times to pull off the lie and rid her head of the thoughts that fogged her brain more than her lack of coffee.

"Dad likes the nautical beach theme idea." Now smiling, Daphne tried to gather her thoughts. She turned to look at Luke again who now propped himself up against the exterior bedroom door frame and crossed his arms over his chest still with the same blushing grin.

"Yeah, sounds good. I love the beach and nautical theme. We'll talk to Mike and see if he has anything I can use, and we'll go from there."

"Yeah, just let me get dressed and we can get going." Luke replied.

Daphne spoke quickly, "Actually, I need to run home and shower too."

Luke looked confused. "Is that even possible? Well, with your bathroom in pieces and..." He paused, "An un-shower-able upstairs bathroom?"

She smiled. "The downstairs *is* in pieces, but shower is still usable. Plus, I need to get some clothes anyway."

Before Luke could reply, Kada looked at Luke, "Hey, Dad, since you guys will be busy, can I go to Sarah's?"

Luke gave a half smile with a questioning look.

"Sure, but check in, in the morning, before school."

She smiled and nodded with enthusiasm and hopped off her seat to run back upstairs.

Now Luke turned back to Daphne, "You could shower here. You can get out of the shower without shoes." He chuckled.

She thought about it, but she still needed her clothes and at least some makeup before she saw his department again.

She smiled, "Okay, but can I borrow your boots to get home, to get clothes and my makeup?"

"Yeah, but Kada might be closer to your size." He went to the mud room and pulled a pair of white boots and handed them to her.

She slipped them on, and they were a little snug but fit.

"Thank you!"

When she tossed on her coat, she gave him a soft peck and ran out the door. He walked to the big living room window to watch her and pulled out his phone and pulled up her sister's contact and hit call.

When a high-pitched female voice answered on the other line. "Hello?"

He took a deep breath and spoke, "Is this Dani Morrison?"

"Yes, who's this?"

"This is Luke Richmond."

He heard a gasp on her end and pause. In a shaky voice, "Oh my god, is she okay?"

The question told him a lot more than what she was asking.

"She's safe. She told me to tell you she is peachy. The tree is still standing, and she'll see you on Valentine's Day."

"Oh my god, Daphne. She really found you."

He heard the tears and gentle shaky breaths as he watched out the window towards her house.

"Yes…. She did." His voice cracked as he rubbed his jaw. He had so many questions but didn't have much time.

"She told me to tell you she misses and loves you."

A silence on the other end made him look at his phone to make sure he didn't lose connection till he heard a kid laughing in the background then Dani spoke, "You love her." A statement not a question.

She continued when he didn't reply, "Does she know?"

He took a deep breath and replied before letting it out, "No."

"Tell her, before it's too late. If this really is *the* Richmond, then you of all people know how fast her life can change. Tell her I love and miss her so much. And glad she is safe."

He looked up at her house and saw her coming out the back and headed for him. "I'll give her the message. Thanks Dani. We'll talk again soon."

"No. Thank you for loving her. Goodbye Luke."

"Bye Dani."

The line went silent as Daphne walked through the back door.

CHAPTER EIGHT

With her makeup kit and set of clean clothes in hand, she stood in the center of a bathroom twice the size of hers. A separate tiled shower with black and gray tones with a porcelain, big white bathtub in the corner, under a frosted glass window, that could easily fit two full grown adults.

Though she had already been in his bathroom a few times, she had to take in the size almost every time before remembering what she came in for.

Luke stood behind her in the doorway.

"Clean towels are in the cabinet, next to the bathtub. Feel free to use anything, even the speakers."

Her eyes grew large, "There's speakers in here?"

He smiled and pointed to the sound system strategically placed around the bathroom.

"Bluetooth. It's labeled, 'Bathroom'."

"Ooo." She pulled out her cell phone with excitement and clicked on her music playlist before opening her Bluetooth and connecting it.

Within a minute, Savage Garden played through the speakers.

Luke smiled again. He never would have pegged her for a Savage Garden lover. He watched her put her make up case the size of a small carry on, on the counter and shower supplies in the shower.

The shower wasn't even on yet and heat was already rising. If He didn't leave now, he might not be able to.

Even in her world now, making herself comfortable in his bathroom, there was no way to not notice him standing in the doorway. His energy sparked like electricity. Swaying to the music and humming with the lyrics was the only thing holding her nerves back.

She placed a set of clothes on the counter and grabbed a towel from the cabinet next to it. Now she was just ignoring his presence as he stood there watching her comfortably move around his bathroom like she lived there.

She reached in the shower and turned on the water and adjusted it to the temperature she liked.

Back turned to Luke, she stripped off her black tank top and soft, purple pjs revealed cute little blue lace panties that also fell to the floor. Still ignoring him, she walked into the shower stall, and let the steaming water hit her face and run down her body.

She heard the bathroom door click shut and heard the lock click. Her heart stopped.

Rough hands touched her waist and slid down to her hips. She released her breath as electricity crawled through her veins. She turned to notice him still fully dressed, with bare feet as he got wetter by the minute. Her full body on display, a twitch of discomfort and humility stayed in her spine, so she crossed her arms over her stomach.

He immediately shook his head in disagreement, "Nah, ah. You are gorgeous. Don't hide from me."

He pulled her hands away and held her wrists as he bent to kiss her soft lips to her jawline, down her collarbone with soft pecks. He released her wrists to hold onto her waist as he worked his way down over her breasts to her ribs, kissing every beautiful scar down to the cesarean to linger there.

Her hands, still hanging in the air, drifted to the wet shoulders of his t-shirt as a soft moan escaped. He rose again taking a more forceful deep kiss that left both their hearts racing. She slid her hands up the bottom of his shirt and slid it off over his head to splat on the floor of the shower. He pushed his body weight against her until she was pinned against the tiled shower wall. Hungry for his lips, she deepened the kiss, tasting him, letting her tongue dip inside. Now he moaned, rubbing his hands down her sides and getting overflowing handfuls of her luscious cheeks.

With need, she slid her hands down to undo the button to his soaking, wet jeans and pulled the zipper down over his erection. She slid her thumbs into his waistband and tugged down his jeans and boxers just enough to release his erection. She palmed it and stroked it, which gave him a moan against her lips.

He grabbed her luscious ass and lifted her level with him. He moved his hands up her wet soft skin like feathers over velvet. Thumbs under her breasts, fingers around her ribs, he effortlessly pinned her shoulders to the wall as her knees locked around his hips. He released her mouth to watch her as he got closer forcing her legs wider with his hips. His tip teased her lips as he waited for any signs of fear until she took a deep breath as the water continued to rush over them. Her eyes got heavy with comfort as she watched him.

He took her mouth and slowly slid into her. She gasped at his size, that fit her perfectly, as he sank into her. She wrapped her legs around him fully in a need to steady herself. He continued to slowly slide as deep as he could, feeling her entire body for any sign of discomfort or fear. He moved his hands back to her cheeks and lifted her up to get a little deeper and get more leverage.

She felt so soft and silky warm. He wouldn't last much longer, especially how tight every part of her wrapped around him. He took her mouth again and worked down her jawline to her neck, biting as he slowly slid out and thrust back in.

He knew he left a few marks on her neck, but now it was a passion of possessiveness and anger. He wanted to protect her, wanted her to be his. He wanted to kill her ex-husband for her. Water ran over both of them giving off more steam.

Getting in a rhythm, heat poured off them. She breathed hard and let out a soft moan with almost every thrust in.

"Luke..." The whisper left her lips as her grip tightened to climax.

He watched her face and gave one more thrust in and felt her whole body tighten and pulse. Silk poured over him as she finally gave one last soft scream on a deep breath in. The warmth of the silk finally broke him. He dove deeper and gave into his own release. His head came down to her shoulder and he growled out, "Daph..."

She felt every pulse and drop he gave as it consumed her with warmth from the inside. She wrapped her arms around his shoulders and neck, feeling as much relief as he did.

After they both relaxed, he dropped to sit on the shower floor with her legs still wrapped around him, as the shower still poured hot, steamy water over them. She spoke first as he tried to gather his thoughts and breath.

"So, it is true, firemen do get you wet." They both chuckled.

He watched her with his arms relaxed around her waist, as she sat between his legs and bent knees, as her legs laid over his hips. He pulled her hips and torso closer to him.

"Don't let anyone tell you, you aren't beautiful." His smile widened and she gave him a soft peck on the lips.

"Thank you, Luke"

"I guess I should let you actually take a shower now."

"No, stay with me, please."

She ran her fingers over his bare chest and then snuggled in close as he wrapped his arms around her in a comforting hug, and just held her.

He just watched as she washed her hair while he tried to hold back his need to care for her. His resistance shattered when she got her body wash and applied it to her purple loofah. Taking it from her and he gently scrubbed her from the shoulders down over the scars and ran his hands over her breast and a thumb over each scar then down over her cheeks until it was soapy. He gently scrubbed every inch of her body from her chin to her toes as they watched each other with keen observance never saying a word. His thoughts raced.

When he was done, he held a hand around her waist pressing her hips into his. With only his pants on but left unbuttoned, the barrier was needed when he took her mouth, dipping his tongue in and dropping the loofah. He wrapped both his arms around her and pulled her under the shower streams with him. He gave her one last long deep kiss and released his hands and grip, before his mouth then backed up to let her finish rinsing off.

He didn't want to let her go and his hands burned. He wanted to move her into his house, keep her close. He wanted to protect her and show her that life could be amazing with him and Kada. She wouldn't have to be afraid ever again. But would she go for it? Would Kada? The uncertainty left him chomping at the bit. He flexed his jaw as she rinsed her hair and body.

He got lost in the sight of soapy water running down her body and the thoughts that made him the best man to protect her, without coming to terms of why.

When the shower turned off, reality snapped back, and he smiled at the soaking wet petite Daphne standing in front of him. He reached out and grabbed her towel and wrapped her in it, before he could get another erection again. Afraid he would never get his fill of her, ever.

He kissed her forehead and stepped out of the shower as music still played through the speakers. She grabbed for her cell phone and turned off the music as he stripped off his soaking wet jeans and boxers. She inhaled a breath sharply. Her hands tingled with the need to touch him. Both stared at each other for a second. He watched the bruises on her neck darken. He stepped forward, ran a thumb over his marks, and gave her a slow kiss.

She didn't even realize he had backed her up to the cabinets until her cheeks pressed against it. When he released her mouth, he opened the cabinet and pulled out another towel and wrapped it around his waist. She let out a soft breath.

"We could spend all day here and I wouldn't give it a second thought, but we have a bathroom to fix."

She smiled softly.

"I'll let you dry off and get dressed, and I'll change in the bedroom."

He gave her one last kiss before leaving and shutting the bathroom door behind him. For a second, she stood there naked, holding her towel like a lifeline. Now she was falling in love.

Of course, she would be banging the neighbor. That bitch. He couldn't protect her like he could. Well, he would just have to figure out a way around him then continue his plans. He took another sip of his flask and felt the warmth of the liquor hit his toes, then vanish, leaving him colder. Time to go. But he'd be back, he told himself, as he watched the lights turn off in her house, then headed for his car a few blocks up.

When she appeared out of the bathroom looking like a dream in a peachy-tan colored dressy tank top and tight jeans that showed off every curve, hair curled so they bounced when she walked, and makeup done with a professional touch, Luke almost forgot how to breathe.

Since she moved to Birch Valley, everyone noticed her when she walked into a room. Even without makeup or when she kept it simple for work, but now with black, thick, full lashes, and darker tan lips than her skin color, with sparkles, she wouldn't be missed. Even old Ms. Bellwood wouldn't miss her in the car from fifty yards away. His twinge of possessiveness came back with force, especially since now his marks on her neck and shoulders were covered back to her natural skin color.

Damn! His stomach knotted up and he went speechless. Her blue eyes reached his soul and he felt it. She walked to the kitchen counter where he sat and he got a whiff of her soft, fresh perfume that smelt like a soft, ocean breeze. Trying to keep it soft and friendly, he spoke.

"You look good."

She tried to smile, but it fell flat. Watching him keep his distance was disappointing even if she didn't expect to get ravished again.

"Thanks." She replied, then continued. "Hey Luke, thanks for doing this and helping me."

"Of course. You ready to go?"

"Sure, I just need to get my coat and wallet."

Most of the ride was silent and she didn't know why. She felt guilty, like it was her fault that he was now icy.

When he pulled into the station on the bright sunny day, some of the crews were outside talking and they turned to look at him and Daphne in the truck. Luke gave Daphne a smile.

"Ignore anything they say. None of them know anything besides rumors."

She tried for a smile, but it disappeared when she nodded.

"Hey, I'm right here. I just have to file a report quickly and we'll head to the diner to meet up with Mike."

Now she smiled. "Okay."

They got out of the truck and Daphne followed him down the sidewalk to the man door. Luke watched the few crew members outside with keen attention. When firefighter Magar opened his mouth Luke cut him off,

"How many times you wash the Engine today?"

Magar's eyes got big, "Twice."

As Luke reached the man door and opened it for Daphne to walk in, he replied, "Wanna wash it a few more times?"

"No, Lieutenant."

Luke gave him a nod and a stiff smile then followed Daphne inside. Inside the station, Luke put a hand on Daphne's back and led her through the truck bays and down the hall towards his office. He took out his keys and unlocked his office door then opened it for Daphne.

Walking in she remembered the previous time she was in his office.

He flipped on the light and saw her face.

"Don't worry. I got enough to keep the jeans a little looser for a minute."

She grinned like she was just caught till he smiled at her. He leaned down and gave her a soft kiss as he propped the door open and walked to his big office chair and took a seat to turn on his desktop computer.

She sat curled up on his couch and watched him flip from her smiling sexy neighbor to the hot fire dept Lieutenant with a straight face. He worked fast at the computer and pulled a file to read it as he imputed it into the computer and clicked save then send. He flipped through a few more files to sign and double checked them before filing them in the stack of bins on the corner of his desk.

Thirty minutes later, his phone chimed, he checked it, smiled and texted back. He spoke to Daphne without looking at her.

"Mike is at the diner with most of the materials."

He leaned back in the chair before he turned to the side of his desk to face her on the couch in the corner of the office. She had pulled down his thick plush blanket that was on the back of the couch and curled into it as she watched him. He smiled from ear to ear, watching her eyes over the top of the blanket that was pulled up to her nose.

"That blanket stays here."

She gave a small laugh. He couldn't stop smiling as he watched her. Without taking his eyes off Daphne he braced his hands on top of his head and leaned further back in the office chair to speak in a stern tone.

"What do you need, Hastings?"

Daphne's eyes went big as she looked at his office door to see one of the crew members standing in the doorway. When Daphne broke eye contact, Luke turned in his chair to face Hastings over his desk.

"Sorry Lieutenant. Umm, what do you want us to do with the extra winter gear we took off rescue the other day?"

"Put it in the gear room and I'll let Captain Davis know. Thanks."

Hastings looked at Daphne wrapped in Luke's blanket, then back to a stiffer Lieutenant with raised eyebrows.

"She won't give you orders, but I can start printing a list for you."

Hastings lowered his head as Daphne folded in her lips and tried to lose her smile.

"Sorry, Lieutenant," he spoke softly.

When Magar came jogging up to the office door behind Hastings, he poked his head in, "Hey Lieutenant! The valve broke on the Tender. We need you quick."

Luke was already up and moving. "I'll be right back." He said to Daphne as he jogged out of the office and back towards the bays.

She was nearly asleep in his blanket when Luke returned a few moments later. She smiled at him when he walked back in and smiled at her.

"Let me shut down the computer and we can head out before anything else happens."

She took the blanket off and stood up to fold it, when he came over, grabbed her waist, and gave her a forceful kiss. He let go and went to his desk to shut down the computer and clean up any files left. Walking out, she led the way back to the bays after he locked up his office. The bay doors were open now as the crew pushed water outside from the bays. She froze at the water's edge up to the hallway.

Luke continued walking as he picked her up and threw her, stomach first, over his shoulder and held her legs down with his right arm as he walked through the water to his gear rack by the first bay door.

"Oh my God! Luke!" She shouted out of shock.

The crew laughed and watched her brace herself against Luke's back, while holding a hand over the top edge of her shirt to keep it closed. He grabbed a coat off his gear rack and walked out through the bay door and over to the dry sidewalk before he put her down. The crews now watched from the bay doors as she slugged him in the arm and fixed herself as she walked to the truck and climbed in the passenger seat. He smiled and laughed as he jumped in the driver seat.

When they pulled into the diner's back parking lot, she smiled. Giving her half a smile, Luke said, "He had to come in and handle a quick problem, it should only take a minute."

He gave her leg across the center console, a pat and a slight squeeze. She leaned over the console and gave him a kiss. She kept it light. He gave in and deepened it, placing a hand on her jaw and pulling her closer. She released and leaned back to see him. His eyes glowed in the sunlight. He still had a hand under her chin, not letting her wander too far.

"Ready?" He spoke in a soft, deep tone. She smiled and gave a simple nod. Both got out of the truck and headed for the back door. He opened it for her as she strolled in and waited for him.

When he reached for her hand, she didn't hesitate to grab it. Both smiled and held hands as they walked into Mike's office who was on the phone. Mike didn't miss the hand holding and smiles as he watched Luke take a seat in front of the big, dark wood desk with Daphne.

Finishing the phone conversation quickly and hanging up the phone, he gave Luke a glance and smile before greetings from behind his desk.

"Hey Luke, Daphne! So, Luke says you're renovating your bathroom?" He looked at Daphne who was now glowing with her smile.

"Yeah. I hope so. It was outdated anyway, and I think Kada, Luke, and I like the idea of a nautical theme with blues, whites, and tan colors. Luke said you might have some leftovers I could use."

Mike sat up to engage in the conversation fully.

"Yeah, I have a bunch of tiles and trim in the truck. The tub and shower parts I left at home but took pictures for you to see if you're even interested in them."

He pulled out his cell phone from his jacket pocket and opened his gallery, clicked on the pictures, and showed them to her. Her eyes lit up at the sight of the big soaking tub in plaster white.

"Oh my gosh! That thing is huge! You could fit an entire family in that thing!"

Her excitement made both Luke and Mike giggle.

"It is definitely bigger than your upstairs, that's for sure." Luke laughed out loud.

She gave a smirk, unenthused. Mike raised an eyebrow at both of them but kept his questions to himself.

"Can that even fit in my house?"

Luke shrugged.

"We might have to move a couple cabinets and rearrange a few things, but we could make it work."

Daphne's eyes lit up and she did a little happy dance in her seat. She flipped through a couple more photos and nodded her head but kept looking. As she went through the pictures, Mike looked at Luke with curiosity until Luke made eye contact with him. Luke's eyes widened as did his blushing smile when he rubbed his jaw. Mike nodded at him with approval. When Daphne reached the end, she nodded again, and handed his phone back.

Mike took it, stood up from his seat, and said, "I have tiles in the truck if you want to look at those too?"

"Sure. Thank you."

She and Luke both stood, and Luke placed an arm around her back. Mike again gave a glance at Luke. All three walked out of the office, turned down the hall towards the back door, and outside. They then walked over to the big lifted gray Dodge truck with a winch mount on the front and hideaway lights, similar to Luke's. Mike walked around the back, dropped the tailgate, popped the camper shell hatch, and pulled forward two big cardboard boxes and a few long trim pieces. The different shades of blue tiles immediately caught her eye, as she reached in the box and felt the front and back of the light blue tile.

"Oh wow, Mike. I love these."

Giving a small grin, he replied, "Luke thought you might."

She turned to look at Luke standing behind her, gave him a smile, then turned back.

Mike spoke, "Jen had....and loved her beach theme for many years, but she gets bored and does a lot of renovations throughout the house. I've learned to keep and reuse what I can and give the rest away."

She couldn't resist, but merely jumped into his arms for a tight hug. As she let him go, she turned back to Luke and gave him a hug and light kiss on the lips. He ran a hand down her back as Mike watched and smiled again.

"This is amazing. Thank you, guys."

"I don't slack as much as Luke, but I can lend an extra hand on weekends, if you need."

"That would be awesome. Maybe we can have a barbeque with you and Jen when it warms up."

Mike nodded his head.

"Sure thing. We could set up a date night soon, if you two are good with that. There isn't much to do in this town, but Jen and I like the occasional picnic up on the bluff."

She looked confused as Mike looked at Luke.

"You haven't shown her the bluff yet?"

Luke frowned, "No. Haven't had the chance yet."

Mike turned back to Daphne.

"It's gorgeous up there, especially when the sun sets."

"Okay, well, we might just have to go take a look!" She tilted her head and gave a nod and gave Luke a quick swat on the arm.

"Yeah, sounds good." Luke added.

"So, you want to load these into your truck?" Mike asked Luke.

"Sure."

Both the men loaded the boxes of tiles into the back of Luke's truck and secured them, as Daphne looked at the trim and decided against it. She got a new tub and tiles; it was a good start. They talked for a bit about the station updates and their lives at home then about a barbeque and possible dates before they said their goodbyes and headed out after a meal order to-go.

The smell of hot burgers and French fries wafted through the brown paper bags on Daphne's lap and her stomach rumbled. Luke pulled out of the parking lot and looked at her. She was silent, but with a soulful smile as she watched out the window. She did things to him he couldn't explain. Something that made him question his life and the future.

He drove across town, then up an uphill street as it ran out of road. He took a left and stopped.

"The trail gets pretty bumpy from here. Just don't drop our food."

She looked at him, then at the small dirt trail that looked more like an ATV trail as she put an arm around the food bags and gripped the door handle. Luke switched the truck into four-wheel drive and left the road. He was careful, she noticed and probably drove it harder and faster than he did with her. The bumps and rocks had the truck moving side to side and potholes where others had gotten stuck had her lifting off the seat, even with her seatbelt on.

Luke focused on the trail as he turned left and then right. He drove around large trees, and slowly climbed small steep hills until they finally reached a dirt lot. The lot was big enough to fit six trucks and it overlooked the town and Birch Creek in the distance, as the sun was setting behind the mountains that surrounded their valley.

Her eyes widened and her mouth was open as she set the food bag on the console and unclipped her seatbelt to look out the windshield and take it all in. It was their small town of Birch valley, but she'd never seen it from this view, and it was absolutely gorgeous.

He parked close to a small section of trees and nose to the big boulders that lined the bluffs edge. She opened her door and got out to walk to a boulder and take a seat, never letting her eyes move from the scene that laid out in front of her.

When she heard Luke's door open and close, she spoke up.

"This is beautiful, Luke."

When she didn't get a response, she turned to look at him holding the to-go bag and two cans of soda, leaning against the truck, just smiling at her.

He nodded. "I've seen it before, but what I haven't seen is a woman eating one of Mike's big ass chili burgers.... most girls here, go for salads." He smirked.

She watched him and her smile grew. "Well, I'm not the typical woman you probably date."

For a second his heart stopped, hearing the word, 'Date.' Did that mean they were dating? He was kissing her and now, as of this morning, sleeping with her. So, he guessed dating Daphne wasn't that big of a stretch. He just never put a label on anything they had together. It was a small town with not much to do, so people talked. Rumors spread, even the absurd rumor that they were already secretly married. He was used to the rumors, and it didn't bother him...much.

He held up the bag. "There is a picnic table over here." He nodded toward the other side of his truck.

Though snow still covered the ground, it had been a pretty warm day and the last bit was still warm enough to keep her warm and glowing with her smile.

She got up, walked over to the table to brush off the last bit of snow, and take a seat. Still bundled in her nice gray dress coat, she shed it, and laid it next to her on the bench. Her tan, peach colored tank top sparkled in the sunlight as she dug in the bag Luke had placed on the table. He still watched her as he took a seat across from her. She opened the Styrofoam container and smelled the steam that escaped out into the chilly air.

"Mmm. It smells so good."

"Just wait until you taste it. Mike is one of the best firefighters I know, but he is the best cook I know."

"But he's your best friend, you have to brag about him." She laughed.

He watched her take a fork full of the chili and take a bite. Her eyes sank as she stared at him.

"Am I bragging now?"

With a mouth full of food, she shook her head, then swallowed it.

"No! You weren't kidding. This is really good." She took another bite and washed it down with her soda.

"It's a good thing he is married, he'd have every woman chasing him."

Luke chuckled at that statement around his own mouthful of food.

They ate and watched the sun set getting lower. After her burger and most of the fries were gone, he saw her start to shiver. He took off his black hoodie and stretched it across the table to her. She looked at him from across the table and shook her head.

"I have my coat but thank you."

"Put it on till you're done eating at least, so you don't have to chance staining your nicer coat."

She smiled and took it from him. She slid it on, and the combination of a warm, soft hoodie and his scent was intoxicating as it gave her a sense of pure happiness in that single moment. She stopped it just below her eyes, keeping her big grin hidden. She watched him watching her take a deep breath in and sink into the hoodie that was four sizes too big on her. He didn't even hide his grin and small laugh as he took another bite of a French fry.

"Sorry. Old habit. It's a comfort thing."

"Well steal my entire closet if you want to just don't steal anyone else's."

"Deal."

The sun started to touch the top of the nearby mountain. So, they began wrapping up the empty to-go boxes and he placed the empty bag and her coat in the truck and closed the door. She stood there in his big hoodie, now looking confused.

"I wanna show you something quick."

He grabbed her hand and heard the truck lock and beep as they walked towards the woods beyond the picnic table. He only wore a dark gray T-shirt and jeans and still the heat poured off of him in the cooler weather.

He led her down a narrow snow packed footpath that led into the darkening woods. In her boots, she had to take more steps to keep up with his longer, faster paced strides.

They walked through the woods, up another small hill, and helped her cross a little stream that trickled down the side of the hill. Soon, they came to another small opening similar to where they had parked, but this one had a wider view and sat up higher. High enough to see his truck and the rooftops of their houses across the small town in the distance.

Still holding his hand, she walked forward and sucked in a breath just as the last light hit the valley and sent rays of red and orange sunlight up and over the backside of the peaks.

His free hand curved around her back to her waist, then around her stomach from behind, as she felt his chilly nose nuzzle and peck her neck softly. Her hand tightened on his, as she tilted her head to the side so he could reach it better around the collar of his own hoodie. After a few more soft kisses, she turned in his arms to face him. She had to look up at him, but his eyes told her everything. He was falling for her just as much as she had fallen for him.

She wrapped her arms around his neck and stood on tiptoe to reach his lips. Just before they connected, he tightened his hold around her waist and lifted her off the ground in one swoop.

Her feet curled up to her butt and for a moment the world and time itself stopped. She couldn't remember ever being this happy and secure. Nothing could ruin this for her.

When he pulled away, she saw the questions in his eyes, but he said nothing. She took a much-needed deep breath and searched his eyes. Even in the dusky light, she saw his thoughts. They wandered from happiness to curiosity to the disappointment that darkened his golden eyes as he set her back on the ground, but still, he didn't loosen his grip. His lips connected one last time in a deep but shorter kiss that had her tilting her head to give into his need.

When he released, he spoke up.

"Ready to go? It's gonna get dark soon."

She gave a small smile and replied, "Sure."

By the time they reached the truck, only the little light from the town gave them enough to see their hands. When they opened the doors of the truck, the cab light came on for a couple seconds as they got in and shut the doors. He dug his keys out of his pocket and started the truck. The engine came to life with a low rumble and the dashboard lit up as he clicked on the heater vents. She briskly rubbed her hands together before placing them on the vents that blew the semi warm air out.

His arm draped over the console as he carefully backed the truck up and turned it around in the small dirt lot. She watched his hand before he shifted the truck into drive and put it back on the console. She reached for it and laced her fingers through his. He tightened his grip with her hand, without looking at her as he watched the trail and mirrors, working his way back down the hill until they hit the dirt road again.

He took it out of four-wheel drive before starting back towards town, headed for home. Her body relaxed as the truck warmed up and she grew tired. His truck smelled like him with hints of bergamot, cedarwood and smoke, and leather. It was uniquely him. He definitely wasn't anything like the big city guys she was used to, in every way possible.

"Daph. Daphne." She woke to her hair being pushed out of her face that was now on the center console as she curled up in a tight ball in his front seat. The cold sank in as she sat up to see Luke leaning over with her door open. A quick glance around her told her they were in her driveway.

"I was going to carry you to bed, but with your head over there, I imagine my hold would be more like an unconscious victim being carried out of a burning building, either by the feet or over my shoulder." He chuckled softly.

That made her smile, then sit up and give him a soft kiss. She grabbed her small purse from the floorboard and got out of the truck with a hand from him. They walked to her front door, unlocked it, and stepped inside. She slipped out of her boots and set her purse and keys on the chair next to the door, but he just stood there in her entryway.

When she finally turned and looked at him, he just watched her.

"I should probably be getting home. Kada comes home in the morning and we both have work in the morning."

Her head spun trying to think what day it was. *Today was Sunday.* That's right. Good thing he knew. They would have stayed up all night and missed work the next day. Sensible, smart and good looking. One of a kind.

She walked over and stood on her tiptoes to give him another soft kiss until he deepened it, wrapping his arms around her waist and pulling her in closer. When he released her mouth and waist, she felt a twinge of disappointment.

"I'll keep the tiles and stuff in the truck and bring them by tomorrow after work, maybe start on it after dinner, if you are up to it."

Around a sluggish brain, she nodded in agreement with a smile.

"You are tired. Go get some sleep and I'll see you tomorrow." He gave her a quick soft peck and turned around to open the door.

"Thanks for today, Luke. It was nice."

With the door opened, he turned his head to smile at her.

"You're welcome. Sweet dreams."

"Night." She replied, then shut the door behind him.

On either side of the door, both of them took a deep breath with disappointment.

In a black wool dress coat and shiny black shoes, Darryl stood in the snow next to a large spruce tree, across the street. The snow was now packed down from standing there a while and watching this guy leave her house. His temper stirred as he took a sip from a small leather covered flask. His thoughts raced. He found her. Now to make her come home with him. He'd have to find a way soon. This guy, whoever he was, won't mean anything to her.

He watched, hidden by the darkness, as the guy got into his truck and his reverse lights came on. After he leaves, he could try and pick the front door lock, or just knock and get her to open the door. He would get her to listen and come home with him, somehow. But when this guy backed up and instead of heading back into town, turned to go further down the road and pulled into the next house, his temper spiked.

Of course, she would be banging the neighbor. That bitch. He couldn't protect her like he could. Well, he would just have to figure out a way around him then continue his plans. He took another sip of his flask and felt the warmth of the liquor hit his toes, then vanish, leaving him colder. Time to go. But he'd be back, he told himself, as he watched the lights turn off in her house, then headed for his car a few blocks up.

CHAPTER NINE

W hen Daphne walked into the school the next morning the secretary, Miss Jeannie, gave her a big smile and bright eyes while on the phone with a parent. Then pursed her lips and batted eyebrows and fanned herself with her hand.

She gave a silent laugh, and a big smile then blew her friend a kiss while stepping around kids almost her own height. When she reached her office, she had three kids already lined up at the door. Instead of her usual sigh, she gave them a smile. Ready for the day, she unlocked her door to let them in.

"Bye, Sweetheart." Luke said to Kada, as she got out of the truck in front of the school with her duffle bag over her shoulder.

"Bye, Dad. Love you." She smiled at him before closing the door quickly and jogged up to the front to meet Sarah, who was sitting on a bench in the sunlight.

"Love you too." He spoke softly to himself and sighed. Now to the station to face the crew that had been recently updated about his current relationship status by their Captain. Luckily his crew knew better than to blow up his phone, otherwise he probably would have decided on grunt work at home. But at least at the station, he had his own lockable office to hide in.

When he pulled into the station, Mike and a few others had the trucks pulled outside the bays and were washing them on the sunny blue-sky day. After pulling into the parking spot labeled, "Lieutenant Parking Only" next to the captain's and handicapped public spots, he put it in park and shut off the truck. He grabbed his radio and pager off the center console and got out of the truck.

Walking to the door, the crew with both women and men, all dressed in station sweaters and tactical pants, gave him catcalls and whistles with shouts of "Congrats!", "Finally!"

and "Way to go, Lieutenant!". Luke just gave them a wave and shook his head, unwilling to explain, as he opened the station door. Fumbling the keys, as he walked through the hallway, he passed several open doors to various offices. Near the end of the hall, he reached the last door on the left that read, "Lieutenant's Office". He unlocked it, went in, and propped it open after turning on the lights.

When Luke sat in the big chair behind the desk and opened a file, a knock rapped on his doorway. He looked up to see Mike standing in the doorway.

"Come in. I was just gonna get some reports done."

"Is the Henderson report ready for me yet?" He asked as he came in and took a seat in one of the chairs.

In a sigh of relief, he wasn't asking about Daphne, he smiled to answer, "Yeah, I got it right here." He paused to flip through the finished reports section in his stacked paper trays and pulled out a report and handed it to Mike.

"Thank you." Mike took it, flipped through a couple pages, and then closed it.

Luke answered, "Yup, no problem." Then went back to the file in front of him, and only looked up when Mike didn't move.

"What's up, Cap?"

Mike shrugged, "You good?"

"My house is still standing. Kada is at school. Oh, I had this amazing breakfast Kada made this morning with hashbrowns, bacon, and cheese. Oh, you should try it. I do feel like I'm about to have a headache because I don't know who really came to see me, my Captain, my brother or my friend."

Luke stared at Mike with a smile. Mike reached for a sheet of paper in the back of Luke's printer sitting next to him and crumpled it into a ball and threw it at Luke. Both laughed as Luke caught the paper ball before it hit him.

Another rap on the doorframe had both of them turning their attention to the man in an official uniform. Mike immediately sat up straight. "Director, what brings you down here to our neck of the woods?"

He walked over and took the seat next to Mike.

"Well, I see I need to put another request in for paper funding." He chuckled, while Mike and Luke looked at each other before laughing.

After an hour passed talking with the director, he left and there was another rap on the doorframe.

Magar called out.

"Ah. Captain. All the trucks are washed, and truck checks are done."

Mike looked at Luke and said, "Well talk later. Jen wants dinner soon anyway."

Luke rolled his eyes and nodded, before Mike and Magar walked out.

"Finally, I can get some work done." He whispered to himself as he returned to his file and flipped it open before alarms went off echoing through the station making him grumble and get up to jog out of the office. It was going to be a long day.

On his way home, he stopped at the store and picked up a big bouquet of red roses and purple irises, as he remembered her small porcelain plaque with a quote. It also had purple irises around the edge. He knew better than anyone how short life could be and how fast anyone's life could change. He was in a rut after his wife died. It's been eight years and it was Daphne that had snapped him out of it. He was lucky enough to have Mike, his family, and the department and without them all these years, he surely would have fallen in the deep end. He knew what he had.

After he made the purchase, he headed for his truck with a wide smile until he noticed a car parked in the far corner right away. Amongst the beat-up trucks and four-wheel drive SUVs that ran around this old town, was this new shiny silver Mazda nickel. Fancy clean sedan cars didn't have much of a place here where the only pavement was the main street into town and the occasional parking lot.

He walked to his truck and typed the license plate number into his phone for future reference, but with dark tinted windows, it was impossible to see if anyone was inside. Hell, it might be Mrs. Adam's grandchildren who lived out of state now. He wouldn't let it ruin his day, even though his instincts told him it would soon.

He put the flowers on the center console and drove to Daphne's. While turning the corner, he didn't see her car yet and it stopped his heart before it started again when he realized he had a key to her house.

He pulled into her driveway and parked. He jogged to the house and up the few stairs to the front door. He pulled out his pocketed keys and slid hers into the doorknob and unlocked it. The scent of lilies was like a slap to the face. It was so amazingly her, but at the same time it stirred something sinister within him.

He walked to the kitchen island and touched a leaf of one of the six lilies with tulips and a big Hydrangea. He set his bouquet on the counter, then through the window, saw his kitchen light come on. Kada was home. He took one last look at the bouquet of flowers in a pretty new vase and frowned, then walked out and headed home.

Kada was already working on dinner when he walked in the door. Spaghetti again. He didn't complain. He knew she was learning, and Daphne did teach her a few tricks that made a world of difference in her spaghetti, that usually was blander than a saltine cracker. The improvement was enjoyed with his whole heart and stomach.

She stood over the pot of sauce stirring it as he set his radios on the entryway table, walked over to her to give her a hug, and a kiss on the head.

"Hey, Sweetheart. Smells good."

"Thanks, Dad. How's the crew?"

"Good. They say Hi and they miss you." He walked over and sat on the other side of the counter.

"Want to watch a movie tonight?" He asked before she stopped stirring the sauce and turned to face him.

"Actually, Sarah is in my room. We are working on a book report but maybe after we are done."

He smiled, not because she agreed to it later, but because his daughter was sensible enough to be willing to finish her homework first. He was raising a good girl...woman. She wasn't little anymore, and he had to remember that. At least Kada wasn't bringing home flowers from other men. The jealousy stirred again thinking about Daphne's bouquet.

"Dad!" The shout rang out that made him look at her.

"What?"

He was now hunched over the counter propping his head up with a hand.

"You look tired. Go take a shower, eat some dinner, then go to bed."

Now it all sank in, the tiredness and exhaustion.

"Yeah, sounds like a good plan."

She smiled at him as she grabbed for the noodles.

He sluggishly got up and walked to his bedroom for clean clothes, then headed for the bathroom.

After he returned from the bathroom, clean, and in soft, blue snowflake pajama pants and tank top, as he walked straight to the living room window.

The sun was just starting to set, but he could still see clearly to Daphne's empty driveway. He swallowed then turned around to a plate of spaghetti on the counter and the kitchen cleaned up.

He could hear the girls laughing upstairs with music blaring behind it. He sat and started eating. The food only made him more tired.

The shine of headlights made him snap around to see Daphne pulling in her driveway. By the time she opened her car door, he had his untied boots on and a light coat. He walked fast down the street and into her driveway before she even got to the front door.

"Daphne! Where have you been? I thought we were gonna start on your bathroom tonight." His huffing and puffing didn't seem to affect her like it did him.

She slowly turned around to look at him. "Oh Shit. Sorry, Luke. I went out with some of my coworkers and completely forgot. Can we do it tomorrow? I'm really tired tonight."

He jumped two steps at a time up to the porch, grabbed her and planted a hot kiss on her lips. He didn't even know why he did it, but he did, and when he connected, he could taste the fruity tart wine with a wintergreen mint. He held her face, but she only put a hand on his side. When he released her lips, his hands still held her.

"How much have you had to drink?"

Her eyes dropped to a scowl as her spine stiffened and she jerked away.

"Oh, fuck you, Luke! I had two glasses of wine with some coworkers over dinner. Besides, what am I gonna hit? A tree doing five miles per hour, that you can do in this rink-a-dink town. I'm not a damsel in distress and I'm not a princess in a tower, you can't save me!" She shouted with anger.

That fired his blood.

"Daphne, That's not fair. You don't see what I see."

She cut him off to continue as she unlocked her house then paused with the door open.

"And I'm glad for that because I would hate to feel like I have to save the whole world. Goodnight, Luke."

She stepped inside her house and closed the door on him before he could say anything else.

He stood at her door and put his hands in his pockets, feeling defeated and angry.

He whispered to himself. "Not the whole world, just mine."

Then he turned to walk home and stewed the rest of the night.

In the morning, heading to work he passed her house and still saw her car there.

"That's odd." He spoke softly.

"Maybe she slept in." Kada replied.

Nearly forgetting she was with him, he replied, "Yeah. Maybe."

For a minute he wondered if he should go back and apologize but he didn't think she would want to see him.

He dropped Kada off at school and pulled up Daphne's text conversation. He typed out, "I'm sorry. Dinner tonight?"

He pulled into the station and ignored anyone that tried to shout at him. When he got to his office, he let out a breath. He got in a couple phone calls and some paperwork before Mike came knocking.

"Must be PMS week. Jen is too, that's why I'm down here." He chuckled at Luke looking up from his paperwork, then got blasted.

"She drove home on God knows how many glasses of wine last night, then spit fire at me for saving the world!" He paused, took a breath, then continued. "Now she won't answer my texts or calls and slept in past work this morning!"

Mike now shut the door and took a seat. Stuffed his hands in his pockets and leaned back.

"Is that all?" He spoke with a less than enthused tone.

Luke gave a soft thump on his desk with a fist and leaned back in his chair. "I don't know anymore."

Mike took a deep breath in and let it out folding his hands then leaned forward to brace them on the desk across from Luke. "Luke, I've known you a long time. We grew up together. I saw you and Jasmine together, you had Kada, got married, then you left here, and became a big shot city firefighter. And when Jasmine died, it hit us all. Kada was all that held your shell together and like a bad call, you've never been the same, until you and Daphne walked into my office holding hands."

Luke frowned at his friend's words but nodded in acknowledgement. Luke knew how much he cared for Daphne but hadn't realized how empty he was without her.

Mike continued, "My advice. Hang onto her. I don't know why she came here or how, but she chose you for some reason, other than your looks, and I'm happy for you."

They gave each other a look of understanding.

Luke checked his messages again. Still no reply. He stood up quickly and so did Mike. Luke walked to his door and got his coat, opened his door, and turned back to Mike.

"Thanks." He said, then walked out again, ignoring the Lieutenant's questions and shouts from the crew. When he reached his truck, the pager on his side sounded, "Birch Valley Fire. Standby for page." and tones echoed.

He froze in place and so did Mike, who was now by the open bay door that held his command vehicle. Pager tones echoed through the station and outside, as the crew raced to get into their gear.

Dispatch came over again. "Birch Valley Fire, Motor vehicle accident. Mile 11 of Birch Way. Single occupant of a silver Mazda. Unknown condition."

Luke sighed. Guess he'd have to tell Daphne he loved her after he saved the world. He raced to the command truck, grabbed his gear off the rack beside it, and tossed it in the back of the truck cab. Then they rhythmically jumped in the truck. Luke in the passenger seat and Mike in the driver seat. Like a well-oiled machine, each crew member knew what to do and what emergency vehicle to take. Lights and sirens on, they raced out of the station and onto the main road, heading for the edge of town.

After reporting to dispatch, Luke turned to Mike, who was fully focused on the road and radios, but said nothing about his prior sighting of the Mazda.

Nearly Eleven miles outside of town was the long-paved road that weaved around mountains and cliffs. They turned a corner as they saw the overturned, crushed Mazda and the debris of glass, fiberglass, and plastic that scattered the road. Mike pulled up close, careful not to run over the debris, then put it into park, and gave Luke a nod. Luke jumped out and radioed dispatch to size up the scene as the rest of the trucks arrived. Mike checked the driver out and radioed in his condition to dispatch as well.

"Dispatch, one victim trapped, conscious, but not alert with a head wound. BV 5-1, taking command of the scene."

As dispatch replied, Luke put the crews to work. Mike also directed the crews and ran the scene just as easily as he ran the crew at his restaurant. After getting the doors off, Luke and Hastings got the battered man out, who looked like a CEO in his now shredded and blood covered designer suit. As they watched the medics haul him off to the ambulance, Hastings only said what the entire crew thought, "Alaska claims another tourist." Luke gave a soft huff but gave Hastings a warning glare and smirk.

While helping the crew start to clean up, something purple in the overturned car caught his eye. Luke got closer to the wreck and peered inside to see a shattered purple cell phone. He reached for it and as he tapped the screen the picture of him and Daphne came up with "1 missed call" and text from "Richmond". His heart tripped. Moving around some debris in the car, Daphne's purse and its scattered contents came into view. His heart stopped as he immediately took a deep breath and stepped back shouting for Mike.

"Captain!"

Mike jogged over to him and looked over the wide-eyed, shocked Luke.

"What's up?"

Luke leaned over to Mike to talk over the radio chatter and truck engines. "I found this in the car."

He handed him the broken purple phone with him and Daphne on the shattered screen. With cracks and random black spots over their photo it was hard to see but Luke's smiling face was visible along with Daphne's hair and their clasped hands.

"What?" He replied, looked at the cell phone, then crouched down himself to peek inside the mangled overturned car and saw the female purse and its contents strewn about mixed in with the debris.

He looked up at Luke now rubbing his face.

Mike reached for his handset to his radio, "Dispatch, Birch Way command. Vehicle contents show a possible second victim. We are gonna search the area."

The crew immediately stopped and looked to Mike for directions. Mike gave them directions to spread out and search for the possible victim. He looked for Luke who now took off on foot in fear for Daphne. He now was rounding the corner they came from, searching the ditches ahead of the crew before Mike caught up to him.

"Luke, stop! We will find her; you need to go sit and get off my scene. The crews are looking." Even as Mike spoke, he knew Luke wouldn't listen.

Luke walked over to the ambulance just as they shut the doors and took off with sirens and lights. His heart raced. The sounds went muffled. He closed his eyes and took a deep breath to slow his heartbeat.

A flash of the same victim, but in a white Jeep Cherokee brought back memories he had long forgotten. His eyes went wide with fear as he looked at Mike.

The Jeep was down an embankment, Daphne and her husband were pretty banged up. The car was caught on a tree 150 feet from the bottom of a cliff. Darryl was unconscious, but in better condition than Daphne who had shorter brunette hair and with light blonde streaks at the time.

Luke was one of the first to rope up and repel down to extricate them after the crew secured the car. He helped get Daphne out of the mangled car and onto a backboard. Then walked back up the hill with her, and into the ambulance. The terror in her eyes he saw that day, it did affect him as she held onto him up the hill. He knew something was off about the accident but had no proof. When he helped load her into the ambulance, her fearful eyes still hadn't left his. He was running on pure adrenaline and caffeine after a very long day, a sleepless night and now in fire mode while trying to run it as any other scene and trying to get home to Kada and his bed.

The memory hit him like a slap to the face. How had he not remembered this before? It had been a couple years, but Daphne's face was unmistakable and unchanged. The anger stirred inside him. He took another deep breath to slow his heart rate, and something gave him hope. For what, he didn't know yet.

Luke walked to Mike who was talking to another fireman about expanding the search from their 100-foot diameter around the car. After Whitte left, Luke talked with Mike.

"She's alive, Mike." Purposely keeping his name informal. "We've pulled her out of another accident before. One worse than this."

"When? Ok, what's going on?"

Luke rubbed his jawline, then put his hands on his hips and widened his stance.

"Ok." He took a deep breath. "I'm pretty sure, that was Daphne's ex-husband. Three years ago, he brought her up here for a surprise and wrecked on Deadman's Corner going over the edge." He took a deep breath. "I pulled her from that wreck, Mike. That's how she knows me and why she moved back here. She lost a pregnancy that day and several over the next year and he lost his shit."

Mike knew Luke long enough to know what that implied as dread sank to his bones.

"And she's been running since." Mike finished.

The puzzle was complete. He wondered why Daphne got so attached to Luke so quickly. It was more than just sexual and physical connection between them. It was getting very hard to believe that what they showed was all there was. Luke wasn't one to let anything distract him from doing his job and when Daphne had moved in next door, Luke was an entirely different man from then on, confused, but a better whole man.

Mike took a deep breath but understood why Luke didn't say anything. Instead, he held up a finger and grabbed his handset on his shoulder then waited for radio silence to talk to dispatch.

"Dispatch, Birch Way Command."

"Go ahead, Command."

"Yeah, we are gonna need state trooper assistance, get me Dawson at our location, also put Freeman Fire on standby, please."

"Copy. Calling state troopers for assistance, contacting Officer Dawson and putting Freeman Fire on standby." Dispatch replied.

Mike crossed his arms and looked at Luke, who just watched him and waited.

"You better give Kada a bus pass home with Sarah, this may take a while."

Luke gave Mike a pat on the arm and jogged off to the command truck to retrieve his cell phone and call the school. When he pulled out his cell and unlocked it, the same pictures as Daphne's phone popped up. His heart stuttered and clenched like a vice. He took a deep breath and told himself he would find her, alive.

The school knew Luke and what he did for work well enough not to question or deny Kada a bus pass. A common occurrence for her to be told to go to Sarah's when Luke knew he wouldn't be home because of longer calls. After he hung up his phone, Luke tucked the cell into his turnout pants pocket, threw on his turnout coat from the back seat, and joined the search.

Daphne laid in a snow pile that was half melted from the sun that day. She saw the blood but couldn't think about injuries from the crash. She had to stay awake and stay focused. Get away from Darryl. Get help and get to Luke. She grabbed handfuls of snow and packed it around her broken right shoulder. It's been a while since she had been able to feel her right hand. She laid there as she looked up at the trees when her focus began to fade.

"No! No." She used her left arm and sat up to rip a hole in her shirt, just below her left breast, and tuck her arm in and use the shirt for support. She was cold and numb. From her lack of proper clothes, loss of blood, injuries, or the snowbank and weather, she didn't know but didn't care as long as Darryl couldn't find her. Even if that meant Luke couldn't either. She wouldn't go back, not to the crash and not to him, she'd die first.

Luke Richmond. He saved her once and knew he would again. He really did love her and now she missed him more than ever. Where is he? What was he doing? Her mind wandered as she got sleepy. "No. Richmond." She whispered to herself.

She stood up and felt lightheaded. The faint heartbeat throbbed through her head, making it nearly impossible to stand. She widened her stance and closed her eyes while she took a couple of deep breaths and steadied herself. She opened her eyes and saw a boulder about 100 feet up the road. Get there, take a break, then find the next boulder, just keep going.

The crew was spread wide, searching the nearby woods and ditch lines. Luke was wandering a nearby hill in the woods, searching for any sign of Daphne. Whitte and his crew found signs of blood on the passenger floorboard and seat after they turned the car upright. Meaning there was proof of an injury before the crash, which only got Luke to abide by Mike's command even more to stay on scene and help out.

He had to stay level-headed, work the scene as if it was someone else. But the worry and panic stayed in his spine like an ache he couldn't ignore and hollowed out his stomach giving him the same emptiness he already knew all too well.

When Magar came across the radio saying he found something about forty yards northwest of the crash site, Luke sprinted down the hill and back to the road. Magar stood about 120 feet in the woods from the ditch, over Daphne's bloody cardigan sweater shredded from glass and a silver Maltese cross necklace engraved "Richmond".

He recognized the necklace but had never seen it. He stood and reached in his pants pockets under his turnout pants and pulled his truck keys free as others started to gather. Magar watched him, while he bent down and matched the necklace to the Maltese cross shaped hole in his keychain Daphne gave him for Christmas with her key attached. Luke smiled.

He looked at the cardigan and necklace then towards the crash site just around the corner. He knew she was staying hidden from her ex-husband, but still close enough to the road so she would be able to get help from people passing by. And the direction from the crash told him she was headed back towards town.

"That's my girl. You know what you are doing."

Luke pocketed the necklace with his keys and continued to walk 120 feet from the ditch towards town, in front of the rest of the crew.

When he came across the bloody snow pile, he radioed for Mike who drove up in the command vehicle and parked alongside of the road and got out.

The snow print and finger marks told Mike she was icing an injury and with a wide pool of blood in the snow, she was here awhile. He crouched down next to the snow pile and looked at his truck. It was barely noticeable through the trees.

"We passed right by her on our way to the scene. That much blood..."

Luke cut him off. "Yeah, I know!" He snapped out, then called out. "Daphne!" He kept walking.

Mike watched Luke and radioed in the evidence and its location, just as a state trooper truck pulled up to his command vehicle.

"Captain Davis!" He called Mike.

"Yeah?"

"You might want to come with us."

Mike called out to Luke, as they jumped in the command truck and followed the officer down the road. Another male officer was parked along the ditch with its lights on. Luke jumped out of the truck and ran to the officer talking on his radio, calling for an ambulance.

"Where is she?"

The officer pointed into the woods where another officer, about 100 feet in, leaned over an unconscious beaten Daphne on the ground.

Luke's heart stopped as he took off in a full run, jumping the ditch line in full turnout gear and up the small slope to Daphne. Luke grabbed the limp unconscious bloody Daphne from in front of the officer.

"Daphne! Daph, come on, wake up."

Luke checked for a pulse on her neck, a spot he's had his lips several times. He knew her pulse rate when his arms were wrapped around her and now the faint and weak pulse didn't match. He took off his turnout coat and wrapped it around her.

The officer watched Luke holding Daphne in his arms and spoke.

"She was holding a handful of broken glass. In the sunlight, it sparkled as we drove past. That's how we found her."

He looked down at her right hand, laying in the snowy dirt, to see the mix of blood and shattered glass pieces in her hand. He brushed out some of the glass and held her bloody hand and rubbed it close to his chest.

Mike walked over and stood next to him as he gave the ambulance their location over the radio.

The officer finished, "Looks like she's been here for a little awhile."

An ambulance rolled up and medics came running with medical bags and a backboard.

Luke held her tight as tears started to roll down his face.

"Daphne, I'm here. You're gonna be okay. I got you. Stay with me. Come on Daph, please. I love you."

Mike smiled at Luke, "She's gonna be okay, Luke."

Medics got her on a backboard as Luke took his coat off her. They pressed gauze into her wounds to help with the bleeding, then lifted her up and walked her back to the ambulance.

Luke stood and looked at Mike, who just nodded.

"Go."

Luke ran after the medics who were now putting EKG leads on and starting an IV. One of them looked at Luke.

"Her pulse is weak and thready, we are losing her, we need to get her to the hospital now."

"I'm going with!" He said and jumped in the back to reach for Daphne's hand that still held the last pieces of broken glass.

"Stay with me, Daphne."

She woke up still drowsy. Her eyes peered through the light, and she could hear the beeping of her monitors. She tried to speak out of pain, but nothing came out. Her eyes tried to focus and grasped a man standing outside her door, in the window.

Again, she tried to speak, but couldn't. The man turned around and she saw it was an officer in uniform. He made eye contact with her and flagged down a nurse.

When the nurse came in, she spoke softly, "Well look who's awake. How are you feeling?"

She nodded and tried to move her arms, but only her left arm moved. She looked to her right and saw her shoulder in a cast resting on a pillow. Her head throbbed. With her left hand, she felt her head was bandaged up. The nurse checked her monitor and pushed a couple buttons, then watched her feel her head.

"Your head hurt?" She asked.

Daphne nodded.

"Ok, I'll get the doctor and see if we can get you something for that..."

She continued after uncrimping her IV lines.

"You know, he hasn't left since you got here." Nodding to her other side.

She lifted her head up and looked to her left.

Across the room, Luke slept on a couch in his turnout pants and boots with a thin blanket covering him.

Her eyes grew big, and she smiled. The nurse was giving her a shot in her IV and watched Daphne start to cry.

"Do you want me to wake him?"

Daphne nodded fast with a pleading look in her eyes.

"Okay. Let me get a doctor and I'll wake him."

The nurse clicked on her IV monitor and walked out, returning a few moments later.

She walked over to Luke and gave him a pat on the shoulder to wake him. With a jolt he jerked awake and immediately looked from the nurse to Daphne smiling at him. He sat up, pushing the blanket to the side.

"You're awake." He said with the biggest smile he could while getting his bearings. He rubbed his eyes then stood up and took a couple steps to her bedside and took the doctor's rolling stool to sit on.

The nurse spoke to them both.

"The doctor will be in a minute to give her pain meds, check on her, and talk to you."

Daphne nodded with tears still in her eyes. Luke replied, "Thank you." to the nurse gathering up her clipboard and file.

"Of course." Then walked out, shutting the door behind her.

Luke reached for Daphne's good hand, now bandaged up, and held it in his big, scarred, dirty hands. With sad eyes and a smile, he asked, "How you feeling?"

Again, she opened her mouth, but nothing came out. With her left hand, she tried to feel her throat, but Luke didn't release her hand and held it back before she could touch the bandages.

"It's gonna be a few days before you'll get your voice back. But it's okay, I have some vacation time saved up, I can take a few days off so I can help you."

She instantly shook her head with wide eyes and made the headache worse.

"Don't tell me no. You're coming home with me where Kada and I can help you...." He paused and lowered his tone. ".... for a little while."

He now held her hand with both of his and gave a gentle squeeze.

Home. Her home. Her eyes widened as she ripped her hand away and gave a pen writing gesture.

Luke reached over and pulled a pen and notepad off the tray with a big cup of water next to it, then handed her it. She couldn't write well with her left hand, so she tried to take it slow, scribbling out the words, '*My house?*'

Luke read them as she wrote it out.

"I gave the State Troopers my key to your house. Troopers took pictures of the scene and left. Mike, Jen, and some guys from the department are cleaning up the..." He paused and swallowed before choking out the words. ".... the damage."

He straightened his spine but didn't let go of her hand that still held the pen.

Flashes of Darryl throwing her into her kitchen island and the wall, watching the flowers that she knew were from Luke, tossed across the floor and stepped on. They bled together into her wood floor like paint, as he stepped on them with his shoe and his other connected with her ribs and broke them. She laid on the floor helpless, saying nothing to stop him, as soothing wave of numbness crept through her body. Luke's face was the last thing she saw before going unconscious.

She turned her head away from Luke as the tears fell to the knitted hospital blanket. Luke propped a hip on the edge of her bed and pulled her into his chest gently.

"You're safe. He can't hurt you now."

She wiped at the tears and felt the pain of the bruises on her face, then turned back to look at Luke, and picked up the pen again.

She wrote out slowly, '*Where is he?*'

He released his right hand from hers to rub his jawline and looked into her eyes and swallowed. "No one knows."

She closed her eyes and folded her lips inward.

He took a much-needed breath. It was hard when he heard all this himself, but it was harder to tell her now.

"He came in with an ambulance to our clinic to get patched up for his injuries before we knew what had happened. You flatlined in route and had to be medevac'd here to Freeman for life threatening injuries. By the time Dawson figured it out, Darryl checked himself out of the clinic. That is why I put Kennedy at your door. He won't get near you again, Daphne. I promise. I am here and always will be, even after all this is over. Birch Valley is on alert and on a manhunt for him." He growled out the manhunt ending of the statement.

The look in her eyes nearly shattered him.

"Jesus! Daph, I'm so sorry." He took in a shuddering breath and a few tears rolled down his face. She lifted her hand to his face and ran her thumb over his cheek to wipe at his tears. He closed his eyes and leaned into her hand, then leaned over and softly kissed her lips, careful not to hurt her.

When he reached into his pants pocket and pulled the necklace free and showed her the small Maltese cross engraved with *Richmond*, she smiled.

"You dropped this."

He spoke as he wrapped it around her bandaged neck and clipped it.

"It goes with my keychain, doesn't it?"

She gave a smug smile and nodded as he kissed the Maltese cross and then her.

When he released her, he spoke softly, "I love you, Daphne."

She already knew he did but hearing it for the first time made her heart beat harder as she knew she loved him for a couple months now. It was an affirmation she needed. She mouthed the words back, "I love you too."

He then kissed her hand and sat back down on the stool as the doctor came in with two vials of medication and her file.

"How we doing today?" He asked.

She pointed to her head. He nodded.

"Yup, I have something for that, right here."

Luke rubbed a thumb over her hand.

The doctor walked over to the computer and typed some stuff in then unlocked a cabinet and took out two syringes. He got a rolling tray ready, filled each syringe with the liquid from each vile, and injected them through her IV.

"There, that should help with the pain." He cleaned up the tray and vials and took a seat on the spare rolling stool and rolled it to her right side to talk to both her and Luke.

"Daphne. Hi, I'm Doctor Revak, I did your surgeries. You came in with a broken shoulder, clavicle, and fractured ankle. Bone fragments punctured your trachea, but luckily never released still giving you full use of your lungs. You have a few broken ribs and a head injury, but scans and x-rays showed no significant damage beyond that, thankfully."

Daphne nodded in understanding as he talked. Luke still held her hand and gave it a slight rub throughout the conversation.

"I repaired the tissue and ligaments around your collarbone and shoulder, stitched up the punctures to your trachea, which is why you can't talk right now. The stitches are on the outside so you can eat but I'd stick to soft foods for a couple of days at least. Give it a couple days for swelling to subside and you should get your voice back." He spoke quickly before either of them asked.

Daphne looked at Luke but saw he had already heard this as he stayed silent next to her. Which wasn't Luke.

"The shoulder and arm are casted to refrain from too much movement and causing more damage to those areas. Your ankle is braced for a bit. I have faith that the rest should heal on its own. You have a lot of bumps and bruises, but honestly, I think you were pretty lucky. It could have been a lot worse, but you have a well-trained fire department that loves you and that's something special. But even more than that, a fireman that has done nothing but fight for you since you arrived. He's a good one."

As the doctor and Daphne looked at Luke, who now fought back the smug smile and raised Daphne's hand to place a kiss on it. Daphne smiled with her heart and lips watching him, then turned back to the doctor.

"Healing time for full movement is at least 6-10 weeks, so get practicing left hand dominance for now." As he gestured to the scribbles on the pad next to her.

Luke chuckled as she gave a breathless laugh and nodded her head.

"I want to see you back here for a full follow up with me in 4 weeks for cast removal then into a brace but check up with Doctor Clint in Birch Valley in two weeks. If your scans are still clear in the morning, we'll get you checked out with some meds for pain and swelling, and Mr. Richmond here can take you home. Okay? Any questions?"

She shook her head and felt the full weight of it, so she laid her head back to rest on the pillow. The meds were kicking in now and she felt tired and relaxed.

The doctor stood up and patted the bedside rail. "Get some rest. We'll have you out of here soon." Then reached across Daphne to shake Luke's hand and said goodbye.

Luke looked at a less than enthused Daphne. The bruises had darkened on her face, but the swelling had gone down over the last two days they were here.

He tried for a smile that fell flat. "Are you hungry? Thirsty?"

She turned her head on the pillow to look at him and shook her head. She didn't want to think about food when other thoughts took up priority in her mind.

"Ok, well I'm gonna go down to the cafeteria and get some coffee quick. Mike and Kada should be here soon with Dawson to take your statement...written statement." He frowned as he corrected himself.

"Kada has been dying to see you, if she doesn't soon, she'll shred Freeman and Birch Valley." He chuckled.

She smiled and picked up the pen and scribbled out, "Just like her dad."

That made him smile again. He stood and leaned over her bed and kissed her forehead. "I'll be back soon."

Daphne watched Luke leave, still in his turnout pants and boots, and say something to the officer posted at her door before he walked off. The silence sank in and was deafening. It carried a lot of her fears even if she didn't know it before Luke left.

The clock showed 2:35pm, as sunlight shined through her small window to the vast city of Freeman. But still the dark crept up her spine now. She clung to the blanket like a lifeline, pulled it up over her chest. She felt the bandages that spanned her collarbone, neck, and then the necklace. She smiled and then felt up her face to the slightly swollen bumps and scrapes over her jawline and cheeks, to the cut beside her eye and the stitches in her hairline that were covered by gauze.

More tears fell from her cheeks. She closed her eyes and heard Luke's voice, "I love you, Daphne." again. She smiled then drifted to sleep.

CHAPTER TEN

T he door opened and a soft shout from Kada, "Daphne!" had woken her from a sleep she hadn't realized she fell into.

She opened her eyes as Luke came around from her left side again to stop Kada from leaping into Daphne's bed.

"Kada, slow down. She's tired and in some pain. You have to be gentle."

Kada walked over to Daphne's bedside and leaned over to give her a gentle hug. Mike followed with an armload of flowers in a large vase and the other arm held various gifts of teddy bears and chocolates with balloons and a stack of cards in various colors of envelopes.

Her eyes widened as she gave Kada a hug with her one good arm and gave her a kiss on the forehead. Kada saw the necklace with "Richmond " engraved into the Maltese cross and rubbed a thumb over it and looked at her dad who only gave her a smile before walking over to Mike. Kada looked up at Daphne's face and spoke as tears started to roll down her face, "Are you okay, Daphne?"

Luke spoke as he took some of the gifts from Mike's arms, giving Mike some relief, "She's okay, Kada. If everything turns out well, she should be able to come home..." He looked at Daphne before finishing the sentence, ".... with us tomorrow."

Kada's eyes lit up, "With us?"

"For a little bit so she can rest and heal."

Daphne forced a smile. She definitely wasn't used to being dependent on others and now literally had no say.

Mike walked over and gave Daphne a hug and then braced a hand on her bed rail.

"The flowers are from Jen and all of us at the department, the various teddy bears, cards, and balloons are from everyone in Birch Valley including some of your students."

Before Mike could finish, Kada ran to pull a soft, white, and dark pink teddy bear out of Luke's arms and gently placed it next to Daphne, "And this one is from me."

Daphne mouthed the words, "Thank you." Which had Kada frowning, and her eyebrows pulled down.

Luke held Kada's shoulders after setting the rest of the gifts on the window seal and spoke softly over Kada's head. "Sweetheart, Daphne had to have surgery so it's gonna be hard for her to talk for a while, but she says, 'thank you'."

Luke pulled Kada to the other side of the bed to make room for Mike.

Mike finished. "Mrs. Adams, your next-door neighbor.... Your *other* next-door neighbor sent the 'Get Well' balloon with daisies on it and says she is happy to be back at Birch Valley Middle as the school nurse till you can heal and says take your time and don't worry about your job or students. Mrs. Jeannie, your secretary and friend from the school, sent a care package of lotion, hairbrush, and feminine products you girls use when you're lying in a bed helpless." He laughed and gave a smirk. Daphne just rolled her eyes.

"And last but not least I guess I have a couple of cheeseburgers and fries in the truck from the restaurant cooked fresh...about an hour ago and a bag of clothes for the both of you. Jen and Jeannie tag teamed your outfits, so don't look at me. Luke, Kada and I also brought a couple pairs for you with your body wash and shaver."

"Oh, thank you." He spoke with a gasp of relief. "I need a shower."

"Or a hose." Mike gave a single chuckle.

Kada sat at the foot of Daphne's bed and gently placed a hand on her leg as they watched each other.

Luke walked over, gave Kada's shoulder a gentle squeeze, "You gonna be okay for a minute? I'm gonna help Uncle Mike get the rest of the bags out of the truck."

"Yeah, I'll stay with her."

"Okay." He replied but withheld his reservations about Kada's capabilities of gentleness around Daphne.

"I'll be back in a sec." He told Daphne, then gave her a smile and puckered his lips in midair, giving her a silent kiss over Kada's head.

Daphne smiled wide and gave a small nod but didn't return the favor in front of Kada.

Over the next twenty minutes, the guys made their way down five stories of the hospital to the parking garage. They grabbed the rest of the bags, talked about Daphne, caught up on station news, and then returned quickly. Kada did all the talking to Daphne about a boy she liked in school, how it wasn't the same without her next door, but how she was used to dad being gone a lot. It made Daphne a little sad to hear that, knowing she was the reason he was gone now.

When the guys returned with a bag full of food and a duffle bag. Daphne's belly rumbled with hunger. The four of them ate and were nearly finished when Officer Dawson, a tall, beefy man with dark blonde hair, knocked on the doorframe. Wearing a full police uniform and vest, he looked a little less than frazzled.

Luke stood up to greet him, and they gave each other a quick manly hug.

"Luke, Miss Daphne, Captain, Miss Kada, how are you all doing?"

One by one they answered with a "Good", except Daphne who answered with a couple of nods, then covered her mouth as she swallowed her bite of food.

"Oh no, Ma'am. You go ahead and finish please. I'll take Luke's statement first."

Luke looked at Daphne and introduced them, "Daph, this is Officer Trey Dawson. He's been a good friend of not only Mike and I's but the Department and is a local friend to everyone in Birch."

Dawson gave a single nod of his head towards Daphne. "Yes, I'd like to think that I am but unfortunately in uniform, is not how I expected to meet you."

Daphne gave a slight smile before nodding her head.

Mike nodded at Luke then jerked a nod towards Kada.

Kada was a very strong and independent young girl who didn't need protecting a lot of the time, but from this she did. Luke knew how Kada felt about Daphne. She had handled a lot after her mother died and when he fell apart, but still grew up a beautiful woman that could take care of herself and even her dad on most days. But Luke knew, she was nowhere near ready to hear Daphne's story or understand it completely.

Luke gave Mike a nod back.

"Kada, Honey, it's time to go." Mike told her.

She looked at her dad, then at Dawson and nodded before walking over to give her dad a big hug.

"See you at home tomorrow?"

"If Daphne gets released, we will be there. Don't give Uncle Mike too much trouble please, and get your homework done."

Kada frowned, rolled her eyes then gave a lengthy, "Yes."

She then walked over to Daphne giving her a hug as Daphne kissed her cheek. Mike said his goodbyes too and followed Kada out.

Luke and Dawson took a seat on the doctor's stools as Dawson opened his notebook to take notes.

Luke sat next to Daphne's left bedside and placed a gentle hand on her leg with his right but kept his back to her as he recalled every detail he could remember from the pager tones to the hospital.

Daphne listened carefully as she slowly ate the last of her burger and fries in small enough bites, not to hurt her throat even while on pain meds. Daphne heard the grovel tones in Luke's voice as he told his story and his painful recollection of grim outlooks for her and about the previous accident. The whole time he held her leg as she ate her burger with her only available hand, but still he couldn't look at her and she understood why. Officer Dawson did though while taking notes and on occasion looked from Luke to her as she nodded through the facts in Luke's story.

Her thoughts raced and flashbacks came and went as Luke told his side, but when Dawson asked about the 1st accident, Luke recalled the minimal details and only remembered pulling her from the car himself. What he remembered was facts according to her, but in her mind, he left out the most important ones.

How he smelled. Though he wouldn't remember, she did, like it was yesterday. His cologne or body wash was like a lifeline. It was musky with sharp amber and cedarwood, different then what he wore now. But for the few seconds her head was on his shoulder before he placed her on the backboard, his scent combined with how he held her hand even in a thick work glove, gave her a sense of security she had thought was gone while the car dangled a hundred and fifty feet from the bottom of the cliff.

She watched his hand now holding hers on the bed beside her and it stirred something inside she hadn't felt yet. His hands though rough and calloused, were capable of so much and right now he chose to hold hers.

He was the main reason she moved to Birch Valley after all. When she found a nice cabin for sale on a half-acre of land in the small town, she jumped at it but never expected to move into the small cabin next to the man that saved her.

She had only expected to thank him for saving her, but as the leaves began to fall, she remembered taking a break from unpacking and organizing what little she managed to keep. She had walked out back and found her little bench that overlooked the creek. She was scared, alone and almost decided to run again when this little dark brunette girl came out of the neighbor's house holding two to-go cups of hot cocoa and gave her one. Kada's hands around that white paper cup, though considerably smaller, were like her dad's, ready to help anyone in need.

She smiled as she watched Luke's thumb gently rub hers on the bed between them, and there was that sense of security again. She was safe. She swallowed the last of her food and drank from the cup of water next to her bed behind Luke. Then placed her hand back in Luke's.

When the officer finished with Luke and rolled his stool around to the other side, he was smiling. He gave Daphne's casted shoulder a soft touch, then spoke softly.

"I know you can't talk, so I'm just gonna ask you a few questions and you can answer with a nod or shake and if you need to say something, you can write it down, okay?"

She nodded.

"Is what Luke told me, correct to your understanding?" Dawson asked.

She gave a nod.

"Did you have any indication that Darryl Ryker was in Birch Valley before Friday?"

She closed her eyes and shook her head. Luke took a deep breath, raised his hand, and spoke.

"I did." Mad at himself for not remembering the Mazda in the parking lot by the store until now, he rubbed his face with both hands while wishing he would have listened to his gut when it told him that the car didn't belong on Birch Valley.

When Dawson and Daphne looked at him in silence, he swallowed and continued.

"I didn't know it was him, but I saw his Mazda parked by the curb next to the grocery store Thursday evening after work. I knew it was out of place in our town, but I swear I didn't know it was him."

He stared at the blanket over Daphne and his thoughts rolled off his tongue.

"Maybe if I had known I could have stopped him, called you. Shit, even called Daphne, then maybe we wouldn't be here right now."

When Daphne touched his arm, he snapped out of it with a jerk of his head and looked at her.

"I'm sorry."

She just smiled and intertwined her fingers with his. Dawson took the notes down and continued.

"Okay, so when did Darryl enter your house? Thursday? Friday?"

When she nodded on the mention of Friday, Dawson wrote it down.

"So, Friday...afternoon?"

She shook her head.

"Friday morning?"

She nodded as he wrote on his notepad. He looked up at her again.

"Okay, so Friday morning. 11am? 10? 9am? 8am?"

She shook every hour he asked. So, he went back further.

"7am?"

She shook her head.

"6?"

She nodded.

Luke took a deep breath. Without looking at him, Daphne tightened her grip, holding his hand as he looked at Dawson.

"She wakes up at 6 to get ready for work, then heads out 'bout 7."

Daphne looked at Luke. He had a painful expression but smiled.

"You saw me coming home from calls and paid attention." He shrugged, "So did I, except that morning."

She frowned now and pulled his hand up to her lips and kissed it remembering their fight before she shut the door on him.

"Ok, so you were getting ready for work. Then what? He knocked on the door?" Dawson spoke.

She nodded, then pointed to her chest, head, then Luke with her left hand.

Dawson's expression brightened. "You thought it was Luke?"

She nodded again.

He took down more notes.

"Okay, so I'm guessing you tried to run..."

The corner of her mouth fell in a frown as she nodded.

"Then what? He hit you and threw you?"

She nodded again.

Luke huffed out a breath, stood up letting his hand slide out of hers, and walked out of the room, closing the door behind him.

She watched him, then crossed her arm over her stomach, and felt the weight of it push on her broken rib and she clenched.

Dawson watched her clench as he leaned forward on his stool and with a sad expression spoke, "I'm sorry Miss Kimble. I just have to get the facts and know exactly what happened to build the case. Are you okay?"

With a somber look, she nodded.

"Luke will be okay. He's one of the strongest men I know. He's been through hell and back and still came out on top. But you have changed his and Kada's life forever and your presence hasn't gone unnoticed in Birch Valley. You have the support of everyone in that town, whether you know them personally or not, and I will find Darryl, I promise. I actually feel safer having you with Luke than my jail cell in the station. Luke won't let anything happen to you and neither will I."

She smiled big as tears fell from her face. Dawson folded up his notepad and got up for the box of Kleenex sitting on the counter and handed it to her. She grabbed one from the box and wiped at her eyes.

"I think I got enough for now. If I need more, I'll come back later after you get some rest."

He gave her bed rail a pat and stood up.

"Get better and get some rest. I'll see if I can find Luke for you."

She smiled again and nodded as she mouthed the words, "Thank you."

He nodded back and left the room saying something to the officer on his way out.

Luke returned a few moments later walking into her room and straight across the room to lean over her bed and brace a hand on each side of her head and give her a hard deep kiss and lingered there for a moment finally releasing to brush a hand down her hair that lay strewn out over her pillow.

"I'm so sorry. I love you, Daphne."

Later that night, he helped her wash up in the shower in her room, with a washcloth and soap. Careful not to get the cast or bandages wet, he took his time washing over the old scars and some of the smaller new ones. He made sure that what was left unbandaged was healing properly.

She sat on a shower chair with what felt like a miniscule towel over her lap and her breasts on display. She never felt more naked than she did at that moment. She hit rock bottom. She was the most independent woman she knew and here she was broken and beaten, as her neighbor had to help her take a simple shower. She was more scared than she had ever been, cause she had others to protect now that she put Luke and Kada in danger. Her heart shattered. In the cover of running water she silently cried, trying not to show Luke, as Darryl's death threats towards Luke and Kada rang through her ears and ate at her like the secret it was.

When Luke, now barefoot, rested her head back on the back of the chair to wash her hair, he gently pulled out a few hidden twigs in the bottom ends of her long, beautiful, chocolate brunette hair. He washed the ends first, then started to work his way up, again careful of the bandages at her hair line.

When he was done, he helped her dry off and into some lace panties. The idea of a bra was too constricting right now, nonetheless impossible with her shoulder cast. She slipped into a pair of her purple and black yoga pants that were loose at the bottom and big enough to stretch over the brace.

Luke went over to the small bag Mike brought and pawed through her clothes looking for a shirt that would work with her bulky shoulder cast that spanned half her chest and arm. He pulled out form fitting tank tops and cardigan sweaters and near sheer blouses. He grumbled to himself then spoke louder as the next thing he pulled out was a baby doll lingerie and held it up dangling the strap on a single finger for her to see.

Daphne smiled and started to laugh,

"Did Jen and Jeannie put anything in here useful.... right now?" he spoke with curiosity as he examined the sheer top closer.

When she stopped laughing, she held her left arm around her ribs, wincing from the pain.

Luke chuckled with a genuine smile.

"There's my girl."

When the rare opportunity came available to toss a random woman around in his hotel room bed on overnight trips alone to Freeman for work, He gave into the release of pressure but never saw it as anything more than that. He always made sure there was no further contact and that they were never close to home or too personal. Sure, women weren't blind and would often try to paw at him even on shopping trips with his daughter but every single one was shot down in an instant as he pushed Kada through the store.

Luke had everything from the washboard abs, large biceps, chiseled jawline, and thighs that could crack a walnut. But Luke didn't crave anyone since his wife died. His needs and wants weren't important, the only thing at the time was Kada, and Luke made sure of that. Any woman that came into his house was either family or happily married to another man and No woman had touched his bed since his wife, until Daphne.

But the first day her candy apple red Jeep pulled into the next house, he watched her take in boxes and bags one by one as he drank his morning coffee. She was undeniably noticeable, and it wasn't just physical. But for the first time in almost eight years, his carnal needs seeped into his bones and became an itch just below the surface of his skin that even now, he knew would never go away. His instincts were working in overdrive trying to love and protect her the only way he knew how and along with that came his sexual desires to show her how she should be treated.

He toyed with the sheer fabric thinking about how happy she was with her big white smile hauling in a box and her big brown curls bouncing with every step up her porch. He could make her happy again, he believed he could, and would.

"Luke?" She breathed out in a shallow whisper. He snapped out of it and looked at her.

"Yeah?" He answered.

She sat in silence with her arm over her chest watching him.

"Yeah, sorry. Lost in thought."

He tossed the lingerie back in the bag and kept searching. Screw it! He had an idea. He pulled out one of his black T-shirts.

"This should fit." He announced as he stood up from the bag and walked back to Daphne. She smiled when he showed her his T-shirt. She raised her left arm up for him to slip it over it, over her head carefully, tucked her right forearm into the shirt, and pulled it over, down to her hips on the shower stool and freed her damp hair.

He faced her now and crouched down in front, resting his elbows on his knees and his hands on her thighs, and looked up at her face.

"You're beautiful, Daph. You always will be to me."

He reached up and tucked at a tendril of hair behind her ear as he rubbed a rough calloused thumb over her soft damp cheek.

She leaned her face into his hand that opened when she pressed into it.

A knock on the outer room door made both of them look at the bathroom door.

"Daphne? Are you doing okay, in there?" a nurse called out.

Luke answered, "Yeah."

He gave her a soft kiss then walked to the bathroom door and opened it for the nurse.

"Just helped her get dressed."

"Well, my, my, you look like a new woman."

The nurse stood by the door, looking over Daphne down to her bare toes.

"Alright, well, let's get you into bed, almost time for your next meds."

Luke and the nurse helped her hobble the few steps out of the bathroom and to her clean freshly made bed and climb in.

The nurse hooked her IV back up and checked her stats.

"I like those numbers. That bath did you some good."

Daphne hadn't really stopped smiling since Luke helped her get dressed, but now she smiled a little wider.

"Okay, well, how you feeling?"

Daphne nodded and gave a raspy, "Okay."

"Okay, well Honey, be careful with that throat, don't strain it too much. If you need anything else, just make him holler for you. Okay."

She gave an empty laugh and nodded.

When she left, Luke got up. "You gonna be okay for a minute while I take a quick shower?"

Again, she nodded.

He walked over to her window full of gifts and flowers and pulled a teddy bear from it.

"Here, hold this for a bit." As he tucked it next to her and gave her a kiss on the forehead.

"I'll leave the door cracked and make it quick."

She clicked on the TV and watched a movie. A few minutes later he returned wearing another black T-shirt, jeans, and tactical boots and held a much thicker duffle bag than before. She wondered if he was at least sensible enough to separate her clean clothes from his dirty turn out pants and boots.   He placed the bag by the couch and took his seat by her bedside, to hold her hand, and watch the movie with her.

Later that night she watched Luke drift to sleep curled up next to her on the small hospital bed. He was far more exhausted than her. But he put in a lot more work than she had the last few days taking care of her instead of his daughter, where he should've been. The guilt eased up her spine and stiffened it.

When he spoke to Officer Dawson, she could hear his shaky tones as he explained the accident and his efforts to find her. Sowing the two sides of their memories together now, she knew he had it harder than she did. Though she didn't understand what it was like to have to worry about someone you share your soul with, she did know worrying about someone you loved was always worse than worrying about yourself. That was something she had gotten used to. She tried to put herself in his shoes but gave up when she giggled at the thought of Luke walking through the woods half-dressed running from an abusive ex-girlfriend. Not a chance.

By morning, Luke helped Daphne check out after tests and scans showed good progress. She grimaced and snarled at the crutches the doctor tried to give her, so Luke helped her hobble to Mike's truck who waited for them in the front of the hospital.

The ride was mostly silent as the gifts, flowers and bags took up the front passenger seat and Daphne leaned against Luke holding her close in the back seat. Mike turned down Main Street and Daphne heard all the whistles and screams as a bunch of her students and parents lined the sidewalks with posters and signs with "Get better soon" and "We miss you, Nurse Kimble". Her heart filled with joy as she rolled down the window and waved.

When they pulled into Luke's driveway, she got out and saw her house and car across the yard. Darryl's screams and bitter words as he threw her around like a rag doll, flashed through her head. She winced at the thoughts. Before Luke came around to her side of the truck, shut her door and told her, "Nope! Don't even think about it." As he carefully picked her up and carried her up the steps to the waiting Jen and Kada.

Luke was the first to give hugs and greetings after setting Daphne down to her feet. Daphne smiled at Jen and pulled her into a one arm hug with a smile. Making Jen smile and give Daphne a gentle hug.

"Sorry I didn't get a chance to visit you in the hospital. I was holding down the fort."

Standing only an inch or two taller than herself, Jen had pinned back waves of golden-brown hair, quite a few shades lighter than her own hair. A smile that could brighten anyone's day and a set of sultry golden-brown eyes that glittered in the sunlight. Mike leaned in and gave his wife a kiss on the cheek and gave her an armload of Daphne's gifts. Daphne just smiled.

Kada waited patiently to welcome Daphne home and gave her a hug squeezed a little tight making Daphne take a deep breath in pain. Kada instantly released and apologized. Daphne just shook her head and gave Kada a kiss on top of her head, then spoke with a whisper, "I missed you."

Kada just smiled, "We have a surprise for you!" As her eyes lit up.

Jen walked in the front door first, carrying an armload of flowers, gifts, stuffed teddy bears, and balloons. Then Mike who held the door open for Kada next and Daphne hobbled inside with help from Luke behind her.

Sarah, Kada's best friend and cousin, held outstretched arms to a dark purple soft chaise lounge chair sitting under one of Luke's bigger living room windows that face her house and the creek. It held soft white pillows and a matching blanket and had a little end table next to it.

Kada spoke first. "It's not your little bay window, but we tried to make it comfortable, and we all had a hand in it. I picked it out, Dad paid for it, Uncle Mike moved it, Jen set it up, and Sarah and I added the blankets and pillows."

Kada folded her hands in front of her standing on tiptoes all proud of herself. "You like it?"

Daphne spoke as loud as she could, but it came out raspy, "I love it! Thank you."

She put a hand over her mouth and melted.

Sarah spoke, "Try it out. I think it's super comfy."

Daphne hobbled to it and sat down as Jen put her flowers on the end table next to it. "Ooo, soft. I love it. Thank you so much."

Luke lifted her braced ankle off the floor and turned Daphne's legs to rest on the chaise. She looked at everyone watching her and felt uncomfortable.

Daphne spoke up as loud as she could, trying not to strain her voice, "Hey Mike!'

He turned to walk to her and Luke, then Daphne stood back up from the chaise as Luke tried to sit her back down. She swatted at his hand and pulled Mike into a hug with her good arm.

"Thanks for the save and keeping his head on straight."

A shocked Mike gave her a gentle hug and released her, "Well you are welcome, but I just kept his head on his shoulders, the rest was him."

He gave a nod towards Luke still sitting on the Chaise next to her.

"He knew what you were doing and where you were going. No man better to protect and save you than him, and definitely no better fireman and friend, I want working next to me."

Luke stood up and gave Mike a smile and pat on the shoulder.

"You have a good one. He won't let you down and though he'll never admit it, he's been kinda crazy about you since you moved in next door."

She smiled and turned to Luke. His eyes went dark.

Then he leaned in for a lingering possessive and passionate kiss for everyone to see, gently placing a hand around the small of her back and pulling her to him and placing his other hand gently on her jaw and neck.

Kada and Sarah screeched, while jumping up and down.

Kada said with excitement, "I knew it!"

Which made Luke and Daphne both smile, then helped Daphne sit and propped her braced ankle and other foot on the Chaise.

"Dad, not ready for a relationship? Pfft! Yeah, whatever. Daphne wasn't ready for Dad and Me!" Kada said with a smile.

Everyone chuckled then Jen snapped her fingers at the two girls to get the rest of the stuff from Uncle Mike's truck.

Mike smiled and walked back to Jen and gave her a soft kiss, and said, "I'll help them."

Luke, who now sat on the edge of the chaise watching Daphne, spoke without moving his eyes off Daphne's.

"I'll help too."

As the girls left. Daphne smiled bigger then chuckled.

"What?" Luke asked. Mike watched on in anticipation.

With an even more raspy voice while holding her throat. Daphne said, "Is this chair to make me feel comfortable or to keep me in one spot to keep your house masculine and functional?"

Mike winced first, "Ooo, shots fired. Pew, pew."

Jen tightly closed her lips and tried not to laugh, but it bubbled up and she released a loud laugh. Then made herself busy cleaning up.

Mike turned and went to help the girls haul stuff in, still laughing out the door.

Luke pursed his lips in a wide smile.

"You want to paint the walls purple, paint the walls purple. Just don't touch the truck or office. If a fuzzy purple seat cover shows up in the truck, there will be consequences."

She winked at him and whispered with her smile widening to an evil grin, "Ooo, can't wait. Fluffy purple seat covers are kinda hard to put on one-handed, but I can try.".

Luke scowled and kept it safe by kissing her forehead and then got up to help Mike and the girls.

Jen finished filling a glass of ice water and hurried over to place it on Daphne's table next to her, then took a seat on the end of the Chaise.

"Thank you." Daphne spoke as she reached for it and took a sip, letting the cold water soothe her throat.

Jen just watched and waited until she was done drinking before she spoke. "So did Luke like the lingerie?"

Daphne choked on air as she set the glass down with a surprised look.

"That was you?" She rasped out.

Jen smiled big and nodded fast.

"Well, me and Jeannie, both thought it would be funny, but I put them in knowing he would find it and probably panic or something."

Panic was not the first word that came to mind when she thought of his reaction in the hospital bathroom, but more like a momentary lapse of unconsciousness would be more like it. Daphne raised both eyebrows.

"Oh, I think he died a little." She chuckled.

Jen laughed, "I knew it. Oh, Daphne, that man has been bundled up tighter than a priest, I swear. I think I actually told Mike to buy him a hooker from Freeman and a hotel room for the night last year for Luke's birthday, but he instead got him a stupid custom radio harness, then when Mike came home telling me, Luke was holding hands with you. I think every woman, married or single, within a 20-mile radius of this town threw a handful of confetti in the air."

Jen, though forward and open, Daphne enjoyed it and laughed with her.

"That man has been a ticking time bomb. You know men actually get pissy when they can't release the pressure? They are worse than an old maid going through menopause. They call our PMS, 'Shark week' but have you seen an adult man that hasn't gotten any in a while? And we are the hormonal ones? Yeah Okay!" Jen rolled her eyes.

They both rolled with laughter again before they saw Mike and Luke walk in front of the window and Luke pointing towards the creek.

"But on a more serious note, Daphne don't even think twice about a young, hot pepper, hugging Luke and giving him a peck on the cheek in the grocery store. We all love Luke, but he has never and will never look at anyone else the way I just saw him look at you. He's in over his head and he doesn't even know yet. He's chasing a wildfire and it's gonna get hot and exciting before he realizes it." Jen gave Daphne a wink.

For a minute, Daphne forgot all her worries and pain and almost even forgot she was injured. Though she just met Jen a few months ago she felt like she had known her for years.

When Kada came in, she was lugging the bulky duffle bag, complaining, "What does Dad got in here? A dead body?"

Jen got up quickly and grabbed it from her, "Oh honey, it's just your dad's dirty turnout gear. Your Uncle Mike will have to take this back to the station and get it cleaned up. Let me just get out the rest of the clothes in here and Uncle Mike will take it."

When Kada walked back out, Jen opened the duffle and pulled out the smaller red duffle with Luke's gear to set it aside then dug out all the other clothes. She whispered from across the room to Daphne, "I think I'll just put these away now." Then walked down the hall to put a little bit of clean clothes on top of the dresser with the lingerie and put the dirty clothes in the laundry basket in the corner then shut Luke's bedroom door.

While Jen was tied up, Daphne watched Luke and Mike out in the yard talking. It was starting to warm up outside. The snow from the trees started to melt and the ground now only held about a four-inch layer of crunchy ice with small open patches of soggy dead grass. Mike had his hands in his pockets while Luke had his arms crossed over his chest and a wider stance than Mike. Whatever they talked about had Luke thinking hard before Mike said something and laughed which had Luke tightening his bottom lip, rubbing his jaw and chin with a couple of nods.

Whatever Mike said next, had them both rolling with laughter as Luke playfully swatted Mike's shoulder, then pointed a stern finger at him.

Mike just shrugged his shoulders with a smile, which had Luke turning his head to look at Daphne through the window, with a flat, but thoughtful face.

When Daphne smiled at him. He forced a smile before turning back to Mike when he said something, then they walked off towards the back of the house.

Later, they all ate Mike's barbeque he cooked for everyone on Luke's grill. Then said their goodbyes as Sarah pleaded with her mom to stay the night. Jen then pushed Sarah out the front door with a reply, "No. You have some chores to catch up on. Kada spent all weekend with us and you two even got the day off from school today to help Uncle Luke."

Mike patted Luke on the shoulder and walked out behind his wife and daughter. Luke closed the door, walked back to Daphne's chaise, and sat down.

"You need anything? You doing okay?"

She nodded. "I'm okay. A little tired and sore." with a raspy voice.

"You want your pain meds? You're about due for another dose."

She shook her head.

"No, I don't like the way they make me feel. Besides, I'm already starting to feel better."

Luke raised an eyebrow. "You haven't even been out of the hospital for 24 hours and you already want to run."

Daphne gave a sly smile, and broke, "Luke, this is torture. I have my own house; I can take care of myself."

His smile widened. "And I have no doubt." He softened his expression and voice. "But what if Darryl comes back?"

She frowned but lifted a brow. "And what about Kada?" She asked him.

Kada, now washing dishes, shouted from the kitchen, still unaware of the full situation. "I can take care of myself, thank you!"

Daphne and Luke just smiled without looking at her.

"Kada, dishes, now. Then homework." Luke spoke in a gruff tone while never taking his eyes off Daphne. "Four weeks until your next check up with Doctor Revak?"

"Two weeks with Doctor Clint." Daphne tried negotiating.

"Daphne Kimble." He spoke.

"Lucas Richmond." She said,

Kada raised her hand from scrubbing a pot, "Kada Richmond!"

Luke tightened his jaw.

"You're so handsome!" She tapped him over the edge.

He couldn't do anything besides give her a very frustrating hard kiss that she accepted, with a big smile.

Then Daphne gave in. "Fine! Four weeks until this cast comes off then I get to go home."

"Okay, agreed."

Now he moved in for a slower softer kiss that made Daphne moan softly.

She touched his scruffy jaw that had some stubble but kept up with clean lines.

He tilted his head to fit better and ran his tongue over the edge of her lips. They both got a sudden surge of heat, Luke released, sat back, and they stared at each other.

Daphne heard a sigh and turned her head to look at the kitchen with Luke. Kada leaned over the bar, elbows propped up on the counter, hands fisted together, and chin propped up on her fists as soapy dishwater ran down her arms. She watched them with a big grin from ear to ear and a little dreamy-eyed.

"Kada Jasmine Richmond." Luke spoke sternly.

She rolled her eyes, dropped her arms, and went back to the sink to pull the plug from a now empty sink. With a huff she dried her hands.

"Yada, yada, yada. I know! Homework. I'm going." Blowing out a breath as she walked up the stairs to her bedroom.

Luke stood up and looked down at Daphne on the Chaise, "I'll go make the bed up."

Then walked to his bedroom, opened the door, and a couple minutes later yelled out with sarcasm, "Really?"

Daphne laughed and smiled as she heard the dresser drawer nearly slam close with a little extra force.

When Luke returned, he had changed into his pajama pants that showed a little less of the extra bulge and in a tank top instead of a T-shirt. And, oh man, he looked sexy. He walked over and crouched down next to her, placed one arm on the back of the Chaise behind her shoulders and leaned his right elbow on his knee and spread his knees wide.

"Ready for bed?"

"Yes." She purred out while watching his eyes, then bit her lip.

"No. Sleep." He smiled, then continued. "Give it a couple more weeks. I want to do it right. You deserve a lot more than I gave you last time and without pain."

He gently reached his right hand across her body to her left side, placed it on her ribs through his black T-shirt she still wore and with the lightest touch, ran all five fingers down her ribs, making her suck in a deep breath.

"See?...... I need something to hold onto." He spoke in a low soft tone with lowered eyebrows and sultry eyes.

She rolled her eyes and sighed, "Okay."

She didn't need to ask if he could last that long, cause according to Jen, he could last a lot longer than she could, but that was before they knew each other also.

He picked her up gently, let her feet touch the floor and helped her limp to the bedroom. He tucked her in on the left side of the bed, so that her better left side would be the side he slept on so he couldn't accidently hurt her. He preferred the right side of the bed anyways as it was closest to the door for calls.

After he had her all tucked in, he walked to the other side, climbed in under his soft firefighter comforter and bedsheet, and laid on his side facing her. He softly touched her good shoulder and ran a finger over her bruised collarbone on her left side and up her neck to the dark purple bruises on her cheek to the corner of her eye. He let out a drawn-out breath.

"I love you, Daph."

She turned her head because she couldn't move from her back position. She smiled and puckered her lips. He leaned over her, tangled a hand in her hair and gave her a long kiss, then released.

"Sweet dreams." He said before moving back to his pillow, leaving his hand tangled in her hair and holding her left hand with his left.

She drifted to sleep as he played with her hair.

CHAPTER ELEVEN

O ver the next couple of weeks, Daphne was able to walk and talk fully again and Luke was loving every minute. He also loved having her closer, sleeping next to her every night.

They became like a family. Kada always had supervision, not that she needed it and someone she could talk to that understood her better than he could. They made dinner more often and ate at the new small dinner table Luke bought and tucked in the corner of the living room by the mudroom. Luke looked forward to coming home to Daphne after every call and workday, especially the bad days. Over time she got used to random alarms and pager tones throughout the 24 hours in the day and even got used to the kisses before he left and after he came home.

Though Luke hardly ever saw Daphne out of the Chaise or bed very often, He noticed laundry and dishes were kept up more often than not and never needed to ask if it was Kada or Daphne. He knew she stewed, hated it and tried to keep busy. She taught Kada more recipes and how to cook them, how to pretreat different stains in the laundry, and even sow and patch up clothes. Luke didn't know what hurt worse, the fact that he couldn't teach her himself or knowing that she never got the chance to learn from her mother. But he smiled that at least she had the chance to learn.

Luke tried not to push his luck on doing everything he could for Daphne and found his own ways to fight himself against trying to cut her steak for her or apply makeup on her worst days. Not that he knew how but there was no doubt he would watch every YouTube makeup tutorial known just to make her feel better for a day. He hated watching her lose herself slowly over the passing days that turned into weeks.

When Doc Clint at Birch Valley gave her good healing reports, Daphne went home with Luke and Kada with a smile bigger than Luke's.

They pulled into the driveway and walked into the house. Kada went to her room to do homework while Luke put his keys and pager on the entryway table and watched Daphne walk to the Chaise, curl up in it and look out the window.

Luke crossed his arms over his chest and leaned back on the front door. The bruises were nearly gone, the scars mostly faded, and her smile got brighter everyday it got closer to removing the cast. She hated it, and even now that she could walk and talk, Doc still wouldn't give her the green light to return to work just yet. Being a middle school nurse required more range of motion than just her right-hand fingers. Even her wrist stayed nearly attached to her waist.

She chomped at the bit a little more often than not. Even if she tried to hide it, Luke knew. When he went on quick errands to the store or station, he usually left with the sole purpose of giving her time to go for a walk or go to her house. He never stayed away longer than an hour unless it was a call. Which usually gave him enough time to catch up with Mike and the crew or put some time in at the station and do needed errands. Daphne never told him she would leave, so he never said anything about finding her shoe prints out the back mudroom door, down the hill to her bench beside the creek.

Luke never worried or had to remind her of what she could or couldn't do with her shoulder in a cast, and he was proud of her for never testing the limits. She was smart and always conscious of her injuries, never pushing it. Unlike any other human he knew, especially himself, that would likely get mad from restraint and push the capabilities of an injury, making it worse. But he was thankful she never did.

When Luke moved from the door, Daphne looked at him. He walked to the chaise and sat down beside her.

"How you doing?"

She gave a fake smile, "Good."

"Wanna go for a walk with me?"

"Sure."

After Luke helped her into a coat and boots, they walked out of his mudroom and instead of taking a right to Daphne's house, they turned left to go deeper into the woods.

He held her left good hand and followed a path that was starting to overgrow with new branches from the unused years. They swerved and wandered deeper into the woods. Luke kept a slower pace for her but led the way without talking.

"Luke, where are we going?" She spoke but got no reply.

She looked around but saw nothing except trees and bushes. The further they got; the more snow was on the ground with small handfuls on a few branches left over from where the sunlight hadn't hit yet.

Soon she heard the trickling sound of the creek again and soon walked into a small opening a couple feet from the creek surrounded by big solid birch, cottonwoods and evergreen spruce trees that shaded the area right to the edge of the creek.

With a quick jerk of her left hand that he held, he turned around and sent her stumbling forward as he caught her hips and filled his hands while watching her.

"Luke!" She shouted with a scowling look. He held her close, forcing her to look up to see his seductive, but stern expression.

"What do you want, Daphne?" He spoke with a low growl.

Close enough to feel his hot breath on her cheek, she felt him thumbing her hip bones, as his big chest expanded with every deep breath he took.

"I don't know." She now spoke in a low tone with somber eyes as they stared into each other.

"Not good enough. What do you want?" He asked again.

She took a deep breath, "To not live in fear."

"And what do you fear?"

Even as he asked the question, he thought he knew the answers. But he was wrong.

"The future."

Bringing his eyebrows down, he asked.

"What's wrong with the future?"

"The uncertainty. Not having or able to plan."

He pawed at her hips, while keeping his hips touching hers.

"What's so bad about the unknown?"

"Luke, I've been running for almost three years, and I will have to do it again, but for the first time in those three years, I don't want to."

"Then don't." He spoke with force before he moved his right hand to her jawline and neck and pulled her in for a kiss, careful not to bump her cast.

Heat poured off him in waves as her heartbeat raced under his hand. He deepened the kiss by tilting his head to the right and taking her full mouth. She opened her lips and his tongue dipped in, as he tasted her. His fingers tightened on her neck and hip, holding her in place. She felt the familiar bulge in his jeans that pressed against her. She moved her left hand up to his ribs and dug her fingers in as they shared each other's taste.

When he finally released her lips, he didn't let her go but looked into her eyes, as his darkened with emotion. He paused a moment before rubbing a thumb across her cheek.

"You need to go home." A statement not a question.

She squinted her eyes in confusion, looking into his, for answers.

"I'll lose you completely if I don't let you go now." He spoke with a softened harshness.

"Luke?"

He continued to rub his thumb on her cheek, but still held her close.

"Kada and I will still be next door if you need anything. I'm not going anywhere, I promise. But we are going tomorrow to see Dawson and get you a gun."

She smiled, then it fell flat. "I don't know how to shoot."

Still with a low tone he said. "I'll teach you. We'll buy you something you can handle, and we'll go to the range. I'll teach you how to use it, so, both of us are comfortable enough knowing you can protect yourself."

Now she smiled. "Thank you."

He smiled, "You're welcome, but no more running. Stay. With me."

She stood upon her tiptoes and kissed him. He sank into it. Before she knew what was happening, her back side pushed against a wide birch tree, and her left shoulder laid against it. He devoured her mouth, taking anything, she gave. He moved his left hand back down to her hip and slid both hands down her thighs until his fingers caught the backside of her knees. He lifted them until her long, sexy legs in tight jeans wrapped around his waist and his erection pressed hard into her.

His mouth moved from hers to her jaw and up to her ear lobe. She moaned. He nosed under her bouncy curled brown hair that smelled like a bouquet of flowers and kissed the sensitive spot on her neck, just behind her ear at the base of her skull that had her moaning louder and longer.

"Luke! Oh My god!" She moaned out.

He sucked at the sensitive spot as heat poured off of them both. He then pinned her to the tree with his hips and got his left arm under her for better leverage. He kept sucking as his right hand moved down to her belly and under the big coat to undo the button on her jeans, and slide the zipper down enough to slide his hand in.

"Lucas!"

Every time she said his name, he ached. He nosed her coat collar away as he kissed over her left shoulder and down to the collar of his T-shirt she wore over the cast. His fingers against the tight jeans, moved her thin panties to the side and found her clitoris and ran his thumb over it, making her gasp and push her chest into his face and arch her back.

He stopped kissing her and found her with two fingers and watched her face when he pressed them into her. She let out a near silent scream that had him taking her mouth again as he thumbed her clitoris and sinking his fingers deep inside her.

His erection strained the fabric of his jeans. With each movement of his thumb, she moaned against his mouth and took everything he gave, till they found a rhythm.

She moaned louder with each stroke. He released her mouth again to watch her face as she got closer to the edge.

"Yeah, that's it Daph."

She threw her left arm over his shoulder and pulled him closer. Her breast stretching the fabric of his soft cotton T-shirt, he put his mouth over her breast and found that she wasn't wearing a bra. So, he sucked on her nipple through the soft, thin fabric as she screamed his name. "Luke!"

When she climaxed, he looked up to watch her face as she gave one loud moan and her entire body clenched tight around his fingers as he felt the ribbons of warm silk slide over them. Her body pulsating with aftershocks as her thighs squeezed his waist. Her left arm wrapped tighter around his neck to steady herself.

When she finally went lax, he slid his fingers out and let her feet drop back to the ground as he slid his wet fingers in his mouth and sucked them clean as she watched him.

"Mm, so sweet."

He then helped her zip up her pants and button them. Then he readjusted the shirt and zipped the coat back up. He rubbed a finger across the hickey he left intentionally, again, marking what was his and smiled.

"Oh, God, Luke."

"See, told you, I needed something to hang on to."

She tried for a smile but instead swallowed her ruffled nerves.

"You weren't lying."

He placed a hand on the tree on either side of her head and gave her lips a soft quick peck. She held tight around his waist with her left arm and leaned against the tree because her legs were shaking and weak.

His eyes were still smoldering and leaning down close enough to feel his longer drawn-out breaths. He didn't smile as she clung to him for support. When her breathing slowed, he spoke while staring at her.

"Don't run, Daph. Go home if you have to but Kada needs you as much as I do."

Before he could continue, she cut him off.

"How...." she looked at him in confusion before cutting herself off.

Still not smiling, he frowned. "I saw it in the hospital. I know it's only getting worse staying with me."

She nodded now in complete understanding of how he worked, as the irritation began to stir. "Of course, you would use Kada and sex as your weapons of choice."

The corner of his mouth tipped up as he shrugged a shoulder.

Oh, that smile almost made her lose her knees, as anger and lust swirled through her veins, so she grabbed a fist full of his shirt and he dropped his right hand to grab a handful of her luscious cheek to hold her up.

"They are what work best for this battle."

She shook her head gently.

"But she's also my weakest point. She could get hurt, Luke."

His temper sparked without warning and his fist hit the tree trunk next to them with a loud crack sound. Out of reaction, she flinched and her whole body jerked away from him.

His eyes widened in shock and worry.

"Shit! I'm sorry, Daphne. I didn't mean to scare you. Daphne? Daph, I'm sorry. I don't like how he has so much control over you......." His voice got louder as he continued till it became a shout. "...... He won't get close enough to Kada and I'll make sure of that, but you can't keep running!"

Still facing away from him with a shaky voice, she replied, "It's all I know. You don't know him and what he's capable of. I'm sorry, Luke."

He lowered his voice to a soft tone, "Daphne? Look at me, please." He didn't dare touch or reach for her, he knew better, so he stuck his hands in his coat pockets.

She wouldn't show him her tears and fear.

"I'm heading back home; I'll see you tomorrow."

She walked down the path back home as the bits of snow crunched under her boots, her left arm wrapped around her ribs over her right arm in the cast. She walked with her head down watching her feet as tears dropped from her cheeks.

He growled out his frustration and gave a 1, 2, punch to the tree trunk again, now making his knuckles bruise. Now he was pissed, at himself and at her ex, as he watched her walking away. He had to do something. He had to make a call...or two.

When she got back to Luke's, she walked in the back door, through the mudroom and inside. Kada stood at the kitchen bar drinking a cup of water when she saw Daphne coming in with tears streaming down her face.

"Daphne? What's wrong? What happened? Where's Dad?" Kada began to panic.

Daphne said nothing and walked to Luke's room to grab a big tote bag and start filling it with clothes and anything that was hers that she could find.

Kada came in and wrapped her arms around Daphne and Daphne shattered. At nearly the same height, Kada rested her head on Daphne's shoulder and Daphne wrapped her arm around Kada.

"I love you, Kada."

"Oh, Daphne, I love you too."

The familiar thud of the back door had them both turning to see Luke coming in as he watched both of them with his hands in his pockets, stiff spine and facial expressions that spoke volumes of pain, anger, worry, and sadness as he took a seat at the bar to watch them through the open bedroom door and prop his head on his hands on the bar.

Daphne gave Kada a good squeeze and kissed her forehead.

"I'm going back home."

"I'm going with you."

Daphne immediately shook her head, "No. You need to stay with your dad."

"No! I'm going with you." Kada nearly shouted.

Luke just watched them with a hand on his chin while his elbow rested on the counter. Daphne looked at him and he didn't protest his daughter's demand.

"Go, get your stuff. I'll meet you over there."

Kada ran out and around to the stairs that lead to her bedroom and up. Daphne walked out of the bedroom and over to Luke still on the stool. He turned and rested his elbows on his knees and folded his hands together with a tight jaw.

"I'm sorry, Daphne. I love you."

With her tote over her left shoulder and keys in her hand, she lowered her head and gave him a kiss.

He placed a hand on her cheek and softly rubbed it. She pulled back with a smile.

"I know."

When she didn't reciprocate it, he broke more.

She placed the hand with her keys over his and leaned into it, for a second before turning, walking out the back door and heading for her house.

When Kada came running down the stairs with a backpack, she stopped in front of her dad.

He faked a smile even if he knew she saw through it.

"I love you, Daddy."

Now his smile turned real as he stood up and gave his daughter a hug.

"I love you too. Call me if anything happens or you guys need anything, okay?"

He now tilted her chin up with the edge of his fist when she didn't respond quick enough. "You hear me?"

She noticed the darkening bruises on his hands but didn't question it and rolled her eyes, not really understanding anything that was happening.

"Yes, Dad."

She gave him a peck on the cheek and one last hug before running after Daphne. When the door shut, Luke walked over to the window and put a knee on the chaise to watch Kada reach Daphne's back door as Daphne walked inside. Luke sighed and shut the curtains, making the house darker, then pulled his phone out of his pocket and hit speed dial number 3.

When Daphne stepped foot into the house. She took a deep breath in, enjoying the moment of return before Kada pushed through the door beside her and put her backpack on the couch, saying, "Should we watch Gilmore Girls?"

Daphne smiled and shut the door.

"Sure, I'll make the popcorn."

She looked around to remember then flinched at the memories.

The house was back together except the bathroom which was still broken but the shattered tiles and debris were now cleaned up. Daphne opened her bedroom door to put her bag in there and it felt cold and empty. She frowned and threw her bag onto the bed and took her coat off.

Luke's black T-shirt covered her down to her hips. She grabbed the collar and pulled it up to her nose and breathed in his scent. Her heart shattered as tears fell from her face, soaking the T-shirt, as she gasped for air.

"He's next door." Kada spoke from behind her.

She turned around and pulled Kada into a tight hug with her one good arm.

"I know."

"Daphne, what's wrong? Dad won't talk to me."

Daphne took a breath, wiped at her tears, and sat on the edge of the bed with Kada.

"It's complicated, but my past followed me here."

"That wasn't just a car accident like Dad said it was, was it?"

Daphne wiped at more tears as she shook her head.

"No."

Kada gave a frown.

"Kada, I may have to leave for a bit to keep you and your dad safe."

A now shocked Kada stepped back in a huff and raised her voice to a shout.

"No, you don't! Dad can protect you! I already lost one Mom! Dad loves you, like a lot! We're a family!"

The tears started to roll down her face. Daphne held a hand over her heart then reached out for Kada's hand. Kada gave in and gave her, her hand to hold.

"You have to trust me, Kada. I don't want to leave you or your dad. I love you both so much and when it's safe, I will come back, I promise. But I have to keep you guys safe."

She nodded through the tears and threw her arms around Daphne's neck, not caring about the cast. Making Daphne wince but was happy for the full-hearted hug as they held each other for a long minute.

"Now, let's go watch some Gilmore Girls and forget about this."

Luke took a cold shower and cranked the rock music after the phone call. It didn't settle him like he had hoped it would. So, Luke took some energy out on cleaning. Then he took the soft white blanket off the chaise and put it on his bed where she slept. He laid in bed, but tossed and turned, trying to fall asleep. He grabbed his phone off the nightstand and pulled up her texts. He started to text then saw her text bubble pop up, then turn off.

He took a deep breath then deleted the message and set the phone aside. His phone chimed a few seconds later. He pulled up her message and saw a picture of Kada asleep in Daphne's good arm in bed with her and a *"Goodnight, Luke"* text message.

He smiled, and replied, *"Sweet dreams, Daphne."*

He plugged in his phone and looked at her picture again to save it to his phone and put it on the nightstand. Then rolled over finally drifting off to sleep.

Daphne woke in the morning with her arm still holding a sleeping Kada close to her side. Daylight brightened the room as Daphne smiled and yawned. Coffee, she would need a pot of it to wake up. She slipped her arm out from under Kada and slid out of bed in short black shorts and Luke's black T-shirt then she went in search of coffee.

When she opened the bedroom door, Luke stood at her kitchen island holding two to-go coffee cups dressed in nice jeans, a dark gray button up dress shirt, and a black leather coat. He looked different and not just because of today's style choice.

He stretched out a cup and as she walked over to take it, she noticed his now dark bruised knuckles.

"A peace offering. Add in my sleepless night and your fridge of rotten milk and creamer, I figured this was a better way for us to start the day."

She cringed at the thought of her fridge.

"Shit, I forgot to go grocery shopping."

He chuckled, "It's okay, we can go later."

She rolled her eyes and took the first sip of coffee and let it seep into her bones.

"Mm." She closed her eyes.

He watched her over the rim of the cup as he drank his.

As her brain started to work properly, she noticed Luke was distant. Friendly, but colder. He didn't say he loved her. Didn't give her a kiss or even touch her. He was different and it bothered her, but she wouldn't say anything. She already missed his touch, even a simple kiss but maybe this was better, easier for both of them. She had to hurt him to keep him safe, so it was her own fault.

Luke's hands ached with the need to touch her, to hold her, tell her how sorry he was and how everything would be okay. But if she wanted, needed space to stay, he'd give it to her to keep her here. He would keep her here, somehow. He'd make sure of it. He had a few ideas, but if those didn't work, he'd figure something out. But she wouldn't leave without a fight, and he was prepared and as of last night and this morning, so were a few others. Space and time, that was all she would get from him.

"How'd you sleep?" He asked.

She scrunched up her nose and tilted her head side to side in between sips of coffee.

"Kada still asleep?" He asked.

"Yeah. I talked to her last night."

To hide his nerves, he took a big gulp of his coffee, then asked. "What did you tell her?"

She raised her eyebrows while swallowing a sip.

"More than you. Luke, she's twelve, not five. You have to give her more."

She sighed and looked at his golden-brown eyes, that gave her more of a reply than his mouth.

She continued when he didn't, "I didn't give her details, but more of an understanding. She's upset and spent all her breath trying to keep us three together. She puts all her faith in you. You're the hero in her life and she knows it. She also said that she's lost one mom already."

Nothing Daphne told him surprised him, but it was a side of Kada he didn't see or talk about much. Making him love his daughter more hearing it from Daphne, but it pained him to hear Kada mention losing one mom. He knew what she implied, but unfortunately couldn't confirm it for Kada. The only thing he could confirm is that she was definitely his daughter which made him smile with pride.

Kada fought for him and just as much as she fought for herself. Richmond blood. When they knew what they wanted, they went after it, Fighting anything or anyone in their path. An admirable trait, especially for a 12-year-old girl, in Luke's mind.

Daphne confirmed his thoughts like she read them. "She is definitely your daughter, Luke. She is you. Just in female form, 20 years younger and with a voice."

Luke chuckled, then sighed as he drank his coffee. Voice? Did she not think he had one? He had plenty to say if that is what she wanted but he didn't think it would change anything. He saw more than she realized and spoke when he needed to but let her make the final decision on what she saw and heard from him. A lesson he had to learn the hard way with Daphne.

He smiled at her as the bedroom door opened and out came Kada with narrow fierce eyes. It didn't take Luke or Daphne long to realize she had been awake for a bit and probably listening. Kada walked over to her dad, who put an arm around her and gave her a kiss on her forehead.

"Hi, Sweetheart. Sleep, okay?"

She scowled at Daphne. "Crappy, knowing she is breaking up our family."

Luke gave a sharp warning, "Kada Jasmine!"

"What, Dad? It's true."

Daphne sucked in a breath and gave a frown.

"She doesn't want to leave, but still is. It's not fair, Dad. We already lost mom and now Daphne...."

"Kada. Enough." Luke cut her off with a low sharp tone.

"No, Luke. It's okay. Let her get it out."

Luke took a deep breath and gave Daphne a look then Kada.

Kada turned her sights on Daphne, as Daphne set her cup on the counter and folded her hands in front of her.

"You love us, I know you do, so why are you leaving?"

"Kada, it's complicated. I love you..." She looked up to Luke then back to Kada, "...both, very much. That is why I am leaving. I have to keep..."

Kada cut her off and started to raise her voice before Luke gave her a soft light swat on the butt as a warning.

"Safe? No! You're running because you're scared of actually having us. You love Dad! You have our name on a necklace and you two are always kissing. You guys have that kind of love soulmates share. I know you guys do; I've seen it! And me, you love me. Why are you taking that away from us?"

Daphne watched her heart bleed through her words, and it was painful but even more so to look up at Luke and see the same words come from his eyes from behind Kada. As Kada started to break and hurt, the more anger she showed. Something she'd seen in Luke a couple of times and knew it was pure reaction.

"Life was good before you came, we were fine! Then Dad fell for you, and we became a family and then you two took a walk, you came back upset with a hickey and now Dad's hands are bruised. Let me guess Dad got too close and you panicked? Now Dad is just gonna let you run away cause he is just as scared." She hissed out.

Luke stood up quickly and stepped in between the two facing Kada, while holding up both arms with a hand still holding his coffee.

"Ok, that's enough Kada! Say your peace but don't talk about things you don't understand."

Kada looked up at her dad and broke as the tears rolled down her face. Then the sobbing started as she ran out the back door and ran for her house barefoot. Daphne got up and walked to her kitchen window to watch her running across the soggy grass until she reached Luke's back door and inside, then sighed loudly.

She didn't even hear Luke but felt him place his hands on her hips as he watched out the window over Daphne's head.

"*That's* why I don't tell her a lot. She'll be okay. Give her time. But I would like to know where my daughter is picking up this knowledge of hickeys and what else she knows...hmm maybe not."

Daphne turned in his hands and gave him a slight smile, "You do realize, Kada is a little over a year away from high School, right?"

"Shit! Well thankfully she has you and I. Plus me and Mike know everyone in this town." Luke said with another smile, dropping his hands before turning to walk back to the kitchen island and take a seat on the stool.

Daphne turned around, leaned against the counter bracing herself with her arm.

"I'm not her mom, Luke. I don't know how to be a mom. I tried and failed with my own and even my body told me no."

Luke turned on the stool to face her over the kitchen island, his eyes with some heat. He braced his elbows on the counter and his chin on his thumb before looking her in the eyes, His anger stirred as he tried to hold it back. "You never failed, not once. *He* failed you several times and your body told you to wait." He growled out with some anger before continuing with a softer voice. "That's not failing, that's healing. Don't confuse the two, Daph. You will always have Kada, no matter what happens between us, because that is what she wants and someday..." The words came out before he could stop them, "... you will have your own, I promise."

She went speechless and just smiled at him. He smiled back. He didn't know why he made that promise or how he would keep it but he'd figure it out even if it wasn't with him. He'd have to, for her. He took a deep breath and it started to sink in before His phone chimed, snapping him back to reality. He pulled it from his leather coat pocket, checked the message and texted back. He put his phone back in his pocket and stood up.

"Almost time to go. You need to change into some...real clothes." He choked out the words as he took in Daphne's sleep wear from head to toes, taking his time again.

Still sad a little, she tried to smile as she walked to her bedroom and opened a dresser drawer to pull out clothes till, she heard the bedroom door close. She turned around in a jerk as Luke threw up his hands.

"I'm just here to help, that's it."

Frowning, she turned her back to him and lifted the baggy black T-shirt with her one good arm, up and over her head and over the cast to let it fall to the floor almost seamlessly in one fluid movement.

She's getting good at that. Luke thought to himself.

The new scars were starting to fade to her natural pink and peach skin tones. His hands remembered what it was like to touch her skin and begin to itch with renewed need. He flexed his hands in his pockets out of sight, as she picked up the clean shirt and slid it on just as effortlessly as she took the old one off with her one good arm.

Taking off the shorts and panties were no different as she chose a pair of black yoga pants that tied in the front to which he helped with. The waist band covered her cesarean scar, so he rubbed a knuckle against the small old scars, up to her casted arm, up the neck, to the hickey that he left yesterday.

"See, healing." He smiled.

She noticed him getting closer again then he took a step back and put his hands back in his pockets. She thought he was adorable when he tried to turn icy but couldn't. He stood there at her door with his hands still in his pockets, stiffer than a security guard, but unable to leave in case he was needed. His instincts battled his thoughts, and she watched the war rage within him.

After she grabbed a light coat for the sunny day and her purse, they walked out. Mike stood on her porch, leaning against the railing with his hands in his pockets and a pistol holstered to his thigh over his dark blue jeans.

"Hey, Daphne. Ready to do some target practice?"

She wouldn't cower now. She would take charge of her life. This was how.

"Yes." She smiled.

She looked up and noticed Luke's truck beside her car, then Mike waved towards Luke's house. Mike's truck was parked in his driveway and Jen in the driver's seat, smiling at them through the open passenger window.

"Have fun! See you in a bit." Jen yelled across the yard and Luke threw up a hand in a single wave.

Luke and Mike walked down the couple of porch steps in front of her. Luke jumped in the driver's seat and shut the door. Mike walked around to the front passenger door and opened it for her, while lending a hand to help her get in.

"Thank you." As she watched Luke texting on his phone, as she slid into the front seat. Mike shut the door and got in the back seat.

Daphne watched Luke text a message with one hand and caught a glimpse of his pistol on his hip that was hidden under his jacket. Never did she know it was there until now. It kind of scared her how secretive and stealthy he could be. She never knew what he was gonna do next, or anything about him other than he saved her but yet something told her, she could trust him. Daphne then heard the sound of a paper bag as Mike spoke from behind her.

"Hey, Luke told me to bring the food, so I hope you're hungry."

She smelled the food before Mike slid two sandwiches wrapped in foil wrappers with two small paper bags of hash brown nuggets onto the console. The steam and smell wafted out of the bag. She was so happy to get something to eat since Luke didn't give her a chance before they left.

"I hope you like egg and sausage croissant sandwiches?"

Daphne grabbed up one sandwich and opened the wrapper.

"They really are amazing." Luke spoke from next to her.

"Yeah, cause he doesn't know any better, Daphne. Don't let him fool you." Mike chuckled.

Daphne took a bite with her stomach growling. It was soft and buttery and full of flavor down to the garlic and herb seasoned egg. It was a delicious sandwich. Luke nodded with wide eyes and a smile around his own mouthful, then his phone chimed. He finished his bite before looking at the message.

"Gotta go." He put the truck in reverse and backed out of her driveway.

By the time they pulled into the police station, Officer Dawson was locking the front door, dressed in his full uniform with his vest like last time she saw him. He walked over after he was done and leaned on the hood of the truck with an elbow.

"Hey guys. Hey Daphne." He spoke as the three of them left the truck and got out. Luke came around behind Dawson and Mike stood next to her as Dawson spoke to her.

"So, Luke says you want to protect yourself and learn how to shoot?"

Daphne smiled and nodded her head. Mike gave her a careful and gentle pat on her casted shoulder. Dawson gave a strong nod and smiled bigger.

"It's a smart move, Daphne. Because even with the entire state of men armed and guarding your house, the best protection is yourself and the ability to handle any situation."

"I hope so." She spoke.

"You'll do fine. I remember when I taught Mike's wife, Jen. Now she's running what....85% accuracy."

Mike scoffed at that. "Yeah, she wishes."

"Hey Luke, do you remember who won the last shoot out?" Dawson poked.

Luke just laughed, "I'm pretty sure that was Jen, Dawson."

Mike jerked back in a joking surprise.

"She got the head start!" He said with a little force and then chuckled.

All three men now laughed. Daphne enjoyed watching the men joking and laughing, especially Luke. When Luke looked at her, she gave him a smile, he gave a half smile with saddened eyes back.

Luke and Mike nearly matched heights, but Dawson, nearing his 50's, stood a few inches shorter than them. He also kept a beard, neatly shaved short, versus the other two who kept clean shaven, unless they had a few days off to let some stubble grow. Which Daphne always preferred on Luke; he was sexy with his stubble which made her scared to see him in full turnout gear. She hadn't seen him yet since the first accident but knew what she imagined probably wasn't even close to what he would actually look like. Her skin sparked with energy with her imagination. She knew the gear and uniform could only amplify what she already saw and loved about Luke. Everything she saw of him beneath the uniform and gear was already appealing and nothing could change that.

When Dawson spoke, Daphne had realized she had dazed off staring at Luke, lost in her thoughts.

"Okay, so let's get you armed."

He turned and led the way to the backside of the station. Mike stepped around Daphne to follow him with a kind of excitement in his step.

When Daphne looked back at Luke, he had a wide smile he tried to hide, while staring at Daphne. As she turned to follow Mike a few steps behind, Luke from a step behind her asked in nearly a whisper, out of earshot of Dawson and Mike,

"What were you thinking about?"

Still following the others, she jerked her head to Luke who still had a small smile, while his hands stayed in his pockets. Not wanting to say anything, she asked, "Why?"

"Cause, I've seen that look before..." He paused and the corner of his mouth raised, "right around the time you got that bruise on your neck."

She nearly stopped dead in her tracks with shock. She didn't think she had *that* face. Her eyes wide while looking at Luke. He put a hand to her lower back and pushed her forward with him to keep her walking.

"No, don't stop. Dawson and Mike will start to ask too many questions."

When she returned to full speed, he put his hand back in his pocket.

"I need you clear headed, Daph. You need to know how to protect yourself in case..." He paused again and took a deep breath. "...In case I'm not around."

She gave him a scowl not understanding her instant anger.

"I'll be fine, Luke." Then charged ahead to catch up with Mike and Dawson, who reached the storefront on the backside of the police station.

When Dawson unlocked the barred door and opened it for everyone to enter. She stepped in at the small store that held a variety of rifles and shotguns on shelves behind a glass counter that held the pistols and knives with a few other weapons. It had outdoor gear on racks around the store and a little bit of everything you would need for survival in the Alaskan woods.

Luke came in behind her and walked to the glass counter with Mike. Dawson let the door shut on its own and followed the guys and walked around to the other side of the counter. Mike and Luke looked at the pistols like a kid in the candy store.

Daphne just smiled and stepped up next to Luke to look at them. Dawson pulled out a few with safety locks on them as Daphne felt them in her one good hand and asked questions that all three of the men would answer.

After nearly an hour, Daphne liked the Springfield 40 in her hand and with tips, tricks and info from the guys, she felt confident that recoil wouldn't be too much for her weaker left arm, but still powerful enough for self-defense.

Dawson nodded his head in agreement.

"Good choice. It suits you. I just need to see an ID and I'll get the paperwork started. Daphne dug in her purse and pulled out a North Carolina driver's license with her name and photo, as she gave it to Dawson. Both Luke and Dawson glanced at each other quickly while Luke worked his jaw. Dawson frowned seeing the ID. Before Luke had time to ponder her ID, his arm next to her held out his credit card to Dawson.

Daphne gave Luke a scowl as Dawson took both the cards.

"Luke, No. I got it."

Dawson froze in place holding the cards. Luke looked at Dawson sternly.

"Dawson, run the card, please."

Dawson slank away while tightly holding his lips closed and shared a look with Mike who also backed away to wander the store and head for the fishing gear section. Daphne huffed out a breath and threw up a hand.

"Why did you do that, it's my gun, I can pay for it."

"Cause I have money and you need a pistol."

"Luke, you have Kada to take care of ..."

He cut her off.

"She's fine and has everything she needs. I'm not touching her college fund and paying for this won't break me. So don't worry about it."

Deliberately changing the subject Luke asked.

"You do like it at least?"

Daphne now smiled. "For now, we'll see how well I can handle it with this damn cast on."

Luke smiled and his eyes brightened.

"I'm right here." He reminded her and his resistance broke. So, he leaned down and gave her a slow hot kiss and she took it. Dawson deliberately tapped the computer keys a little harder, making more noise. She used her good hand to brace herself on the glass counter as Luke pulled his hands back out of his pockets to frame her face and tilted his head to deepen the kiss. When he pulled back, he watched her eyes open.

"Keep your head clear." He spoke softly but with a serious tone.

That, was his worry? That's why he's been so cold? Or was there more?

"I will. Thank you, Luke."

He searched her eyes and gave her one more soft kiss but kept it shorter.

When he pulled away, he looked at Dawson who was still typing on the computer on the far end of the counter and acted like he didn't see anything. Still watching the computer, he quickly glanced in their direction, he spoke.

"This may take a sec, go find her a holster."

Luke took her over to the holsters and found one that would work with her purse and after paperwork went through and Luke signed it and the receipt as Dawson kept his head down.

On the way out of town to the shooting range, Luke held her hand over the center console between them. His thumb rubbing her gently. Mike just smiled from the back seat and texted his wife.

A few miles out of town, Luke turned right down a dirt road and followed it a mile back to a locked gate and he just pulled off the side and waited. Daphne looked at Luke and Mike confused until Dawson pulled up behind them in his patrol truck, got out and unlocked the gate and opened it.

Another mile down the dirt road that got bumpy in places shaking Daphne around, making Luke smile as he slowed for the potholes and bumps, they pulled into a parking lot with three big sections. A long range, a short range, and a tactical range. Daphne's eyes lit up as Luke parked into a spot closer to the short range, then got bigger as Mike's truck pulled next to them as Jen drove up with a smile. Daphne gave a small scream as she opened the door and Jen did the same. Now armed with a pistol on her side too and gave each other a hug.

"Oh my gosh. You're practicing too?" Daphne asked Jen while Jen took off her coat and tossed it in Mike's truck.

"Of course, can't let the guys have all the fun!"

Mike got out and Jen gave up the truck keys to Mike with a big smile and gave him a soft kiss and a small chuckle. "Ready to get beat again?"

Mike rolled his eyes, "I'll be the only one doing some whooping around here, woman." As he gave his wife a soft swat on her ass.

As Luke came around to greet them. Jen asked Daphne. "So, what did you get? Can I see?"

Getting excited, Daphne opened the truck door again, got her purse and got her new pistol out to hand it to Jen barrel down. Jen, more comfortable with it, took it, unloaded it, cocked it, and with both arms, aimed it down the range.

"Hell yeah! That's nice. It fits you. I hope you enjoyed spending Luke's money. He needed to let the spiders and moths out of his wallet."

She laughed as Mike put an arm over her shoulder and pulled her into his side.

Luke stood behind Daphne now and put his arms around her waist and pulled her back against his chest and kissed her temple.

Mike and Luke shared a smile.

"Happy for you man. Luke's a good guy, Daphne. I haven't seen him happy like this in a long time and Kada just loves you to death...." Mike said.

Jen cut him off. "Yes! She tells me how fun you are and how you nursed her ankle. You are a blessing to both of them."

Daphne smiled with her heart. "Aww, thank you. They are amazing and so are you guys and this town."

Daphne didn't know what Luke had told them about their current relationship or why they were really there, so Daphne didn't say anything, but tilted her head back to stare up at Luke as he gave her a smile and kiss.

So, Luke didn't say anything about them. So, were his kisses real or a show?

Dawson pulled up and walked over to them. "Aww. You all look so cute, but did we come here to love on each other or are we teaching this girl how to shoot?" The group gave a unified laugh.

Jen handed Daphne back the pistol and they all walked over to the benches. They all gave Daphne points and safety tips and showed her how to load and unload and how to be safe. When she put on her safety goggles and earmuffs, they all watched her load it, cock it, and aim with her one good arm and very little help from Luke.

Luke stepped on her left side, braced her right heel with the instep of his right foot. Put an arm across the back of her shoulders for extra support and braced her left arm for recoil support.

"Go ahead. Aim for the center." The whole group watched in anticipation. Daphne flipped the safety switch and BANG! When she opened her eyes, they all stared at the target.

Top right outer edge was hit.

Jen cheered as Luke said, "Good Job. I'd say that would be a shoulder shot. Next time keep both eyes open."

Daphne smiled and was proud.

"Go ahead. You have 16 rounds. Hit the target."

Bang! Bang! A couple more shots fired. Her holes got closer to the center.

When she emptied the mag. She put the gun down on the bench and took her glasses off and saw the numerous holes around the center then blinked to get a better look. Three small holes in the center red circle.

She got excited as she jumped up and down giving Luke a one arm hug and kiss.

Dawson from behind Luke, spoke. "Not bad at all for your first time and one handed! Great job, Daphne!"

Mike and Jen walked over from shooting their own targets and looked at Daphne's target.

"Damn, girl! Yeah, that will deter a bear." Jen applauded Daphne's effort.

Is that what Luke and Mike told her? That she was protecting herself from wildlife?

Mike gave her a nod, "Good job!"

Luke looked at Daphne with a proud smile. "You ready for some more?"

"Yeah, let's do it." As she put her glasses back on as Luke reloaded the mag for her.

Daphne spent two hours unloading a couple cases of bullets through her new pistol as Luke now watched on with pride and did some practice of his own.

Daphne's accuracy improved greatly, but her precision needed some work. Still Luke didn't say anything, knowing she was only shooting with one very weak arm and left-handed, but he had the confidence that he needed. She could now handle herself and was comfortable with her new pistol.

After packing everything away safely, they all said their goodbyes and made plans for a big family picnic the weekend after she would get her cast removed and Luke and Daphne headed off on their own.

Luke held her hand again over the console as they rode the rough road back to the main road into town and kissed her knuckles as they turned onto the main road.

They drove through town without a word and took a left onto their street, driving though the small neighborhood sparse with houses.

Luke turned the last corner. Daphne watched him as he focused on the road and pulled into Daphne's driveway. He put the truck into park and turned it off as he sighed and looked at Daphne.

"What are we doing Luke?"

The question surprised him a bit, but he didn't falter in an answer.

"I don't know but I will never stop loving you no matter what you decide."

"But, why me?" She asked in confusion.

Again, without a pause he answered, "Because you are the only one that reminded me and Kada what it was like to have a mom and wife without the ring and birth certificate and all without even trying."

He paused and continued when she didn't say anything.

"You are not Jasmine. But you are Daphne and so much more than a past. You are strong and brave, a fighter and the most caring nurse of an entire middle school but you are also scared and stubborn and trying to do everything on your own."

Her eyes widened as a single tear fell.

"I see it all Daph. You are an amazing woman. You say you're not a mom, but Kada I know sees it as you two watch your girly movie and things. You took care of her ankle and her period, let her grow and be independent. You talk to her and listen and even understand. That is being a mom, not cause some piece of paper says you are. Forget about what I need or want but Kada needs you just as much as you need us."

He knew Kada was her weak spot and would crumble or break when he used Kada against her. She leaned forward and looked over at his house.

He read her thoughts. "Kada is over at Sarah's working on a project and cooling down from this morning."

Daphne's eyes went wide then closed and dropped her head in regret.

Luke leaned over the console and grabbed her chin to look at him.

"Hey, it's okay. She'll be okay. She is twelve and changing every day. We will talk to her tomorrow, maybe go out for a picnic or something."

"Luke, I hurt her."

"Maybe, but luckily us Richmond's have thick skin, are resilient and forgive pretty easily." He rubbed her chin and smiled.

"I'm sorry Luke."

He closed his eyes as he gave a slow nod then opened them.

"It's okay but you have to promise me you will stay and stick this out. Stop running."

She took a deep breath and tried for a smile. "I'll try, I promise."

He leaned over and gave her a soft kiss then leaned back in his seat and reached in his pocket and pulled out a key on a keychain and gave it to Daphne.

"So, you know you always have a home to run to."

Daphne looked at him in shock and took the key and key chain.

It was a silver heart engraved with "Luke" and "Kada" on either side.

More tears fell from her face, and he wiped at them.

"It's not in a personalized engraved box but you have it."

She kissed him and leaned back to hook them to her keys.

"So, you get out some aggression today?" Luke spoke to change to a lighter subject.

Her eyes went big in surprise.

"Actually, I did!"

"I saw. You were going at it for a minute, and I think that was when you hit the target. You get it all out?"

Understanding the question, she answered with a smile. "Yeah, I think I did."

He smiled. "That's my girl."

He leaned over and gave her a harder longer kiss letting their tongues tangle and when she started to lean into him, he pulled back quickly.

"A little over a week and if everything checks out, I promise we will both get our fill of each other. But first, let's get the cast off."

A little disappointed but she gave a small laugh and agreed.

"So now my terms."

Luke leaned on his fist on the console and raised an eyebrow. "Okay, What?"

"Stay with me tonight."

He smiled big, " No other place I'd rather be."

They got out and he hit the key fob lock button as the truck lit up and horn honked. They walked up the porch holding hands and since he had her only available hand, he unlocked the door with his key and let her go first as he held the door open then closed it behind him.

CHAPTER TWELVE

In the morning Daphne woke to a Kada smiling propped up on her arm and no Luke in her bed. Daphne pulled the blanket tighter over her nearly naked body.

"Hey Kada. What's up? I thought you were at Sarah's?"

"I was. I got back this morning. Dad is on a call. He said you wanted to talk."

Looking at the clock to get her bearings, it showed 10:26am, nearly four and half hours past her usual time.

Gasping, Daphne flung up and almost lost her blanket around her.

"Dad said to let you sleep and to be nice. You are staying, aren't you?"

Still gathering her thoughts, Daphne blinked to see more clearly while holding the blanket with her left arm.

"Yes Kada. I'm staying. I'm so sorry, I hurt you. I didn't mean to."

Kada jumped in place on the bed and tackled Daphne back down making her wince in pain.

"Oh, Sorry Daphne." Her voice turned soft and full of worry. "But you said you had to protect us, but from what?"

Daphne needed coffee for this.

"Let me get up and we can talk after I get a cup of coffee."

"Okay!" She got excited and left to room, closing the door behind her.

After she got dressed, she got coffee and sat at the counter with Kada. She laid it out leaving out the gory and finer details making it PG-13 for the twelve-year-old.

When the coffee sank in her brain waking her up and Kada told her "Sorry" and "Love you" then they hugged. Though it made Kada nervous, she understood why now her dad was being so protective and why Daphne came...more like running home. It all fit now, in Kada's mind, all except the bruises on both her dad and Daphne. That got left out, but Kada didn't ask.

With that taken care of Daphne could breathe a little easier and decide to make breakfast while turning on some music and dancing while her and Kada flipped pancakes and bacon. For a moment the world was right again, and when Luke texted "I love you." She felt as giddy as a teenager in love.

She texted back, "I love you too. I miss you."

She set her phone down to finish plating the bacon then her phone chimed again. Daphne smiled and reached for it, Kada snuck a piece of bacon off the plate before Daphne could slap her hand away.

Kada watched Daphne go all smiles and dreamy eyed while reading her dad's text and couldn't help but smile at the happiness she wished for her dad and wanted for Daphne.

Over the bite of bacon, Kada teased, "Ooo. What is Dad saying?"

Daphne couldn't stop smiling as she hid the phone screen against her chest.

"He said sorry he wasn't here when I woke but hoped you were a good enough replacement and asked if we want to go have a picnic later."

Kada tilted her head back and forth quickly as she took another bite of bacon and swallowed it, "I had plans with Sarah, but I can change them."

Daphne texted again and put her phone back down while jamming to the music and plated the last of the pancakes. When Daphne grabbed the plates and walked them to her small table set up for three, her phone chimed again. Kada snagged it off the counter and ran around the kitchen island while opening the text message.

"Kada! Don't! Give that back!" Daphne giggled and gave chase, doing a couple laps around the small island before realizing Kada had a lot more energy.

While reading the text, Kada fluttered her eyelashes at Daphne.

"Ooo, He says 'sounds good, he is off the call but has a couple more things to do quick then he'll be home and that he loves us and he'll see us soon.'"

She texted back as she spoke what she wrote, "Okay Dad, we love you too! Kiss kiss!" and hit sent just before Daphne snagged it back as Kada laughed.

Daphne looked at the message and sent her own reply then chased Kada around the island again.

Over pancakes and bacon and toast with orange juice, thanks to Luke's stocked fridge and what Luke packed up for Daphne for Kada to bring over. The girls talked boys and of course, Luke. After breakfast, Daphne took a quick shower in her still busted up bathroom and then braided Kada's hair the best she could.

Luke walked in the front door while the sun shined brightly through the kitchen window, lighting up the whole house with a soft glow. He smiled big, putting his keys on the kitchen island before Daphne and Kada noticed him over the loud girly pop song coming from Daphne's TV.

Daphne was the first off, the couch, clicking off the music then running to Luke with a smile, all giddy still. Luke had to catch her as Daphne leaped into his arms and kissed him. Luke gave a soft throaty moan and a soft squeeze around her waist careful of the cast then setting her back to her feet.

"Eww. It was cute when Daphne went all gooey over her new boyfriend texting till, I saw her making out with my dad." Kada spoke with a disgusted face.

Both Daphne and Luke laughed. Then Luke's face turned serious as he turned back towards Daphne.

"We need to talk."

Her face grew with concern.

"Ah Oh! What happened? You have to go to work?"

"No. We are all still going on a picnic if you want to after I talk to you."

Luke took a seat on the kitchen stool and sat Daphne down in front of him. Kada walked over and stood next to Daphne.

"What is it, Luke? As long as we are still together...all of us..." She pulled Kada to her side. "...Not much can ruin this day."

He smiled at her and gave her a soft kiss.

"That's why I love you. Remember that what you just said. We are all fine and healthy and together, and you will always have me and Kada."

She smiled, "Okay, so get on with it!"

Daphne heard a couple of vehicles pulling in the driveway and grew confused.

"I've already done the paperwork and made a few calls but...both our vehicles were vandalized sometime last night. Magar had to pick me up for the call this morning."

Her face dropped in shock as she stared at Luke.

"Hey, it's okay. It's material. We are okay."

He leaned over and put his hands on her legs and without proof he wouldn't mention who everyone was thinking did it, till Kada said it.

"Do you think it was her ex-husband?"

Luke glared at Kada now as Daphne got up and ran for the front door ripping it open, before gasping at the damage. Dawson was taking pictures, while Mike walked around both vehicles with another officer in uniform, inspecting the damage.

Daphne's car only had "Whore" in neon green paint written all around it but Luke's truck tires were all flattened with knife marks, had broken headlights, windows, windshields, and dents in the hood and sides.

Daphne was frozen on the front porch, taking it all in. Luke walked up behind her and put his arms around her in a tight hug.

"Hey Daph, it's okay. I can get it fixed or buy a new truck. Insurance already has my report. They are just waiting on Dawson's pictures and reports. It's okay."

Kada stepped outside, "Oh my gosh! Dad, your truck!"

Luke sighed and gave her a look, "Thank you, Kada!"

Then turned to watch Mike and the officers investigate the damage with Daphne in his arms.

Daphne turned around in Luke's arms and looked up at him. "I'm so sorry Luke!"

He scowled at her. "Why? Cause you did this? You knew this was gonna happen? It's a truck, Daphne, not my life."

She scoffed, "Yeah. Yup. I snuck out of bed in the middle of the night while sleeping ever so comfortably with my boyfriend......."

Kada looked at her dad and smiled from behind him.

".... And smashed his truck and wrote 'Whore' on my own car."

Luke's face went into a smiling shock.

"Well, what the hell did you do that for?"

Daphne gave his chest a light swat as he started to laugh.

Kada watched the officer taking pictures of her dad's tires.

"Oh my gosh! It was Daphne's ex, Dad!" Kada shouted loud enough for everyone to hear.

As everyone including Mike and the officers looked at Kada, Luke looked down at Kada with a more pissed off look, as Daphne's head fell forward to thud against his chest.

"Again, thank you, Kada." Luke spoke with a gruff tone.

She looked at her dad's angered face then to Daphne tucked in his arms and chest, then gave a frown and a silent "Sorry."

Luke jerked his head toward the front door next to him as Kada went inside. He bent his knees to get a tighter grip on Daphne's waist and lifted her off the ground, forcing her to look at him.

"Hey, it's fine. Really. Insurance will cover it. Nick..." Nodding at the tow truck driver that just pulled in with a big flatbed truck, ".... will take it to a body shop in Freeman and I'll have it back in a week. For now, we can scrub off the paint on yours and I'm gonna borrow Mike's Dodge while he uses the Station's command truck."

Daphne watched him then gave him a kiss, as she wrapped her arm around his neck. He leaned into it and gave her a teasing love bite. She smiled against his lips and then he did.

"You are so amazing. Thank you."

"You are welcome. Now go inside, get ready for a hike and picnic, let me clean out my truck before they take it and I'll be inside in a few."

Daphne smiled and gave him a soft peck and got set down when Luke let her feet touch the porch again. She walked away and went inside.

Luke walked down the steps and over to Mike taking in the damage around his headlights. "I'm gonna kill this asshole!"

Mike looked up and saw the now pissed off look on Luke's face and clenched fists.

Dawson spoke up as he and the other officer took notes by Luke's driver door.

"You will not, Lieutenant!" He then walked over to them and spoke with a serious tone.

"Look, Luke, I know what he is doing to you guys. I get it. Really, I do. He's scaring her and baiting you into doing something stupid. But if you go after him, I can't help you, at least not legally." He gave a smirk that Mike caught and laughed at, but Luke ignored it.

"He beat the shit out of Daphne which she barely survived the first time none less the second time, kidnaps her, and only god knows where he was taking her before she wrecked the vehicle to get away, is still healing from that and now he's threatening us! Find him Dawson, before I do!" Luke raised his voice.

Mike held up a hand towards Luke, palm out, "Luke, breathe man!"

Luke sucked in a breath and punched his truck on the side panel above his front fender behind his headlight, leaving another small dent.

Mike spoke, "Really man?"

Dawson looked at the truck and its new dent and snapped a picture with his phone camera before pointing at Luke, "I'm gonna tell the shop to leave that dent just for you. Now knock it off Luke! We will find him I promise. It's a small town and unless his CEO suit and tie is camo, he's not blending in with the wildlife, so he can't go anywhere but out!"

Luke hated it but nodded in agreement and put his hands on his hips and took a deep breath.

Mike pulled out his keys and held them out to Luke. "Get them out of here, go on that picnic and I'll take care of this."

Luke was never hot headed so it was a new experience for Mike and Dawson to see him amped up over protecting Daphne and also gut wrenching knowing what he could be capable of, if it became necessary.

Luke took the keys and gave Mike a pat on the shoulder. "Thanks man."

When Luke walked away to retrieve his gear and radios through the broken windows of his truck, Mike poked him verbally, "Hey Luke......"

Luke turned around to raise an eyebrow at him.

".......keep the seats clean."

Luke didn't smile but threw up his hands while holding the radios and gear, "No promises."

Mike frowned and dropped his head.

Dawson laughed and clapped a hand on Mike's shoulder as Luke turned back around and took his gear to Mike's dark gray Dodge truck with a camper shell on the back.

Mike and Dawson watched him.

"He's fully involved." Mike said.

"Now I see your guy's fascination with fire. So destructive but yet beautiful. I can't look away." Dawson finished as Mike laughed.

After Luke put his gear in Mike's truck parked at the edge of the yard, he headed back for the house. At the front door, He took a couple of deep breaths, thought of Daphne and didn't even have to force the smile as he opened the front door.

Daphne and Kada were talking, smiling, and jamming to music again like nothing had happened. Now Luke really smiled. Those girls that were smiling and laughing, they were his. When they noticed him standing there they laughed and began packing for a hike and picnic. While making sandwiches, snacks and water bottles, Luke made a trip home to get his hiking backpack and mosquito dope.

When they finished packing, they hauled it to Mike's truck which was now backed into Luke's spot where his truck sat just an hour before. He helped Daphne get into the taller truck, he gave her a kiss and shut the door. Luke locked up the house and made sure everything was secure and got in. The girls were talking about a boy, Daniel, at school.

"Wait, what? Are you dating Kada?" He jerked around to face Kada in the back seat.

"No! Dad! He's just a boy in my class that likes Sarah."

Luke spoke softer, answering now, "Ok. Good!" He told himself to tell Mike when he got home.

Luke drove through town and hit a dead end at Birch creek. Daphne looked confused before Luke turned the drive switch to 4x4, gave it a second to engage and then applied the gas softly.

Daphne sat forward as they crossed the creek going over a boulder and rocks the size of the tires. She bounced around in the front seat as Luke took it slowly climbing the boulders and dips in the creek bed from others that didn't know how to cross.

Her curiosity made Luke smile as his left hand steered, and he leaned on the console with his right to keep him steady. Once he crossed, he turned left and ran along the dryer creek bed for another mile then turned right to follow a shallower creek upstream into the mountains.

Daphne was fascinated watching all around the truck with genuine curiosity, as a few branches scraped along the side and hit the window with a *thwack* sound, making Daphne jump nearly across the console into Luke's lap. Kada and Luke both laughed at her. Daphne gave a smile and swatted her hand at Luke who caught it, kissed it and let it go as they rounded a corner and climbed a steeper hill. Daphne saw nothing at the top over the hood except sky.

"Luke! Where is the trail?"

Kada laughed in the back seat, "Daphne, it's okay. Dad knows where he is going."

Luke stopped the truck, nose up in the sky and smiled then laid his hand open on the console for her to hold. She smiled and grabbed it. When she did, he let go of the brake and turned to the left putting the truck in a nosedive down a hill.

"Luke!" Daphne gave a push back into her seat, holding tight to the door handle and Luke's hand on the console. Luke smiled as he slowly climbed the truck down the hill as Daphne clenched to his hand and finally let it go when they reached the bottom.

Luke worked his right hand and shook out the claw marks between his knuckles. Then took a small path through the woods and to the left that led to a small crystal-clear blue lake. The lake that on the Southside, fed into the same Birch Creek that passed Luke and Daphne's houses.

The sun was shining brightly against the lake making it look like blue glass all the way to the bottom of the crystal-clear water. On the Westside across from them, trees surrounded it, shading that part of the lake. Beside them to the North, mountains towered over them with a small glacier tucked in between two of them. Behind them to the East and Southeast over the treetops, laid out Birch Valley, giving Daphne a wide view of the beautiful small town with the sun directly over it. Her eyes were big as quarters taking in the scenery in front of her with her mouth wide open as she sat on the edge of her seat.

When Luke pulled up to the edge of the water and turned the truck around to back up to it, Kada jumped out. Now with the truck facing the mountains, Daphne leaned forward over the dashboard to get the full view in the windshield. Luke sat back in his seat satisfied with just watching her take it all in.

When she finally sat back and looked at him, he spoke, "This is Glacial Lake. For obvious reasons it was named cause Kavrak Glacier feeds into it."

He pointed up to the glacier on the mountain in front of them.

"It's cold up here, so bundle up before you get out."

Daphne smiled, "This is...I don't know if they even have a word for it. Wow!"

She pulled Luke's hood of the sweater she wore over her head. She tucked her loose hair in the hood and opened the door to get out. Luke got out while pocketing the truck keys and then walked to the back of the truck to pop the tailgate down, pop the camper hatch up and pull out a couple logs of firewood.

Daphne and Kada walked around the small lake to walk and explore as Luke started a small campfire between the truck and the water's edge to keep warm. When Daphne returned from exploring about 30 minutes later, her teeth were chattering.

Luke smiled and chuckled sitting on the tailgate. He spread his legs and scooted back making room for her to sit in front of him and closer to the fire so he could rub her good arm and a leg to help warm her up.

Kada skipped rocks across the lake or looked for odd rocks and things to collect then roasted marshmallows as Luke and Daphne talked.

"So, tell me about Danielle." He asked.

"What do you want to know?"

"Anything. Everything." He shrugged.

She leaned back on his chest as the fire snapped and crackled.

"Well, it's just us now. Dad left when I was little and I don't remember much about him, so Mom raised us by herself. She worked hard doing odd jobs during the day and night school while we slept, to become a nurse. Shortly after I graduated college, Mom passed away from a stroke. Me and Dani always were and still are as close as sisters can be. When I ran from Darryl, she supported me 110%. Shortly after I moved in with Dani after everything with Darryl went south, he found me a year later and attacked Dani and probably would have killed her if Trace hadn't shown up when he did."

When Luke stayed silently behind her, she continued,

"Trace is her husband. Married 14......nope 15 years now. He is an architect and owns his own firm in Raleigh.... where they live. They have three kids. Maya 11, who is tough as nails, a lot like Kada. Levi, 7, and absolutely fearless as most boys and men are...."

Luke chuckled behind her.

"...and Jaclynn, 3, the baby and so spoiled."

She stopped and looked up at Luke who was silently staring at the fire then looked down at Daphne in his arms.

"What does your sister do?"

"What doesn't she do?" Daphne scoffed.

"She is mostly a stay-at-home mom now, but she substitutes teaches at her kids' school ever so often and she helps Trace design buildings. She was also a midwife before she had her own kids and she occasionally helps out at her best friend's daycare, plus keeps her house and family running."

"Wow. She really does everything." Luke said with surprise.

They both watched Kada turning a marshmallow on a stick as it turned from white to golden brown and caught fire when she looked at Daphne and asked. "Do you miss her?"

Kada blew it out and ate it off the stick, as Daphne and Luke laughed before Daphne replied.

"Yes, I do miss her very much. She's my best friend and knows everything about my life. Until I moved here, but we both agreed that the less she knew the better when I ran here to find...." She choked on her words as she watched Kada's curious facial expression.

Luke gave Daphne's leg a small rub for reassurance.

"Before you came here to find what?" Kada asked.

Daphne smiled at Kada. "Your Dad, as it turns out."

Kada licked the sticky marshmallow off her fingers as she looked confused. "So, you knew Dad before you came here?"

Luke just chuckled while Daphne sighed and answered."No. I'd seen him once. He helped me on a call, and I came back to thank him."

She tried to keep it lighter for Kada.

"Well, I think it worked!" Kada said with a wide grin.

Luke gave a full laugh behind Daphne as he leaned back on his hands now.

Daphne gave a softer laugh than Luke, "Yeah, I think he knows how much it meant to me."

Luke leaned forward again, wrapping Daphne in his arms and gave her a soft kiss on her cheek.

"Man, I wish Dani could meet you guys. She would love you two. She would get a kick out of Kada. She's gonna flip when she finds out I fell in love with Richmond."

Luke gave her a small gentle squeeze and sighed.

She turned her head around and gave him a kiss.

"We should probably eat, I'm getting hungry." Luke spoke.

Now that Daphne thought about food her stomach rumbled.

After they set up the picnic on the tailgate, Luke sat and leaned on the bed frame, letting his right leg hang off the edge of the tailgate while eating a sandwich.

Daphne leaned her right cast into his chest and propped her right leg over his leg and Luke pulled her into his side with his left arm resting around her waist and ate with his right hand while watching the horizon.

Kada smiled from her camping chair next to the campfire watching them eat and snuggle. She couldn't resist pulling her phone out and taking a picture of them. Luke and Daphne smiled for the picture then kissed, as Kada took a second picture. Kada knew how much Daphne made him happy. It was a new side of her dad after years of being alone and fighting the aftermath of losing his wife, her mother. She hoped this would last, as she watched them and took a bite of her own sandwich.

After they were done eating and cleaned up, they locked up the truck and took a hike around the lake and through the woods. Kada led the way as Luke and Daphne held hands and held back making small talk.

When they rounded a corner, Luke stopped and turned left pointing down the hill. Daphne looked but saw nothing but trees and Birch creek. She squinted hard and Mrs. Adam's house came into view in the distance. Her eyes followed the creek up to the spacing of trees to the right.... her house....and Luke's. In the distance they weren't any bigger than a dime to her as she smiled and gave Luke a kiss.

Kada tapped her foot, "Come on, I wanna reach the waterfall."

"Kada, we will get there." Luke said.

A surprised Daphne looked at Luke. "Waterfall? How much further?"

Luke smiled, "About two miles."

Daphne smiled and tried to run but wouldn't let go of Luke's hand, so he gave into a jog with Daphne but ended up walking shortly after they started.

Soon she heard the falls before she saw them with more excitement, she took off in a run with Kada after she let go of Luke's hand.

He just smiled at them running together and slowed himself down to stick his hand in his pocket to play with the lid on a small velvet jewelry box. He thumbed the rim and smiled so big thinking of Daphne.

He wanted her in his life and Kada's forever and knew that since the day of the accident as he searched for her in fear, thinking he would lose her completely.

When she rounded the corner, Daphne watched the big waterfall come into view, over a cliff about 500 feet up the mountain that came down into a river, led down the mountain side, and disappeared into the trees.

Daphne jogged up to him and gave him a long romantic kiss with her good arm around his neck. Luke took a deep breath and wrapped his free arm around her waist lifting her off her feet.

"I love you, Daphne." He spoke against her lips.

"I love you too, Luke! Thank you for today. We all needed this today."

"Yeah, we did."

He paused and looked at her eyes which were sparkling with pure happiness watching him.

His heartbeat raced. Was this the right time? Could he make this better for her? He searched her eyes. Was she ready or would she run again? He wanted her but did she really want him, and Kada, forever? He released the jewelry box in his pocket and wrapped his now empty hand around her.

"We should probably get headed back soon. Sun is setting, it's gonna get dark quick."

"Okay but first I want a picture of us to remember this!"

She ran to find a nearby tree and propped her phone up on a branch facing the waterfall and Luke and Kada, then set the timer on her phone. She ran to Luke's left side hiding her cast in his side as his arm came around and Kada stood in front, so Luke and Daphne put a hand on each of Kada's shoulders.

"Smile!" Daphne said before her phone clicked.

Daphne and Luke kissed, and Daphne moved her hand to his chest and Luke turned to face her.

Click! The camera took another photo.

When they got back to the truck, the sun was almost set, putting an amber glow over Birch Valley and the lake. Daphne took a picture on her phone quickly before she jumped in the truck, Luke had warmed up the minute they got back. He made sure the campfire was out and didn't leave anything and got in.

Luke smiled at Daphne and put the truck in drive and hit the trail headed for home. By the time they hit their street, the last of the sun glimmered across the sky in orange and red streaks. Kada fell asleep in the back seat and Daphne leaned over the console to rest her head against his shoulder. His thoughts wandered the entire trip back home.

When they turned the corner, Daphne saw a silver Explorer parked behind Daphne's car. Daphne's heartbeat tripped and went into a full gallop and Luke readjusted in his seat and pulled into her driveway next to it.

Daphne watched out her window as her sister in the driver's seat came into view.

"Dani!" Daphne screamed, waking up Kada in the backseat.

When Luke parked Daphne and Dani jumped out and gave each other tight hugs.

While they were busy, Luke pulled out the jewelry box, turned it in his hand for a second and stuck it in the locking compartment under the center console and locked it with the key before sighing and getting out with a smile.

Kada stayed frozen and silent in the back seat with wide eyes wondering what was in the jewelry box. Then smiled at her dad through the windshield as he walked around the truck to greet Daphne's sister.

When Luke came around the front of the truck. Dani's eyes got big. Being obvious, she leaned towards Daphne, "That......" Making a one finger gesture from Luke's head to feet and back up again, ".... is Richmond?"

Daphne gave a wide smile at her sister with a laugh, "Yes Dani. Be nice."

She gave a soft low moan "Ooo. So much better than Darryl."

Luke smiled overhearing her as he walked up and stood next to Daphne. Dani watched him and looked him over, reading body language and clothing and facial expressions.

He stuck out a hand to her.

"Hi, Dani, nice to finally meet you.'

Dani smiled at her sister then looked back at him then pulled him into a hug.

"We are family. We don't shake hands."

Luke nodded with a wide smile, "Fair enough."

When she was released, he stepped back next to Daphne and pulled her into his side. The truck door opened and out stepped Kada. A confused Dani looked at Daphne and then back to Kada

"Dani, this is Kada. Luke's daughter."

Her face turned to shock, "Luke's...Your daughter?"

Luke smiled, "Yeah."

"I mean I'm sorry, Daphne's letter said you had a sweetheart and Daphne's best friend, but I guess I pictured 6, not 15."

Though Kada smiled, she shyly spoke, "I'm 12, turning 13 next month."

"Oh my gosh, you are so gorgeous!" Dani said loudly with excitement.

Kada sleepily smiled. "Thank you." as she ran fingers through her hair trying to get out the bed head look from falling asleep in the back seat.

"Hi Kada, I'm Dani. Daphne's sister."

She stuck her hand out to Kada. Kada took it and gave it a quick shake.

"Hi." She spoke as she stepped into Daphne's side.

Daphne looked up at Dani, "So how long are you staying? How did you get here? or...know how to get here?"

Dani looked to Luke and back to Daphne.

"What?" Daphne spoke up.

"Daph, Luke brought me here. He paid for my plane ticket and rental car, for almost two weeks. He said you needed me."

"What? Why?"

Luke shrugged and turned to face her. He moved her hair behind her ear and rubbed a thumb against her cheek.

"Extra help to keep your feet on the ground *in* Birch Valley and to help with healing."

Daphne opened her mouth to talk but Luke finished talking,

"And no, not physically. I know you don't need anyone for that." He smiled as he looked into her eyes through the dark. She closed her mouth and smiled.

"Thank you. I love you."

"You're welcome. Figured she could visit and help you while I'm gone on call at least till after you get your cast removed."

He leaned down and gave her a hot kiss that had Dani fanning herself as she watched them.

Kada rolled her eyes then looked at Dani, "They do that a lot!"

Dani raised her eyebrows, "Yeah, I bet they do."

Daphne and Luke both laughed, breaking the kiss and moment.

Luke looked over Daphne's shoulder, "Kada, get the food out of the back and take it inside please."

He looked at Dani, "I'll get your bags."

"Oh! Okay. Do I have to tip? I don't have cash, but I think we can...."

Daphne cut her off, "Dani!"

Luke looked at Dani, worked his jaw with a scowl then looked at Daphne. "Get her inside before she gets too much fresh air." Then kissed Daphne on the forehead and headed for the Explorers trunk.

Dani clicked the fob towards it and popped the trunk open as she watched Luke walking away. Daphne grabbed Dani's right arm with her good left and hauled her inside.

Luke thought this was gonna be fun. Dani was a touch wilder than Daphne. Even her looks showed it with a short pin straight bob haircut to her chin. The tips of her hair professionally dyed almost to a platinum blonde, highlights over a lighter caramel brunette and a lot of makeup he thought was done by a professional. They couldn't have been more different. Luckily, he made plans to go back to work so Daphne could catch up with her sister.

When he heard a short scream and a "Oh my god!" that Luke knew Mike could hear on the other side of town, he rolled his eyes. He hauled in Dani's three luggage bags that he knew would be filled with high heels and beauty products mostly.

"Dad, can I go to bed?"

He carried the luggage up a couple steps behind Kada.

"Yeah, say goodnight to Daphne."

When they got inside Luke heard them upstairs. Kada put the ice chest from the picnic onto the kitchen island and headed upstairs. Luke followed with the luggage effortlessly and into Daphne's spare room where Daphne and Dani made up the spare bed with clean blue sheets. He set the luggage down by the door and smiled at Daphne.

Kada spoke, interrupting Daphne's conversations with Dani.

"Goodnight Daphne."

Daphne looked at Kada. "Going to bed?'

"Yeah, the hike wore me out, plus I have school tomorrow."

"Okay goodnight. Love you." as she walked over and gave Kada a one arm hug.

"Good night, Dani, Night Dad. Love you!"

"I should probably join her." Luke spoke from the doorway.

"Oh No! Luke, I have so many questions and I wanna hear about this...." She reached over and grabbed Luke's empty sleeve of the sweater that Daphne wore.

Luke nodded with a smile, "What about the arm she has wrapped around me?"

Daphne smiled at Luke.

CHAPTER THIRTEEN

After putting away the picnic stuff, Luke sat in Daphne's bay window with Daphne between his legs, her back to his chest, and his arms wrapped around her. Dani sat on the couch across from the bay window and sat forward in anticipation.

"So, I know how you guys met, so start from there."

Luke looked confused and stayed silent. Daphne spoke "Deadman's corner, 1st accident. She knew I came to find Richmond."

Luke stayed confused with so many questions but kept them to himself. He kissed her head and leaned back against the window frame.

Over the next hour of Luke and Daphne telling her on their last eight months together, every emotion filled Luke as Daphne laid in his arms. When Dani asked questions, Daphne filled in the blanks. Dani cried, smiled, "oohed" and "awed" through nearly most of it, only to end up on the floor next to the window hugging her sister's legs.

"So how long have you lived here, Luke?"

"All my life, mostly. Dad was a firefighter with Birch Valley, Mom and her parents moved here in 1976 and they fell in love and had me. Dad died in a house fire on a call when I was ten. I grew up with Mike and a few others at the station. Mom passed away shortly after I graduated high school and joined the department."

Daphne heard the change in his tone in his voice and turned to look at him as he told his story, that she was even hearing for the first time.

Luke continued, "After a bad call, I found immediate comfort in... A friend..." He swallowed trying to gather his thoughts and held Daphne tighter.

"... Nine months later, Kada was born. I fell in love with her mother, Jasmine, married her, moved to Freeman for a while..."

Dani propped an elbow up on her knee and put her hand under her chin. Daphne rubbed Luke's thigh for comfort, and he looked down at Daphne, remembering it all.

"We got pregnant again and decided to move back out here to be closer to her family and our hometown. A drunk driver hit her on the driver's side, taking my son, Kyler Lucas Richmond and my wife, Jasmine Danita Richmond-Davis. Kada survived in the back seat with a few scrapes and bruises."

He took a breath and looked up at Daphne, who was frozen in a state of shock.

Dani looked from Daphne to Luke and back in confusion. "What?"

Without taking her eyes off Luke, she turned her head towards Dani and spoke, "Luke married his best friend's sister. His late wife, Kada's mother, is Mike's sister."

Luke gave a rueful smile then dropped his head again. Daphne took a deep breath. She knew him well enough to see the guilt in his expression. She used her one good hand and lifted his face to look at her.

"Hey, it wasn't your fault. It's not your fault. It wasn't a house fire you could have prevented or put out. You still have Kada."

Luke started to smile. "And you. I have you."

"Yes. We still have each other. Our steps lead us both here."

Daphne looked at Dani, who gave a frown and nod. Daphne placed a hand on Luke's knee as she now faced him fully. Her feet now tucked under Luke's thighs and around his ass that stretched the fabric of his jeans. Her knees almost to her chest as she sat in between Luke's legs in the bay window and took a deep breath. Luke watched her with a smile.

Dani got up and gave Daphne a kiss on her head and headed up stairs.

When she disappeared out of sight, Luke spoke with curiosity. "Talk to me, Daph."

She looked up at him with tears in her eyes, he wiped them away with his hand.

"Luke, when you pulled me out of that 1st accident, it was the safest I felt in the last five years and not just because you were a fireman and that is your job, but you were different."

"Cause I saw beneath the physical scars." He spoke with a soft tone.

"I think so, but Luke, I didn't just run here to thank you and away from Darryl..."

Luke's eyes widened with understanding as he took a breath, "You only came because of me."

"Luke, I'm so sorry."

If Daphne expected anger, she got the opposite.

Luke grabbed her hand and pulled her into his chest and gave her the tightest hug he could manage without hurting her or the cast, then tilted her head up with a finger under her chin, "I'm glad you did."

"Luke, I didn't know I bought the house next to you, or about Kada, or if you were married. I just figured if I was in the same town as you, I would be safer. When Kada came to see me, I swear I still didn't know it was you. Not until you gave me your card, when Kada spent the night, did I make the connection. But by then, I already fell in love with Kada, and she felt like a daughter. Then you were there standing in front of me, thee Richmond, the one that saved me more times than just once over three years, and even after I moved here. Every time I ran from Darryl, you made me. I searched for the security and safe feeling cause you gave that to me one time. I never found it, till you tripped over my washer and caught me of all things which I'm still working that one out in my head." She and Luke both chuckled.

He framed her face with his hands and looked into her eyes with his golden eyes going a deep gold color. "Daphne, Kada is yours. She's ours. Kada knew that before either of us did."

"And now you guys are in danger because of me." Daphne's heart shattered.

"Daph, I'm in danger every day, risking my life for strangers and the people of this town and even some not from this town, but I don't love them, not like you and Kada. Everyone is worth saving but no one more than you and I'm pretty sure Kada would agree with me."

Her heart over-filled and by reaction leaned in and gave him the softest sensual kiss. Luke couldn't handle it anymore. In one swift movement, he wrapped his arms around her and stood up making her legs wrap around his waist and her good arm around his neck.

"Luke, No. My sister is upstairs."

She gave him a dead stare and he just laughed, loving where her thoughts went. He walked to the front door, opened it and closed it quietly, with her still wrapped around him.

"Luke....Where are.... No! Not my car!" Her eyes got really big.

He laughed again and gave her a quick peck on her lips and said "Shh."

Before stepping down the few porch steps and passing by her car and in between Dani's rental and Mike's truck. He opened up the passenger door of the truck and set her on the seat facing him.

With even bigger eyes now and a tone in her voice, "NO! Luke, we can't! Mike will kill you!"

Luke really laughed now, "Wouldn't be the first time."

He raised an eyebrow and jerked his shoulder up. When he reached behind her making her lean back, she smiled really big.

"Luke, I swear to god, If Mike ever asks me, I will sing like a Canary, I can't keep secrets!"

Luke looked down under him and gave her another soft peck with her still wrapped around his neck, "Shh! He won't ask you anything."

When he tried to open the compartment under the console, he remembered it was locked. Luke dug out the keys from his pockets and unlocked it as Daphne watched with curiosity. He had no smile but was happy and serious as he rummaged through the compartment.

"Luke, what are you doing? We don't need protection. I can't get pregnant, plus if I could, it would be from the last shower we took together."

Now he had an irritating look, "Shh!"

When he finally sat up straight, Daphne raised with him as she still held her arm around his neck and then let go to relax a little as she watched him with curiosity. With nothing in his hands, he placed both palms down on her thighs and looked into her eyes.

"First off, this is not how I expected to do this, but Daphne Kimble...."

Her eyes went big again.

".... You belong here with me and Kada. Maybe not here but over there."

He nodded towards his house.

"You never needed rescuing, just the tools and support to save yourself. You're a very strong woman, Daphne. Strong enough to save a fireman and his daughter. Kada gravitated towards you not because she thought I needed a wife or even that she needed a mom but because she saw you needed us. And honestly, I can't argue with her, cause I felt it too that day in the diner. But more then that, I found out how much we needed you."

He placed his right hand on his chest.

"This is me. You know it all now, except for the years we never knew we needed anything else until you needed a Richmond. Maybe the fireman, maybe the daughter or even the neighbor, but I do know you got all of them willing to take a chance and risk their lives for you. Daph, I want to show you what a real man can give you and I promise it will never come from anger. Stop running. Marry me and give me and Kada, a wife and mom to love and protect."

With a flick of his thumb, he turned a ring around on the end of his middle finger around reveling in the moonlight a beautiful emerald cut Ametrine with four little sparkling diamond accents and a small amethyst on each side set in a rose gold setting, that closely matched her necklace and earrings from Christmas.

She gasped looking from the ring to his eyes and the tears broke leaving streams down her face. Still silent, she nodded. So, he took her left hand and slid it on her ring finger. A perfect fit.

Without saying a word, she hooked her left arm around his neck and kissed him.

He braced his left arm on the seat and climbed over top of her, pulling the passenger door closed with his right hand. Daphne smiled against his lips.

"Shh, I'll get it professionally detailed." He spoke softly.

He let go of her lips and moved down her neck digging both his hands up the big sweater dragging it over her left arm and head to toss in it in the driver seat while dragging her over the console and to the backseat.

She used her left hand to slide under his shirt and up his washboard abs before he pulled it off himself, tossing it on the seat next to them. Then continued down her neck to the button up blouse just as his mouth worked down her left shoulder and over her breast. He spent a minute putting soft kisses there as she gave soft moans with each kiss, "Luke, No. I need you now."

Never taking his mouth off her, he looked up. "No. I want to enjoy you and do this right this time. Just don't scream too loud."

Her eyes rolled back as her hand tangled in his hair.

He worked his way down over her soft scars till he found her cesarean scar and took his time kissing every inch of it then pulled at her jeans before he unbuttoned them and slid them down to the floorboard.

"I need you to lay down for me, Daph."

She let her cast slide against the back, down to the seat till she laid as flat as the curvy seats would let her, resting her head on his shirt he discarded.

He took a full view of her completely naked with just her thin little black panties and spoke softly, "God, you're gorgeous."

Daphne smiled with stars in her eyes.

Luke with one hand undid the button on his jeans and unzipped them over his hard erection, to release some tension. Then he bent down to place a kiss on her lower belly and breath in her scent moving down, placing a hand on each of her thighs to spread them further apart. He tucked two fingers in her panties, and pulled them down to her bare toes, letting all his fingers glide over her soft legs and over them. He kissed the back of her leg as he freed the panties and dropped them to the floorboard.

"Luke, I need you."

When his hand moved back to her leg, he kissed back up her leg to her thigh.

"Oh Luke," his name and soft moan escaped her lips, which made him hotter with need. He kissed over her swollen lips and sucked on them.

"Lucas."

His tongue dipped inside, tasting her soft sweetness and took it all, till he found her clitoris. His tongue ran over it gently making her body clench tight. He looked up and watched her arch her back and tighten. He gave it a gentle suck, making her legs rise so he moved his hands back to her thighs to hold them down over his shoulders.

His tongue worked down and found her dripping with sweetness and gave his own moan. Her fingers ran through his hair, nearly breathless giving her own moan.

He looked up and dipped his tongue inside and out making her pulse with need and sucked with his own hunger. His hands slid down her thigh and found her clitoris again. His thumb rubbed it gently as he sucked with his whole mouth and used his tongue to taste her.

Her entire body tightened, "Lucas," she gave a throaty deep moan. He dipped his tongue in and out of her making her clench to his hair. He moved his hands to her hips grabbing handfuls of her luscious hips and cheeks. He gave one last suck and ran his tongue up and back down taking everything.

"Richmond!" She gave a soft scream as her back arched and thighs clenched around his head, holding him there.

The warm silk came like a wave as his hands ran up her hips and over her sides grabbing and pulling her down as he drank every drop of the sweetness, as her entire body pulsed.

When she went limp, he raised up and shoved his pants and boxers down completely releasing his hard erection, as he watched her relaxed smiling face. He climbed over her bracing a hand on each side of her head then moved his left hand forward to the edge of the seat and dropped his elbow down next to her cast and the back of the seat, as he watched her face.

Her eyes got brighter when his tip found warmth and wetness. Her right leg moved up against the seat to his hip and wrapped around him. He smiled and pressed the tip into her. Her mouth opened, but nothing came out as her blue eyes darkened in the moonlight.

He sank deeper with his own raw carnal need as he pulsed with heat, taking a few fast deep breaths, and dropping his head to her shoulder. He slid out and pushed back in. His entire body sparked with energy as her hips raised with renewed need.

When he pushed deeper, she turned her head, finding his shirt under her crammed between her head and the door. She took a deep breath of it, taking in him and his scent, taking her fill. Finding a rhythm together as her left arm held around his ribs. Her hand spanned his lower back then clenched tight, digging her nails into his back.

He looked back up to her face, and her eyes reached his soul. He took her mouth and sank his tongue in tasting her and taking everything she gave. He knew he would never be able to get enough, even in his lifetime.

She moaned against him, so he released her mouth to watch her, "Daph."

He slowed and pushed deeper and gave her long slow strokes in and out.

Her eyes closed as her mouth opened, "Lucas." Her body clenched and her left leg came over his other hip and wrapped around and locked her feet together, not letting him back out just go deep as he could go, as her face went into shock.

"Richmond!" Her back arched pushing her breasts close to his face as he watched her and gave one last deep push in as far as he could and heard her breath catch as more warm silk wrapped around him, the shock of it sent him into his own release as he wrapped a arm around her arched back pulling her down on him, giving his own deep moan as he pulsed with her, together.

"Daphne." Her name on breathless release escaped him as he pulled her up with him to sit on his thighs and lean forward under the low ceiling of the cab. He took her mouth again and went lax.

When she released him to fall back to the seats, he smiled at her and leaned down over her to give her a soft sensual kiss. He held his weight on his right forearm over her. Then moved down to her jaw and onto her neck.

"Luke." she spoke but got no reply or halt.

When they couldn't move a couple hours later the windows had fogged over and both of them were breathing heavily as she laid on top of him now and he held her cheeks and thighs, looking up at her from the seats.

"Luke, no more. I can't move."

"That makes two of us."

Her left hand over his chest bracing herself over him, as he gently rubbed his right-hand fingers up and down her back and over her cheeks down and braced his head up with his left arm behind his head as he watched her.

She thumbed the ring on her hand, turning it between her fingers. When she didn't say anything, Luke smiled and did.

"You aren't a classic diamond solitaire, or a big fancy gold ring. You're unique, vibrant, colorful, and drop dead gorgeous Daph."

She smiled big watching him as her eyes got heavy, "I absolutely love it! It's so gorgeous."

"I love you, Daphne." He spoke.

She rested her head back down on his chest next to his chin tucking into his neck, so he kissed her head.

"I love you too, Richmond."

He smiled, knowing she said his last name for her own reassurance and gave her a gentle squeeze with his arm.

The tap on the window had them both jerking awake, then the back passenger door opened. Dani looked them over as they all tried to grasp what they were seeing. Daphne laid over Luke, both naked.

Dani was the first to go into shock. She covered her eyes and turned around with a scream. "Oh my god!".

Luke sat up releasing the shirt from under him and Daphne grabbed it to cover herself as Luke grabbed for his boxers and pants on the floorboard.

"Dani! What are you doing?" Daphne shouted.

Dani still turned around facing her car with the truck door open, holding the inside door handle as Luke and Daphne scrounged for their clothes.

"Umm, I could ask you two the same thing..."

Luke gave a grin and small laugh now, "But you wouldn't need to."

Daphne glared at him and gave his chest a soft smack with her hand.

Dani laughed, "Yeah....anyways. Luke's daughter is inside, asking where you two are and wondering if she has to go to school today."

Luke slid on his pants, buttoned them and remembered his phone was inside the house and the watch was at his house.

"What time is it?" Luke asked

Dani spoke, "Umm, about 8 O'clock."

"Fuck!" He spoke in a rush and went to help Daphne get dressed having troubles with her one and only free hand.

"You, know what? Don't even worry about it. I'll take her to school. If that's okay with Luke? Where is it?"

Luke replied, " Straight across town and Main Street, can't miss it. Kada will show you."

"K. I'll cover for you guys, today. Just stay down. I don't need her asking *me* too many questions. I'll be back soon."

Dani took a breath in and shut the door without looking and walked inside the house.

Daphne and Luke both laughed then groaned.

Luke spoke first, now half-dressed but not well. "Ugh, I need coffee and maybe an IV. I feel like I got two hours of sleep after a ten-hour marathon. Three-day training wasn't even this hard to recover from."

Daphne, still holding Luke's shirt over her bare chest, leaned back in the seat.

Luke bent forward and picked up Daphne's blouse off the floorboard and gave it to her, in trade for his shirt. He helped her put her blouse on and then put his shirt on.

The sounds of voices and sight of Dani and Kada coming out the front door through the windshield made Luke and Daphne drop to the seat quickly and out of sight. Luckily, Mike's back windows were at least partially tinted making it harder for anyone to see in, but not impossible.

Dani's voice was loudest, "Umm, I don't know where Dad and Daphne are, but I think school is important. My kids are still going to school even though I'm not home."

Kada gave Dani a look, "But Dad's cell is on Daphne's counter and his pager and radio are at home. He never leaves those."

Luke huffed out a silent breath and rolled his eyes. "Shit." he spoke softly as Daphne tried to hold in the laugh and her breath.

Kada was too smart and observant for her own good and this was the only time he could remember he wasn't proud of it. He watched the windows with nerves, hoping she wouldn't look in her Uncle Mike's truck as she passed by. Kada walked around the front of Dani's car and jumped in the front seat away from the truck.

Daphne and Luke held tight to each other, like they were criminals being hunted by the police. Dani's car started, backed out of the driveway and headed down the street. Daphne and Luke sat up, let out a breath and hurried up to get dressed and inside to shower together quickly.

When Dani pulled back in the driveway within 20 minutes. Luke was filling an Outer Banks mug with coffee at Daphne's counter, looking tired, but in clean clothes. Daphne was slouched over the kitchen island on the stool holding her own coffee cup, looking nearly dead with wet tangled hair. Luke turned around and leaned against the counter next to the sink and took his first sip of coffee. Holding himself up with his right arm. Both of them looked like they haven't slept in a week.

When Dani came in trying not to smile as she looked at them. Luke spoke first, "Thanks Dani."

"You're welcome."

Daphne looked at Luke making eye contact, as she slid her left hand under the island counter. He took another sip of coffee, watching her. Dani took her coat, hanging it up by the door and toed her shoes off. She watched them both, as she walked over to sit next to Daphne.

"You guys have fun.... in the last 10 hours?"

Luke just laughed, nearly choking on a sip of coffee as he smiled at Daphne. Luke waved a finger up and down towards Dani's head to toes and back, mocking her, "And *that*...is your sister?"

Dani's mouth dropped then smiled.

Daphne laughed, smiled and nodded as she watched her sister. "The strong brew version without the filter, but yes."

Luke gave another chuckle and took another sip of his coffee looking at Dani, "Sorry, lack of sleep."

"Okay, what is going on? You guys look like death and are all nonchalant. And I know it's not just from a night of some very hot sex."

Daphne and Luke made eye contact, as he smiled over his coffee cup while taking a bigger gulp of coffee this time. Daphne deliberately pulled her left hand out and drank her coffee as she watched Luke giving him a slight wincing look. Luke rolled his eyes.

"Daphne? Luke? What is goin'...." Then she noticed the ring and let out a scream that now had Luke cringing. Daphne put the cup down before she grabbed her hand and pulled it toward her to examine the ring.

"Ahh, my sister is engaged! Ooo damn Luke, you do have amazing tastes. First my sister, then this ring." She spoke as she tilted Daphne's hand back and forth watching it sparkle in the kitchen lights.

"No, that credit goes to Kada. Kada found her, Kada brought her home, and Kada picked her out a similar necklace and earring set last Christmas. I just fell in love with her and found a matching ring with more diamonds."

He smiled at Daphne who smiled back with sparkles in her eyes as her sister jerked her hand back and forth, still watching the ring sparkle. Luke drank the last of his coffee. "I better get to work and cross my fingers we don't get any calls today."

Daphne smiled, "Got time for a quick breakfast...at the diner?"

His smile went sly.

"That is playing with fire in a very dry field of tall grass."

Daphne gave another wide smile, "I know."

"Food does sound good, and I could use anything for energy right now, but you better take that guilty look off that face unless you want to raise Kada alone."

Daphne gave a hearty laugh as Dani looked confused. "Ok. I'll put on some mascara."

Both the girls walked out to the bedroom then upstairs to the bathroom.

Luke smiled, put his empty coffee cup in the sink, took his cell off the counter, and pulled up Mike's text conversation.

"Nah, better do this over the phone...Nope. Text."

He wrote it out and double checked it.

Hey, Daphne's sister is in town for a visit. The three of us are headed for the diner for breakfast, then I'm headed to Station for paperwork. He clicked 'Send'.

He heard Dani's voice yelling down from upstairs, "Hey Luke?"

"Yeah?"

"Before I forget, Kada wanted you to pick her up from school. She told me to make sure and tell you!"

"Okay, Thanks!"

Crap! Kada. He needed to figure out how to tell her, as this was even a surprise to him before he had a chance to talk to her.

"Hey Daph, I'm gonna run home and grab the radio and pager and lock up the house quick."

"Ok. I love you!" She walked down the stairs halfway to see him.

He looked up and smiled at her, "I love you too."

When Luke walked back in the back door, Daphne wore a peach and pink ombre light hi-lo sundress with heeled sandals that showed a few scars on her legs. Her hair half up with more curls framing her face now beautifully colored and softly blended with makeup.

Luke stopped dead in his tracks and just looked at her with a smile.

Dani spoke first as Daphne just watched him standing next to the counter, tucking a curl behind her ear. "What do you think?"

He didn't answer and just stared until Daphne spoke. "My cast is ugly and bulky."

Now Luke rushed to her and tossed his radio, pager and keys on the counter to grab her waist, lift her up to sit on the counter then tuck his hips in between her legs. He gave her a hard, possessive kiss, ignoring Dani in the same room just a couple feet away.

When he let go of her mouth, he spoke with a stern tone while looking her dead in the eyes, "You, future Mrs. Richmond, are beautiful and never think otherwise."

She smiled and gave him another kiss. "I love you, Richmond."

He smiled wide, "I hope so. Cause, you're kinda stuck with us now."

He pulled her off the counter gently, setting her feet back down to the floor.

"Are we taking the truck?" She spoke, giving him a sly smile.

He raised his brows with a wide smile. "Show Dani where it is, I'll park the truck at the station and walk over, so I can go straight to work after."

She laughed and gave him a warning smile, "Uh Huh..." and finished the sentence in a high-pitched voice, "Canary!"

He hooked his fingers under her chin and lifted up, "Then I suggest you better get something really good to eat."

She smiled and sashayed away as Luke gave her ass a soft swat through the thin fabric of the dress.

"Damn, you two are so cute!" Dani spoke and headed for the front door.

Daphne grabbed a lace white cardigan out of the closet by the door and Luke helped her put it on. After they locked up, Luke helped her into Dani's car, he gave her a kiss, and closed the door.

He walked over to Mikes truck, opened the drivers' door and saw his sweater Daphne had yesterday, still in the driver seat. He moved it over to the passenger seat and looked in the back seat for any evidence. Back seat showed some signs of excitement, so he sighed. He drove it to the station to clean and wiped down the entire cab.

"Thank God for leather seats" he spoke softly. Otherwise, he would have been here for another hour. He deemed it good that Mike would never know, and he could live the rest of his life happily married.

When he walked into the diner, he saw Dani and Daphne in the far corner where he saw Daphne the very first time. He smiled and walked over to them.

Dani had a grin watching Luke walk to them and slide into the booth next to Daphne. She was chewing a piece of toast, so he kissed her temple and put his arm on the back of the booth seat behind her.

Dani leaned over the table talking softly which Luke was thankful for, "She has been chomping at the bit. Your friend Mike has already come out to check on us and the waitress, I think already noticed the ring, but hasn't said anything. She just keeps smiling at Daphne."

Luke grinned at Daphne, still chewing on toast. "Okay, well I suggest if we want to tell Kada first, then we might want to take this to the office."

Daphne drank her orange juice, finally swallowing her food. Luke got up and helped Daphne up. He looked at Dani and gave a jerk of his head, "I'm gonna need you as an ice breaker."

Dani smiled then jumped up with enthusiasm. As they walked through the diner a few customers gave them smiles. Luke suspected that they hadn't even seen them together and was still getting used to that idea.

Luke spoke to the waitress as he walked by, "We'll be back. Save our table please, Katy."

She watched them walk by and gave a wide smile as Luke held Daphne's hand hiding the ring, "Sure thing!"

Luke led the way, followed by Daphne then Dani behind her, as they walked around the corner, through the kitchen swinging doors passing the smiling waitresses and waiters. They passed through the kitchen, and the crew never even gave them a glance. He headed back further, and took a right at the hallway, then down a few doors to the office on the right with windows where Mike sat hunched over papers and keyboard, typing away.

Luke gave a tap on the frame but didn't bother stopping to wait for permission.

"Oh, hey Luke, Daphne, Dani! Food good?"

Daphne nodded with a wide smile which made Mike drop an eyebrow with a smile and look at Luke.

"What's up?" Mike asked first.

"Have you met Dani?"

Mike smiled and sat back crossing his arms, "Yeah. I just met her out there in the diner."

Dani gave a short wave, as she stayed in the doorway. Luke and Daphne took the two chairs in front of Mike's desk, Luke on the left side holding Daphne's hand in his lap and playing with her ring, covered by the desk from Mike.

Luke looked back at Dani, then to Mike, "You might want to close the door for this."

Mike sat forward and braced his arms on his desk and gave Dani a nod to close the door, which she did.

"Richmond, what's going on?"

Luke also sat forward still holding Daphne's hand.

"We haven't told Kada yet so only Jen can know till after school, Captain."

Returning the formality as an understanding only they knew.

"Okay." he scowled at Luke then over to the grinning Daphne.

"I asked Daphne to marry last night after the picnic."

Daphne threw their clasped hands up on Mike's desk so Mike could see the ring as she blushed and danced in her chair.

Mike with a shocked look, had to blink a few times, then look at the ring. "What? Really? Wow! Congrats man!"

He immediately stood up and came around to hug Luke first then Daphne. He reached and held Daphne's fingertips to examine the ring closer. "Wow! That is a rock." He watched it in the light as he turned her hand.

Mike pulled out his cell phone to take a picture and Daphne moved to Luke's other side hiding her cast in his side. Something nobody questioned or gave a thought to. She placed her left hand on Luke's chest displaying the ring. Both smiled as Mike took the picture, then took a picture of the ring as Daphne and Luke held hands. He typed on his phone and hit send.

"Wait for it!" Giving Luke a look and smile.

Luke rolled his eyes and pulled out his cell phone to set it on the desk in front of him as the three of them took their seats again.

He turned to Daphne and Dani, "He told Jen, his wife.... my other sister-in-law."

Dani smiled and Daphne winced.

Mike looked at Daphne and Dani, "Welcome to the family."

Dani spoke first, "Waited 37 years for a brother."

"I win! I get a husband, a brother, sister in-law, niece, and daughter all at once!" Daphne smiled at Dani behind her, dancing in her seat, like she just won a competition.

Dani stuck her tongue out at her like two little girls fighting.

Luke and Mike laughed as Luke smiled wide and leaned over, giving her a lingering kiss till his phone rang on Mike's desk.

"Jen Davis" popped up on his screen.

Mike and Luke gave each other looks and laughed before Mike spoke, "Might want to put that on speaker unless you want to blow your eardrum."

"Too late, Dani did that this morning."

Dani laughed and winced at the same time as Luke answered and put it on speaker.

"Hi Jen. You're on speaker phone in the office."

A loud scream came through the phone making everyone cringe and laugh.

"My brother is getting married!"

Luke looked at Daphne and gave a laugh as he answered Jen, "That's the plan."

"I need to see this ring in person, I'm on my way!"

Mike spoke first, "Honey, hold up! They haven't told Kada yet."

"Oh...." a pause before she caught the drift, "Oh, gotcha. When you guys gonna be home?"

Luke put his empty left hand to his chin propped on the desk over the phone, "Daphne's sister is in town for a visit, and we were gonna eat some breakfast before I head to work, but Daphne and Dani should be home in another hour."

Daphne spoke up, "Go to Luke's though, I wanna be there when Luke and Kada get home."

Luke smiled and kissed her temple.

"Sounds good! Oh My god! Congrats you guys! I'm so happy for you!"

Luke and Daphne both said, "Thank You!"

Then Luke, "Love you, sis!"

"Love you too, Luke! See you guys in a bit."

Luke clicked 'End' on his phone then looked back up to Mike.

Mike now sat back in his chair with his hand folded on top of his head. "So, you pick a date or season yet?"

Dani spoke first, giving a sly smile, "I don't think they've had time yet."

Luke and Daphne both turned their heads and gave her a glare, as Mike just gave a wide smile and nod.

"Uh, huh. Yeah, I figured Luke would consummate a marriage *before* the wedding, He did the first time too." He glared at Luke, who just ruefully smiled.

Daphne flooded her lips inward and bit down and tried not to smile. Mike looked at her and Luke.

"Okay, well when you slow down and the stars and Northern lights stop spinning, let me know. "

Daphne and Luke gave Mike a solid nod before Luke spoke.

"Best man?"

Mike smiled, "Honored. Though we will have to call Freeman in for coverage."

Luke nodded.

Mike got up again and gave them all a hug including Dani and said "Congrats" one last time, before they walked out to the diner to eat.

When they were finished eating, Mike took their ticket, signed it, and waved it at them from across the diner with a smile at Luke. Luke threw up a hand at him.

"I guess breakfast is on Mike." He told the girls.

"Well fine, he's got breakfast, I got the tip." Dani spoke as she dug into her purse pulling out a twenty-dollar bill and putting it on the table.

"Thanks, sis!"

"Yeah, thanks Dani."

"No, thanks needed. Just take care of my lil sis."

"Done! Well, I got to get my exhausted butt to work. See you after I pick up Kada?"

"Yeah, we will be....at your house."

"Ours." He corrected and smiled as he stood up from the table.

Luke leaned over and grabbed her jaw with a hand and gave her a lingering kiss that had a few people gawking at them and screaming, "Yeah, Lieutenant!"

Luke waved a hand in the air and smiled without taking his eyes off Daphne.

"Love you."

She smiled and replied, "Love you!"

"Give Jen a hug for me."

Daphne gave him a nod.

"Bye, Dani."

"Bye, Luke."

Luke waved at the waitresses and some people as he left.

Chapter Fourteen

Dani parked at Luke's and Daphne used her own key for the first time. Smiling as she opened the door, she walked in. She wasn't used to being here without Kada or Luke. This was the first time without them. She will never get over how it smelled like him and hoped it would never change. She gave Dani the grand tour before they sat at the bar to sister talk.

"I'm so happy for you, Sis. I just can't get over that it's him, Richmond! Thee Richmond that saved you and now you are engaged to him. He has the most adorable daughter, and Oo, you're so happy and glowing! You more than anyone else I know deserves...." She held out her pretty manicured hands palms up and waved them around Luke's home. "...this and him!"

"Thanks, Dani. Now, if we could just find Darryl. I hate not knowing where he is or when he'll show up."

"If he shows up."

"Dani, this is Darryl, watching me date my hot firefighter neighbor."

Dani gave a grim frown. "Let's not worry about that, Luke wouldn't let anything happen to you. He has trouble not kissing you every 10 minutes. That man isn't about to let anyone break down his door and take his future wife."

"Daphne Richmond." Daphne spoke, getting a grasp on her future.

Dani smiled at her.

Daphne got curious so she asked. "How many times did you talk to him?"

Dani immediately spoke up, "Three. Once, to tell me you were fine and with him. And that was when I knew he was in love with you and called him out on it."

Daphne's face went into shock. "No. You didn't!"

"Oh, yeah. He wasn't very chatty and I didn't hear you. I just knew."

"Oh my god. What did he say?"

"Nothing, only that you didn't know yet and I told him to tell you." She gave Daphne a half frown.

"The second, was three days later, when you were in an accident and in the hospital cause of Darryl. He told me you were okay and sleeping after surgery. He had a few medical questions about you for the doctors and said he was pulling all his resources to find Darryl. Then the third, was three days ago. He said you and him had a disagreement, he was worried about you, and that you needed me. He gave me a day to get ready and flew me straight here."

Daphne knew exactly what disagreement she talked about. She took a deep breath. "I got scared. I fell in love with him and worried I might lose him and Kada if Darryl came after me again. So, to protect them, I wanted to run.... again, and he got upset, and I walked away."

Dani showed a grim face, "Oh, Sis. I don't think you could lose him. He has no fear especially when he knows what he wants and his daughter is him, in half the package with hormones and hair. Don't fuck with her. She'll whoop Darryl's ass and not break a nail!"

Daphne laughed and smiled because Dani didn't have to know Luke and Kada 24 hours to know who they were. She got up and gave Dani a big, long tight hug.

"I love you, sis."

"Oh! I love you too. He's a good man, Daphne. Fight for those two."

Daphne smiled over Dani's shoulder.

They heard footsteps as the door flung open and Jen came through. She closed the door, but didn't bother taking off her shoes or coat, before jogging across the living room to Daphne and Dani at the kitchen.

"Ooo, let me see. Let me see!"

Daphne proudly stretched out her hand with her ring on display for Jen to examine closely.

"Oh, even prettier in person. Damn, my brother has some good taste."

Dani and Daphne both laughed as Dani agreed.

"Jen, this is Dani, my sister. Dani, this is Jen, Luke's sister in-law, Mike's wife, and Kada's aunt."

Dani and Jen shared hugs and greetings.

The girls spent all morning and early afternoon talking about wedding ideas and their future. It all had Daphne's head spinning, but for her and Luke, everything since she moved in next door was a whirlwind. Life...her life happened fast, and she was still trying to get her feet under her, but she was excited for the future which now looked brighter as she looked around Luke's house, saw nothing but him and Kada, and smiled with her whole heart.

Jen searched Luke's kitchen and found ingredients to throw together some sandwiches for them and joked, "Need to stay healthy for the honeymoon. If my brother can't stop kissing you...well, I'll have a lot of nieces and nephews to watch soon."

Daphne took a deep breath and let it out. Dani closed her eyes and pulled her sister into a hug.

"What?" Jen asked as she plated the sandwiches.

Dani turned to Jen, "Daphne can't have kids. Her ex-husband...."

Daphne cut her off with a soft tone, "Dani."

Jen's face went into shock, "Oh my god, I'm so sorry, Daphne. I didn't mean...I'm sorry, I didn't know."

"It's okay, Jen."

Daphne took a breath and gave her the quick version of her past and Luke and Daphne's beginning...the first beginning, then finally why she came back to Birch Valley.

Jen gave Daphne the biggest tightest hug. "Sounds like Luke. Well, there isn't anyone better for you than him, Daphne. Luke has a heart of gold and knew exactly who to give it to. Give it time. You will heal and be able to have kids again. No doctor, especially Doc Clint, will tell Luke no or that it can't be done." Jen laughed, making Dani, and Daphne laugh too.

She continued, "We love you, Daphne. You came in and saved him and Kada. Nobody in Birch Valley will forget that, especially Luke, Kada, Mike, and I."

Daphne smiled and pulled up Luke's texts on her phone.

"I love you."

In a near instant reply, her phone chimed.

"I love you too. How is it going?"

"Good." She texted back.

"Good. Hey, I have an idea on how to include Kada. Trust me?"

"With my life."

"Xoxo. I'll be home soon."

As Daphne smiled at Luke's replies, Dani texted Trace to check in, tell him about Daphne's engagement, and her trip so far. Jen texted Mike to grab Sarah after school, come to Luke's, and that he wouldn't want to miss what was coming. The girls made plans for a girl's day out with Kada and Sarah, for this coming Saturday after Daphne got her cast removal on Friday. It scared Daphne not knowing how her arm would look, but she smiled and agreed anyway.

When they heard the guys pulling in with their trucks, Mike's Dodge with Luke and Kada and the pristine white command truck with gold printed *Birch Valley Fire Department* on the sides, with Mike and Sarah. Daphne got up and ran to sit on the Chaise and wrap up in the blanket to cover her hand. Jen and Dani stayed at the bar by the kitchen.

When Luke, Kada, Sarah, and Mike walked in, Luke and Daphne immediately connected with a smile.

"Hi Kada. How was school?"

Kada took off her coat and her backpack with Sarah, setting them by the door, then walked over to sit with Daphne and give her a hug.

"Good. Where were you guys this morning? Dad won't tell me anything."

Daphne looked to Luke who stuck his hands in his pockets, walked over to her, and gave her a quick peck. Then over to give Dani and Jen a hug as Mike held Sarah's shoulder, steered her towards Jen's lap to sit with her mom. Mike went and got a beer out of Luke's fridge and leaned on the counter.

"We were busy."

"Dad left his phone on the counter with his pager and radio."

"Kada! Enough, Daphne is trying to talk to you." Luke gave a sharp warning.

Kada pulled her eyebrows down as the others looked at Luke.

Luke looked at Mike and walked to the bedroom and when he came back out a second later, he looked at Mike again with a rueful smile.

Mike looked at Dani, Daphne, and Kada and it clicked.

"You mother...Luke! We are gonna talk about this later!"

Daphne yelled out, "Canary!" then laughed making Dani and Luke laugh too.

Luke looked at Daphne and tried to say her name between laughs.

Luke ducked his head and walked towards Daphne and Kada, "Yes, Captain!"

Jen, Sarah, and Kada held confused facial expressions. Dani looked at Jen and leaned over to whisper in her ear so Sarah wouldn't hear. Jen's eyes grew confused then went big.

"Daphne! Luke!"

Now Sarah and Kada looked around the room.

Luke spoke up, "Later guys. Not now." he spoke towards the kitchen then looked at Kada.

Kada looked at everyone watching them, "Dad, what's going on?"

"Me and Daphne have some news to tell you. Kada, you wanted a mom for so long and while we both healed from losing mom, your Aunt Jen stepped up and played that role for you."

Jen shed a tear and laid a hand over her heart then grabbed for her phone to video the rest knowing it was gonna be good.

"I'll always be grateful for that, but now I have a chance for us to get what we both want."

Kada's eyes lit up with a smile and looked at Daphne.

Daphne took over, "Kada, can I marry your dad?"

Kada wrapped her arms around Daphne not caring about her cast. "Oh my gosh! Yes!" then released Daphne to leap into her dad's arms crying. "I love you, Dad!"

Luke replied holding Kada, "I love you too."

Then back to Daphne to hold Daphne.

"But Kada, I think your dad has something else to tell you."

Everyone held their breath not knowing what was going to happen next,

Jen spoke, "Mike, pass the popcorn!"

Everyone laughed.

Kada looked confused and turned to face Luke, taking a seat next to Daphne as she put her arm around Kada.

"Kada, just because I'm marrying Daphne, doesn't mean Mom is gone. Me, Your Uncle Mike, and Aunt Jen love Mom very much and that will never change."

Kada's eyes began to fill with tears as she wiped at them.

"I miss her so much, Dad."

"We all do, sweetheart. It's okay, but this is to remember her and the promise that you will always have this family. Uncle Mike, Aunt Jen, Sarah, Me and now, Daphne and your Aunt Dani."

Dani and Jen scooted up to the edge of their seats to watch as they both cried.

Luke dug in his pocket and pulled out a small wooden box and opened it to reveal a small black pearl ring with tiny diamond accents in a silver setting.

"Dad, That's Mom's!"

He nodded. "It was Mom's engagement ring. I gave it to her when I found out she was pregnant with you."

Now Kada had rivers flowing down her face. Daphne rubbed her back and smiled at Luke. Luke crouched down in front of Kada and pulled the ring out and a small silver chain. He slid the ring on and wrapped it around Kada's neck and clipped it, moving her hair out of the way. She held the ring on the chain and stared at it.

"We will get it resized for you next week so you can wear it."

She leaped into Luke's arms, and he hauled her up into a hug as she cried in her dad's neck. As Daphne looked up, everyone had tears including Mike who drank his beer, then she stood up to fold herself into Luke and Kada's hug.

In the aftermath, after a box of Kleenex went around the room, Kada and Daphne showed off their rings and hugged as Mike pointed at Luke with a finger and scowl. Both of them laughed. They had a celebratory dinner while talking about the possible dates and seasons of a wedding and their future together.

After a long week, Daphne and Luke dropped Kada off at school Friday morning and headed for Freeman for Daphne's checkup and cast removal appointment.

Besides sleeping together every night, mostly in Luke's bed, this was close to the only time alone they had gotten together since the engagement. When it leaked out to Ms. Bellwood, it caught like wildfire, the town sent congratulations and questions every day.

Daphne and Luke were both happy for the break. Luke was relieved that Daphne hadn't had a second to think about Darryl and the problems he had caused so far. She stayed over the moon happy as he went to work and came home to her every night and after every call. He reminded himself every time he walked in the door what it was like to come home to just Kada, and some days, no one. He swore to himself that he'd never take Daphne for granted because he knew what the other side was like for him.

When Luke talked with Dawson after he heard the news of the engagement and came to the station, Dawson gave him the news that Darryl had not been found, seen or heard from yet, but was following some leads. It gave Luke a twinge of worry that he kept from Daphne and never said anything to her about Dawson's visit.

He drove the highway to Freeman holding Daphne's hand as she talked about the planned girl's day out to celebrate tomorrow with Dani, Kada, Jen, and Sarah. She worried what her arm would look like after the cast removal, but the excitement of the use of a second arm took most of the worry away. Luke smiled and kissed her hand and the ring on her finger.

When they got to the hospital they waited for scans and tests and one by one, they came back positive. Some relief. Next was the cast removal to see how it looked on the outside. She clenched tight with her left hand to Luke's, sitting next to her in the doctor's office as the doctor cut through the cast and opened it. Some dead skin and red scar tissue covered most of her shoulder. The doctor gently moved her arm and shoulder judging the range of motion and mobility. He deemed it good enough for a small brace that can be taken off and on for the next two weeks and that her healing was doing great.

Daphne let out a big sigh of relief as Luke smiled at her and gave her a gentle kiss. When they checked out, Daphne kept stretching her arm out and moving it trying to release the tension in her shoulder. Her and Luke got to the truck, and he sent a wide group text to Dani, Mike, and Jen telling them the good news and updates, then turned off his phone before anyone could reply.

When his phone chimed turning off, Daphne looked at Luke with curiosity.

"Luke?"

His left hand laid on the steering wheel and he turned to brace himself on the console between them while rubbing his jaw.

"It's our turn to celebrate our life. Mike and our crew are watching Kada and Sarah, Jen is hanging out at the two houses with Dani, and I have a hotel reserved for the night for us. Then tomorrow when we check out, Mike and the girls are coming in, you will go with the girls and Me and Mike are gonna go pick up my truck at the shop and head home."

Daphne smiled wide with shock.

"Aww, Luke. You didn't have to."

"Yes, I did. If we didn't have company at one of our house's, then we were being watched by the town now that it's out. I need you now and to myself. The others understood and said to tell you to enjoy yourself and...me."

She laughed, "Dani?"

He rolled his eyes, "Yeah."

She smiled and laughed then kissed him. He deepened it and leaned into her and opened her mouth with his tongue to dip inside then pulled back quickly.

"No! Mike will kill me now!" he laughed and put the truck in reverse to back out of the parking spot at the hospital.

When he pulled into a tall luxury hotel, Daphne's eyes got big as she looked at Luke as he parked. Luke got out and walked around pulling out the small duffle and large rolling suitcase out the bed of the truck. He then shut the tailgate and locked the truck with the fob. He looked at Daphne.

"Dani and Jen packed your bag with a few suggestions."

"Suggestions? Luke?"

He shrugged a shoulder, smiled, and gave her a kiss.

"Don't worry. Let's go check in and get settled. I need you soon!"

She glanced down at his pants that were now bulging.

He tucked a thumb under her chin and pulled it up as he kept a straight face. "Up here or we'll never make it to the hotel room."

He threw the duffle bag over his shoulder and used it to block anyone else's view until he got it under control as they checked in. The clerk checked them in, gave them the room card keys, and told them, "Enjoy your stay with us, Mr. and Mrs. Richmond."

Throwing Daphne off guard as her heart missed a beat. Luke smiled at her and kissed her, taking the room keys from the clerk and turning with Daphne to walk away. They rode the elevator in silence to the 19th floor and got off and walked down the hall to the end. Luke slid the key in the door, opened it, and held it open for Daphne to walk in first as he smiled.

Her eyes lit up as rose petals lined the short hallway opening up to the king bed with more rose petals. Candles and a bottle of Champagne on ice lay on the small table for two next to the large floor to ceiling, tinted windows that overlooked the city. A large bathroom with a jet tub that could fit five adults in it was filled with bubbles and more petals and candlelight. When she turned around to find Luke. He put the bag down by the bed and stood in the hallway entrance watching her with a wide smile.

"This was how I wanted to propose and how I should have done it to begin with."

Daphne smiled, "No. It was perfect. It was an amazing day and an even more amazing ending." She smiled. "This is perfect, Luke! Thank you!"

She jogged and jumped into his arms and wrapped her arms and legs around him. She was happy to have both her arms back. He gave her a sensual kiss and walked to the bed to flop her down on the white plush down comforter as petals flew up around them.

"I knew you were different." She spoke with a soft tone.

Her eyes turned a darker shade of blue as he sat up on his knees and pulled his sweater and shirt off, tossing them off the bed before devouring her mouth.

The whole evening had them both never thinking about anything except each other. Daphne dug through her bag to find out what Jen and Dani packed this time. She pulled out the same lingerie from the hospital, making her smile and laugh. Also, her gorgeous black silk cocktail dress that hugged all her curves with matching strappy stilettos and clutch. They got dressed up. Luke in a dark gray dress shirt and black dress pants with a black tie. She wore her Amethyst necklace and earrings Kada and Luke gave her for Christmas, that now matched her engagement ring.

Five years ago, this was a common occurrence to dress up. Now as she looked at herself in the bathroom mirror. She smiled at knowing who the effort was meant for this time, especially knowing Luke appreciated it and never expected it from her. To Darryl she was just a trophy for status at his company parties. So, dressing up and staying quiet on his arm was mandatory regardless of how she felt about it. Now, she loved stepped out of the bathroom and making Luke speechless. Something she told herself she wouldn't take for granted.

Luke took Daphne to a formal dinner and talked about their future and plans over Champagne and a King crab dinner. They skipped dessert and went for a swim in the hotel swimming pool and hot tub then took a shower together in their hotel room, before exhausting themselves to sleep, wrapped around each other near three in the morning.

At nearly 7am, Daphne woke up in a daze, still wrapped in Luke's arms. It was the best night sleep in over the last six weeks since she had her cast.

"Morning, Beautiful."

She looked up to him, looking down at her and smiled. She would never tire of that smile of his in the morning. After they got up, Luke showered alone as she sat eating a slice of toast, watching the tiny city streets below her window. After he got out, they ate breakfast together and enjoyed coffee and the view, before a knock sounded on the door. Daphne smiled and looked at Luke who ate a slice of bacon and drank coffee with a smile.

She jogged to the door and opened it for the girls and Mike. Greetings and excitement spread about the room and view. Luke and Mike talked while the girls talked about their plans. Luke watched Daphne holding Kada next to her with a relaxed pose at the small room table, laughing with them as he held her foot on his knee, under the table, across from her. His heart smiled, he never thought he would be this happy again.

After they checked out, Luke took the luggage from Daphne as Kada stood next to her. Dani, Jen, Sarah, and Mike had already started to head towards the vehicles. Luke stepped away from the counter and Luke pulled his card from the wallet he held and held it out to Daphne.

"For you two, to do some shopping together."

Daphne's eyes got big as she shook her head. "Luke, no! You've already spent enough. I can handle it today."

"No. You got the last shopping trip with Kada. This one's on me. Go buy a wedding dress and Kada a dress and whatever else you need, to tell me 'I do.'" He smiled.

"Daphne, Dad is letting us go shopping. Take the card, now."

She smiled, but reluctantly took it and slid it into her purse, leaning up and kissing him softly. "Thank you!"

He smiled and wrapped his arms around her. "See you tonight."

"Love you, Richmond." She said near his lips.

He smiled, "Love you, both!"

She let go and turned away with Kada under her arm as they walked to Dani's car and got in.

Luke walked to Mike's truck, stuck the bags in the back seat and got in the front passenger seat with a big smile at Mike.

The girls went to lunch and spent the rest of the day going shopping at boutiques and wedding shops. Daphne tried on wedding dress after wedding dress in all sizes and shapes, while the girls all tried on bridesmaid's dress. Though Daphne was having fun, and laughing with the girls, it wasn't real until she tried on a fit and flare, lace, long sleeve, off the shoulder, beaded bodice in Ivory white.

Dani zipped her up and buttoned it. Daphne hadn't even looked in the mirror yet and felt something tugging on her heart. As Dani smiled at her, Daphne joked, "Ok, dress number 1432 coming out!"

Dani laughed.

When Jen and the girls went into shock, Daphne asked, "What, does it look that bad?"

Kada spoke first, "Daphne, you need to look in the mirror!"

"What? Why?"

As she stepped on the pedestal and turned in the five large full-length mirrors, Kada and Dani fixed her train. Daphne stared at herself. Her heart stopped and she went silent. For the first time she felt gorgeous. But how, she hated the dress on the hanger. But this dress fit her in every way. So, she denied it.

"No! I don't even have a wedding date yet. No! We are just looking."

"Dad sees you in that, he'd be marrying you tomorrow! You are so gorgeous, Daphne!"

Daphne smiled and got off the pedestal to hide herself from the mirrors and before the girls could stop her, a shop attendant came over.

"Oh wow! That is absolutely stunning on you! Should we try a vail with this one?"

Before Daphne could tell her no, all four girls shouted, "Yes!" in unison. So, the attendant went to get one.

When she came back, she held a long floor length beaded veil to match the dress, pinned it in Daphne's long loose hair, and tossed the edges over Daphne's shoulders. The attendant put a handout to help her back on the pedestal. Daphne stepped up, then looked up.

"Daphne, you're a bride! My Dad's bride!" Kada spoke, taking Daphne to tears of joy. Daphne pulled Kada into her side for a hug as all the girls got up and got in a big group hug.

Dani spoke first as they all broke to tears.

"Who's calling Luke?"

They all laughed till Kada spoke up. "I will!"

She asked Daphne to use her phone and then got it from Daphne's purse. Daphne watched as Kada pulled up "Richmond " contact, making Kada smile. She clicked on the call button next to their last name and family picture of them three at the waterfall. Kada smiled and waited for her dad to answer.

"Hey Beautiful! Having fun?" He answered.

"Dad, It's Kada."

"Oh, hi sweetheart. You guys, okay? What's wrong?"

"Yeah. Mom...I mean Daphne found her wedding dress."

Her voice started to crack. Luke stayed silent for a moment, letting Kada catch her breath as the other girls all talked and played with Daphne's dress in the background. Kada walked over to the chairs and sat down.

"Kada, you, okay?"

"Dad.......... I have a mom. Like an actual mom." Tears started to stream down her face as the room got silent.

The girls all turned to look at Kada crying into Daphne's phone.

Daphne stepped off the pedestal and hiked the bottom of the dress up to jog to Kada and pull her into a full hug in her lap. "Oh, Kada."

Daphne took the phone from Kada wiping at Kada's tears, then clicked Luke on speaker.

"Hey Babe, you're on speaker."

"Hey. How's Kada?"

"She's crying here in my lap...in my wedding dress."

"OK, well if that dress can do that to her, then you have to buy it. Kada, sweetheart?"

Kada stopped crying into Daphne's shoulder and looked down at the phone in Daphne's hand, "Yeah, Dad?"

"It's an amazing feeling, isn't it? The feeling we had when Mom was here. Someone to love us the same way Mom did."

"Yeah." She looked up at Daphne and smiled.

"Daphne showed me how to raise you when I was trying to raise a little girl. I hated it, because it meant that Mom was really gone and that you were growing up, both of which are things I tried to stop for the last 8 years. I'm so sorry Kada. I failed us both. I was on autopilot just getting to the next day not realizing how I've been keeping us both from moving forward. Then I saw these two beautiful women walking towards me at the restaurant, my daughter and her mom and for the first time I had to accept I was not the hero, Daphne was. She rescued us. Today it was your turn to see it, as she stood in a wedding dress, probably beautifully glowing. Huh? She's ours, as she's been since.... you had to go bug the new neighbor when I told you not to. But I'm glad you did cause we both fell in love with her."

Everyone laughed, including Kada. Luke and Mike's laughter echoed through the phone.

Kada hugged Daphne and gave her a kiss on the cheek with a smile.

Sarah stepped around Jen and over to Kada wrapping an arm around her, "Hey Kada, your mom, is our school nurse. Next year Mr. Parks has to send you to see Nurse Richmond and...... For 8th grade formal, our moms can chaperone while Dad and Uncle Luke go to work at the station."

Kada's eyes grew big with a big grin. Both Mike and Luke spoke at nearly a shout through the phone their complaints and comments as all the girls laughed.

When they all quieted down from laughing, Luke spoke.

"See Kada! She's ours and so is Aunt Dani. So, make Mom buy that dress, I want to see it and get yours, then I'll see what I can do about changing her last name, soon."

"I Love you, Daddy!"

"I love you too, sweetheart. Now let me talk to her for a sec."

Kada gave Daphne another hug and kiss on the cheek with a big smile. "I love you."

"I love you too, so much!"

Kada jumped down off her lap and walked away with Jen, Dani and Sarah as Daphne took Luke off speaker.

Daphne answered, "Hey Babe."

"Hey. I was waiting for that to happen."

"Yeah, she's 12, but for her to call me 'Mom'. Luke, I never expected that."

"I did. She doesn't need dad at this stage. She wants to share mom's clothes and shoes and needs someone to understand her. Friend, and neighbor, Daphne and Nurse Kimble were never gonna last too long."

"Luke...."

"No, I'm actually pretty happy about it that she gets to experience it. I can't hold her forever, Daphne. but I never expected you to slap me that hard to get me to realize it."

He got silent and her phone chimed. She looked at it.

Text message from Mike Davis

She clicked on the message, and it pulled up the picture of the three of them at lunch in Freeman. Luke's hand on Daphne's leg under the table as he and Kada smiled at her. She smiled at the picture; they looked like a family.

"But everyone noticed before I did, so I guess I deserved it. But it's something me and Kada haven't had in a long time, so it's taking us a bit. We are Richmond's, but we are still human."

"And heroes." She spoke softly in reply.

Luke chuckled softly. "I love you, Daphne. Go enjoy your time with our daughter and buy that dress! I want to see you in it soon."

"I love you so much!"

"I'll see you guys tonight after you get home."

"Okay, bye Baby."

"Bye, Beautiful."

She hung up as the others were now drinking champagne and sparkling cider and watching her.

Jen and Dani Both held their arms open, with wide smiles and spoke in unison, "Sis!"

Daphne walked over for a group hug in her wedding dress then bent down to squat in front of Kada, "Will you be my Maid of Honor?"

Kada smiled big and threw her arms around Daphne.

The rest cheered.

When they left, Daphne held her wedding dress and Kada's dress in a bag with most of their accessories.

As Dani pulled into Luke's as Daphne smiled at Luke's truck next to them, just the same as it was. She never thought she could miss seeing his truck as much as she did until she got excited seeing it again. An overwhelming joy spread through her as she watched his truck while getting out of Dani's car.

She didn't stop smiling as she got out to take her dress home to stash it over at her house so Luke couldn't see it. She jogged across the yard with her big dress bag, as the girls walked into Luke's.

Daphne put the dress bag in the bedroom closet, closed the doors then walked to the front door with a wide smile and pure happiness until she opened the front door to see Luke. He stood there leaning against the frame with his hands in his pockets, a painful expression, and a fire in his eyes.

"Daphne Ryker?"

Her eyes got large as her smile fell flat.

"I'm not sharing my wife!" He spoke with a low growl.

She took a deep breath, but before she could answer he held up his hands.

"I know, you were kinda busy staying alive and finding me. but If I want to marry you next weekend, I need that option to be available. You are mine, not his!"

"Luke, I am Daphne Kimble. I never took his name." She spoke with guilt.

"But you are still... right now, married to the same man that nearly took your life?"

"Yes. But I'm working on it, I have papers."

"Fill them out and get them filed." He spoke with a fire as he stepped back from her. "What else is in Dawson's background check?"

"I told you everything else. Luke, I haven't been married for a long time. I played the role, but I wasn't happy. I'm happy with you. I am going to marry you. Today with Kada, I became Daphne Richmond, and I don't think my feet have touched the ground since. Please believe me Luke."

Her eyes told him guilt, and sorrow so he gave a slight smile and kissed her.

"Come here...." She took his hand and led him down the steps and into the middle of the shared yard facing the creek, then turned to face him.

"This is where I want to show you, my dress. This..." She spread her hands wide to stretch between their houses. "......This is us. This is where our story began. And over there..." She pointed to her bench in the back. "That is where I met Kada. You, I met at the diner, but I found Richmond, here. This is where we fell in love, and this is where I think we should get married."

Luke smiled and picked her up to his level.

"It sounds perfect. When?" His face holding no expression as he asked.

"I'll have papers filed and be divorced soon. I promise. But I think we should get married on July 26th."

His eyebrows came down in confusion.

"The day I met the Richmond's. It's our day."

He smiled again and spun her around, still holding on to her waist while planting a hot kiss before she pulled back.

"Luke, lunch is about to come back up. Stop please!"

He laughed and stopped. Over her shoulder, he saw Kada standing in his living room window watching them.

"That's a little over three months?" He said.

"I know. It's a long time to wait."

"You? You waited three years. Me, I've been trying to pin down your feet for the last nine months. But three more won't hurt I guess as long as this stays on."

He held up her hand and kissed her ring.

She smiled, "Forever."

"So, we have a date?"

"We have a date!" She said in excitement.

Luke waved at Kada as he kissed Daphne. Kada and the others came out to stand in the brown grass that started to grow new sprouts already. Daphne turned her head to see them coming out as Luke held her.

"We are getting married, July 26th." He told everyone that gathered around.

Everyone cheered and Kada hugged Luke and Daphne.

"Oh, and Kada is my Maid of Honor. She's mine for that day!"

Luke scoffed, "Hey, she was mine first!"

Kada clung to Daphne as their eyes went wide and they turned to run as Luke gave chase.

"Dad! No! " Kada screamed, holding on to Daphne's hand running with her!

Jen gave chase, "No! She is my niece!"

Kada giggled and laughed as she got chased around the yard with the biggest smile Daphne had seen on her face.

Over the next week, Daphne got the okay to return to work and smiled at their family picture at the waterfall that sat on her desk and next to another with a silver frame that held a picture of Kada and Luke sitting on the front bumper of one of his white and gold fire trucks.

Luke and Jen got to spend time with Dani that week showing her around the town, taking her off road and meeting the town.

At dinner at Daphne's cottage with Luke, Kada, and Daphne, Dani swallowed a bite of her food, gave Daphne a look.

"So, are you gonna tell him about next week?"

Daphne gave Dani a straight face, "No."

"He's gonna find out."

"Na ah. Not unless you tell him."

Luke looked back and forth to Daphne and Dani, chewing his own mouth full before swallowing it. "What?"

"Nothing." Daphne spoke and kissed him.

He looked at Dani and smiled, "What? April 24th?"

Daphne froze. "Dang it!"

Dani laughed. "Yeah, that day!"

"Already got it covered!" He smiled wide and looked at Daphne.

He pulled his phone out of his back pocket and smiled at Kada, "Should we show Aunt Dani?"

Kada gave excited nods and smiled.

He leaned away from Daphne to pull up the picture and handed his phone to Dani.

"Ah! Kada! You traitor. You knew too!" Daphne smiled and scowled at her.

"Dad told me." She laughed.

Dani took the phone and put her fork down to look at it as her eyes got big at the picture of his back living room window next to the mudroom. Then he swiped to the next photo, The design plans for a large bay window, big enough for a small family and room for him to stretch out.

"Oh my god, Luke! You're serious?"

"Yeah! I kinda love her! But I need some help with it." he told Dani then chuckled and smiled at Daphne.

She blew up the picture and looked at the plans closer.

"Of course, I'd love to help. She's gonna flip!"

"What? What is it?"

Dani pretended to pull a zipper across her lips and throw away the key.

"Dani! Luke?"

He reached over and took the phone back from Dani and clicked the screen off and stuck it in his back pocket then smiled and kissed Daphne again.

"Soon."

She smiled and took another bite of her food.

Kada spoke next to Dani. "Mom, you are gonna love it! Dad has the best ideas!"

She swallowed and smiled at Kada, "Yes, he usually does."

Chapter Fifteen

On April 24th, Daphne woke in her bed to a single red rose and purple iris on her pillow next to her. She smiled and turned to look for Luke but found her bed empty. She got up in her satin purple shorts and tank top and opened the bedroom door to see Luke leaning on her counter drinking coffee while talking to Kada and Dani. Her heart stopped when she made eye contact with Luke, and he smiled. He was so sexy, inside and out, and he was hers. She still had trouble believing it.

"Mm, Good Morning! Happy Birthday." He said as he set his coffee cup down and met her halfway to the kitchen to pull her into a hug and kiss.

"Happy birthday, Mom!" Kada sprang from her stool at the counter and ran to Daphne to join the hug.

Daphne pulled Kada into a hug, then kissed Kada on the cheek. When she stood up, Dani was right there pulling her into a hug. "Best birthday ever!"

"Happy Birthday, Sis!"

"Aww. Thanks! So glad you can be here!"

"Thank Luke. He called me."

"Just had to make sure I knew what I was getting me and Kada into." He laughed and smiled.

"Hey Dad, I love my Aunt Dani!" Kada spoke and wrapped her arms around Dani.

"Aww! Did you hear that, Sis, I'm Aunt Dani and she loves me!" She grinned from ear to ear.

Daphne went wide eyed and smiled, "I know and I'm Mom!"

Dani and Kada hugged again a little longer. When Kada released Dani, she smiled at Luke who now held Daphne.

"I must have been tired last night; I didn't even hear you get up." Daphne spoke.

Luke walked to the kitchen and poured Daphne a cup of coffee, doctored it to her liking and gave it to her as she kissed him.

"I had to pry you off me to get coffee." Luke chuckled and drank his coffee.

"Yeah, didn't feel a thing."

Dani looked at Kada then to Luke and Daphne, "What time did you guys go to bed?"

"Daphne hit the bed at about 11. I followed shortly after."

"And *after* that?" she scowled at Luke and Daphne.

Luke got confused not catching on until Daphne gave Dani a smack on the shoulder, then Luke rolled his eyes.

Kada, not paying any attention to them, jumped up and down.

"Kada, wait. Let Daphne wake up first." Luke spoke, still holding Daphne.

Daphne looked at Kada who had a wide smile.

"What's up?" She asked Kada,

"I wanna give you, my present."

She looked at Luke who just shrugged his shoulders.

"It's one large present that everyone had a hand in, including your sister, Mike, and Jen." Luke said with a smile.

Daphne smiled at him then looked at Dani.

"It's actually pretty amazing. I got to hand it to Luke, he did good."

"But mine first!" Kada spoke.

"Okay." Daphne stated as she went to take a seat on the bar stool.

Kada ran to the entryway and picked up a big box wrapped in purple wrapping paper and a rose gold bow!

"Aww. Look, it matches my jewelry!"

"That was also Kada." Luke spoke over his coffee cup, reaching for the pot then refilling his coffee.

She set it down in front of Daphne, who unwrapped it and opened the box. She pulled out soft purple and gray couch pillows in all different shades and sizes.

Daphne smiled. "Oh my gosh, they are so soft! I'm definitely using these for my window and couch. Aww, thank you, Kada!"

Kada and Dani laughed and looked at Luke.

Luke put down his coffee and pulled his phone out of his pocket and walked to Daphne. "They aren't for this house. They are for our house."

He pulled up the pictures and showed her the bay window designs, plans, and the picture of his back corner in the living room next to the mudroom. A large deep sunken bay window with couch built in and foot tall bookcase built in under the windows and storage underneath overlooking the creek and side view of Daphne's house. It was like hers, but bigger and better. Her eyes lit up as she took his phone and looked at them.

"You are getting me a bay window that could fit our entire family in it?"

"That's the plan of course if you give Mike the go ahead."

"Oh my gosh, Luke! I love it!"

Dani spoke to Luke. "Told you!"

He smiled and gave Daphne a kiss.

"Wait? Mike?"

Luke smiled. "That's the part we all are in on. Me and Mike are building it, Jen and Dani helped design it and Kada is decorating...with supervision. Otherwise, you would have had it pink and purple. We all agreed on gray and purple for you but also for my sanity and other decor." He chuckled.

"I love it! Thank you." She gave everyone a hug.

She hung onto Luke's phone and pulled up a new group text to Jen and Mike!

"This is Daphne. Luke just showed me the bay window plans. You guys are amazing! Lots of love! Thank you!"

Almost an immediate text back from Mike. *"So, this means I got the approval?"*

Daphne texted back as Luke watched over her shoulder. *"Yes!"*

"Awesome! You are very welcome. Happy birthday, Daphne!"

Jen finally answered back, *"Yay! Happy birthday, Daphne! Tell my brother to give you a hug! We'll see you for dinner tonight!"*

Daphne looked at Luke as he spoke with a frown, "Kinda a bittersweet dinner. A goodbye to Dani, but a birthday celebration."

Daphne looked at Dani.

"I gotta leave in the morning. Trace is going nuts with the kids."

Daphne laughed and smiled. "Yeah, I bet. But aww! Okay."

She got up and gave Daphne a hug, "But we already made plans to come back in July!"

Daphne smiled and hugged her sister tighter.

"Man, my sister is getting married..." Dani said

She left Daphne's arms to step over to Luke and Kada and pull them both into a hug.

"......to you! Thank you for everything you guys have done for her!"

"We didn't do anything, she found us, remember?" Luke smiled, giving a hug back squishing Kada in between them.

Dani smiled before she let Luke and Kada go. "But Sis, I have one more present for your amazing window. It's from Me, Trace, and the kids. Like your bay window, it was a group effort."

Daphne smiled. Dani walked over to the counter and pulled a small rectangle package down, wrapped in a shiny blue paper. Daphne sat at the counter and opened it as Kada, and Luke looked on with curiosity.

She pulled out A wooden picture frame with clear resin and sea glass in shades of blue, tan and white put together to look like a beach and ocean, with seashells and sand filling in the bottom just enough to still let light through like stained glass.

"Home."

She started to cry.

"It's made with everything from our beach."

Luke smiled at Daphne and rubbed a hand on her back as Kada gave her a hug.

Luke spoke softly over Daphne to Dani, "Outer banks?"

Dani nodded. "It's where we grew up."

Daphne looked up.

Luke smiled and nodded towards her coffee cup collection.

"Next time you want to hide, coffee cups from every place you've been might not be a good idea to have. At least out where neighbors can see. Cause then they do research and dig even before the background check." he smiled.

She scowled. "It's the only thing I have left and being 4,000 miles away from home isn't easy."

He smiled, "Well now you are 100 feet from home."

She shook her head, looked up at him and smiled, "No."

She bent down, picked up Kada to set her in her lap, and wrapped Luke's arms around both of them.

"I'm already home, just as I was 3 years ago."

He smiled big and leaned down to give her a kiss around Kada.

"Eww, I don't want to be stuck between you two! Let me go!"

Luke and Daphne in unison, held each other tighter, and squished her even more.

"Ahh! Dad! Mom!"

Dani laughed with Luke and Daphne. "Get used to it, Kada Kid. It's what parents do. I do it all the time to mine."

Kada smiled at Aunt Dani when she gave her the new nickname.

When Luke's pager went off, he reached down and turned off the alarm. Daphne pulled back and looked at him.

Luke spoke before Daphne could, "Mike can handle it."

"No. Go! It's okay. I'll hang out with the girls."

He smiled. "No, It's your birthday."

"It's fine! Go! Just don't rescue any more stray women."

He gave a hearty laugh, smiled and gave her a hard kiss then headed for the door before turning to look back.

"I love you both! I'll be back before dinner."

Her and Kada smiled back and replied, "We love you too!"

He smiled, bolted out the back door to his house, out the front now with his radio, and into the truck to flip on lights and sprint down the road. Kada and Daphne ran out the front door to wave to him as he passed. He smiled at them as he reported to Dispatch on his radio.

When he got to the station, Mike radioed to him to grab the rescue truck as Mike led the way. Luke slammed on the brakes in his station parking spot, jumped out, and pocketed his keys. He jogged into the station to grab gear, put it on, and jump in the rescue truck with Magar in the front seat. Hastings, Whitte, and two others sat in back as they pulled out of the station.

When he pulled onto the scene, he jumped out to throw commands to the crew for tools and walked to Mike standing twenty feet from the wreck. Mike turned to Luke and held up a hand to him, "Hold up Luke."

He took note of the informality and turned his head sideways. A banged-up silver Mazda, in similar style to Darryl's, laid on its flattened tires with broken windows and crushed hood. Luke's eyes got big and full of fire.

"Is he in there?" Luke spoke with force.

"Luke, back up!" Mike gave a stern command.

"Mike! I swear I will finish him before Dawson even arrives!"

"Lieutenant! Step down, now!" Mike held a hand to his chest now.

Mike's radio activated with dispatch, "Birch Valley command?"

"Command, Go ahead."

"State troopers responding. ETA 5 minutes."

"Copy. AST five."

Luke's eyes flared. Mike stepped sideways to block him and then grabbed with both arms around Luke's waist. Luke blocked and elbowed him in the chest before Mike could lock his arms, knocking the wind out of Mike as he hooked a leg and dropped his knee and hip under Mike's efficiently taking him down for a second, till Mike pinned Luke's arm, than shifted his weight and rolled a knee into Luke's chest pressing on his sternum, pinning him to the ground as Mike looked down at him with a hold on his turnout coat with his free arm. Luke shifted his weight and hips to throw Mike off balance and over his head. Hastings and Magar ran to break up the fight, grabbing Luke's arms and prying him back. Whitte helped Mike up as Hastings and Magar held Luke back.

"Mike!"

Mike looked at Luke dead in the face, "Don't do it, Luke!"

Luke took a deep breath and looked at Mike, full of rage.

"Luke!"

In two swift motions, he threw his head and helmet back into Magar's nose and tripped him before knocking him back. With his now free arm, he punched Hasting in the throat making him release to grab his throat as he gasped for air. Luke ran for the car, as Mike followed. He stopped short of the colorful birthday wrapped present in the front seat with a tag that said, "Happy Birthday, Daphne."

Mike and Whitte grabbed his arms before he could reach for the present through the shattered window. At the last second, Luke, Mike and Whitte heard the tick tick sound before the car blew, throwing the three men across the road, into the ditch and trees. The red Lieutenant helmet bounced on the road as the scene went silent and smoke filled the air.

The girls were smiling and laughing at Luke's house with Jen and Sarah when Dawson called Jen's cell.

"Hey, Dawson! What's up?"

Everyone turned to look at Jen on the phone as they had lunch.

"Yeah, Daphne's here. Dawson?"

She laid the phone down on the counter with a concerned face and hit the speaker button. Daphne leaned forward towards the phone.

Daphne held Kada in her lap at the counter.

"Hey, Dawson, What's up?" Daphne answered.

"Daphne, Jen, there's been an accident. Three members of the department are on their way to Freeman hospital in critical condition. Two of them are Luke and Mike. You should probably head there. I'm on my way, myself."

Daphne and Jens' faces filled with fear and tears as they hung up the phone and ran to grab keys and purses.

Dani shouted, "I'll drive!"

They left Luke's and jumped in Dani's car. Kada, Sarah, and Jen in the back seat of the explorer. Daphne and Dani up front. Kada and Sarah crying and screaming in Jen's arms as Dani pushed the speed limit all the way to Freeman. Daphne took a deep breath and turned in her seat to face Kada.

"Kada. Sweetheart. It's gonna be okay. Dad and Uncle Mike are strong. I need you to stay with Dani while Me and Jen go check on them when we get there. We will meet you in the waiting room as soon as we can, I promise!"

Kada could only nod through the tears.

Dani got verbal commands from Jen on how to get to the hospital once they hit the edge of town and when they pulled up to the Emergency doors. Daphne and Jen gave Sarah and Kada hugs and kisses and got out, leaving them in the car with Dani to find parking and running inside to the front desk.

"Where is Michael Davis and Lucas Richmond? They are our husbands!" Jen told the clerk.

She pulled them up on her computer, "They are both in surgery, but a doctor will be with you soon."

Magar and Hastings in turnout gear ran up to them and pulled them into hugs.

"Jen! Daphne!"

Jen and Daphne started to cry. "Oh my god! What happened?" Daphne asked them.

"We don't know. There was a silver Mazda and Luke and Mike got into a fight, then the car blew up with them and Whitte next to it."

"Oh god, Jen!" Daphne screamed and crumpled to the floor.

Jen bent down to Daphne with tears of her own, "Daphne. Daphne listen to me! They are going to be okay. You hear me? Luke and Mike will be okay!" She spoke with force.

Magar and Hasting bent down beside them to help Daphne get off the floor.

"Come on, Daphne." They said as they helped her up from the middle of the floor so others could get around them. When she stood, Jen threw her arms around Daphne in a full tight hug.

"Our men are strong. They are gonna be okay."

Dawson walked up to them in his full uniform and folded Daphne and Jen into a hug. "Hey, any news?"

Magar shook his head at Dawson and crossed his arms across his chest.

"Hey, they are the strongest men I know. They are gonna come home to you guys, they will."

Dani came in with Sarah and Kada as they ran to hug Daphne and Jen.

"How's, Dad?" Each of them asked Daphne and Jen.

Daphne and Jen both wiped the tears off their faces and looked at the girls.

"We don't know yet. We can't see them yet." Jen answered as Daphne held Kada tighter.

Magar bent down to face Sarah and Kada. "Both your dads are gonna be fine."

Daphne's stomach turned. She stood up and grabbed Hastings for support to steady herself. Jen watched Daphne turn pale, "Daphne, you need to sit."

They all walked to the waiting room as Hastings pulled out a bottle of water out of his turnout pants pocket and handed it to Daphne. She took a drink as she walked down the hall and wiped at her tears.

When the rest turned into the waiting room, Daphne kept walking, went into the women's restroom, and threw up in the trash can. She cried and tried to catch her breath. Jen came in behind her, filled with her own tears.

"It's just stress. It passes and will get better each time."

Daphne looked at Jen in shock. Jen, through her own tears, gave her a sad look and rubbed her back and took a deep breath.

"Their job is to save lives, ours is to support them, and fortunately for us, Mike and Luke are some of the strongest. They will survive."

Daphne grabbed a paper towel and wiped at her face. Jen grabbed the water bottle off the counter that Daphne put down when she came in and handed it to Daphne to drink.

"Water helps."

Daphne pulled the cap off and chugged half the bottle at once before replacing the cap and felt a little better. She looked in the mirror and ran a hand through her hair. She wanted to shatter. Her rock and strength to live was now laying in the hospital.

After two hours of waiting for news, Daphne fell asleep against Magar as Kada laid across his lap and Jen and Sarah against Hastings. Dani sat next to Daphne reading a magazine and a few other firemen and officers, laid stretched out across the various chairs and benches as Birch Valley's entire Emergency crews and a few spouses took up the waiting room.

When the doctor came in calling out, "Richmond." Daphne and Kada jumped up out of a dead sleep making Magar jump.

"Yes, that's Me! I mean mine.... ours!" Getting her bearings as she held Kada next to her. She pushed at her hair again and blinked to see clearer. "How's Luke?"

The doctor smiled. "He's gonna be just fine. He's pretty banged up and was in surgery for a couple hours getting what small glass and metal made it through his gear, removed. Though the force of the blast was powerful, whoever built it made it more for show then harm. So, his gear took most of the force and what little shrapnel there was. Besides minor damage to some tissue and skin, nothing made it deeper so he's pretty lucky. Scans and x-rays look good, so I'm confident it's mostly just scrapes and bruises. He will have to stay overnight tonight to be monitored and if he does well, I can release him in the morning. He is just waking up from surgery so he's gonna be pretty tired, but you can see him for a few."

Kada and Daphne let out a breath of relief and hugged each other as the firemen and Jen, Sarah, and Dani did the same behind them.

The doctor held another clipboard and called out, "Davis."

Jen and Sarah stepped up and he gave them the same positive news as Daphne and Kada. Everyone hugged and cheered with relief. And again, the same news for Firefighter Eric Whitte.

Daphne walked out of the waiting room with Kada and down the hall as Kada clung to Daphne's hand. When they came to his room, they looked in the window and saw Luke lying in bed with bandages on both arms, some bruising, small bandages, and scrapes on his face. He appeared to be asleep until Kada squeezed Daphne's hand tighter, and Daphne rested her other hand over it. Luke jerked up making immediate eye contact with Daphne then Kada and smiled.

Kada ran in with tears in her eyes. "Daddy!"

"Hi, sweetheart!"

Daphne moved to the doorway and softly shouted, "Kada, be careful! Dad is still in some pain."

Kada sat on the bedside and snuggled into Luke's arms around the IV tube and wires, putting an arm around his ribs. Daphne still stood in the doorway watching them as Luke looked up at her and made eye contact.

They didn't need words to talk and with a few shared facial expressions of pain, sorrow, and fear, Luke's eyes darkened as Daphne's filled with tears and wrapped her arms around herself. Luke gave her two small shakes of his head as Daphne wiped at her tears. She looked back up at him as their eyes shared their fears, but very different fears. Her eyes searched his, as she gave a few silent sobs. He gave one solid shake of his head as she dropped her head and took a step back into the hallway.

"Daphne!" He spoke with fear but softness.

She turned to walk down the hall.

Kada looked up just in time to see Daphne pass the window.

"Where is Mom going?"

"Just to give everyone updates." He inhaled and let it out, watching the empty door frame where she just stood a minute ago. He didn't like lying to Kada, so he changed the subject.

"You have fun today?"

She smiled and began to tell him about hanging out with the girls.

Daphne got up to a slow jog as she weaved her way through the halls as tears streamed down her face. She dodged doctors with clipboards and nurses with medicine and passed by the waiting room with Dawson and the crew.

When she passed the waiting room, Dawson and Magar noticed her as she passed and jogged after her. Dawson pointed down the south hallway, "Get Jen." Magar kept jogging and turned left down the hallway.

Daphne passed the front desk, ran out the emergency doors as they rolled in another patient, and kept running through the parking lot to the manicured lawn with a few trees and small pond. She paused at a tree to brace herself as she took a few deep breaths of fresh air as tears streamed down her face. Before she could gather her thoughts, a deep voice spoke behind her.

"Daphne?"

She turned around to watch Dawson walking up to her. She wiped at her face and hair.

"Oh. Hi, Officer Dawson."

"Please, it's Trey. I'm not on duty right now."

When she didn't respond he walked up and stood next to her with his hands tucked in his duty vest. He took a deep breath and just watched a duck paddle around the pond.

"He spooked you, didn't he? Because he's actually human and not invincible like you thought? I'm guessing you have some guilt over that cause whether it was Darryl, this snapped you out of a dream and into reality, even when you had doubts that Luke was everything you thought. He's been saving you and now you don't know how to save him. Now you know different that Darryl can hurt you both and you want to run, again."

Feeling a little crucified, her knees buckled making her fall to the soft grass and the sobbing came like a wave. Dawson knelt beside her and placed a hand on her back.

"Not a single damn word of that is true! Fight, flight or freeze response has taught you that running will save everyone. It's a lie. Though fighting might require some training, luckily it doesn't require certifications, textbooks, or tools. Just the same courage they possess. " He spoke softly, but with force before he saw her pain and anger.

"Luke knew what Darryl is capable of and still chose you and will always choose you. At least that's what he told me the last time I talked to him and told him I hadn't found Darryl yet. I was sworn to secrecy because he didn't want to ruin your engagement glow. So, if you are gonna run, you better find the lost city Atlantis because he'll never stop chasing and fighting for you now. He'll destroy everything he knows to save the only world he wants."

She started to cry harder as he kept rubbing her back.

He spoke with a softer and lower tone now, "Daphne, you don't know the other side of Luke, the side before you. We did and let me tell you, Lucas is not the same man. He was a shell; you gave him a life and purpose. You loved him even when he didn't know how to love himself or anyone else and don't even get me started on Kada. Jen tried her best, God bless her, but Kada lost both parents when her mom passed and now, she has both of them back."

He looked back at the parking lot to see Jen running with Magar towards them and then turned back to Daphne.

"Daphne, please don't leave them. Fight back. Fight with him. I can promise, Luke and Kada are worth the fight through this. Luke is alive and needs you, just as much as you need him and Kada."

He stood up just as Jen and Magar reached them.

"Daphne! Oh my god. Are you okay?" She looked at Daphne sitting on the grass then up to Dawson who just gave her a small sad smile.

Jen bent down in front of Daphne and pulled her into a hug.

Daphne just cried it out on Jen's shoulder, thinking about what Dawson said. Maybe it was true. Magar sat down next to her in his turn out pants and boots and pulled out another bottle of water from his pants pocket and handed it to her. She drank it, then looked up at him. Light blonde hair, buff build, younger than Luke and Mike.

"You know from our perspective, hero or not, our bravery doesn't come from a badge or paycheck. It's from our families at home that support us. That's our strength. He needs you Daphne to do his job. Saving strangers doesn't matter unless the ones we love are safe. Lieutenant was just starting to come back with a smile, he doesn't live at the station anymore and he is giving us the fun exercises. Please don't make me go back to keeping the lawn manicured and trucks polished."

Daphne gave a small laugh.

The three of them laughed and cheered. "Hey, she's back!"

Daphne smiled and wiped away her tears and leaned against Magar, who put his arm around her and gave her a tight one arm squeeze, then helped her up.

She took a deep breath. "Thanks guys!"

She gave them all hugs. Jen threw her arm around Daphne and her head on Daphne's shoulder as they walked back in with Magar and Dawson following them.

"It's okay Sweetie, Magar and Dawson will go with you to talk to Luke. Me, Sarah, and Kada will go get some ice cream with Dani."

Daphne wiped a little better at her face and hair and Jen swatted at her hand.

"Stop that. You're fine! You could be wearing a trash bag and Luke wouldn't even notice. This is the process almost every fire wife goes through. It's normal. I did it with Mike but trust me it gets better. Eventually you'll realize that he has a heart too big to do any other job and the only time we get to even come close to understanding them is tomorrow, when they walk out of here and radio dispatch that they are available to respond and back in service area. Because that is who Mike and Luke are."

Daphne took a deep breath, smiled and rested her head on Jen's shoulder as they walked inside the hospital and down the halls.

The sounds of men's laughter got louder as they got closer. When they rounded the corner, firefighters and police overfilled Luke's room spilling into the hallway.

Magar stepped in front of Daphne to push them through the crowd. "Hey move it! Coming through!" when he reached Luke's bed Daphne heard a "Hey man! Thanks for the save. If it weren't for you and Mike decking each other, we all would have been on the car and lying next to you."

Luke's voice spoke, "Yeah well, no fire textbook I know will teach you how to save lives by fighting your Captain either."

"No, just your small-town Lieutenant." Magar laughed with the rest of the men.

"But anyway, I brought someone to see you."

"Do I actually get to meet the new Magar addition?"

Magar sounded a little disappointed, "No, not today, but soon I promise." He paused, " But take it easy though Lieutenant, this one is also fragile. It took some time and convincing but Me, Dawson, and Jen put some pieces back together for you."

Luke's face went from a smile to flat as he sat up to look around with wide eyes as he was now dressed in his jeans, but shirtless as the monitors and IV still hung from him around the small bandages.

"Hey guys, clear out!" Magar spoke loud enough for everyone to hear.

When they dispersed and started to leave the room he caught a glimpse of Daphne's chocolate brown hair and his heart tripped. When she finally came into view, Jen and Dawson stood behind her. Luke got up out of bed and started to walk towards her and got caught up by the IVs and wires. With one jerk, he ripped them off and tossed them at the bed next to Magar.

He grabbed Daphne in one swoop and lifted her up not even caring about the pain from his bruises, bandages, and scrapes that scattered across his chest and arms.

"I'm so sorry, Daphne." He grabbed her face with one hand to look at him. Her eyes filled with tears.

Magar and Dawson gave Luke a pat on the shoulder on their way out. Jen spoke up, "Where's Kada?"

Still watching Daphne, he jerked his head to the right, "In the waiting room with Dani and Sarah."

"Okay. We are going for ice cream. We will be back."

"Thanks, Jen."

"Hey, love you, Bro!"

"Love you too!" He replied.

Now alone, Daphne wrapped her arms around Luke's neck. "I'm so sorry, Luke. I thought I lost you, then Kada looked to me, and my head got dark when I saw you and I don't know....my feet just ran. I'm not strong like you."

Now he kissed her hard and long. When he released her mouth, he released his hold and let her slip back to the floor.

"You will never lose me, but you have to stop running, Daphne. When I saw you leave, I thought you were gone, and I had no way to stop you."

Daphne smiled. "You almost did, till Dawson...or Trey talked me back from that ledge then Magar and Jen jumped on the bandwagon. Magar said I had to come back because he didn't want to do station yard work anymore."

Luke rolled his eyes and gave a chuckle. "Damn. Now I gotta give him that promotion."

When Daphne softly chuckled and smiled, Luke smiled even bigger.

"There's my girl. My beautiful future wife."

He took a couple steps back holding her hand, sat on the edge of the bed, lifted her up, braced her knees on either side of his hips.

"I love you so much, Daph!"

"I don't know why, but yes I love you too!"

Luke smiled. "Because every time I lose you, I lose myself."

"I'm so sorry, Luke, I never meant to......."

He kissed her again with more hunger. Daphne and Luke both smiled. Luke spoke softly rubbing a thumb over her cheek, "Let's go home, so I can at least catch the rest of your birthday."

"Sounds amazing."

Luke got dressed and grabbed his bag of personal items off the rack taking out his cell, keys, and wallet to put back in his pockets. Then put on his dirty and hole torn turnout coat for cover since his shirt was trashed.

He held Daphne's hand while they visited Mike and Whitte, who were also checking themselves out, against the doctor's recommendations and a few protests from the crew. After paperwork and meds, Mike, Whitte, Luke, and Daphne walked out as Dani pulled up with Sarah, Jen, and Kada.

"Daddy!" Luke caught Kada in mid-jump from running across the parking lot as Mike gave Sarah and Jen both kisses and hugs.

Jen looked at Daphne, "See!" and gave her a big smile and a wink.

CHAPTER SIXTEEN

While Mike and Luke took it easy for the next couple of weeks healing from the accident, they remodeled Daphne's bathroom and built the bay window in Luke's living room for Daphne.

Daphne was sad to leave her house mostly empty. She took one last look around and grabbed the last packed box from the kitchen counter, shut off the lights and walked out the back door as Luke walked across the yard. He took the box from her and gave her a kiss.

"Ready?" He asked as Kada, Mike and Jen came up behind him.

She sighed, "Yeah."

"It's still here, and it's just the guest house now. Dani, Trace, and the kids will be here soon to fill it for the wedding."

She smiled at him now and looked at his house that was now theirs. He leaned down and gave her another kiss and turned to catch up to Mike and Kada already headed back to Luke's.

Jen dropped back to lean in and whisper to her, "When you gonna tell him?"

Not really shocked but surprised that Jen figured it out when she herself was still denying it.

"Depends on how long I can hide it…" She placed a hand on her belly now, "…Hope fully after the wedding."

"Daphne, he'll know before then, you need to tell him. He's gonna be excited."

"I just don't want him to feel the heartache I had to get used to after losing a pregnancy. He's lost a wife and child; he doesn't need another."

"But in two and half months he will marry his wife, pregnant with his child. He's gonna find out, He is kinda trained in emergency medical care. Plus, Richmond's are some of the strongest people I know. He'll never quit on his kids or you."

Daphne smiled at Jen. It was hope she never had before.

A month before the wedding, it was getting harder and harder to hide the morning sickness from Luke and Kada, who assumed she was getting sick, but the symptoms were not going away. Daphne still denied it herself, telling her it was a combination of sympathy over her loss and baby fever.

Dani flew in to help with the wedding and the bachelorette party. Daphne and Kada drove to Freeman in the morning to pick her up from the airport.

"Mom?"

Daphne looked to Kada as she parked her Jeep in the airport parking garage and put it into park, then looked over to Kada.

"Yeah?"

"What's it like having a big sister?"

Daphne brought her eyebrows down, "It's kinda like having a best friend that is always around no matter how much you fight or love each other. Someone that understands you and that can hate and love you at the same time because of it."

Kada smiled.

"Like Sarah?"

Daphne nodded with a half frown.

"Yeah, if you lived with Sarah for 18 years and shared everything you own with her."

Kada and Daphne both laughed.

They got out of the car and Kada ran around to Daphne to give her a hug.

"Hey, we haven't spent much time together, it's been pretty crazy lately. Maybe we should do a Gilmore Girls night soon before the wedding, huh?"

Kada smiled really big and gave Daphne a tight squeeze around her stomach.

"Oh, Kada. You are getting stronger."

Kada dropped an eyebrow and an arm leaving one wrapped around Daphne. They walked into the airport and rode the escalator down through the lobby and back up to the arrivals gate.

When Dani's plane landed and Dani walked through the gate, Kada and Dani both shouted, making everyone look at them.

"Aunt Dani!"

"Kada Kid!"

They ran to each other and into a big hug as Daphne hung back from that group hug, smiling at them both. Dani looked up to Daphne then down to her belly and instantly dropped her eyebrows with Kada still wrapped around her waist and walked towards her sister. Daphne widened her eyes, not really shocked that Dani pegged it right off the bat. But laid a finger on her lips to keep her quiet.

"Hey sis!" Dani spoke as she reached Daphne while Kada let go.

Dani wrapped her arms under Daphne's and placed a hand on her stomach. Daphne hooked her arm under it and pushed it up to her shoulder with a smile.

"Hey Dani! Missed you."

"Oh, My god! Did you hear Jackie's daughter is pregnant?"

Daphne sighed and rolled her eyes at Dani.

"Supposedly Jess is pregnant, but it's not confirmed."

Kada watched them and then spoke up, "Who is Jackie?"

Dani looked at Daphne and without missing a beat Daphne spoke, "Jackie was our mom's best friend, who kinda took us in when our mom passed. Jessica is her daughter, who grew up with us, just like you and Sarah."

"Oh! Okay." Kada smiled and walked on the other side of Daphne holding her hand.

Dani smiled at Daphne and gave her a look.

"Do you think Brian knows?"

"No. If she hasn't confirmed it, why would she tell Brian? Brian put her on a pedestal and has no plans to take her off, she wouldn't give Brian any more reason to make her more fragile." Daphne looked to Kada and smiled and gave her a gentle squeeze as the three walked to the escalator and rode it down to the baggage claim. To keep up the facade for Kada, Daphne kept going, "As long as she hasn't changed since I'd seen her last, Jess is cautious."

"Well, what about Jess's best friend.... What's her name?"

Daphne dropped her eyebrows showing her irritation.

"Julie?"

"Yeah, the one married to Brian's brother?"

"Julie. Umm, I don't know. I would assume she's guessed by now. They are pretty close."

Dani slugged Daphne in the arm making Daphne stumble.

"What the.... Dani!"

"So, you and Julie both knew about Jess being pregnant before I did?" She nearly shouted.

Daphne looked to Kada who was now just as shocked as Daphne, then back to Dani with a mean scowl and now with a low growl clenched her teeth together, "It's just a rumor! Jess and Julie talk a lot, it doesn't mean anything. Jess is probably just sick. Jesus, Dani!"

Kada looked at Dani with a confused scowl.

"Sorry, Kada. Just old town gossip."

Daphne switched hands with Kada, as she rubbed her shoulder on the opposite side when they reached the luggage carousel. After they got Dani's four bags of luggage, Daphne asked as they walked back to Daphne's car, "When are Trace and the kids supposed to come in?"

"On the 19th. Just a week before the wedding. Trace has to work, and Jackie is down to help him take care of the kids."

"Oh Okay. I miss them. Can't wait to see them."

Dani gave her a hug. They miss you too. Maya is so big now." She is almost as tall as Kada."

Daphne's face went into shock as she looked at Kada and back at Dani.

"Yeah. It's crazy. These kids eat twice as much as we did and never stop growing."

"Well, Kada eats like her dad and if Maya is still the same rugrat that I remember, then yeah, I can see it."

They both laughed as they reached Daphne's car.

On the ride home, Kada watched Daphne and Dani talking and catching up, soaking in the sisterhood that she never had.

When Daphne pulled up at her old house, Luke immediately came out and walked across the yard to meet them.

"Hey, Dani."

"Oh, Luke!" She stopped to look up and walk over to greet him and give him a hug.

Luke wrapped his arms around her tiny shoulders.

"Oh, feels like you are doing better than the last time I seen you."

Luke laughed. "Yeah. Finally, I have no limitations at work. I thought I would get soft just redoing Daphne's bathroom, building a window, and playing with the sirens." He chuckled.

"Well from where I stand, I can't notice, but I'm sure my sister would have told me something if you got too soft."

Luke smiled and side stepped closer to Daphne.

"Dani!" Daphne looked to Luke, "No! I wouldn't have."

Luke laughed and now folded his arms around Daphne and lifted her up to plaster a hot kiss. Then move her to his side and pick up Kada on his other side.

"Soft isn't part of my job description." he chuckled.

Kada laughed as Dani nearly screamed. "Luke! Oh my god! Put my sister down!"

Luke dropped his eyebrows.

Daphne glared at Dani, stuck in Luke's grip with a uncomfortable look.

"Before you hurt yourself. Jeez. You're still healing."

"I'm fine, Dani. Daphne is light. I hauled more redoing her bathroom." He laughed but put Daphne and Kada down.

Kada watched Daphne and Dani make eye contact and took mental notes.

"Okay, well I'm gonna get Dani settled in and we'll be over shortly." Daphne spoke.

"Okay. Well, Mike and Jen are coming over in a bit for ribs. Mike wants to talk about some bachelor party ideas. No clue." Luke smiled.

"Uh, huh. Just remember who you are marrying next month."

Luke placed both hands on Daphne's hips as Dani looked at Kada, "Uh, huh. Kada Kid, will you help me with the bags since Mom and Dad both have their hands full."

Kada laughed, "Yeah. They may be awhile. They may even skip dinner too."

Dani, Luke, and Daphne all laughed as Kada took a bag from Daphne's trunk and hauled it into Daphne's cottage while Dani followed.

Luke turned back to hold Daphne, "So how are you feeling?"

Daphne smiled as her stomach turned, "Good."

Luke smiled, "You look like you are doing better. I know you've been sick lately. Just get rest and fluids now because I don't need you sick over our honeymoon. Have you decided where we want to go yet?"

She gave him a thoughtful look, "Umm, No. But I don't think I'll be ready for a bikini anytime soon."

"Daphne you are gorgeous, why won't you believe me? Scars are just trophies."

Daphne smiled again and leaned up to kiss him.

"Because you are the only one that I need to look beautiful for, And I'm just now accepting that."

"And you are absolutely gorgeous. But I personally cannot wait to see you walking down that aisle towards me in this dress that had our daughter crying."

Daphne's stomach moved again, so she let go of Luke to drop back on her heels and further away from him. "Mm. Soon, Mr. Richmond. Soon."

"My wife."

They both smiled.

Dani screamed from inside the house as Daphne turned to look at the front door. "I think she just saw the bathroom."

They both laughed.

"Ok. I'll let you handle that. Mike and Jen should be here soon. So don't take too long."

"I'll try not to. Hey! Wanna take Kada with you so I can visit with my sister?"

Luke wasn't even surprised at the question and nodded as he walked with her to the front door and called for Kada.

"Kada, come help with dinner please. Sarah, Jen, and Uncle Mike should be here soon."

Kada came walking around the stairs from the bathroom as Daphne walked in. "Aunt Dani likes the bathroom." Kada said, rubbing her ears with a painful wince.

Luke laughed and kissed Daphne before turning and walking out with Kada in tow.

Dani came around the corner as Kada and Luke disappeared out the front door.

Dani spoke softly but with excitement now, "Oh my god, you could give birth in that bathtub!"

Daphne laughed and put her finger up to lips to keep her quieter.

"Mike gave it to me. It was left over from their renovation projects."

Dani moved to the kitchen window to watch Luke and Kada go inside Luke's front door then turned around to stare at Daphne.

"So, when are you due? What is it? And why haven't you told Luke yet?" Dani spoke as her tone got louder and fiercer.

Daphne smiled and rubbed her bloating belly.

"I don't want to get his hopes up. You know how pregnancies go for me and besides, it's not even confirmed."

"Well, we are just gonna have to fix that. Make a doctor's appointment tomorrow and I'll go with you and if it turns out to be just the flu..." She looked down at Daphne's swollen belly, ".... with some constipation.... then Luke will never know, but if it's not, then you have to tell him Daph."

Daphne smiled. "Fine. But in Freeman. Doc Clint, out here, wouldn't be able to hold that secret."

"Ok. And while we are there, we can do some shopping for Luke's wedding ring like we talked about and anything else we need for the wedding."

Daphne smiled.

"Ok but you need to tell him you are taking me out, so Kada doesn't start asking questions."

"Do you think Kada would.... sing like a canary?" Dani laughed.

"Mm, maybe, but I think it would be because of excitement for a sibling. You know she asked me how it was having a big sister today?"

Dani grinned and placed her hands over her heart.

"Aww! See, even Kada wants a sibling. You need to tell them."

"I will, if it's true and when I'm in the second trimester."

"Call in for an appointment and we will find out."

Daphne smiled.

When they heard Mike's truck pulling down the road to Luke's, they went out and grabbed the rest of the luggage as Jen jumped out with Mike and Sarah in Luke's driveway.

"Hi, Dani!"

Jen spoke from across the yard, then carried in a bowl wrapped up with saran wrap into Luke's with Mike and Sarah. Dani smiled, waved, and spoke through her teeth tightly clamped together. "Oh, she is so dead for not telling me, my sister was pregnant."

"Dani, be nice. She didn't know much either."

Dani glared at Daphne as she rolled in the bigger of the suitcases.

A few moments later Jen came walking through the front door.

"Hey! Luke said you guys were getting Dani settled in and having a sister's moment."

She looked at Daphne then to Dani with confusion when either of them didn't say anything.

Dani walked across the living room and took her purse off the counter to smack Jen with it.

"How come you never even texted me that my sister was pregnant, Jen?"

Jen, now shocked, looked from Dani to Daphne, who had her hands up.

She spoke with excitement, "So you confirmed it?"

"No, not yet. Probably tomorrow."

"Oo! I wanna go!" She said now, really excited with big eyes.

"You two, Luke is gonna kill me already and if I drag you two to the doctors with me and it is true then he's gonna kill all of us. Luke, Mike, and Trace are gonna be single raising our kids."

Dani laughed. "Might do Trace some good."

"Yeah, Mike won't starve. And he'll probably be happy not having to keep up with all my projects. Sarah is practically old enough to care for herself."

Daphne just laughed and held her stomach that turned again, sending her running to the bathroom to throw up.

Dani and Jen both stood in the doorway watching her.

"Oh, I do not miss that." Jen spoke softly.

Dani laughed and turned to get Daphne a glass of water from the kitchen and hand it to her beside the toilet. "You're pregnant, Sis."

Jen smirked and nodded in agreement. "You won't be the only addition to the Richmond family, that's for sure."

Daphne smiled. "Oh my god. This is getting so hard to hide from him and especially Kada. She is so observant. Where did she get that from?"

Daphne looked at Jen now standing closer and leaning against the sink.

"Her mother. Jasmine knew everything just by looking at someone for the first time. Mike has it too. It's a Davis thing." Jen rolled her eyes and smiled at the thought as memories ran through her head.

"Great, so I not only got to hide from Luke and Kada, but Mike now?" Daphne groaned.

Jen waved a hand through the air and rolled her eyes again. "Oh Honey, Mike already knows. He's been pillow talking that you might be for the last month but without confirmation from me, Luke or you, He hasn't said anything."

Daphne now looked to be in pain before groaning and throwing up in the toilet again.

Dani spoke from the wall next to Daphne, "Yeah they are observant. I swear Kada was gonna bust Luke and Daphne in Mike's truck that morning of their engagement." Dani laughed.

"If it was Luke's truck, she might have. But being Uncle Mike's, she probably didn't think mom and Dad would be *sleeping* in there." Jen chuckled

"We need to tell the guys we are taking Daphne shopping tomorrow in Freeman so we can get her checked out at the hospital and figure out a way to keep Kada and Sarah here."

"I'm on it! Luke won't ask me questions." Jen grinned

"Jen, just be nice. He's got a lot on his plate, and this will not just be a side dish."

"No, but firemen are always hungry." She grinned and giggled.

Dani and Daphne looked at her with a smile while they both rolled their eyes.

When they got Dani settled and Daphne was back in order with some added makeup to keep her looking better, they headed back to Luke and Daphne's. They walked in laughing as Luke and Mike looked at them from the kitchen. Mike and Dani hugged and greeted each other.

"All settled in?" Luke asked her then looked at Daphne walking with Jen.

"Yup! But it's gonna be weird being over there by myself."

"Well, you could have the couch here if you want it."

"No. His house is getting smaller every time I see it."

Daphne kinda giggled as Mike and Luke looked at each other. Luke walked around the counter now, over to Daphne to wrap his arms around her, and give her a soft kiss making Daphne's stomach move again. He looked at Daphne and searched her eyes.

"Hey, Jen and Dani want to take me out tomorrow and do some shopping. Kinda like a sister's day just the three of us?"

"Yeah! We have to visit a couple stores for the honeymoon, and I have some prepping ideas to get her ready to be a Richmond." Jen spoke.

Dani mumbled under her breath, "Be or have?"

Luke, not really hearing, looked at Dani who just smiled at him.

"I mean yeah, whatever you got to do. Mike and I have some meetings at work, and I have to do training with a couple of the guys, but Kada and Sarah can hang out here. Mike and I will check on them."

Daphne jumped a couple of times with excitement before she smiled wide and kissed Luke again.

He saw Dani and Jen's faces of shock behind Daphne and watched it fade when Daphne wrapped her arms around Luke's neck and shoulders.

"I love you Richmond."

Now he smiled and forgot everyone in the room. "I love you. We need to figure out where we are going for our honeymoon soon. I don't want to see this house for at least two weeks after we walk out of here."

Daphne smiled. "Soon. I promise. We'll talk."

He kissed her again, making Daphne's stomach turn again.

"It's cold in here." Daphne shivered and walked to the bedroom, coming out a minute later pulling Luke's Station sweater over her head and down over her stomach to her thighs.

Luke smiled then handed Mike the platter of kabobs and burgers for the grill across the counter with a shared look between them. "We better get started on dinner."

Later that night, when everyone said their goodbyes and Luke said goodnight to Kada, he walked into the bedroom to find out Daphne had already passed out. He stripped his clothes off and slid in the blankets and rubbed a hand up her side feeling the soft material of one of his cotton t-shirts. He smiled and stretched out beside her wrapping an arm around her waist and pulling her closer to him and kissing the back of her neck.

"Mm." she moaned softly.

He rubbed his hand up and down her side and kept kissing her neck. Sleepily, she rolled over and tossed her leg over his hip as he continued to kiss her neck now down her collarbone. He worked at the bottom of the shirt to pull it up.

She rolled their hips, so she sat over him and freed herself of the shirt, putting her upper body on display in the dim lighted room leaving shadows over her. He searched the shadows of her face and held her hips over his.

Running his thumbs over her hip bones and up over the growing stomach he took in everything. He ran his fingers gently over her scars and small stomach, touching every single scar softly.

She felt the rise of his erection under her and laid over him bracing a hand on either side of his head to kiss him letting her tongue dip inside.

He ran his hands back down her sides and to the edge of her shorts and pulled them and her panties down over her cheeks as he pressed his hips up. She released her legs free of the shorts and kissed along his neck. She slid her hips back over him and down pressing him into her slowly.

Luke gave a moan.

"Daph...." His breaths caught as he closed his eyes and arched up to her.

She rolled her hips pushing down and back as he held her waist to refine from too much movement.

"Daphne, I'm not gonna last."

She closed her eyes and took a deep breath as she sat up and pressed him deeper. "I don't care, I need you."

"Daph...No." He groaned in pain from resisting.

She braced her hands on his chest as she rocked her hip back and forth ever so gently. His hands spread wide on her waist as his thumbs moved over her stomach for a full grip and he tried to slow her. He felt how hard her belly was and looked at it and up to her face, but she kept her eyes closed as she rode him. Forgetting now about what he thought, he was sent to the edge.

"Daph. Daphne."

She kept her eyes closed as her hips rocked back and forth pushing him deeper and sliding out.

"Daph!" On the edge of breaking, he nearly shouted as she kept her eyes closed and kept pushing him till he broke. He pressed deep into her as he held her hips down moaning as his shoulders pressed down into the bed, raising his hips, and giving into his release.

"Luke...Oh my god." She kept riding him as the warmth filled her.

When he relaxed into the bed, she laid over top of him and hurried for her own release. He watched her face now as she tried for her own. He felt her start to pulse as she quickened her movements, he had to hold her hips to stay inside her. She threw her head back and arched as her fingers held his waist pulling him up. He pushed as deep as he could and sat up to wrap his arms around her waist and pull her down as he took a mouth full of her bare breast.

"Richmond. Oh my God!"

Her entire body tightened. He looked up to try to see her face, but she arched her back and kept her face from his view. He felt the warmth hit him just before he slid free when she moved her hips. Her stomach still hard made him rub his hands over her belly as she straightened again and looked down at him.

When they made eye contact in the dim light, Luke knew, but said nothing as he smiled.

She saw it in his eyes and rolled off him to her side of the bed and laid on her back.

He placed his big hand on her stomach and rubbed his thumb back and forth and smiled.

She frowned and turned away from him. He pulled her hips back towards him and wrapped his arm around her waist careful not to squeeze. Snuggling in close to her as she curled into a ball.

In the morning, Luke sat at the bar drinking coffee and checking his email and messages for work when Dani knocked at the back door. He gave a wave in as she opened the mudroom door, then the inner door.

"Hey! Where is Daphne?"

"Still sleeping."

Dani wore a long light blue floral print sundress that reminded him of Daphne, but with lighter shorter hair and more makeup.

"What? Still? Ahh! We need to go."

Luke grinned over his cup of coffee at her and nodded his head towards the bedroom door. Dani marched over to their door and opened it letting light in. She walked in slowly and saw Daphne laid out on her stomach completely naked, still sleeping

"Sis! Sis! Wake up!"

She rolled over putting her breasts and torso on display, along with the small curve in her belly. Dani pulled the bed sheet over her sister and sat on the edge of the bed on Luke's side.

"Luke?" Daphne mumbled.

"No, that is your sister." He spoke from the bedroom doorway drinking his coffee leaning against the frame watching them.

Daphne opened her eyes and looked at Dani and then at Luke, pulling the sheet tighter around her.

"Dani! What are you doing here?"

"Umm, it's almost 8 o' clock. We have to go pick up Jen and head to Freeman, remember?"

She glared down at Daphne out of Luke's view.

Daphne drew her eyebrows down and rubbed at her face. "Oh, shit! Yeah!" Now sitting up in bed still holding the sheet.

"Ok, well get up and get dressed like now. We need to be leaving soon."

"Ok. ok. I'll be out in a second."

Dani got up and headed for the door when Luke stepped forward and out of Dani's way of the door.

"Na, ah! No way Romeo. She doesn't have time. Let's *go that* way!"

She pointed out towards the kitchen, blocking his view of Daphne.

He smiled as she grabbed his arm and walked him out of the bedroom, closing the door behind them. Kada came down the stairs now.

"Hey, is Mom awake?"

Luke responded before Dani could, as he refilled his coffee and took a sip. "Yes, but she's getting dressed and ready to leave with Aunt Dani and Jen."

"Ugh, I need her." Kada pouted.

Dani walked over to Kada, "What's up, Kada Kid? Can I help?"

Kada nodded toward the stairs, and they walked away and up to Kada's room before Luke heard the bedroom door close.

Luke smiled and drank more coffee when Daphne emerged from the bedroom still looking tired in soft purple PJ pants and fluffy bathrobe. She walked over and gave Luke a kiss that he deepened as she reached for his coffee cup in his other hand.

He smiled and laughed against her lips trying to keep the coffee out of her reach.

When she pulled back to reach for it, He raised it in the air over their heads. "You don't need coffee."

"Luke, come on. I don't have time for my own cup and I'm really tired."

She pulled on his arm trying to reach the cup.

"Lucas, give me the cup!" She snapped.

He backed up to drop his brows at her but not his arm with the coffee.

"We are making a doctor's appointment for you soon." he dropped his arm and handed her the cup.

She took one sip then another. He watched her and her belly keenly with his own nerves.

"Ok. that's enough." He took the cup away.

She growled as she ran a hand through her hair and stocked off down the hall to the bathroom.

Luke pulled up Mike's text conversation.

Hey, I'm taking the day off. Move meetings. Girls are up to something.

When his phone chimed, he pulled up Mike's message: *I figured that at dinner yesterday when I canceled them. Be safe.*

When Dani came back down, Luke looked at her. "What are you girls doing today?"

She shrugged. "Just wedding and honeymoon shopping."

He smiled. Like her sister, he could read the lie but didn't really know what the truth was.

Daphne emerged from the bathroom looking a little brighter, she smiled at Luke.

He propped a hip up on the counter and leaned on it as he watched her in loose jeans, and his hoodie.

"Ready?" She asked Dani as she walked to Luke.

Dani nodded.

He smiled at her and wrapped her in a hug. "Love you. Have fun."

She smiled and kissed him. "We will. Love you too."

He smiled and grabbed her hips rubbing his thumbs over her stomach through the thick sweater, as his eyes darkened. She smiled wider.

"I'll be back before dinner."

"Okay."

She walked out grabbing her purse and keys by the door.

On the way to Freeman, Daphne talked with the girls. "Luke knows I'm pregnant."

Both the girls gave their own shouts and questions.

"What? How?"

"Did you tell him?"

Daphne smiled as she watched the road, "No. He just knows. I can read him like he can read me. Plus, he can't keep his hands off my stomach since last night while we were.... in the mood."

"Daphne!"

"What? I'm sorry, he touches me, and my hormones go all berserk."

Dani turned to look at Jen in the back seat, "*That's* how he knows."

Jen nodded in agreement with a smile.

"But you haven't confirmed or denied it?"

"No. He didn't ask, so I didn't tell."

Dani gave her frown from the passenger seat. "Well, you should have just told him what we are doing then." She threw up her hands.

"No. He's waiting for me."

"Well, we'll know today."

Daphne smiled and laid a hand on her belly.

While Jen and Dani waited in the waiting room for Daphne, they read magazines and watched the fish tank full of colorful fish until they heard Luke's voice at the front counter,

"Hey, Abby. Thanks. Where is she?"

"Hey Luke, sorry. I didn't know. She's in room 7. Through the doors, down the hall and to the right, third door on left."

"Thanks."

When he turned around, Jen and Dani stood up, wide eyed. He walked past them to the hall door with his hands in his pockets and spoke with a stern voice not giving them a chance to talk.

"Go home, both of you. Me and Daphne will be home soon."

Daphne waited for the test results in the doctor's office. She looked at their picture on her phone and smiled. Her stomach turned with anxiety making her queasy. When the doctor came in, she smiled with nerves.

"Well, the test is positive, you are pregnant. So, let's do an ultrasound and find out how far along. If you want to come with me, we'll head to the ultrasound room and take a look."

She got up and walked out of the room to follow her down the hall when Luke walked around the corner with a dead stare.

"Luke!" Now in panic mode she stopped in her tracks and so did the doctor.

He marched up to her and plastered a hot kiss on her lips with his truck keys still in his hand.

When he pulled back, he didn't say anything, just stared at her.

"Luke, how did you know I was here?"

He swallowed with a straight face, scaring her more than if he showed his anger.

"I know you're pregnant. Mike has been thinking you might be, but I told him that it was impossible. Then Dani comes to town, you three disappear without Kada. I knew something was off. You've been tired more often. No period. Sick and a hard belly. Jen is getting jumpy. Dani can't keep a straight face. So, I followed you to Freeman with a lot of very different emotions, Daphne. Then I sat in the parking lot hoping it was for Jen or Dani, until Abby your nurse, also our paramedic, texted me with 'Congratulations Luke.'"

"Luke, I'm sorry. I just didn't want to know and then if we lost it......"

He interrupted her, "*If* we lose it then we will try again. I made you a promise, so I'll do anything it takes for me to keep that promise Daphne. But you have to talk to me." His voice stern.

"I'm sorry Luke. I love you."

He kissed her hard and pulled her closer wrapped both his arms around her then pulled back to look at her. "I sent Dani and Jen home with your car. Mike has the girls, and I took the day off."

She smiled. "Well...." She looked at the doctor patiently waiting for them, ".... we are just about to do the ultrasound and find out how far along we are."

He smiled now, "Sounds good." He kissed her forehead after finally reaching the calm he tried for all morning.

They got settled in the dark room with the screen projected on the wall in front of them as the Nurse raised Daphne's shirt and touched the wand covered in gel, to her belly. Immediately a heartbeat sounded throughout the room over the speakers. They watched the screen in anticipation as the nurse moved the wand around and pushed a little harder. Then two heart beats came across the speakers. Daphne and Luke looked at each other in surprise and held hands before two babies showed up on the screen.

"Oh my god, twins?" Daphne exclaimed.

"Looks like twins to me." The nurse said as she moved the wand around. Luke, still in shock watching the screen, then back to Daphne with a big grin. "We are pregnant.... with twins."

Daphne looked at the nurse, "How far along? Are they okay?"

Luke rubbed her hand in his and watched the nurse for an answer.

"Umm......"

She moved the wand around Daphne's belly and took a few pictures and did some measurements.

"......looks to be about 12 almost 13 weeks, and yeah, they look healthy."

Daphne broke as tears rolled down her face. Luke leaned over and kissed her.

The nurse printed out a few pictures of the twins before Luke asked, "Do we know the gender yet?"

Nurse shook her head, "No. It's still a little too early, but hopefully in another 4 to 6 weeks, we should be able to tell."

Luke looked down at Daphne, who was now thinking and then answered her thoughts, "Yes, that would make it our engagement night."

Daphne looked at Luke who smiled from ear to ear as he watched her face brighten. Both spoke at the same time, "April 5th."

Luke raised her left hand and kissed her ring.

They walked out of the hospital, both with smiles from ear to ear. Luke held Daphne's hand and looked at the ultrasound pictures as Daphne held her belly with her free hand. Luke pulled his keys out, walked Daphne to the passenger side, and opened the door and helped her in. He gave her a kiss and rubbed his hand over her stomach before he buckled her in his front seat, then closed her door with a big grin still holding the ultrasounds. He got in the driver's side of his truck and tucked the ultrasound pictures into the frame of his map lights over the center console and smiled at them then at Daphne as he leaned over and kissed her again before he put it in drive and left the parking lot.

Darryl watched them leave, from his parking spot across from where Daphne and Luke just left. He gripped the steering wheel, waited till they were almost out of sight, and followed them as he kept his distance.

CHAPTER SEVENTEEN

When Daphne and Luke pulled back up at home, Daphne saw her car parked back at her house and Mike's command vehicle was parked next to them.

Luke still held Daphne's hand, so he kissed it as he turned off the truck and looked at her.

"Ready?"

She took a deep breath. "Yeah."

He got out of the truck and walked around to help her out. They both walked up the steps to the front door and inside to the waiting crowd. Kada was the first to greet them with hugs and smiles. Luke smiled at Kada then at Daphne. "Mom has some news to tell you."

He kissed Daphne and walked away to the kitchen where Mike, Jen, Dani, and Sarah stood. Dani and Jen gave Luke a hug as Daphne walked with Kada to the Chaise to sit.

"Hey, Kada. You are gonna be a big sister."

Kada smiled from ear to ear and threw her arms around Daphne as Dani and Jen cheered. Mike gave Luke a one arm hug and pat on the back.

Dani asked first, "How far along are you?" She looked to Daphne then to Luke when she didn't answer.

Luke couldn't stop smiling at Daphne as they smiled at each other. Luke leaned back against the counter facing them.

"Go ahead, might as well tell them." Daphne smiled and blushed at him.

Luke grinned from ear to ear as he rubbed his face. "Doctors tell us we are 12 weeks pregnant...." He paused and looked at Daphne and Kada, "With twins."

The screams and cheers started as Kada ran straight to her dad and jumped in his arms.

Dani walked to Daphne as she got up from the Chaise to give her sister a hug. "Wow! Twins? Really?"

Daphne gave a hesitant nod.

Dani frowned and with the rest of the family distracted gave her sister another tighter longer hug. "It'll be okay."

Hugs and congratulations went around as Daphne and Luke smiled at each other.

"12 weeks, huh?" Mike looked at Luke with lowered eyebrows.

Dani yelled out, "Canary!" and everyone laughed, including Mike as he rolled his eyes.

Luke looked at Kada now standing next to Daphne with her hands on Daphne's belly, then walked next to Mike at the kitchen counter. He tightened his lips, smiled and nodded. "Sorry, Mike."

Mike took a deep breath then smiled. "I'm happy for you two. So when is her due date?"

Everyone turned to Luke.

Luke Answered, "With Twins doc told us it could be as early as Thanksgiving. But full-term twins are 37 weeks, putting us on December 20th, 5 days before Christmas." He smiled at Daphne, "Best Christmas presents ever."

The energy in the room shifted as Luke straightened his smile and spine.

"Now that's out of the way, I have a bone to pick with my sisters." Luke spoke with a stern voice as he looked at Dani and Jen.

Jen raised both her hands, "Hey I told Daphne to tell you two months ago."

Luke went into shock, "two months ago?" He looked at Daphne and asked, "How long have you've known?"

Daphne frowned, "Known.... about two hours, guessed....Shortly after your accident. Jen said it was stress shock at the hospital, yeah, well she was wrong."

"I know my sister well enough to peg it coming off the plane yesterday, but you almost lost your wife, Mike. Not telling me my sister was pregnant!" Dani clenched her teeth together as she spoke to Jen who just shrugged with a half-smile.

"Yeah, think how I felt." Luke spoke sternly at Dani and Jen, now both frowning and wincing at him.

He walked over to Daphne and placed both his hands, under his sweater she wore, on her stomach.

"Luke...."

He gave her a shake of his head. "I know. It's okay. They are healthy and doing good. That's what matters right now."

She kissed him as she withheld her fears.

Kada came over and barged in between pushing Luke back. She laid a hand on Daphne's belly waiting.

Luke placed his hand next to Kada's and looked at her. "It's a little too early for us to feel movements."

She smiled at her dad.

"But trust me when I say Dad can make me sick or settle them, just by talking." Daphne said with a grin.

Kada dropped her eyebrows and looked from Daphne to her dad.

Luke watched Daphne with a wide smile and gave her belly a small rub.

"It's your voice. They get excited when they hear you."

Jen laughed behind Luke, "Yup those are my brother's kids, not that there was any doubt."

Daphne leaned to her left to look around Luke at Jen. "Yeah, and you know how hard it is not to lose your lunch and hide it, when your fiancé talks cause his kids are making you sick? And don't even get me started on these hormones, it's hard enough not to eat, scream, cry, sleep and..." She glanced at Kada and Sarah before finishing, ".... *hug* Luke at the same time. Well, no wonder, I'm carrying twins, *his* twins!" Daphne pointed to Luke.

Daphne glanced around the room at the adults' grinning smiles, trying not to laugh, but Mike and Luke both gave into the laughter.

"So does this change anything for the wedding?" Jen asked quickly to change the subject.

Luke and Daphne looked at each other as Luke smiled. "I'll leave that up to Daph. I will fit in my tux either way."

She smiled as everyone watched her for an answer.

She watched Luke but spoke loud enough for everyone to hear, "I'll have to do some dress alterations to fit it and I don't want to hear any complaints when I throw up or cry at the sight of you or while you say your vows."

Everyone cheered and laughed as Luke and Daphne smiled at each other.

"I wouldn't expect anything less from my beautiful pregnant wife."

Luke leaned over and pushed Dani and Kada out of the way, grabbed Daphne's hips and lifted her up to wrap her legs around his waist and hold her. "You, future Mrs. Richmond, are a mother."

Her eyes went wide as she looked at him. He was right, she hadn't thought about it till now. She never thought she could have kids and now she was pregnant with twins. Her heart bloomed and nerves sparked, as she stared into his eyes then leaned down to kiss him.

Over the next couple of weeks while planning and organizing the simple yard wedding, Daphne slept a lot and ate usually twice as much as Luke. Luke watched her belly grow just a little bigger each day and loved making the twins move when he talked to them.

The week before the wedding Daphne was packing a small bag for a two-night outing for the bachelorette\bridal party, Luke sat on the bed watching her gather clothes from their dresser into the small tote bag.

"Do you know where they are taking you?"

"No. All they'll tell me is a relaxing girl's weekend. But I made them promise to behave with Kada, Sarah and Maya coming along." She spoke as she folded a tank top then stuck it in her bag.

Luke smiled and replied, "Just be careful please. No strippers and no drinking."

Daphne smiled over her shoulder at him, "Anything else or should your secretary fax my secretary a list of dos and don'ts." She laughed.

He glared at her.

She smiled and turned around to face him, "Yes, I know. I will be careful. You know I will, Luke."

"I know. Sorry, I just don't know what I'm gonna do without you and Kada for a couple nights and not being able to talk or text you."

She walked over to stand between his legs on the edge of the bed and wrap her arms around his neck over his shoulders.

"You will have your bachelor party Saturday night. Enjoy it. Our last break from each other before you can't get rid of me and last time you will be single."

He smiled. "Yeah, I haven't been single since you moved in next door.... umm nope, Take that back, since our lunch in Freeman during training."

She drew her eyebrows together.

"I slept with a female firefighter from the Freeman Department the first night at the hotel. It was a stress release because you had me tied up in knots."

She gave him a smile and kissed him. "I knew you weren't bundled up tighter than a priest like everyone told me. Which yeah, Kada and Jen, both told me you were."

"Yeah, not even Mike knew my sex life, so a lot of people probably thought that."

"Yeah, well while we are on secrets here, I also had a one-night stand."

His eyes widened but not his lips, "Yeah? With who? Because if he is from Birch Valley, I probably know him."

She smiled, "Just some hot fireman I met in a diner once. He was so sexy in his turnout pants and boots. He drank coffee and kept staring at me, so I had to have him. Sorry." She gave a sly smile.

"Oh Yeah? I think I do know him. Six foot one, Dark blonde?"

She nodded with a frown, "Yeah, that's him."

"Yeah, sorry to burst your bubble but he's taken."

"Mmm, too bad, he was a lot of fun. Him in his sexy turnout gear and watching me over coffee. Man, I had dreams about him for a week after that."

Luke smiled, "I bet you did, I watched you check me out from head to toe."

"Well yeah, you kept staring at me like I was a clown. I wondered what your problem was."

"No problem, just no one else needed my attention more than you did at that moment and I'm glad I paid attention. I saw the fear and memories in your eyes. I knew you needed help. Then I saw it again when I met you at the bench with Kada, then again when I gave you my card. It was then I knew it was something with me."

"Luke, it's always been you and will always be you and I couldn't be happier. You are the only reason I'm here. Not just on Earth but in Alaska. Of course, there is no one else I'd rather see at the end of that aisle next week than Richmond, my Richmond."

"Then you will see me there and Kada. Sorry, package deal. Two Richmond's for the price of one."

"Best deal ever."

She kissed him and slid her hands up under his sweater and over his head as he grinned helping her take it off. She tossed it towards her packed tote by the bedroom door, leaving him in a t-shirt.

He placed both hands on her belly and placed a kiss there. When Kada knocked on the open bedroom door.

"Mom, I'm all packed."

Daphne turned her head to look at Kada as Luke still held her waist and belly. "Ok, just *one* bag right."

"Yeah." Kada answered as she walked over to Luke and Daphne and placed her hand next to her dad's. "Are you ready Dad?"

Luke smiled up at Daphne and Kada, "For a family and wife, with you four? Yes! Kada just make sure Mom takes her vitamins, they are in her purse and lots of water."

Kada smiled at Daphne then looked at her dad, "Dad, she will be fine, we will be fine."

Luke smiled, "I know."

Daphne smiled at Luke, "I love you, Richmond."

"I love you too." He spoke, giving her a quick light kiss.

Kada smiled, still feeling Daphne's belly, "Why do you keep calling Dad by our last name?"

Luke and Daphne both looked at her, but Luke answered, "Because that is all my turnout gear says."

Confused, Kada answered, "But you weren't wearing your gear when you came home."

Daphne smiled and turned around in Luke's arms and sat across his lap as she watched Kada.

"You haven't been told the full story yet, so you better hear this before we get married."

Luke smiled as he held Daphne and watched Kada.

Daphne continued, "When I left my ex-husband, I got into a car accident. Dad pulled me out......."

"Wait, Dad went down the states to pull you out of that car accident?"

"No, I came up here for a trip with my ex and got in a car accident. Dad pulled me out and saved my life, and not just that once but several times over the next 3 years. During that accident all I could remember was his golden eyes, his cologne and his last name from his crew calling him Richmond. It stuck with me. For the next three years, it was what kept me running and fighting to stay alive, till I had no place left to run to but back here to that fireman who saved me the first time. Then one day, I was talking to my new neighbor's daughter, who came to share hot cocoa with me and then a fireman with golden eyes came trudging across my yard pissed off that his daughter snuck over to me."

"So how did you know it was him?"

"The night you came over to spend the night with me during his training. He gave me his station card which had Lieutenant Lucas Richmond, then I knew without a doubt it was him, but I already fell in love with someone else."

Kada grew shocked, "What? Who?" She spoke with some force.

Luke and Daphne both gave a soft laugh before Daphne answered, "You."

Kada blushed, smiled and then hugged Daphne.

Luke spoke up, "That was my turning point. I knew I wasn't getting you back unless I married her."

"Wait what? How long have you two been together, together?"

Luke smiled at Kada, "A little while. We had to be sure."

Daphne reached for Luke's phone on the side table and searched through his photos. She pulled up their truck photo of Daphne laying over the console as Luke drove and holding hands to show Kada.

"Wait, what?"

Kada took the phone and looked at the picture of her parents happy as Daphne smiled holding hands with her dad in his truck.

"I played hooky from work, and we went Christmas shopping in the beginning of December, after I dropped you off at Sarah's one day. She stayed home that weekend pretending to be sick and we snuck out and spent the day together, made the agreement to figure us out before we told anyone else." Luke smiled at Kada.

Kada had a smile from ear to ear as she looked from Daphne to her dad. "Oh my gosh! I knew you got more from Dad than just my snow gear that morning we went sledding!"

Daphne and Luke laughed before he spoke, "Swipe left."

Kada did.

"What? Ah! Dad! Mom!"

Luke gave a full laugh. Daphne looked confused and took the phone from her and looked at the picture of her, Luke and Kada at lunch in Freeman with her leg over his and his hand on her leg under the table as Kada and Luke both smiled at Daphne. Daphne smiled, remembering when she first saw it at the bridal shop then looked at Luke.

"Another firefighter at training took that to tease me at work and it got sent to nearly everyone at the fire department and training as everyone tried to figure out who you were and what was going on with us. Another reason I came home early the next day. I ran them two miles with forty-five-pound weighted vests. I don't know if I was mad at Jackson for taking that picture or if I was mad at myself for losing my grip on what I thought was my life."

Daphne leaned over and kissed Luke and lingered over his lips.

"You lost your life but found mine." She smiled at him before continuing, "We better get going. Dani is gonna come over here looking for me and Kada if she doesn't see us soon."

Luke gave her another soft kiss and ran his hand over her small baby bump.

"Aww. I know my parents' story." Kada smiled.

Daphne just gave a small laugh and swatted a hand through the air at her, "Let's go!"

When Jen pulled up in her Tahoe with Sarah, Dani and Maya, Luke helped Kada, and Daphne load their luggage in the back as they jumped in. Luke and Daphne gave each other one last kiss. "Love you!"

"Love you too, be safe. See you soon."

Jen backed up in the cul-de-sac and waved at him.

Jen drove to the edge of town and hit a small dirt road a couple miles outside of Birch Valley and down to the sight of another creek following the small dirt road that turned into a narrower driveway.

When she pulled up to the large rustic cabin, Daphne's eye grew bigger as she leaned forward to take it in through the windshield. Daphne looked at Jen with a wide smile.

"You can thank Magar and your Fiancé when we get back. Luke didn't want you wandering too far from him but still left us secluded. It was Magar's before he married and had a family. This was his bachelor pad, complete with surround sound system, all the alcohol me and Dani can drink, 10 acres of land and 3 days and 2 nights of nothing but us and the woods."

Dani cheered in the back seat with Kada, Maya and Sarah, as Daphne smiled and hugged Jen.

Later in the evening the girls danced with the surround system cranked and ate a variety of finger foods. Daphne smiled as she watched the girls singing and dancing. The twins were not happy with all the dancing she had done and had to sit with Luke's sweater for extra comfort. Dani came over and sat next to her breathing hard as they watched Jen, Maya, Kada and Sarah dancing.

"You okay, Sis?"

Daphne, smiled. "I'm great! I'm so happy you are here. I'm getting married in a week to Richmond."

"Aww. I'm happy I get to be here. But I have Luke's number on speed dial if anything happens. I'm not taking any chances with my nieces or nephews. "

Daphne smiled. "I'll be fine sis. Don't worry."

"I know. I just see how he is when he is around you...."

Daphne laughed, "What suffocating?"

Dani Laughed, "No, protective. He lost his wife and unborn son; he's scared to lose you too."

Daphne took a deep breath. It was a different view; she hadn't given much thought too.

"I think I'm gonna go outside for a minute to get some air. The twins are not happy right now."

Dani smiled. "They miss Dad."

Daphne smiled and nodded and placed a hand on her belly.

Dani took Luke's sweater and slid it over Daphne's head and over her belly, rubbing it into her belly gently.

"I love you sis." Daphne said

"Aww, I love you too. Go get some air but don't take too long, we have some games planned. I wanted to do 'Pin the dick on Luke' but Jen nixed that idea with the girls here." Dani said with a chuckle while rolling her eyes.

Daphne gave a solid laugh as she held her belly.

"See there's my sister." Dani gave her a hug.

Daphne stood up and walked out on the front porch to lean over the railing. She took in the sight of Willow Creek that was closer to Magar's house then Birch Creek was to her and Luke's. It rushed within just a few yards off the side of the cabin and along the driveway. The sound was soothing compared to the loud music inside.

She bent down and sat on the porch steps taking it in till she heard the *click click* of a pistol cocking. She looked up to see Darryl rounding the side of the house. Her heart tripped as she opened her mouth.

"Na. Ah. Don't scream or I'll shoot."

He walked to her as she stood and tried to back up. His eyes held an intense emptiness that scared her because for the first time he wasn't evil. Now he was running on nothing except pain which would make him even less predictable.

"No. You stay right there."

He slowly walked towards her and held the gun level to her head.

"So, you're pregnant with his kids and getting married now huh? Yeah, I don't think that is gonna happen. I'm gonna take everything from him just like he took it all from me."

He grabbed her arm turning her around to face the front door and held the gun to her head.

"Call his daughter."

"No! She has nothing to do with this. Leave her out of it."

He pushed the gun barrel into her head, "Call her!"

She took a deep breath. "Kada!"

A couple of seconds later Kada came running out the open front door and screamed when she saw Daphne being held with a gun to her head. "Mom!" Tears immediately broke down her face as she took a breath.

"Kada. I'm okay. Stay there!"

"No, Mom! Mom!"

"She is not your mom!" Darryl spoke over Daphne.

Dani, Maya, Sarah and Jen came out behind Kada, "Kada, what's wrong?"

When they looked up and saw Daphne and Darryl, they took a deep breath.

Dani spoke first, "Darryl."

"Hey Danielle! Long time no see."

"Darryl. Let her go. Don't do this, please. She's pregnant."

"I know with that piece-of-shit fireman's kids. Twins even. Well guess what? I'm gonna take it all from him. Just like he did me."

Daphne held her belly and looked at Dani. She curled her three middle fingers in making a phone sign. Dani looked at it then back up to her expression and brought her eyebrows down. Daphne glanced quickly towards Kada then back to Dani. Dani pulled out her cell phone slowly while staying hidden behind Kada and hit Luke's speed dial number and turned the call volume all the way down.

When it lit up that he answered the call, in her hand, she spoke loudly.

"Darryl, Let Daphne go!"

"No! That fireman doesn't get to have her, and my kids!"

Dani looked at Daphne and wrapped an arm around Kada and slid the phone into Kada's back pocket and pulled Kada's big sweater over it.

Kada cried and shook. "Mom. Mom."

"Kada, it's gonna be okay."

Dani rubbed hand up and down Kada's arms trying to calm her.

"Down the steps, now! The truck is on the other side of the shed. Get in." Darryl spoke gruffly.

"Mom?"

Darryl moved him and Daphne forward, "You four stay there and don't move, Or I'll kill them."

Kada walked down the steps holding herself.

"Kada, listen to me. We are gonna be okay. Just get in the truck, please."

More tears started to roll down her face.

"Mom, no! Please no."

Jen, Sarah and Maya watched on in fear as Dani stiffened her spine and stepped forward in front of them to block any possible shot at them.

"Kada, listen to mom please. Dad will find you guys soon, I promise. But listen to mom."

"Shut up, Bitch!" And a gunshot went off making Jen, Sarah and Maya scream as Kada stepped to Daphne and clung to her.

Darryl had his gun raised in the air. "Get in the truck! Now!"

Kada hurried across the driveway and to the old Chevy truck next to the shed and got in the back seat.

As Darryl held Daphne at gunpoint and walked backwards to the truck. When he stood next to Jen's Tahoe, he held the pistol to the hood and shot, making fluids leak under it.

Dani stepped forward again, "Be careful Sis. I love you."

Daphne clenched to Luke's sweater she wore and dropped her hand next to her and then opened her hand to drop something shiny on the ground without Darryl seeing. "I love you too."

Darryl turned and walked Daphne towards the truck and quickly shoved her over the console to the front seat.

Daphne looked at Kada scared in the back seat who opened her legs and showed Daphne the phone still on with Luke then closed her legs to hide it again.

Daphne nodded and smiled. "It's gonna be okay Kada. Buckle up."

"Shut up! Get in the seat."

"Darryl Let her go! She is not ours. She is Luke's daughter. She has nothing to do with this! Take me but let her go!"

"I said shut up! That asshole will lose everything he ever loved! Including the woman, he should have left for dead at the bottom of that cliff."

He slammed the older Chevy truck into reverse and floored it down the driveway, back out to the road, then down the highway.

Dani yelled at Jen, "Call Mike! Kada has my phone with Luke on. Find out where Luke and Mike are."

Jen ran inside to get her phone and saw Daphne's phone sitting by the couch.

Dani ran down the driveway to where Daphne dropped something.

She looked around till she saw a flash of silver and bent down to pick up Daphne's necklace with "Richmond" on the small silver Maltese cross.

Dani heard the sirens as Mike's command truck was first to whip in the driveway and slam on the brakes followed by Luke's truck and then Dawson's patrol truck.

Luke jumped out and ran to Dani in sheer panic and fear, still holding his phone next to his ear. "Where is she? Where did they go?"

She frowned and took a deep breath. "He took them."

She held out the silver necklace to him.

Mike ran to Jen and Sarah and held them. Jen walked over to Luke and gave him a hug as he listened on the phone. What little conversation he heard was mostly muffled but most of the time he couldn't hear anything.

Mike and Dawson ran to Luke who was pacing while listening to the phone with Dani and Jen next to him.

"What's happening? Luke? What is going on?" Dani asked next to him.

He shook his head. "I can't hear anything. Who has it?"

"I called you and turned down the volume and stuck it in Kada's back pocket. She was the only one I could reach. He had a gun to Daphne and wasn't letting us get close to her."

He hugged Dani, "You did good."

His demeanor scared Dani. He was in full methodical mode and rather calm for just having his pregnant fiancé and daughter kidnapped by her ex-husband who told them he was gonna take everything from him.

His eyes were glossy, and breaths were long and deep.

He ran inside the cabin and searched till he found Daphne's phone and stuck it in his back pocket then walked back out to Mike.

"Call Magar."

Mike pulled out his phone and pulled up Magar's number and hit call then handed it to Luke. Luke took it and walked back in and down the hall to the master bedroom.

When Magar answered Luke cut him off, "Magar, What's combination to the gun safe? Daphne and Kada were kidnapped by Darryl."

Luke handed his phone to Mike and held Mike's cell as he opened the closet and moved some clothes to reveal a large gun safe built into the wall. Mike listened to Luke's cell. Luke dialed the number on the safe and unlocked it, opening to reveal several rifles, a couple of shot guns and a small shelf of pistols and ammo. He pulled out two pistols for him and

Mike now standing behind him and handed one to him. They checked the ammo and mags in both and tucked them in the small of their backs and pulled their shirts over it.

"Thanks, I'm going after him. Get to the cabin and help Jen and Daphne's sister please. Thanks."

He disconnected the call and tossed Mike's phone back to him as Mike handed his back.

"Luke..." Dani spoke from the bedroom doorway, breathing hard.

".... He'll kill them the moment he spots you coming. That's what he wants, they are the bait."

Luke looked at Mike and then back to Dani. He took a couple steps to her and pulled Dani into a hug. "She'll be okay Dani. I'll find her, I promise."

Daphne's necklace flashed through his memories. The blood-spattered necklace laying on the ground next to her cardigan. He pulled Daphne's necklace from his pocket and rubbed a thumb over it in his hand.

Luke's eyes and smile widened. "I know where he's going."

Luke sprinted out, bypassing Dani and Dawson as they asked questions. Mike stayed hot on his heels kissing Jen on his way by, "Stay here."

Luke jumped back in his truck and connected the phone to his Bluetooth in his truck as Mike jumped in the passenger.

"Luke! Where are they going? We need Dawson!"

"Not anymore." He growled out with anger as he slammed his truck in reverse then back into drive as he peeled out of the driveway.

He flipped on his emergency lights and ran out to the highway and passed Magar as Luke turned onto the highway back towards town and took the left just before the turn to Birch Valley. He followed the mountain side pushing well over the speed limit as Mike held on.

Daphne's voice and screams came over the phone and truck speakers.

"Darryl!"

Mike picked up Luke's phone and held it as Luke drove the narrow road along the mountain side pushing the limits of his truck and the curves and turns of the road. Mike never questioned Luke's driving skills as he cut the corners and tires rounded the shoulders edge with steep drops and cliffs.

Luke listened to the call as his pregnant fiancée and daughter screamed and pleaded with Darryl.

"Daddy isn't gonna save you." Darryl's voice came over the speakers as Mike looked at Luke now staring out the windshield while hitting the curves at high speeds.

"The lodge is under construction, there isn't anyone up there Darryl!"

Daphne's voice came across the speakers as Luke gave a grin and gripped the steering wheel tighter.

Mike pulled up Dawson's texts on his phone and sent him the message, *They're at the Lodge! Get there!*

"I know, it's perfect. The one place your fireman wouldn't think to look, in his own back yard."

"Darryl, no! Let Kada go!"

"Mom! No! Please stop! Mom!" Kada's screamed with fear.

Luke let off the gas for a sharper corner then sped back up after rounding it halfway through, with the precision of a professional driver on a well-known course.

"Kada! No, let go of me! Kada!"

Luke's pulse raced as his engine revved and his tires hummed on the road.

Two gunshots sounded through the speakers. Luke let off the gas as he and Mike glanced at each other with fear as Kada let out a blood curdling scream and a moment of pause before she spoke.

"No! Mom! Where are you taking us? Dad!"

Luke's jaw tightened as he sped back up.

"No, stop! Mom! Stop you're hurting her! Please stop! Mom! Mom, no!"

"Kada run!" Daphne's scream shouted through the speakers.

Gunshots sounded in the distant background as the phone started to static with bad reception.

"Dad! Dad! Daddy!" Kada's shaky voice came through the speakers

Mike answered. "Kada! Kada! Are you okay? Where's your mom?"

"He took her! He hurt Mom! I'm in the woods." The phone started to static again.

"Kada, stay there! We are on our way. We are almost there. We will find you. Stay there and stay hidden! Don't move!"

"Where is Dad? He took Mom! He hurt Mom! I need Dad. Where is Dad?"

"I'm right here Kada! Don't worry about Mom, she'll be okay. Are you hurt? Can you walk?"

"Yeah, I think so..." The phone continued to static.

"Kada, we are losing you. Stay right there, Honey. We are pulling up to the lodge now."

"Dad.... scared... the truck.... gun.... Mom."

"I know Baby, I'm coming. Don't move."

They rounded the last corner and saw the older white Chevy truck with open doors sitting in the cul-de-sac of a parking lot at a big lodge and pulled up next to it. It was empty. Mike took Luke's cell and disconnected it from the truck's Bluetooth.

"Find Kada." Luke spoke sternly as he checked his pistol again.

Mike gave a nod then pulled the pistol from his back and loaded it. They opened the doors and got out, looking around the area.

Mike and Luke followed the little narrow manicured trail around the lodge and up the mountain side.

Kada's cry came across. "Uncle Mike?"

"Yeah Kada, I'm here. Where are you?"

"I'm in the woods. I hear Mom screaming." Kada's voice started to break.

"Kada, we will get mom. Stay where you're at sweetheart. Me and Dad are coming up the path towards the glacier."

They walked fast but carefully up the pathway and rounded a corner before they heard Kada's voice through the phone first then off in the woods, "Dad!"

Mike and Luke both looked to their right and saw Kada sprinting out of the woods towards them. Now in full tears she ran to them and wrapped around her dad. Luke bent down as Mike kept watch. He hauled Kada into a hug.

"Kada!"

Luke's hands shook as they wrapped around Kada, who still held Dani's phone.

Luke checked over Kada who now had a bruise and small bleeding gash showing on her cheek and jaw with a ripped collar of her sweater.

Kada barely got the words out on a shaky voice as tears streamed down her face, "Dad, Mom fought him to get him to let go of me and he kicked her in the stomach, and I think she is hurt...."

"Hey!" He snapped out at his daughter and instantly regretted it, before taking a deep breath. "It's okay. Mom will be okay. Go with Uncle Mike and I'll find Mom."

He looked up at Mike trying for a calm through rage, "Get her out of here."

"No. Dad, no!" Kada cried.

Mike looked at him, "Luke, I'd wait for Dawson."

"He doesn't have that much time."

Luke pulled his pistol out and turned to walk away headed further up the trail into the woods.

"Dad, no! Dad!" Kada screamed now struggling in Mike's tight hold.

Luke didn't turn back and paid no attention to Kada's cries.

"Kada, Lets go." Mike spoke to her.

Daphne's screams and more gunshots echoed through the woods making Kada scream. "Mom! No!"

Mike picked up Kada and hauled her back towards the direction of the parking lot. Luke turned to watch them heading back and then turned back to the trail and towards the direction of Daphne's screams. As Daphne's screams got closer, Luke headed into the woods off the trail and through them toward Daphne's voice.

"No! Darryl! Please don't!"

He came over a small hill and saw Daphne fighting Darryl next to a cliff and crouched down beside a thick cottonwood tree.

She was dirty and bruised, with scrapes that bled around the face and looked like her arm was hurt as she held it over her stomach. His stomach knotted and his jaw tightened.

"Darryl, let go of me! You already hurt his kids. Best if you just run now before he finds us both! You'll never touch Kada again."

He stuck the gun to her head again, "You'll have to do. When he finds your pregnant body, it'll be enough to teach him to never mess with another man's wife. You should have never ran to him."

Luke stood up next to the tree making Daphne squint to see him. She smiled at him then turned her head to look at Darryl. Darryl held an arm around her shoulders and chest. Daphne grabbed it with both her hands and dropped her weight, throwing him off balance as she reached for the gun. Gunshots sounded from Darryl's gun as Luke came out from the woods in a run towards them.

Luke aimed at him but was unable to get a clear shot at Darryl.

Daphne used her forearm to block Darryl's aim at Luke as they battled for control till, he turned the gun on her. Her fear sank to her bones as she watched the fear spread across Luke's face. She closed her eyes and held onto the image of Luke's eyes pulling her from the first accident, as tears began to stream down her face.

Another gunshot rang out, making Daphne scream, as Darryl's body went limp. His grip on Daphne loosened as they both stumbled and fell forward to the ground. Darryl's body laid limp over Daphne in the dirt.

"Daphne!" Luke now in a full sprint towards Daphne as he checked for where the gunshot came from. His left side, on the main trail, showed Mike holding his pistol at Darryl's body on the ground over Daphne. Luke reached Darryl and Daphne and with ease threw Darryl's limp bleeding body off Daphne. He hauled her up into his arms to hold her.

"Daph!"

He wrapped her into his left side away from Darryl's body and shot him again with his right hand, making Daphne jump and cry now.

Mike put his pistol in his back and walked up to them as Luke threw down his pistol to the ground to tuck Daphne into his chest then haul her off her feet and over to the side of the trail to a soft grass section and set her down.

"Daph, where are you hurt?"

Mike followed them and crouched down on the other side of Daphne. Luke slid his hands under his sweater Daphne still wore and felt her belly.

"Luke!" Mike spoke in a stern tone as Daphne screamed and cried as she laid back in the grass.

Luke looked at Mike who nodded towards Daphne's jeans that were partially covered with the big sweater.

The inseams were soaked with blood.

CHAPTER EIGHTEEN

N o! No!" Luke picked up Daphne and sprinted down the trail back to the truck and lodge parking lot.

"Kada?" She asked through the tears as he ran with her in his arms.

"She's alive and okay, thanks to you."

Daphne started to cry more, "I'm so sorry Luke."

"Daph, no! You and Kada are alive, that's what matters."

"But I don't think the twins are."

Luke held her tighter. He turned the last corner, and the trucks came into view with Dani, Kada and Mike's command vehicle with Dawson and his patrol truck.

Kada came running up to them, "Mom! Is she okay?"

"I don't know Kada." Mike answered for Luke.

Luke ran to his truck. "Kada, open the passenger door."

She did, as Luke set Daphne in the front seat and laid it back while Dani and Dawson came around. "Hey, Med Flight is on their way."

"K, tell Cap!"

Luke looked at Kada crying next to him then up to Dani with his own fear.

Dani gave a nod. "Hey Kada, come on. Let Dad check out Mom. She'll be okay."

"Kada, I'm okay. I love you." Daphne spoke weakly.

"I love you, Mom!" Kada spoke through tears, as she turned to walk away with Dani.

Luke held Daphne's hand and looked at her, rubbing two fingers over the darkening bruises on her cheek and under her eye. "Hey, I need to check you and the twins out. Okay?"

"They're dead Luke. I haven't felt them move." Daphne sobbed as she watched him through her own pain.

"Hey, we don't know that. Medics are coming but for right now I need to make sure you are okay. If you aren't then I can lose you and the twins. They can't survive without you Daph."

Luke lifted the sweater and Daphne's shirt to look at Daphne's dark bruised stomach and deformed rib cage that was usually pretty prominent on her small bone structure. His heart sank. He lightly pushed his fingers around her stomach starting at her hips and worked his way up the sides and softer over the belly as she winced in pain.

"Ow! Luke!"

"I know Daph. I'm sorry. I'm trying to feel if there is any other damage. Hang in there, Baby. I'm right here. Stay with me."

He felt the slightest movement when he talked. He pushed a little harder only to watch her cringe in pain as he spoke again.

"Daphne, you did good. Darryl's gone and Kada is safe. Stay with me Baby. I love you." He felt the slightest movement again. Luke took a deep breath.

"I love you too." She answered with her head turned away from him.

He smiled at her, deciding to not tell her anything yet, then he moved his hands up her sides and to the ribs. Where he not only saw them broken but felt the crunch of bones under his lightest touches, making her scream in pain.

"I'm sorry, Baby."

He checked over her as Dani and Kada watched on out of view.

Mike came over and opened Luke's front driver door and leaned over the console, handing Luke the small medical bag from his Command vehicle.

"Hey Daphne." He smiled at her. She looked up at him.

"Mike, the twins are dead." She sobbed out as tears streamed down her face.

In shock he looked at Luke now, who tightened his lips and gave him a grim expression as Luke put the stethoscope in his ears.

"Hey Daph, let's worry about you right now. Luke won't survive without you. We need you here for Luke and Kada. You saved Kada, now you have to save Luke."

Luke used a stethoscope and blood pressure cuff. When he released the blood pressure cuff, he looked at Mike and worked his jaw and shook his head. Mike's eyes went wide.

Dispatch and Med Flight came across Mike's radio, and Mike walked away from the truck to answer. Luke heard the helicopter approaching.

"Daph, Med Flight is gonna take you to the hospital, we'll meet you there."

"No, Richmond. Don't leave me please!" She started to cry again.

Her plea struck a nerve with him, and he nearly shouted at her, "Hey Daph, I'm not leaving you! I promise! I'll be right behind you with Kada and Dani, okay?"

She held tight to his hand now, not letting him go.

"No. Luke, no!"

"You have to go, Daphne. I'm not losing you and the twins."

"Luke please. No! Richmond!"

The wind started to pick up as Mike landed the helicopter in lodge's front yard and the engine shut down. The flight medics came over to Luke's truck and climbed in the driver seat and another on Luke's side. Luke leaned over to whisper in the medic's ear and the medic nodded. Luke tried to move out of the way, but Daphne wouldn't let go of his hand.

"Daphne! Honey, let go. The medics need to check you out." Again his anger snapped. She cried. "No, Richmond! Please! No! Richmond, don't leave me please!"

Luke let go of her hand and pulled it from her grip then moved out of the way for the medics in the small, confined space of the truck cab, making Daphne scream for him. Luke leaned against the truck bed next to the back door and waited for them to check her out as tears started to fall from his face. Dani and Kada came around as Luke tried to wipe the tears away and smile for Kada, but he looked up at Dani and broke again as more tears fell.

Daphne screamed in pain as the medic checked her out. Kada looked at Luke then to the medics bent over Daphne inside the truck and gave her dad a hug.

"Hey Kada, I need you to do me a favor. You too Dani. Before they transport her to the chopper, tell her she will be fine, and we will meet her at the hospital."

Tears fell from Kada's eyes as she nodded.

Dani looked at Luke and shook her head, "Luke I can't lie to my sister."

He stiffened his jaw and spine, and like a switch, flipped to Lieutenant mode and looked in Dani's eyes as he spoke, "You aren't lying, she... will be fine."

Dani's eyes widened in shock as her hands covered her mouth, "Oh my god, Luke! No! No! Please no!"

Luke quickly wrapped her in a hug as Dani sobbed into Luke's shoulder. He whispered in her ear. "We will try again. Let her heal and we can try again. I promise I won't give up Dani."

"Dad..." Kada looked at Luke. "...is mom gonna be, okay?"

He took a deep breath, thankful for the easier question. "Yes, Mom is gonna be okay. We'll see her at the hospital in a few."

Dani looked at Luke, "You aren't going with her?"

He shook his head. "I can't. They have to take just her. It's okay though, they can get there safer and faster without me and they can take better care of her."

Dani hugged Luke, "Hey you found her. You knew where she was. If it wasn't for you, we might not have found her or Kada in time."

Kada threw her arms around her dad again.

"Still wasn't fast enough."

"Luke, don't. She's alive. You still have her. She still has you!"

Now he tried for a smile that fell flat, "It's not good enough."

One of the medics looked at Luke to get his attention. Luke walked over to them and leaned in.

"She with you?" The male medic asked,

"Yeah."

They talked with him about medical care and her stats, as she sleepily watched him, he tried his best to smile but couldn't look at her without breaking so kept his focus on the medic and just gently squeezed her hand that now had an IV in it. When they loaded Daphne onto a backboard, He let go and stepped back as he looked at Dani and Kada, "She's sedated for flight, so make it quick."

Dani and Kada each took their turn telling Daphne they loved her and that she would be okay.

When they stepped back, He heard the helicopter starting up in the yard a couple hundred feet from where they were. He pulled Daphne's necklace free from his pocket and placed it in her hands and kissed her forehead.

"I'll see you soon." He tried not to look at her but now couldn't.

Her eyes were heavy as she tried to look at him. They were the emptiest he'd ever seen them. She always held so much emotion and thoughts in them and now it killed him to see them so empty. He began to miss her.

"I love you, Daphne."

He gave her a small quick kiss to which she had no muscle strength to return. As his heart shattered, he let the medics take her. He watched them walk her to the helicopter and get her loaded. When they shut the doors, he watched them start on board medical care through the small window before lifting off the ground with Mike standing nearby on the radio with the pilot. They took off and flew over as Luke looked at his front seat and saw the pool of blood from Daphne, making him crumple to the ground to his knees as tears streamed down his face.

"Hey Luke, come on. Daphne will be okay. You said it yourself." Dani bent down next to him.

"Dad, come on. Let's go see mom! Dad, please. Mom needs us."

Luke was unresponsive as his arm that held the seat covered his face as he stared down to the ground. Mike walked over to him as he talked over the radio to Dawson holding the fire and police crews back.

"Hey Luke, we are about to have a 20 crew here. Get it together, man."

Luke stood up straight and snapped, as his blister red eyes went wide and turned to Mike.

"What the fuck do they care? Magar, Hastings, Whit, they could care less about what I just lost or what Daphne just went through! They're only here to clean up the blood and clock out!"

He slammed the truck door closed with a force that had Dani and Kada jumping back.

"Dad! No, Dad!" Kada tried to yell as Dani held her back and Luke ignored her, setting his sights on Mike.

Mike took off his radio harness and set it on the ground, and shouted at Luke, "Ok. So, this is how we are gonna do this? Ok! Ok! What about what you have left Luke? What about Daphne laying in the hospital in a minute asking where Richmond is? What about your daughter over here watching her dad lose his shit, again? What about the opportunity to try again, Luke? Does that mean anything to you? Don't tell me Magar and Hastings and Whit don't give a damn when we are the only family you have left Luke! Guilt, that's what you are feeling right now. Well suck it up and face the facts Lieutenant, you could have lost a lot more, like a sister and nephew!"

Luke's hands clenched tight, "You son of a bitch!"

"Dad!" Kada screamed out as Luke walked towards Mike.

Mike stepped up to Luke. "Come on, get it out!"

At nearly the same height they stared at each other with very different emotions.

Luke, full of rage and grief, Mike with regret and worry.

"Come on! Get it out now before you go and face that woman lying in the hospital because she said yes when you asked her to marry you."

That was the match that lit the fuel. Luke stepped forward with his left foot and with all his force bent his right knee, dropping his shoulder and slammed his fist into Mike's ribs sending him forward enough for Luke to throw a left-hand punch into his chest knocking him back on his ass. Mike stood back up and brushed off his pants and sweater then stepped up again just as the rest of the fire department crew came running to them.

Mike held a hand to them as he watched Luke, "Stay back! Let him go!"

He watched the anger in Luke's eyes and tight jaw, like fire in his blood. His hands in tight fists, stark white, ready to fight again near his chest and side. Squared shoulders told Mike he wasn't gonna back down, yet.

"Come on Luke! You buried one wife and child, now you have to bury your twins, yeah, I'd be fucking pissed off too, except that's not anger Luke. And you know that!"

"Fuck you!" Luke hooked a fist into Mike's ribs then a right hook to his jaw. A second too fast for Mike to block, knocking him down again. Luke bent over Mike and let loose on him on the ground, as Mike dodged and blocked some of the punches. Luke punched the dirt and gravel driveway occasionally hitting Mike's jaw before Mike hooked and kicked out Luke's legs to trip Luke next to him.

When Luke hit the ground with a solid thud next to Mike, Mike tensed and prepared to roll as he waited for more strikes till Luke broke with tears and breathed heavily trying for a solid breath of air. Mike relaxed and took a deep breath now watching his brother shatter. The crews reach them both as Mike sat up next to Luke. Mike worked his shoulders to release the tension and sore muscles then braced his arms over his bent knees. He looked to Luke who laid out flat on his back next to him.

"Come on. Let's go. We got to get you to the hospital. When Daphne comes out of it, you're gonna be the first one she asks for."

Magar, Hastings, Whitte and the rest of the crew stood in a wide circle around Mike and Luke until Dawson came over and pushed through the small crew around Luke and Mike.

"Hey, Dani said you two were going at it and Kada is over there crying. What the fuck is wrong with you two? This is not the time to fight over who's doing the paperwork on this shit show."

Luke sat up now and wiped at his face and took a deep breath.

"Luke just needed a minute to get out some pent-up aggression." Mike spoke as Dawson helped him up, making Mike wince and hold his ribs then rub his darkening jaw.

Magar reached a hand out to Luke, who took it and pulled himself up.

"Thanks." He told Magar then turned to Mike and swallowed, "Why?"

Mike shrugged, "Why not? You're her strength, she is yours. The fuel and the fire. Don't ask those questions, especially when I'm beginning to not understand what she sees in you."

Luke's jaw clenched again as he tried not to smile, then rubbed his hands over his face.

"Now go get her out of the hospital so she can marry you and take you off my hands. I'll sign whatever custody paperwork she needs for you. I'm done with you for the next month! Take a LOA, get married and get the fuck off my crew, Lieutenant."

Luke smiled as the crew laughed, "Thanks Man."

"Go! Get off my scene. Take the command truck. I'll check in after I mop up." He nodded his head towards the trucks.

Luke gave his arm a pat and pushed his way through the crew and over to Kada who still held on to her Aunt Dani.

"Kada! I'm so sorry sweetheart. Let's go see mom." He pulled her into a hug and kissed her cheek then looked up to Dani, who smiled.

"You know how to do some patch work?" He asked Dani.

Dani drew her eyebrows together. "Yeah, why?"

"Good. Let's go."

He jogged over to his truck and grabbed the smaller medical kit out of the med bag still sitting on his console while staring at the pool of blood in the front passenger seat. He took Daphne's keychain off his keys to throw his keys in the cup holder and ran over to Mike's command truck. Dani jumped in the front seat of command and Kada in the back seat as Luke put the truck in reverse and weaved his way out of the now crowded parking lot. He gave Dani the small minor medical kit and showed her his hands that were bleeding with gravel and dirt embedded in them.

"Oh My.... Luke." Dani spoke from the front passenger seat as Luke drove back towards town weaving alongside the mountain.

"Dad, are you okay?"

He glanced in the rearview. "Yeah sweetheart. Daphne just...."

He didn't know what to tell Kada. He didn't have the same way with words like Daphne did. He hated himself for the way he acted but it was a new emotion for him he didn't quite understand.

"Turns you inside out?" Dani spoke as she used gauze and alcohol wipes to clean his right free hand, laid out over the console between them.

Luke smiled at her. "Yeah. She does."

"You do the same to her. My sister wouldn't just move across the country for any memory. You held her might have held her hand for five minutes, but she held yours for three years." She smiled over her thick lashes as she cleaned around some open wounds.

Luke kept his eyes on the road but gave a small frown and nod.

Almost two hours later when they pulled into Freeman hospital, His hands were now bandaged up. They walked in and were told Daphne's room number by the front desk clerk. They jogged to her room to find Daphne asleep, still curled up in a ball on her side. Luke laid next to her, facing her and noticed she now wore her "Richmond" necklace. He smiled and pulled her into his chest. Kada laid behind her and wrapped an arm around her waist. Dani stood at the foot of the bed watching them, as tears streamed down her face.

The doctor came in and Luke immediately got up.

"Stay here Kada."

He walked over to the doctor and out to the hall with him and Dani.

"How is she?" He leaned over and put an arm around Dani's shoulders ready to brace for any news.

"She's stable. She has some broken ribs, mostly refractures but she's doing fine. A lot of bumps and bruises mostly."

"And our twins?" Luke started to snap out.

"Luke!" Dani gave a warning as she glanced at Luke.

The doctor took a breath, "The twins are alive...."

Luke and Dani went into shock, "What? They are alive?" They both asked the doctor.

"Yes. But baby number two took a pretty good hit and I see some placental abruption and although minor right now, it's our top priority and I'm worried about ruptures and oxygen and nutrient deprivation. If that is the case, then I'll have to abort that baby so at least baby one and the mother can have a fighting chance. We are keeping a close eye on all of them and so far, numbers are looking better, and I have good hopes for them, but their numbers are not where I would like them to be for approval of their release. She will be on strict bed rest for a bit where we can watch them closely."

"Of course! Thank you, Doc." Luke replied while trying to slow his breathing.

Dani shook his hand, and Luke leaned back on the wall to take a breath. He pulled out his cell phone and sent a text to Mike, as Dani hugged him.

Mom and twins are alive. Baby two is at risk right now. Keeping Daphne on strict bed rest and on monitors in the hospital but all are still alive.

Mike instantly replied.

That is better than we thought! Give her our love. See you guys soon.

Luke and Dani headed back into the room and Luke curled up around Daphne, pulling her into his chest again.

Dani took a seat on the chair and sent her own texts.

Kada's bruises were dark around her face. Luke reached over Daphne and rubbed a finger over Kada's cheek.

"I'm so sorry sweetheart. I love you."

"I know, Dad. I love you too."

Luke smiled at Kada, then moved his hand down to Daphne's belly over the hospital gown and placed a hand under the thin hospital blanket and sheet covering her.

"How's my babies doing?"

No movement. Luke frowned and took a deep breath and tried again. He spoke but didn't know who he was reassuring, "I'm here. Mom and Sister are okay, and you guys are gonna make it. Stay with us. Mom needs you two to be okay."

He felt the slightest movement, making Luke smile and kiss Daphne's forehead. He rested and put his arm around Daphne and Kada and gently pulled them closer as he rested his head on Daphne's.

"Richmond?" Daphne spoke softly.

"Hey. I'm here."

His left hand moved to hold her left hand between them. She looked up at him and smiled.

"Hey, how you feeling?"

She started to cry. Kada wrapped her arm tighter around Daphne's chest.

"Hey Daph, the twins are alive. We still have them, both."

"Oh my god, Luke!" She gasped for air and cried tears of joy now.

Dani walked over the bedside behind Luke to smile at her sister.

"Really? We still have them?" Daphne asked.

A voice from the door, "I told you, my brother makes some strong kids. The Richmond's are fighters. Every one of them."

They all looked towards the door to see Mike and Jen standing at the doorway when Mike spoke. "And since you have the qualifications, I have no doubt you application will be approved."

Kada was the first to jump up and run to Jen and Mike and pull them into a hug, Then Dani followed but Luke didn't move from Daphne's bed and still held her close. Daphne turned over to her back and sat up. Luke helped and propped a pillow behind her. Daphne saw Luke's hand bandaged up.

"What happened to your hands?"

Luke frowned, so Mike answered. "That's just Luke fighting himself."

Daphne looked at Mike, who had a dark bruise on his jaw.

Dani spoke, "A side I hope you never have to see, but if you do, understand he fights for you." Dani smiled at her sister.

Kada spoke now from Daphne's other side. "Dad went after Uncle Mike and the ground won."

Mike laughed, "She's not wrong."

"Ok, enough. I'm not the one in a hospital bed...right now." He finished the sentence before anyone else could and laced his fingers through Daphne's and kissed her forehead. "Right now, we still have a very whole, healthy and complete family and a wedding in a week."

"Oh my god! I'm getting married next week!" Excitement spread across Daphne's face. Everyone laughed and smiled.

Luke bent down with a big smile to kiss Daphne then her belly.

On July 26th, a week later, Daphne looked at herself in the mirror, beaming with a smile in her form fitting wedding dress, thankful for Dani's makeup skills and a built-in corset to help keep her ribs from moving, as Daphne didn't just look like she got released from the hospital two days ago.

"Oh Daphne, you look amazing!" Both Jen and Dani said in unison as Daphne glowed with emotions of happiness and excitement.

The girls spent the night getting ready at Daphne's house, while Luke and his groomsmen were getting ready at their house.

Vehicles filled the ditch lines, both the driveways and cul-de-sac, leaving Luke's now-decorated truck unblocked in their driveway and with "Just Married" signs and white paint.

Big soft, double layered, flowing white sheets of chiffon fabric lined the big green shared yard blocking out any view from the road, except what can be seen through the small archway decorated with purple iris, red roses, and white lilies, leading into the beautiful wedding ceremony space. The shared yard was lined with rows of white wooden chairs and the aisle decorated with the red, purple and white flowers as they hung off the ends of the rows of chairs. The sun was out, and it was a beautiful day for The Richmond wedding in Birch Valley.

Puppies barked as two small Dalmatians chased each other around Kada's feet.

"Keep them quite Kada, at least till your dad can't just leave me."

Kada smiled and laughed. "But Mom, they are so cute!"

"Ok, we'll have to figure out a way to tell Dad."

Daphne smiled as her stomach turned and placed a hand on it to try and settle it. Dani, dressed in a long silver beaded chiffon dress, looked at her. "Uh-oh! I know what you need."

When she ran off, Daphne turned to where she just stood and gave a shout, "It better be a six-foot one-inch warm body named Luke!"

A moment later, Dani returned with Luke's station sweater that Daphne and Kada slept with all night. Dani wrapped it around her belly and smiled. "No, but just keep them happy for about another hour and then they can have Dad."

Kada smiled next to Daphne in her beautiful purple dress in a similar design to Daphne's off the shoulder long sleeve white wedding dress. "Dad is going to go speechless, Mom. He may not even say 'I Do'." She laughed

"Well, he better talk, I'm counting on it to keep his kids happy long enough to steal his last name, before I throw up." She gave a smile at Kada just as her stomach turned again, making Daphne lift her dress with one hand and run to the bathroom, jumping over the puppies as she covered her mouth with her other hand.

"Nope. Not good enough. Okay. I'll be back!" Dani smiled at Jen, also wearing the same dress as her, and walked out the front door with Luke's sweater in hand and marched across the yard barefoot to Luke and Daphne's house.

Jen, Kada, Sarah and Maya, all looked at each other and walked to the bathroom to watch Daphne throwing up in the toilet.

Jen handed Daphne the glass of water that sat on the new counter with blue tiles.

"Oh sweetie. Let's get you finished so we can get you to him. His kids are not gonna let you eat, and you need to eat."

Dani came running in with a different Station sweater and prescription bottle, "I love your fiancé. I might just marry him and divorce Trace."

"Mom!" Maya spoke in shock.

Dani flipped the hand with the pill bottle, through the air and rolled her eyes, "Oh it's just a joke, Maya."

She came jogging into the bathroom to sit on the floor next to Daphne.

"Here! He and Doc had these filled for you. It's Zofran, to help with the nausea and to help get you through the ceremony, and a fresh Luke sweater."

She smiled as tears started to roll down her cheeks.

"Oh! No! No! No! Stop that. Here, take this." She took out a pill from the bottle and handed it to her as Jen handed her the glass of water again.

"And we are just gonna put this right here." She put the sweater over her shoulder and rubbed the end of it on Daphne's belly gently.

The puppies came running in to climb into Daphne's lap.

"Oh No! Kada, Sarah, Maya, take them out before they ruin Daphne's wedding dress." Jen spoke as she nudged the spotted puppies towards the bathroom door.

Kada and Sarah each picked up a puppy and walked out to the living room with them.

"And Luke sends the message to hurry up. He wants his wife and three kids back. And oh my God, Daphne..." Dani pressed a hand into her chest with an open mouth, wide face and eyes. "...that man! No wonder you are pregnant! You sure he's a fireman? I thought he was supposed to be putting the fires out, not starting them!"

Daphne laughed.

"I told you; women everywhere are still throwing confetti because of you." Jen bubbled with laughter.

"Better then singing Canary! I know if they had the same image burned in their brain as I do, they'd be throwing something else, I'm sure." Dani scoffed then shuddered.

The three women now laughed till A deep voice sounded from the back door, "Daphne."

Jen smiled at Daphne then turned to answer, "We are in here, Honey!"

"Is it safe?"

Daphne laughed while still sitting next to the toilet with Dani. "Yes, Mike."

"Oh, Shit! Dalmatians!"

Jen, Dani, and Daphne laughed over hearing Mike, Kada, Maya and Sarah in the living room.

"Hey Uncle Mike! Daphne, and Aunt Dani got them for us. The brown spotted girl is Phoenix, and the black spotted boy is Chief Louie. Aren't they cute?"

"Yeah. But your dad needs a bigger house!"

Sarah pleaded now, "Oh Dad! Don't tell Uncle Luke please! Daphne wants to die a Richmond at least."

Everyone laughed.

"Yeah, let's get them married first. Luke's been waiting long enough. And I would clean off the puppy hair before you walk down the aisle Kada, or he'll know something is up."

Mike came around the corner to stand next to Jen in the bathroom door. He wore a black suit coat and pants with a white dress shirt, a dark red vest and tie and a purple iris boutonniere and still with a slight coloring on his jaw.

"Luke is pacing and wearing ruts in your floors, wondering how you are doing. I came to find out for myself since he can't and hasn't been able to for the last twenty-four hours."

He took in the complete picture of Daphne in her wedding dress with her hair and makeup all done, Luke's sweater over her shoulder and belly as tears rolled down her face and arm over the toilet lid, looking very tired and sick.

"Oof." He winced at the sight then took a deep breath. "When was the last time you ate?"

Daphne swallowed to talk but Dani answered, "Ate? As in held something down longer than five minutes. Umm, I'm guessing about twenty-five hours ago."

"Okay. Well, let those meds kick in and I'll go see what I can cook up and give your man the update...." His lips drew up tight in thought, "...That you are beautiful and doing great! I'll be back."

He kissed Jen and rubbed a hand down her side. "Mm, you bringing that dress home tonight?"

Jen laughed, "Get out of here. Go prep your boy for his beautiful wife."

Mike smiled wide and kissed her again before turning and leaving.

"Ok. Let's get you ready. If we don't keep moving here, He'll be delivering his kids before He says 'I do'"

Daphne smiled and got up.

They walked out and Kada was standing at the kitchen window looking out.

"Mom, look at Dad! I've never seen him in a suit! Is that even Dad?"

Daphne smiled big and started to run, before Dani and Jen grabbed her arms.

"Slow down! Luke will kill us if we don't send all three of you down the aisle at the same time."

She smiled again and picked up her dress to walk to the window next to Kada and look out at Luke. He was in a black suit like Mike's with white dress shirt, but with a white vest and tie and red rose boutonniere. He was helping set up a couple more chairs and occasionally gave a look up at Daphne's house to reveal a clean shave along his jaw and cheeks and a circle beard around his lips and chin that was trimmed short. His usual head of hair was shortened to a couple inches long and trimmed around the edges for clean cuts and lines.

Kada and Daphne smiled at him.

"Yum." Daphne growled out.

"Mom!" Kada said in shock next to her.

Daphne went into shock forgetting about Kada next to her and pulled her head into her chest holding her ears and head tightly as she looked at Dani and Jen laughing.

"Oh shit!" Then folded her lips inward and sealed them before letting Kada go.

Daphne picked up her cell phone and sent a text to Luke.

There is a hot fireman in my yard that is not my Richmond. Where did he go cause, the new edition is starting fires in my house! Send.

Daphne and Kada both watched out the window as Luke set the chair down and straightened another chair and pulled out his phone to check the message. Luke grinned from ear to ear and looked up at Daphne's house and glanced around him before texting back.

"Can he see us in here?" Kada asked.

"No. I've done my research over the last year."

Kada's mouth dropped open as she looked at Daphne.

Jen grabbed Kada's shoulders. "Ok. Let's go get your hair done." And nudged her towards the bathroom.

Daphne's phone chimed and she pulled it up close to her chest to keep it out of sight.

Richmond: *Mm, Give the new edition a try. It's called a husband and he like more heat than the fireman and doesn't wear protection.*

Daphne gasped quickly and held her phone and hand to her chest and other hand around her belly, making Jen and Dani run in shock to check on her.

"Daphne!"

When Daphne stood up straighter with a big smile and blushing cheeks, Dani and Jen took a deep breath and glared at her.

"Luke!" Dani gave a shout with a temper.

Mike walked in the back door with a plate of food and looked up at Dani and Jen holding Daphne up.

"Daphne! Oh my God. You, okay? What happened? What's wrong?" He quickly stepped to the kitchen, putting the plate of food down before grabbing Daphne off her feet to sit her on the bar stool.

Dani answered, "Yeah, she's fine. But if your boy doesn't stop texting her, He's gonna be spending his wedding at her hospital bedside and not getting married."

Mike smiled and chuckled, "Well at least they are both doing better." He gave a shrug as Dani smiled and swatted at Mike's chest. Jen just laughed.

Dani pulled up Luke's number on her phone and hit 'Call'. Jen walked back to Kada and directed her towards the bathroom as Sarah and Maya played with the puppies. She put it on speaker on the counter as Daphne ate some grapes off the plate Mike handed her.

"Hey Dani. Everything okay?" He spoke with a softer tone like he wasn't just smiling from ear to ear.

"No! Whatever you are texting to her, stop now! Or you will be headed to the hospital with her instead of getting married!" Her voice spiked.

Luke gave a wholehearted laugh. "Sorry. How is she? And all my kids?"

Daphne spoke up around a bite of a sandwich, "She is fine! Fat and tired, but fine. Two of your kids are not happy, they haven't heard their dad in a while. And Jen is doing Kada's hair as we speak."

"You aren't fat, you are pregnant with our twins and from what Mike told me, absolutely stunning."

Mike spoke up, rubbing a hand up and down her back, "She's beautiful. Can't even tell she was through hell this past week."

"I have no doubt. And as of today, she'll never go through Hell without me carrying her."

Daphne smiled and tried to wipe away the sudden flood of tears.

"I love you Richmond."

"I love you too. Hey, do we have an ETA when I get to marry you? The yard is getting pretty crowded out here."

Dani spoke, "We aren't Dispatch, but as I hear you didn't sleep well, your bride, and all your kids didn't either. So, Jen, Sarah, and I are the only ones to help get the other four Richmond's that aren't used to lack of sleep, ready. So, it's a little slower here, but the bride is trying to feed two of your kids now, Kada is getting her hair done, then a couple fixes to makeup and hair, then I'll drag her butt down the aisle to you in about an hour."

Daphne picked up Dani's phone and walked to the window again to look out at him when he replied. "I can't wait."

He was smiling ear to ear, looking at the kitchen window.

Mike walked out the back door and around the house to stand next to Luke as Magar and Hastings came out from Luke's house and walked over to Luke and Mike.

"I love you, Daph."

She smiled. "I love you, Richmond. See you soon."

When she put the phone down and hit 'End', she saw Luke do the same thing as Magar and Hastings in the same suits as Luke and Mike but in silver colors matching Dani and Jen, gave Luke a pat and steered him back to his house.

When everyone was seated, Luke stood with the Officiant in the front, with their flowing creek for background. Bridesmaids and Groomsmen lined up to walk down the aisle together as Magar and Hasting's wives helped get everyone in order.

The music started. Jen and Hastings locked arms and walked first. Then Dani and Magar and then Kada and Mike. Luke bent down to kiss Kada on the cheek as she walked by her dad with a big smile, as Mike moved to stand behind him.

When their wedding song started to play and the crowd stood, a light lit up behind the curtain, showing Daphne's silhouette against the curtain and showing the curves over her chest, belly, back, and hips to her butt and then flared out in the form-fitted dress as she held the bouquet of flowers over the bigger baby bump. Her hair was up in a loose bun leaving single curls to hang free over the clipped in vail under the bun that stretched over the back of the dress matching its full train length.

Luke's heartbeat began to race. Mike placed a hand on Luke's shoulder.

Luke saw Daphne's hand come up to her face, stay there a minute and then come back down to her belly. He whispered to himself, "Come on Daph, walk to me."

Mike gave Luke's shoulder a gentle squeeze.

Daphne took a single step turning herself into the archway as Magar's wife turned the train and fixed the veil behind her. When she looked up, Luke was glowing with pride and a smile in his soul that reached hers, calming every muscle and their twins while she walked towards him. The same golden eyes that had saved her was now waiting for her at the end of the aisle.

His lips smiled when she reached him. She handed her bouquet of red roses, white lilies and purple iris wrapped in a white silk ribbon to Kada, then placed her hands in his, as the secure and safe feeling she had holding his in thick work gloves, flooded her senses.

Everyone watched in awe of the heartfelt emotions, as Luke and Daphne said their vows and exchanged rings.

As Daphne slid on Luke's wedding ring, she watched him and swallowed. He smiled and placed his right free hand on her belly and rubbed to soothe the twins. When he looked down at the ring she slid on his ring finger, it was a black titanium band with the small steel cable that wrapped around it. He smiled at her, knowing exactly what it was meant to symbolize.

Luke dropped his hands to her belly as she weaved her fingers through his holding her and their twins, as the officiant wrapped up the ceremony.

"I am proud to present, Mr. and Mrs. Lucas Richmond! You may kiss your bride."

Daphne laughed and pulled back as Luke's eyes went wide with excitement.

"Lucas...."

She got cut off when he took her mouth stepping around her dress and dipping her back and under him as her arms wrapped around his neck. He held her entire pregnant body up just a couple feet from the ground as the crowd cheered.

Dani stepped around Kada to hit Luke with the bouquet "Oh my god Luke, careful! That is my sister and your kids!"

He released Daphne's mouth as Daphne laughed, to scowl at Dani with a prideful smile, "And she is now my wife and the mother to our three kids."

He slowly straightened, bringing Daphne up with him as the crowd continued to cheer and clap.

Mike looked to Magar, who picked up a fire helmet next to him and handed it to Mike who put it on Luke as the wedding party backed up for the photographer to get a good shot. Just then the puppies barked, making Luke turn to see Daphne's back door as Sarah and Maya opened the back door and out came the two Dalmatian puppies.

Luke's face dropped, as he looked at them running towards them while Kada called them, "Phoenix, Chief, come here!"

Mike chuckled, "Congrats man! You now have five kids and a wife. We are gonna have to build you a bigger house."

Luke glared at Mike with a half-smile.

Daphne smiled big and gave him another light kiss. "Now there are seven Richmond's. Who would have thought Kada bringing hot cocoa to the new neighbor would have given us both a family of seven a year later, less than twenty feet from that same spot."

Luke looked back over Mike to Daphne's bench remembering his own irritation then turned back to Daphne before gently picking her up under the knees and shoulders with the biggest prideful smile while he wore his fire helmet and plastered a hard kiss to her lips. Daphne hooked both her arms around Luke's neck.

Daphne's belly bump showed through the fitted dress as she laid across Luke's arms. Kada threw Daphne's bouquet up, next to her and Luke as the Dalmatian puppies crowded around the bottom of Kada's purple dress. She smiled for the picture holding an arm around her parents as the purple, red and white petals floated down around them.

Snap! The perfect moment was captured in a single picture.

·

Made in the USA
Columbia, SC
14 October 2024

43574545R00188